THE KING'S CHAMELEON

*A thrilling Kit Faulkner naval adventure, set
in turbulent historical times*

England, 1659. Captain Kit Faulkner's house
is prospering; his eldest son, Nathaniel, has
recently returned from a profitable trip to
Jamaica in the good ship *Faithful*, and his
daughter, Hannah, has made a suitable match
with a young sailor. But the resignation of the
Lord Protector, Richard Cromwell, throws
England into uncertainty. Will the republic
flourish, or will a King return to the throne?

Kit is content to let matters take their natural
course, but his younger son, Henry, is an idealist with political ambitions. It soon becomes
clear that Henry is in much deeper than Kit
first realised, and Henry's actions may threaten
everything that Kit holds dear...

*Further Titles by Richard Woodman
from Severn House*

The Kit Faulkner Naval Adventure Series

A SHIP FOR THE KING
FOR KING OR COMMONWEALTH
THE KING'S CHAMELEON
DEAD MAN TALKING
THE EAST INDIAMAN
THE GUINEAMAN
THE ICE MASK
THE PRIVATEERSMAN

THE KING'S CHAMELEON

Richard Woodman

Severn House Large Print
London & New York

This first large print edition published 2014
in Great Britain and the USA by
SEVERN HOUSE PUBLISHERS LTD of
19 Cedar Road, Sutton, Surrey, England, SM2 5DA.
First world regular print edition published 2013 by
Severn House Publishers Ltd., London and New York.

British Library Cataloguing in Publication Data

Woodman, Richard, 1944- author.
  The king's chameleon. -- Large print edition. -- (The Kit
Faulkner naval adventure series ; 3)
  1. Faulkner, Kit (Fictitious character)--Fiction.
  2. Sailors--Great Britain--History--17th century--
Fiction. 3. Seafaring life--History--17th century--
Fiction. 4. Great Britain--History--Puritan Revolution,
1642-1660--Fiction. 5. Historical fiction. 6. Large type
books.
  I. Title II. Series
  823.9'14-dc23

  ISBN-13: 9780727896919

Except where actual historical events and characters are being
described for the storyline of this novel, all situations in this
publication are fictitious and any resemblance to living persons is
purely coincidental.

Severn House Publishers support the Forest Stewardship Council™
[FSC™], the leading international forest certification organisation. All
our titles that are printed on FSC certified paper carry the FSC logo.

Printed and bound in Great Britain by
T J International, Padstow, Cornwall.

For Arlo

Into this Universe, and *why* not knowing,
Nor *whence*, like Water willy-nilly flowing;
And out of it, as Wind along the Waste,
I know not *whither*, willy-nilly blowing.

From *The Rubaiyyat of Omar Kayaam*
Translated by Edward Fitzgerald.

Tumbledown Dick

May 1659

'So, you have had a successful voyage, Nathaniel, and in such uncertain times that is most gratifying.'

Captain Christopher Faulkner paused. Both his son, Nathaniel, and his brother-in-law, Nathan Gooding, held their peace, anticipating some further remark.

The older Faulkner looked up from his diligent perusal of the papers before him, raising his eyebrows. 'Have you nothing to say?' he asked of his son.

'I am sorry, Father,' replied Nathaniel. 'I thought that you had not yet finished speaking.'

'Huh.' Faulkner turned to his partner. 'Nathan?'

'Likewise, Kit. But if comment is necessary I would say that Nathaniel's voyage has proved most encouraging. The Jamaica trade is like to flourish, and that our house should profit thereby is, once more, evidence of God's infinite mercy.'

Faulkner rolled his eyes at his son who had remained standing while his voyage accounts were scrutinized by the senior partners and owners of his ship. He then settled his gaze upon Gooding, soberly clad in black with the plainest of ruffles at his throat and wrists as befitted a Puritan. 'Heaven forefend that we should omit God from our accounts,' he said with a heavy sarcasm, 'though I suspect that the skills of Nathaniel here in seamanship and navigation may well have seen him through his venture.' Faulkner paused and, just as his brother-in-law roused himself to defend his remark, turned to his son. 'What say you of the matter, Captain?'

'I, er...' Nathaniel looked awkwardly at both men. 'I am sure,' he temporized, 'that God over-saw us.'

'Only *sure*?' quizzed Gooding. 'Did thy faith not bear the conviction of certainty?'

'Come, Nathan, you are not a seafaring man,' Faulkner intervened. 'What explanation would you have tendered had young Nathaniel's ship been overwhelmed in a hurricane? That he had sinned to such an extent that God had wrought his infinite justice upon him and his crew? We deal in realities, the laws of cause and effect, and so do you when you take off that confounded large black hat of yours and stare at a ledger. We have enjoyed a handsome profit, whatever the price of rum and sugar in London town.'

'I would not deny that,' responded the dis-comfited Gooding. Faulkner's ready wit was too quick for him, while his brother-in-law's easy habit of command brooked no interference as he rumbled on:

'Well then, let us praise God by all means for our good fortune and drink a cup of wine to Nathaniel's success.' He indicated the jug and glasses on the table. The young master-mariner performed the office, and Faulkner smiled at Gooding as he took the proffered bumper. 'Praise God by all means, Nathan, but do not confuse the divine with the commercial. Thank him that we were not committed to the Baltic trade when war broke out there, or that we have avoided capture in the Mediterranean where English ships have been seized.'

Pressed with a glass of wine, Gooding succumbed to his brother-in-law's charm. It was difficult to stay angry with him for more than a moment or two, no matter what his conscience told him. There was that confidence in the old seaman that Gooding so envied, for he had always been a man of business, and he knew himself inadequate to the task of commanding a ship. Nevertheless, he knew that his own skill in negotiating freight-rates and brokering deals was fundamental to the continuing success of their joint enterprise. He also knew, with the deep-seated conviction of a fierce and private faith, that much of this was directly attributable to his personal devotion to the Lord God and the godliness of his own life. Sometimes, however, he feared that God would set aside his personal rectitude and take issue with the casual blasphemies of Faulkner, his partner and brother-in-law, notwithstanding the additional saintly atmosphere engendered by his own sister and her children, to whom Faulkner, the erstwhile cavalier naval officer, had returned after a long estrangement. Gooding had a habit of regarding life not, as Faulkner did, as a series of causes and effects to be batted at or manipulated, but as an ever rolling balance sheet in which good was constantly weighed against bad and from which consequences flowed. The question that constantly tormented Gooding was whether or not those consequences included an eternal life in the Holy Presence or ... He could never quite comprehend the pains of eternal torture in Hellfire but, alongside what he feared, the public hanging, drawing and quartering of a condemned traitor seemed a mild enough fate.

Faulkner was untroubled by such frightful perturbations. 'How were the men?' the old sea-captain asked of his son.

'Tolerable, Father. I had trouble with two who roistered ashore at Port Royal and debauched themselves most savagely. I discharged them when they returned to their duty and left them to rot where it seemed their fancies took them.'

'And you did not want their labour on the homeward passage?'

Nathaniel shrugged. 'We were fortunate in the quality of the rest of the people.'

'Such men are not to be encouraged,' Gooding put in. 'There are far too many of them in the merchants' service.'

'Most, no doubt, dispossessed Royalists,' Faulkner added drily. 'Which,' he went on, 'brings me to the matter of your brother, Nathaniel...'

'Henry? He is not a dispossessed Royalist. Quite the contrary.'

'Indeed. But Henry possesses the same hot righteousness.'

'But what of him?' Nathaniel stared at his

father. 'Do you purpose to send him to sea? If so, he will not agree.'

'He is become a danger to himself,' Faulkner continued, his tone now serious.

'He is *political*,' Gooding intervened, relieved of his brief mental anguish. He would have said more had Faulkner allowed him to.

'Your uncle is a secret admirer of his younger nephew,' Faulkner explained to his son. 'He thinks Henry destined for a career in politics, God preserve us.'

'He has radical views which your father does not like,' Gooding put in sharply.

Nathaniel put down his glass, grinning broadly in an echo of his father's winning smile. 'Please, gentlemen, please desist for speaking the one for the other...'

'Ah,' said Faulkner with a laugh, looking across the table at Gooding and raising his glass in mock salutation, 'he has us to a likeness, Nathan. It is a besetting sin to express another's thoughts, but too often done, I fear.'

'A presumption, I agree,' responded Gooding, 'but why not quiz the young man himself? I hear him on the stair.'

Henry Faulkner burst into the room without ceremony; he was flushed and panting with exertion. He stood for a moment, his hand against the door-frame, catching his breath as the three men he had interrupted turned at the intrusion. Quite clearly Henry was the bearer of news.

'He ... he's gone! Resigned!'

'Who?' Gooding asked, sitting up expectantly.

'Sit down, boy,' ordered Faulkner in the

peremptory tone he habitually used to address his younger son.

Gooding shot Faulkner a glance of disapproval; ever since Christopher's return to live again with Nathan's sister and her children, the relationship between Henry and his father had been strained and abrasive. He observed the young man's eyes flash pure venom at his father before addressing his remarks to Gooding alone.

'The Protector! Richard Cromwell!'

There was a moment's silence broken by the entry into the room of Judith, accompanied by Hannah, the Faulkners' third child. Both women had been in the parlour below and heard the commotion of Henry's boots upon the stairs. The men rose, and then, as Judith sat at the table, they resumed their seats. Only Henry remained defiantly standing, his chest still heaving.

'Where did you glean this intelligence?' Faulkner asked coldly.

'I have been at Westminster.'

'And you are certain of it?'

'The whole of London knows by now,' said an exasperated Henry, thinking his news was not believed on account of his father's lack of faith in him.

'It is as well to be certain, Henry,' Gooding temporized.

'Well, it is not altogether a surprise,' Faulkner ruminated. 'Dick is no likeness of his daddy...' It was an unfortunate remark, though made without a shred of disingenuousness. Faulkner's rational reference to the worthy but ineffectual son of Oliver Cromwell, who had picked up the mantle

14

of Lord Protector after his father's death the previous year, was not intended to be an implied criticism of Henry, but the young man bristled and flushed scarlet, only too ready to think so. He caught his mother's eye and would have spoken out sharply had not she made a negative motion with her hand.

Again Gooding temporized. 'Ever since he dissolved Parliament at the insistence of the Army,' he said, 'his position has weakened, while the finances of the state leave so much to be desired that it was all but impossible for him to govern...'

'But who *will* govern us now?' put in Judith. 'What will happen? The Army ... a resumption of civil war? Why has God forsaken us?'

'No!' Faulkner banged his hand on the table and stood up. He went to the window and stared down into the street, as if the solution were to be found there among the citizens of Wapping as they ran about their daily business. 'Not God, Judith, not God!'

'Would you have a King back?' Judith rounded on him, and everyone in the room braced themselves. Despite his distinguished service in the Commonwealth Navy, no-one in that room was insensible of the fact that Captain Kit Faulkner – Sir Christopher, if he wanted to assume the rank and dignity of knighthood conferred upon him by an exiled King-in-waiting – had also served King Charles the Martyr in the late Civil War.

Faulkner turned from the window with a wry grin. 'Despite your fears and suspicions,' he said slowly, looking round at them all, 'it is not up to

15

me. I am an Englishman who must do what, at the time, seems right for my country. No man can – or is expected to – do more.' There was a silence; then Faulkner asked, 'What are the rumours, Henry?'

The young man was still hot with resentment at the implied rebuke to his character and for a moment had no answer.

'You must have heard something,' prompted his uncle. 'Such news is rarely unaccompanied by speculation at the very least.'

'Well,' began Henry, ''tis said the Army will assume power ... What alternative is there in such circumstances?'

'They will offer the Protectorship to another,' said Gooding.

'But who?' asked Judith.

'God forbid that it should be Fleetwood, or Disbrowe,' Gooding ruminated, following his own train of thought.

'Cromwell rose from the ranks of the Army; where else shall we look for governance?' put in Judith, whose political views and right to express them were a well-established feature of the household.

'Perhaps there is someone of sufficient standing to command respect, at least in some measure,' added Nathaniel with the awkwardness men of the sea have when discussing matters of which landsmen are better informed.

'Well, Harry,' said Faulkner in an unbending and conciliatory moment, for he had seen and guessed the reason for his younger son's heat, 'as our resident politico, what sayest thou upon the

16

matter of which you have brought us notice?'

Called upon for advice Henry gathered himself. 'The Army is divided,' he began. 'The younger officers, all for a republic, are nonetheless largely responsible for the resignation of the Protector. Some older men of the New Model, keen to retain the status quo, would have served under Richard for as long as he drew breath, provided he did not deny the Army its rights—'

'Whatever they are,' breathed Faulkner under his breath.

Undeterred by this interruption, Henry pressed on. 'The senior officers have been corrupted by power and have lost touch with the men they are supposed to command, so it would seem that the Rump will be recalled and directed to establish a new republic with no head of state!' Henry's eyes were glowing with excitement at the contemplation of this Utopian dream.

Faulkner laughed. 'No head of state! Why now, there is a high-road to disaster,' he said dismissively. 'Surely not. More likely a triumvirate of republicans such as Vane, Ludlow and Heselrige will guide this nation of ours.'

'And all Christians will be allowed to practise their faith,' put in Judith.

Henry, meanwhile, smarted at his father's rapid analysis of the likely outcome. He had not thought of such a solution. Henry was an idealist, not a pragmatist.

'Provided it be not Popery or Prelacy, I trust,' interjected Gooding.

'Indeed not, Uncle,' Henry said, recovering

himself. 'What is being mooted is that a legis-
lature should reflect the will of the people and a
senate be appointed from which would derive a
council-of-state, and that Fleetwood should be
made commander-in-chief of the Army. To this
end, Parliament has been recalled.'

'Well, well,' said Faulkner as Henry looked
round the assembled family, judging the impact
of his intelligence. 'It only remains to get the
agreement of all parties to this marvellous plan.
As for us, my dear Nathan,' he said, nodding at
Gooding, emptying his glass, rising to his feet
and clapping his son Nathaniel on the shoulder,
'we must haul down the old *Faithful* and refit her
for another voyage to Jamaica, I think.'

'Aye,' Gooding said, closing the books in front
of him. 'Life goes on.' He rose from the table,
gathering both ledgers, papers, pen and ink, indicating that Hannah might help. Both withdrew
from the room, followed by Judith. There seemed little more to say, and all knew they would
reassemble for dinner. Nathaniel made to move,
picking up his hat, while Henry, after a moment's
havering, made for the door.

'Wait, Henry, I would speak with thee alone,'
Faulkner said, nodding to Nathaniel as his elder
son paused on the threshold and then passed
from the room, closing the door behind him.
Faulkner turned to Henry. 'Please sit a moment.'

'I prefer to stand.'

'Do please sit.'

'I prefer to stand,' Henry repeated.

Faulkner paused and studied his younger son;
then he shrugged, leaned back in his chair and

reached for his pipe, which he filled with slow deliberation. 'As you wish,' he said at last, picking up a taper and inserting it into the small fire of sea-coal that burned in the grate. 'I had not meant this to seem like an admonition that you must stand thus before me.'

'Indeed, Father? It seems that everything you say to me is an admonition. I am not used to such solicitude.'

Faulkner drew the flame of the taper down onto the tobacco packed into the pipe-bowl, still taking his time. After he had extinguished the taper with a shake of his hand, he threw out a plume of blue and curling smoke and smiled. 'You are right,' he said in a conciliatory tone, 'we have not seen eye-to-eye, and I blame that upon my own faults. You are in want of curbing, and that is not to be wondered at.' He held up his hand to stem Henry's response. 'I understand all the opprobrium you think attaches to my person—'

'Do you, Father?' Henry interjected, unable to restrain himself any further. 'Do you really know what damage you caused my mother by your wanton conduct?'

Faulkner had heard much in this vein from his censorious son and it no longer goaded him. He contented himself with puffing at his long-stemmed church-warden and let the younger man have his head. When Henry had delivered himself of his moral lecture, Faulkner laid his pipe aside with a sigh and drew himself up to the table.

'I am not going to refute your argument; all

you say is true, and I have never denied it. Notwithstanding my guilt in the eyes of God and man you must understand, or try to understand, that it was my misfortune never to have a home, nor a mother beyond the age of eight; that I grew up in rough circumstances and upon occasion let my heart rule my head. After many years in a bleak land, a man plucks at the first fruit he sees; he has yet to know there are other fruits, other occasions ... You have that lesson yet to learn, Henry. Man is imperfect and, despite the cant of the Righteous and Godly who presently consider themselves our masters and with whom you are hugger-mugger, he is incapable of the final remedial improvement necessary for redemption...'

'Without God, of course not!' spluttered Henry in some indignation.

'Let us leave God out of it, at least for the time being, because I wish to propose a course of action that will, perhaps, expose you to wider vicissitudes than you have thus far experienced in your life.'

'You propose sending me to sea.'

Faulkner nodded. 'I do.'

'I shall not go.'

'If I command it, you shall. You are yet short of your majority, and your reluctance is evidence that I have too long neglected your education. You eat from my table at my expense and I hear scarce a word of thanks for it.'

'Your own lust sired me, sir. It has a price!'

The effrontery of this remark struck them both. Henry's heart lurched as he saw the colour drain from his father's face so that his eyes were no longer those of an ageing man, for they had become chips of ice. He opened his mouth to apologize, but Faulkner spoke first.

'If you ever take the high tone with me again, *sir,*' he said, aping his son's mock politeness, 'I shall have you thrown out of the house. I mean what I say, *sir.* A taste of the gutter will curb your damnable insolence.'

Henry swallowed hard, aware that he had gone too far. There was something forbidding, even terrifying, about his father; Henry had forgotten – or perhaps had never properly realized – that his father had held high command and disposed of the lives of seamen at his will. Faulkner went on: 'Such a remark betrays the over-familiarity you have had with this abominable sect of self-righteous, mealy-mouthed hypocrites that set themselves in judgement over us. Are you a Leveller?'

Unable to speak, Henry shook his head. 'Father,' he said, in a croaking whisper, 'I, er...'

'Speak up, I cannot hear you.'

'Whatever you say, Father, but I cannot go to sea.'

'Why not? I can make it as comfortable for you as possible. You can sail as supercargo; you should know enough of the business from your uncle. I will not send you with your brother, but another of our ship-masters.'

'I cannot go, Father. I will not. That is my last word on the subject.'

Faulkner frowned. 'Cannot? Will not? These are words driven by imperatives, yet what imperative has laid you under obligations of such determination, eh?'

'I am ... I am engaged to the Parliament.'

'*Engaged* to the Parliament? In what capacity, pray? A sitting Member? I think not!' Faulkner paused, but Henry made no response, as though unwilling to say more. Faulkner leaned forward, the suspicion forming in his mind crystallizing into a certainty. 'You are an agent!'

Henry said not a word, but the flicker in his eyes as he met the accusation of his father's told Faulkner everything. London, if not the whole of England, was full of such quasi-spies, tell-tales, gossip-mongers and self-appointed purveyors of intelligence. They formed a network, paid for by the leading Parliamentarians on commission, which informed on decent men, and marked them for casual persecution: not attending church, not agreeing with the policy of the late Lord Protector, not paying dues, even smuggling and moral turpitude. It suddenly occurred to Faulkner that he himself had many times risked apprehension but, thinking he had earned some immunity by his services to the state, had never considered he had more likely hidden behind the political shielding of his younger son.

'You have protected me from arrest, have you not, Henry?' he said quietly.

Again the young man said nothing beyond the merest inclination of his head.

'Then I am obliged to you.'

A silence hung between them, broken at last by Henry, who pulled out a chair and sat down, opposite his father. Faulkner stared at his strong, handsome features, a masculine version of Judith's face. 'So you see, Father, I *cannot* go to sea.'

'I see that you cannot go by your own reckoning.'

'You have been once in the Tower.'

Faulkner smiled. 'Aye, and more than once I have stared down a cannon's mouth; do you seek to frighten me? Besides,' he said, visibly brightening, 'with Tumbledown Dick in the gutter, who knows what changes are presently afoot?'

'John Disbrowe—'

'Disbrowe, Heselrige, Lambert, Fleetwood! Pah! Name whom you will, I care not a fig; none will end up in power though the whole devil's cauldron of them set their bleeding hearts at becoming Lord Protector.'

'I told you there will be a Council...'

'No Council will hold this country in one piece longer than a sennight.'

'Come, Father, that is ridiculous! Pure prejudice! Rest assured there will be no more Kings.'

'I would not be too sure of that, my boy. Kings represent stability, and this country is eager to resume its trade and traffic. It needs stability, firm ground upon which money can grow. Many of us are keen to line our pockets with honest toil, not the ill-garnered taxes of honest men seized on the sword points of the New Model Army.'

'But a King guarantees none of that! Better a republic...'

'I would rather a King that one may curb and

23

lay about with strictures than a republic where any jackanapes may rise to the top through coercion, exploitation, dispossession and damned lies! I have stood close to Kings and know they have feet of clay – no, worse than that, morals that might put the entire Puritan faction to flight overseas in search of a heavenly kingdom – but such immoralities can be held in private camera while the excesses of republicans wreck the lives of ordinary mortals.'

Henry shook his head vehemently. 'How can you claim such to be true, having lived in the reigns of two Stuarts, the one perverted, the other of such arrogance that he alienated an entire people?'

'Except those that remained loyal to him,' Faulkner said, lowering his tone and aware that both their arguments were incompatible and their very dissonance had ripped England apart for far too long. 'The country is weary of this bloody debate, Henry. In the end, circumstances will play themselves out and people will settle for what seems to them the best. Perhaps neither of us should predict the outcome, but let matters take their natural course.'

'But I must have a part of that process, Father. I am determined upon a seat in Parliament.'

Faulkner was about to condemn this ludicrous notion, but he curbed his reaction. For the first time since he had come home to live again with this lad's mother, Henry was speaking without choler. 'You would become a Member of Parliament?' he asked. Henry nodded. 'But you require money, opportunity, party...'

'That is what I am presently engaged upon.'

'Ingratiating yourself with Disbrowe...?'

'No, not him, but I cannot say with whom. It is a matter of confidence, of honour.'

'And I must perforce respect this?'

Henry bit his lip. It was clear that he too knew they were in uncharted country. 'I should be very much obliged to you, Father.'

'And if I respect your position – I cannot at this moment say that I second your endeavours – if I respect your ambition, then...' He paused to add weight to his words. 'Then this is a reconciliation.'

The two stared at each other across the table. Faulkner sighed, smiled and extended his hand. Henry flushed then seized it in a strong grip.

'What on earth are we going to tell your mother?' Faulkner remarked drolly.

'I don't know, but I must needs leave that to you.'

Faulkner nodded. 'Yes, you must.'

'I am prepared to make my own way in the world, Father.'

'I am not unaware that your uncle has made an allowance for you.' Henry looked taken aback. 'You are surprised I know of it?'

'Well, to be candid, yes.'

Faulkner chuckled. 'I daresay Nathan would be surprised too, but neither of us need tell him, and besides, I see your mother's hand at the bottom. Let it lie quiet between us.'

Henry nodded and rose, then paused, as if recollecting something. 'There is one other thing, Father...'

'Yes?'

'Hannah wishes to marry.'

'Good heavens! You and Hannah are closer than I had thought.'

Henry shrugged. 'I discovered her reading a letter. It would be a love-match; Mother does not know yet the object of Hannah's affections.'

'Do I?'

'I think not. The matter embarrasses Hannah for some reason that I cannot determine.'

'You know the fellow?'

'Only by sight, but I am inclined to think–' and here a twinkle of intimacy entered Henry's expression, a hopeful mark of the changed relationship between father and son – 'that the young man in question might make a better sea-officer than myself.'

'Indeed. Then we had better make enquiries.'

Part One

Restoration

1660–1662

Honest George

February – May 1660

'Wake up, Husband, wake up!'

'What...? What the devil is it, Judith? What o'clock is it?'

'I don't know, but ... There it is again!'

The knocking at the door was unmistakable, and Faulkner could hear the servants stirring above him. He swore, to his wife's disapproval, and reached for a robe, wrenching the night-cap from his bare head. A thin light could be seen through the chinks in the shutters, marking the approach of sunrise, as he left the bed-chamber, bumped into a squealing kitchen maid, and descended the stairs, bawling that he was coming as if the person in the street was aloft on the fore-topsail yard and a gale of wind was blowing. Drawing the bolts of the front door he beheld a tall man wrapped in a cloak against the chill, a hat upon his bewigged head and his face in the gloom of its brim. Faulkner had no idea of the man's identity but this did not arouse his suspicion; his first thought was that one of his ships was on fire in the tiers and this stranger had been sent to bring him the news. His second followed as swiftly: that the deteriorating state of public order, the misconduct of elements in the Army that went wandering about the city demanding taxes at the point of the sword, and the prevailing turbulence of the resentful citizenry had provoked some riot. But the street as far as he could see remained quiet and the man that stood before him clearly had a message only for Faulkner's abode. The first thought flared up again, the entire circular process having taken no more than a split second.

'Cap'n Faulkner ... Kit Faulkner ... You don't recognize me?' The man snatched off his hat, and in the gloom Faulkner perceived a once familiar face.

'Harrison? Brian Harrison?'

'The same, Kit, the same.'

'Great heavens, what brings you, but come in, sir, come in.' Faulkner called for mulled wine and drew Harrison into the parlour, shouting for wood and, picking up the poker, stirring a glow amid the embers. In a moment the two men were seated, the maids and the scullery boy fussing about them as flames licked up through the hastily revived fire.

'What brings you here at this hour?' Faulkner enquired of Harrison, whom he had not seen for some years. Both men had once been Elder Brethren of the Trinity House, and both had, what seemed now to be a lifetime earlier, served together, commanding ships sent against the Sallee Rovers on the coast of Morocco. Here they had maintained a squadron on a lee shore and bombarded the port until a number of Christian slaves had either run away to swim out to the ships or been released by their captors. Not since the outbreak of the Civil War and his own escape from London with Sir Henry Mainwaring and the fugitive Prince of Wales had Faulkner been in touch with the Trinity House. He had heard that its affairs had been suspended by Parliament, the members of which considered it tainted by its loyalist leanings. In consequence its funds had been plundered and its Court replaced by Puritan Commissioners who had neglected much of its business, especially its relief of poor and indigent seamen and their dependants. He had heard of an assembly of some of the Brethren some eighteen months earlier, but their political colour, conforming too closely to the Commonwealth, had dissuaded him from attending. Thus Harrison's sudden dawn intrusion came as a complete surprise.

'The Brethren are to reconvene. Now that Fleetwood and Lambert are discomfited, the Army has no right to raise taxes and Monck has declared that no power, not even the Army, can subordinate Parliament.'

'Monck?' queried Faulkner. 'Where is Monck? I had heard that he was in Scotland.' Faulkner recalled his old commander, the bluff soldier who served in the State Navy as a General-at-Sea, the Commonwealth's denomination of a senior admiral.

'He will be in London at the head of his troops this very day. Fairfax is in accord and holds York. These forces are all loyal to the principle of Parliamentary rule of law. The southern Army is undone.'

'That is no bad thing; it had become vastly too

large for its own riding boots.'

'Quite so.'

'I had heard Heselrige and others of the Council of State had sent Monck a commission as Commander-in-Chief of all the forces in England and Scotland...'

'And Lawson has declared his loyalty.'

'He commands the fleet in The Downs, does he not?'

'Exactly so.'

'So Monck aims at the Protectorship?' Faulkner hazarded, adding: 'He is in my opinion the only man of rectitude at large.'

'Perhaps he is, but I think his intentions are otherwise.'

Faulkner looked up, meeting Harrison's eyes. 'Then he is for the King?'

'That is the scuttlebutt, though it is not yet certain.'

'Ahh, Honest George is playing his cards close to his chest.'

'So would you if you were playing for such high stakes.'

'True. And the Brethren?'

'Must seize the day, Kit. If Monck is for the King, so be it; if not, then we must declare for Monck – for he is the deliverance for which we have long prayed – or lose what little is left to us. Monck as Protector or Monck as midwife to the King are preferable to the present state of affairs. As for our own part, there is much want among mariners, many of whom have wrecked their constitutions in the state's service as you have yourself seen, while the shipping in the Thames is much in need of moderation – as you must surely know.'

'True; I have not found a crew worth its pay in two quarters of the year, for jack must be as good as his master, even when he cannot patch his frock!' The two men laughed and sipped their mulled wine, staring companionably into the fire that now blazed cheerfully in the grate, a symbol of renewed hope.

'So,' Faulkner said, after a moment's silence, 'am I alone in your solicitations, or is the generality of the Brethren recalled?'

'Those the whereabouts of whom we know will be summoned in the next few days,' Harrison explained. 'As for yourself, knowing your services to both King and Commonwealth, besides my being acquainted with your good sense...'

'Did your advocacy placate those that held me a turn-coat?' Faulkner asked.

Harrison shrugged. 'There have been those who have sat affairs out atop the fence and thus slid down afterwards with no mishap to their breeches, more's the pity of it, but there are those who, like you, have acted out of patriotism, espousing the cause they thought best for their country, and shifted their allegiance when circumstances changed.'

'Thank heaven Monck is among that number,' Faulkner remarked ruefully.

'You served with him, did you not?' Harrison asked.

'Aye, and with some approval, I am pleased to say. He is an able commander for all his lack of

33

sea-time.' Faulkner finished his pot of wine. 'So we – the Brethren, I mean – are summoned this morning then?'

'Aye, at Whitehorse Lane, where we shall determine whether to render taxes as demanded, or join those in the City who refuse until a full Parliament, including the excluded members, has ousted the Rump.'

'Well then, I must repair upstairs and don some apparel while you enjoy another bumper.' Faulkner summoned the maid, instructed her to refill Captain Harrison's pot and removed himself. Ten minutes later, as a red and wintry sun rose above the mist lying along the Thames to strike the myriad of masts-trucks of the scores of merchantmen lying at the tiers, the two men left for Whitehorse Lane, Stepney.

It was four days before Faulkner returned home, and the first thing that he did was call for Henry, only to find, as he had half-expected, the young man was absent. Those four days were followed by a fortnight in which tumultuous events followed one upon the other. The Rump Parliament, governed by a clique, held Monck to his principles of submitting to the civil power, insisting his soldiers tear down the gates of the City of London and seize eleven prominent aldermen as a punishment for the citizens' refusal to pay the taxes demanded. As Monck's soldiers, named Coldstreamers for the place from which they had marched, bent to their task of demolition, the assembled populace confronted Monck, shouting that they would rather let their houses be pulled down round their ears than submit to the tyranny of the Rump. Realizing the Rump was wholly unrepresentative of the country at large, Monck wrote to Westminster, demanding the Rump dissolve itself and admit the excluded members. This alone would restore some semblance of legitimacy and authority to that discredited body. The Rump responded by removing Monck's commission as Commander-in-Chief and making him one of four Commissioners, the other three being creatures of the ruling clique. The move was unpopular throughout the army, both with Monck's forces and the remainder beyond his immediate control. Monck summoned the excluded members of Parliament and secured their agreement to paying the army. Having done this he next withdrew the guard on the Palace of Westminster. The consequence was that, on the twenty-first of February, all the members of Parliament removed earlier by Pride's Purge resumed their seats.

News of this event reached Faulkner within an hour, brought by Henry, who reappeared unshaven, begrimed and exhausted. Faulkner had no idea where in this tangle of loyalties, ambitions and blighted hopes his younger son had placed himself, but judging from appearances Henry had learned that matters rarely fell out with the simple elegance the young so often thought inevitable.

That night London blazed with bonfires and the bells of the churches rang peal upon peal late into the hours of darkness.

'The day of the saints is over,' Faulkner said,

ordering wine as, despite the night's wintry chill, he leaned from an open casement, watching the scene in the street and listening to the wild tocsin ringing out over the city. Behind him in the upstairs room the family used for all important assemblies and otherwise served Faulkner and Gooding as an office – the lower floor being given over to the kitchen, parlour and a small servant's hall – the other members of his household were less cheerful. The Goodings were Puritan through-and-through, and marriage had not softened Judith's politics.

'Do close the window, Husband. 'Tis more than the night's chill that affects me.'

Faulkner did as he was bid, closing both casement and shutters before turning to confront the gloomy faces in the room. 'Come, come,' he said, 'these will be more cheerful times, you mark my words. Whatever the outcome, Monck's influence will guarantee a sensible line of government.'

'Will we have a King?' said Hannah suddenly, voicing the thoughts of all of them.

'Who knows, my pretty one, but, let me see, what sayest thee to having a husband?'

'Husband?' Judith was astonished. Then she began to remonstrate until, seeing Hannah flush and Faulkner roar with laughter, she divined something afoot. 'Husband? Hannah?' she queried, turning from one to the other. 'What is all this?'

'My pretty daughter has a gallant, Goodwife. A handsome and comely lad I trow, and I am minded to give her away as soon as she likes. We have had too much of sensible and saintly misery under this roof. Let us celebrate – modestly, of course – and give some thought to the future beyond despatching ships to Jamaica and buying our way again into the interest of the East India Company. Surely you'll drink to that ... Eh, Nathan? Henry?'

But no-one was listening; they had all gathered round Hannah, who was berating Henry for his indiscretion in telling Faulkner and fending off the questions of her mother who feared above all some indiscretion on her daughter's part.

'Well, well,' said Faulkner to himself with a chuckle, 'thus is history reduced to the mundane.'

Later that night, after the explanations and the justifications, and after the name of Hannah's intended had been revealed as one Edmund Drinkwater, the young mate of an East Indiaman, Faulkner lay in bed unable to sleep. Beside him Judith's breathing was slow and regular, for she was as exhausted as her younger son with the passing of these past few eventful days. Faulkner thought of Henry, whose face had worn an apprehensive expression ever since Monck arrived in town. He was, quite obviously, beset by anxiety, and Faulkner was minded to let him mature in the stir he had had a hand in creating. His consideration of Henry's plight amid the welter of political events led him to think of Hannah and the evident happiness his own intervention had brought. As for Nathaniel, he should by now be in the West Indies loading a homeward cargo.

Finally, his thoughts strayed to his own part in the week just past, chiefly of the assembly of the Brethren of the Trinity House in their place at Stepney. The awkwardness of long separation and factive division had melted away as most, thrown back upon their common profession of sea-captains, had recounted their adventures in loud voices oiled by wine. Whatever their part, often in opposition to one another, there was a profound sensation that they had, between them, laid down their arms, metaphorical and real. Faulkner himself had had an encounter with William Batten who, as admiral of a Parliamentary squadron, had sought Faulkner's destruction when off the Isles of Scilly. Batten, a bumptious man, had cordially shaken his hand, aware of Faulkner's later service in command of a man-of-war under Monck and the late lamented Robert Blake.

Alexander Bence, one of the excluded members of Parliament who had assumed the chair, had declared that they should all set aside their differences and, in the interest of the nation, 'all speak with one tongue and be of one name'. A murmur of agreement and an exchange of mutual smiles had greeted Bence's opening remark. They should, he had gone on to say, 'forsake all rancours and animosities and build anew from the ashes of the past which must, of necessity and practicality, be condemned'. The assembled company had roared their approval and, turning aside, had shaken hands, each one with his neighbour. Before he finally dropped off to an uneasy slumber, Faulkner wondered what their next and more formal meeting would achieve.

Six weeks prior to the assembly of the newly elected House of Commons, the Brethren of the Trinity House gathered again at Stepney. Assembling in full Court, they elected Bence their new Master, he having access to Parliament, and they resolved to do all in their power to restore their finances in the interest of the poor. After this effusion of good intentions, they retired to dine. Faulkner enjoyed a convivial conversation with Harrison during which the latter congratulated him on the formal betrothal of his daughter to Edmund Drinkwater.

'Thank you, Brian, but the wench weeps copiously since the lad is for the East Indies in a day or so and has already gone aboard his ship.'

'Aye, I saw several Indiamen lying in Gravesend Reach two days hence.' Harrison chuckled. 'Well, she must lie on the bed she has made. It was never easy to be a seaman's wife, but Drinkwater has, I understand, a rare competence, and she has chosen well. If he survives, secures interest and gains command, he may do very well and she with him.'

'I sincerely hope that to be the case. At least it is better than had she fallen for a mate of a Geordie brig!'

Both men laughed together, Harrison raising his glass in a toast to the pair of lovers. By now they had been at the table some three hours and around them the gathering was breaking up. Faulkner rose from the table, and turning aside found Bence approaching him.

The newly elected Master extended his hand. 'Captain Faulkner, I have not had the pleasure of wishing you a good day, such has been our business.'

'Indeed, Master, and my congratulations on your election.'

'Thank you, thank you.' Bence retained hold of him and drew him aside. Lowering his voice he remarked, 'Sir Christopher, you must not take this amiss, but I observed your son Henry, who is known to me through Parliament, is strongly in favour of a radical party determined on opposing reconciliation.'

Faulkner was taken aback. The use of his title fell unaccustomed upon his ears and, for a moment, dulled them to the import of Bence's intelligence.

'You see some danger in this?' he asked sharply, once he had digested Bence's news. 'I had put it down to youthful enthusiasm.'

'I hope that is all it is,' Bence said, 'but I should not dismiss him so lightly. He is, after all, his father's son – and I mean that as a compliment, not a judgement, for you are known from your late triumphs in war against the Dutch.'

'You flatter me too much.'

'No matter; heed my words and look to the lad.'

Bence released Faulkner, leaving him to stand stock-still, staring after Bence as he mingled with the dispersing Brethren.

'Are you well, Kit? Or have you had too much wine?'

Faulkner recovered himself and smiled at Harrison. 'No, I am content enough and not over-loaded.'

'You would not be alone, if you were,' Harrison said with a laugh, nodding at Batten who leaned upon William Baddiley, another naval officer. 'Shall we walk together?'

'Gladly, Brian, gladly.' He made an effort to chat with Harrison as they strolled through the lanes from Stepney towards Wapping, but Bence's warning had an uncomfortable habit of disturbing his discourse so that on three occasions he broke off what he was saying. When Harrison prompted him to continue he was driven to make an excuse, claiming to have been distracted by something.

When he finally arrived home he sought out Henry.

'He is not here, husband,' Judith informed him, 'but he gave me every expectation of his being home for dinner. You will have to possess yourself in patience.' Faulkner grunted, but Judith was in full flood, like the Thames when the moon was new or full. 'So, have the Brethren resolved on putting the nation in order?' she asked with more than a hint of sarcasm.

'We are resolved to help the wretched victims of the times, if that is what you mean.'

'And what of the return of the King?'

'Nothing is certain. We must await the outcome of the election and the decision of the Commons.'

'I hear they are opposed to the reassembly of an Upper House.'

'That I understand too, but Monck is a canny man and will, if I am any judge, divine the will of the people and press for mediation and balance. I think that for him the constitution of the Parliament has a special significance, since he has so trenchantly advertised his loyalty to the principle of its supremacy and his opposition to a ruling minority.'

'You do not think that he swings like a weather-cock?'

Faulkner shook his head. 'No! He is taciturn and says little. The populace are not used to that. In the absence of chatter, they imagine it in detail; he is rumoured to be vacillating, then rumoured to be about to invite the King to land. As soon as that rumour is abroad, he is all for Parliament again.' He paused. 'None of it signifies. Monck will act when he senses the moment is right. It is for lesser mortals to swing like a weather-vane.'

'Some of us hold fast to our faith,' Judith said pointedly. Faulkner stared at her in mock disbelief, knowing that she goaded him. 'Why do you look at me like that?' she asked, her eyebrows raised.

'Because you would have issue with me: that I was once the King's, then, when it suited me, a Commonwealth man. Because I was once another's, then yours, then again hers, and now yours. That is what you reproach me with. Being a wind-vane.'

'But you are not a weather-cock,' she responded sharply, 'for such a thing is reliable in that it truly indicates the prevailing wind.'

'In which there is virtue?'

'In which there is utility. No, you are like unto a chameleon...'

'A *what*?'

'A chameleon.'

'And what pray is a chamer...?' Faulkner asked. 'Some cousin to the camel? I have heard of a cameleopard but never a camer-lion.'

'Not camer-lion – a chameleon. It is a kind of lizard of which I have read and which has the peculiarity of changing the colour of its scales according to its place. Thus it is brown when climbing a tree and green when among the leaves.'

Faulkner laughed. 'Oh, really? Am I to believe such nonsense? You read too much, Judith. Perhaps if not cousin to the camel it is first cousin to the unicorn, no doubt!' he scoffed.

''Tis true.'

'Of course it is true – as true as thy name is Judith.'

'What do you mean?'

'You know very well what I mean. I married a Julia and came home to a Judith. Thou had bent thy name to the changing wind. A Puritan lady must needs have a biblical name...'

'You had wronged me, deserted me, betrayed me. I felt the need of some counter-vailing alter- ation in myself. I was not content to be Julia the forsaken lady. Judith was more to my purpose.'

'Ah ha! Indeed! A woman of vengeance – and my point remains: you changed your colour to suit your condition.'

'I do not doubt it.'

43

'Then thou needs must be Goodwife Chameleon.'

'Thou art not as smart as you think, Husband.'

'Never mind that now; I hear Henry on the stair and must have word with him. Pray excuse me.'

Leaving the room, Faulkner caught his younger son removing his cloak and boots before the parlour fire and calling for beer and a slice of beef-pie. He looked up at his father as Faulkner helped him pull his right boot off.

'Father?'

'When you have supped, come to my private room. There is something that I must discuss with you.'

With that, Faulkner took up a candle, jabbed it on the spike of an empty holder and lit it before withdrawing. His private room lay under the tiles, a small room intended as a sleeping place for a servant but never used for that purpose. Instead it was where Faulkner kept his sea-chest and portmanteau, his swords, pistols, half-armour and other paraphernalia necessary to his business as a sea-officer. Here a roll of stained charts and a case containing a backstaff gathered dust; a bundle of bedding, some top-boots and three pairs of workaday shoes lay under a tarpaulin coat. Each item revealed itself as he held up the candle. Faulkner stared for a moment at the portmanteau. He wondered if, among its contents, there was some item he could give to Henry as an earnest of his desire to end the rift between them. It contained a number of items, including a telescope given him by the late King Charles many years earlier, when the wretched man had been Prince of Wales and he—

Faulkner dismissed the recollection and ran his finger over the cuirass and noted the fine dust of oxidization among that of the soot that percolated through the interstices of the tiles.

'Rust,' he muttered to himself, rubbing thumb and forefinger together. Brushing more dust off the rickety chair that he kept there beside a small ship's desk, he set the candle-stick upon the desk and sat down to await Henry. Looking about himself he wondered why he kept all this; it was unlikely that he would ever serve at sea again, for both age and influence were against him, particularly if the King returned with no money – and Faulkner knew well the exiled Charles had no money – and a pack of obligations to fulfil. He recalled he had created this room not merely as a store, but as a refuge. Here he could escape the recriminations that, in the first months of their reconciliation, too frequently issued from Judith. He did not blame her and had long resigned himself to silence; silence, and retreat to this private lair where the appurtenances of past glory reminded him of what he had once been.

He opened the old desk. Inside lay a manuscript book. He pulled it out and opened it. He had not entered a word for over a year: a year in which he had become increasingly involved in his ship-owning partnership with his brother-in-law. It was ironic that it had been Nathan who had saved the marriage between his own sister and Faulkner, but, in a sense, he had.

Hearing Henry upon the creaking stair, Faulkner shoved the book away, closed the desk and turned as the door-latch lifted. 'Come in, my boy. There is little room but do, pray, sit upon my sea-chest.'

'What is it, Father?' Perhaps it was the light of the single candle, perhaps it was the change between them, but, for the first time since his home-coming, Faulkner felt a wave of sympathy for his son. Henry possessed the intensity of his mother and the activity of his father. In the circumstances in which he now found himself, this combination could prove fatal. His features were drawn, the darkness of fatigue gathered beneath his eyes and there was a restlessness about him which betrayed great internal agitation.

'I am as worried about you, Henry, as it is obvious you are about yourself.'

'I am not worried about myself, Father. I am worried about the future of this country...'

'Come, let us not beat about the bush, whatever concerns you, I have received a warning about you.'

'A warning? From whom?'

Faulkner ignored the interruption. 'I do not enquire what it is you are up to, nor with whom you consort, nor what you might intend, but there are those who, in your own best interest and out of consideration for me, consider what you are about is dangerous.' He held up his hand as Henry tried to interject. 'I do not wish to know anything, Henry, but I am asking you to withdraw from whatever diabolical plotting you are involved in, and to make this easier for you I propose that we ship you out aboard the *Judith*. Soames is about to take her to Jamaica and will be clearing her outwards at the Custom House tomorrow.' Faulkner took no notice of the violent shaking of Henry's head. 'You may collect the manifest from your uncle and meet the good captain at the Custom House and quietly board the ship in his company. I will send your dunnage on board, and by the time you return you will have a profession, some pay to your account and here, I devoutly hope, the political situation will have resolved itself.'

The instant Faulkner had finished, Henry broke in, his agitation near manic in its intensity. 'No, Father! No, no no! And a thousand times no!'

'Damn it, my boy, it is obvious you are into something deeper than you know. You may well hang – think of your mother if such a thing—'

'My mother? My mother would understand!' Henry said, leaping to his feet. For a moment he stood irresolute while his father sat in silence, not knowing what more he could say without physically restraining his own son – and Henry was a strong young man and likely to throw him off easily enough. Then, quite suddenly, Henry seemed to make up his mind. His demeanour changed on the instant, and he became quite calm, putting out his right hand and laying it upon his father's shoulder. He looked his father full and spoke.

'Let us sleep on this, Father. I thank you for your concern and will not press you as to your informer. You are right that I run risks; whether I am in danger depends upon events now in train.

47

Your offer of escape by sea is appreciated, but at least allow me the courtesy of resolving the matter over-night to my own satisfaction.'

Faulkner looked at Henry. The change had been swift; too swift, perhaps. Yet what he suggested was not unreasonable. It was clear Henry was shaken, if not terrified, by his plight. Did the change in attitude indicate Henry was calmed by the offer and would salve his own conscience by a pretence at fully considering the matter during the night? Looking at his son, Faulkner did not think him cut out for some conspiracy; he was strong on rhetoric but, as far as his father could judge, showed no sign of being a man-of-action. Faulkner was inclined to think he had just thrown Henry a lifeline which the young man would seize in the morning.

'Of course, my boy,' he said, rising with a smile to shake Henry's hand. 'And now, I think, to bed.'

In the morning there was no sign of Henry; nor did he return that evening. After three days a boy turned up on the doorstep bearing a letter. It seemed to have been written at Gravesend and bore only a few lines.

Father,

Forgive my unannounced Departure but I could not Accept your Charity. I have, however, taken your Advice and, instead, Shipped out for the East Indies as Captain's Clerk aboard the Eagle, East Indiaman, of which Edmund Drinkwater is Second Mate.

Your loving son,
Hry Faulkner

48

'Hannah!' Faulkner roared. When his daughter, her face still drawn with the pain of separation from her lover, peered round the door, he asked peremptorily, 'What is the name of Edmund's ship?'

'Oh, Father ... why, the *Eagle*.'

'Your brother has seen fit to solicit the post of captain's clerk. I assume you knew of this?'

Hannah shook her head. 'But I am glad of it, for the connection with Edmund—'

'I'm sure the two will do very well together,' Faulkner broke in curtly. 'But remind me who commands her.'

'Why, Captain Bradshaw.'

'John Bradshaw?'

'I think that is his name. He is said to speak highly of Edmund—' She broke off with a sob.

'I am sure he does, my dear.' For the first time that morning Faulkner felt for his daughter and held out his arms.

'Oh, Father...' she sobbed, running into them.

'There, there, my darling girl,' he soothed, stroking her hair. 'You will grow accustomed to it. Let us hope he makes his fortune quickly and we can take him into partnership here. We need young blood, and your uncle and I are hoping to invest again in the East India trade.' It was clear that Hannah cared nothing for these musings, but he did not know what else to say that held out any amelioration of her present woe.

Fortunately for both father and daughter, Judith chose this moment to enter the room, and she took Hannah into her own arms. Released,

Faulkner left them, in order to consult Gooding. There was work to be done, and at least the problem of Henry had been resolved. For a moment Faulkner preened himself; Henry had taken his advice. That was a significant event on its own.

The matter resolved, Faulkner dismissed Henry from his mind, leaving it to Hannah and Judith to weep over these twin departures. He himself was constantly betwixt Stepney and his own business affairs as events in the capital overwhelmed its entire population.

In early April, Faulkner was among the Brethren of Trinity House who welcomed General Monck to a dinner held in his honour. Having served under Monck's flag when the General-at-Sea commanded the fleet against the Dutch, Faulkner was among those selected to welcome him.

Monck looked older than Faulkner remembered, a thought tempered by consideration of the burden he bore, but the old soldier's strong and ruddy features lit up when he recognized his former colleague.

'Cap'n Faulkner, how good to see you,' he said cordially, taking Faulkner's hand. 'What business occupies you these days?'

'Matters of less import than occupy yours, sir, though it is kind of you to ask.'

'I hope that you still have an interest in ships, beyond, of course–' Monck looked about him at the assembled and expectant company – 'this present gathering.'

'I am an active ship-owner, yes, sir.'

'Good,' said Monck, pressing his hand and then releasing it as Faulkner introduced Captain Brian Harrison as his 'particular friend' among the Brethren.

The dinner passed well, and at the toasts Monck rose in response to the Brethren drinking to his health and proposed they raise their glasses 'to the future peace and prosperity of the Kingdom of England'.

After Monck had left there was much speculation as to his use of the term 'Kingdom'. Some saw it as a clear if private declaration of Monck's intentions; others recalled the term had been used by even the Parliament after its rift with Charles I had become open warfare.

'It is just a convention; he might just have readily said Republic or Commonwealth...' someone said.

'But he did not,' responded Harrison, turning to Faulkner. 'You know him best, Kit, what d'you think?'

Faulkner shrugged. 'Honest George is far too circumspect a man to make any declaration until it is made freely. He may be for the King but he may not. I would not attach too much importance to what was a common phrase long after the discomposure of the late King Charles.'

This was followed by a general nodding of heads with only one or two dissenters. Few in those dangerous weeks wanted to show for one side or the other, and the Brethren were only too well aware of their mutual policy of concord. Such disinterest, however, did not stop the ceaseless speculation on the streets as the inevitable moment of decision crept daily closer. Indubitably driven by Monck's careful hand, the incremental moves were made to persuade those of influence to recognize the will of the great mass of a people weary of a bullying Army and a power-hungry Rump Parliament. Business denied Faulkner a close following of the ins-and-outs, of the arguments for and against a House of Peers, but the newly elected Parliament met on the twenty-fifth of April, and all the talk was of recalling the exiled Charles to the throne of his fathers, since there were, among the newly returned members, numerous former royalists. Faulkner learned of the communications between Monck and Charles from which it was revealed that the King had made a formal declaration at Breda, the Dutch town at which he was presently resident. This had amounted to an agreement of terms between Charles and the general's secret envoys. Shortly afterwards the Parliament – now consisting at Monck's insistence of two houses – issued a proclamation that King Charles would resume the throne 'by inherent birth-right and lawful succession'. There followed the departure for Breda of the Commissioners appointed to treat with Charles directly and to arrange his speedy return.

Finally, and without his wife, though in the company of Captain Harrison and other sea-captains among the Brethren, Faulkner stood in the Strand and witnessed the triumphant progress of King Charles. The King made a splendid progress, accompanied by cavalry and infantry to the reported number of 20,000, many of the former brandishing their swords and shouting hurrahs as their horses trampled the flowers strewn in the road by the enthusiastic and equally noisy citizens. To add to the din, the church-bells were again rung, while to the glittering cavalcade of nobles and royalists, among them conspicuous exiles who, but a year or two earlier would have had their persons strung up had they appeared in London, was added the garish adornment of tapestries and bright drapery, flags and even bed-sheets upon which were rudely painted words of loyal welcome. At every balcony ladies in their finery, and backed by their maids, threw flowers and longing looks at the dark-visaged King who was, at some six feet and mounted on his charger, a contrast with his diminutive father. The difference prompted enthusiastic comment, eliciting an optimism: 'Things will be different,' people said to each other. 'He is so unlike his father, and his years of exile will have formed a different man.'

At Temple Bar the Lord Mayor, the Aldermen and the Liverymen of a score of Worshipful Companies stood in their chains and robes to greet the King, while the fountains ran with wine at their expense.

In the following days London was full of people from all over the country wealthy enough to come and see the King, who daily showed himself to loud and enthusiastic public acclamation. Adulation of such intensity left Faulkner cold. He had known Charles Stuart as a young man, had been instrumental in the fugitive's escape from his pursuers at the beginning of the

Civil War and, on the way, had taught His Royal Highness the elements of handling a vessel under sail. But he had also known Charles in exile and had lost his great love, Katherine Villiers, to the casual vice of the idle prince. Charles was, he mused to himself back in his house in Wapping, both King and libertine, and Faulkner had little doubt but that his court would be corrupted by the King's pursuit of his courtiers' wives. Well, well, he thought to himself, he had no need to trouble himself. Despite Bence's reference to his knighthood, conferred in the dark days of the King's exile when Faulkner was among a handful of naval commanders willing and able – at their own expense – to wage war on Charles Stuart's behalf, he was confident that he could now sink into quiet obscurity. The restored monarch would have enough to do repairing his damaged country. The best citizens like Faulkner could do was to advance commerce and thereby help, for the public exchequer was empty and money was needed everywhere. The Army needed paying, as did the Navy, for which the repair and building of ships was a necessity. Notwithstanding the hospitality the Dutch had afforded the exiled prince, the Stadtholder and the wealthy burghers of the Seven United Provinces were not eager to allow the English unfettered access to the Spice Islands.

The reflection brought Faulkner again to the consideration of trading with the East Indies. He and Gooding had had majority shares in East Indiamen in years past, and now, he thought, was the time to renew their investment in the trade.

If, as he supposed, young Edmund Drinkwater stood high in the estimation of the Company's Committees, a union with Hannah could have advantages to the house of Gooding and Faulkner. Smiling to himself, Faulkner began to formulate plans to build a new ship for the trade and wondered whether young Drinkwater would suit her as commander. It would be a dowry for Hannah and a shrewd enough move for all concerned.

Later that day he fell into a discussion over the specification for their proposed new ship with Gooding. The two men were deeply into the detail of conforming with the exacting standards demanded by the East India Company, when a messenger arrived with a note. There was nothing unusual in this; such notes were constantly brought to their door, carried from their warehouse or their counting-house. They concerned the business of their ships, or the ships of others for whom they acted as London agents, then lying in the river.

Faulkner slit the wafer, read it and smiled. Looking up at Gooding he remarked, 'Well, well. The Brethren are summoned to Deptford for the first time in a dozen years. Honest George Monck has been created Duke of Albemarle, and we are to consider – along with some other candidates for form's sake, no doubt – electing him our Master.'

'That is no small honour in itself,' said Gooding ironically, a misunderstanding as to Faulkner's enthusiastic involvement with the Trinity House being the sole item of disagreement between them, if one set aside their religious incompatibilities. 'But it is small beer to a man who might have been Protector, was certainly a King-Maker and is now a Duke!'

'That is precisely the reason why I am pleased, my dear Nathan. The Dukedom signifies that Monck's position is secure, his services esteemed by His Majesty. Should we in turn deserve his patronage, then our position, so shaken by the late civil disorders, is reaffirmed.'

'And that is so important to you?'

'Not to me, Nathan, but to the poor devils who have suffered in the late wars and whose condition we shall be in a better position to ameliorate than of late.'

'One might almost think you a Christian, Kit,' Gooding said with a wry smile.

'I should not go that far,' Faulkner responded drily with a laugh.

'There is one thing that is troubling me in all this universal rejoicing,' Gooding said seriously.

'Only one? Good heavens, Nathan,' Faulkner said, his mood still light, unaware of the solemn note air Gooding had assumed. 'I should have thought a Puritan like you would have feared the imminent opening of the gates of Hell itself!'

'I did not note among the King's returning entourage a certain lady...' Gooding let the import of the sentence hang in the air.

A deathly hush fell between the two men. Then Faulkner asked, 'Has your sister prompted this mention of her?'

Gooding shook his head. 'No, but I know the thought is in her mind, and the apprehension of...' He paused awkwardly.

Faulkner interjected, 'Her name is Katherine Villiers, and, if it pleases you, I have neither heard of her, or heard from her, since I abandoned her in Holland. For all I know she is dead. Besides, she is of like age as myself, or nearly so.'

'She is much younger.'

'Only a little ... But does your sister say that?'

Gooding shrugged. 'I only mean—'

'I know what you mean, Nathan, and I appreciate your concern, but your investment will be safe.'

'I know that; it is not my investment, Kit, it is my peace of mind. I do not think that I could tolerate your absconding a second time.'

'You think I still have feelings for the woman?'

'I do not know. I have never had strong feelings for any woman, but I marvel that those that do succumb to the attractions of the opposite sex are apt – upon occasion – to act like madmen.'

Faulkner looked at Gooding and laughed. 'Come, let us decide who is to lay out this Indiaman for us and forget the past. It is like water passed under London Bridge.'

'Perhaps, but the tide brings some, at least, of it back up the stream.'

That night Faulkner dreamed of building their new East Indiaman. The dream passed pleasantly as the ships rose on the stocks until it came to the day of her launching. Then Judith came screaming, wild-eyed, onto the scene, tearing at her hair which flew about her face. She was followed by

Henry, whose face was that of a pallid corpse, and Hannah, holding a posy and who had been given the honour of launching the ship. The great hull, decked out with flags and ensigns, began to move. The King was in attendance, a great honour conferred upon Sir Christopher Faulkner, one among the greatest of the ship-owners of London. On the river in their barges, the Lord Mayor of London, the Aldermen and Liverymen and the Elder Brethren of the Trinity House paid their respects. Other boats crowded the river and, besides the cheering populace, the merchant ships lying in the tiers all fired their guns in salute. But above it all the sharp keening of Judith rent the air and introduced a note of warning. Faulkner began to sweat in his sleep, to twist and turn as the dream reached its climax.

As the great Indiaman slid down the ways, her transom breasted the dark waters of the Thames and drove a white wave before it. The great stern had passed before he had read her name, and it now occurred to him that the question of the ship's name was unresolved. Yet Hannah had launched it. He could not recall what name she had used! They were in the presence of the King, and as Faulkner turned to look at His Majesty he saw the wide grin below the dark eyes and the black mustachios. Something was wrong; something was terribly, terribly wrong. Then the Indiaman's bow flew past Faulkner. He was now alone and for some inexplicable reason exposed upon an elevated platform level with the passing gun-deck of the ship as, with a roar, she accelerated down the greased slipway. It was then that he knew why Judith wailed so intensely, for the new ship's figurehead sped past him: it was a superb carving of the beautiful Katherine Villiers.

Indemnity and Oblivion

June 1660–May 1661
'I suggest, gentlemen, that you leave your papers with me, and I shall give you a price per ton within the week.'

'She must lade at the standard five hundred tons burthen, Sir Henry,' Nathan Gooding said firmly. Faulkner looked on; he had deliberately allowed his brother-in-law to lead the negotiations.

Sir Henry Johnson smiled. 'I admire your ambition, gentlemen. Five hundred tons is increasingly favoured by the Company's Court and, if you entertain any misgivings as to the likelihood of your vessel being accepted, I think I can lay such anxieties to rest.' Johnson looked directly at Faulkner. 'The past is the past, Captain, and we here at Blackwall look to the future.' Johnson rose and held out his hand; Faulkner and Gooding scraped back their chairs, shook the master-shipwright's hand and, donning their hats, passed out into the bustle of the shipyard.

'I thought him civil enough, in the circumstances,' Gooding said as they stopped and stared about them. Faulkner merely grunted.

Two ships lay in frame on the slips, their curved futtocks rising high above the ground and prompting Gooding to remark on the activity. 'He builds remarkably fast, though I cannot see a slip being free for three or four months.'

'That need not concern us once we have proceeded to contract. I thought him optimistic on our behalf, though he was pointed enough to remind me of my sins.'

'They were my Indiamen you attacked, brother-in-law,' Gooding said, good-naturedly seizing the opportunity to get one-up over Faulkner. 'And good men were killed,' he added in a sober tone.

'On both sides, I would remind you, brother-in-law,' Faulkner responded.

Gooding was minded to remark that his Indiamen had been lying peacefully at anchor when attacked by Faulkner and his royalist pirates, but thought better of it. He possessed the rare good-sense to hold his tongue when no good would come of not so doing.

They stood in the summer sunshine, regarding the two ships and the sparkling river beyond the declivity of the slipways. It was, as always, alive with craft of every size, from riverine stumpie barges and passenger wherries to the dominating form of an ocean-going East Indiaman alongside the sheer-hulk, receiving her mizzen mast.

'Come, let us go,' said Gooding, pulling at Faulkner's sleeve.

'Wait a moment.' Faulkner drew away and walked towards the nearer of the two building-

60

slipways. A rickety scaffolding rose round the massive oak frames that stood every few feet, rebated and bolted to the horizontal keel, a huge timber below which lay a false keel. Above the cross-sections of the futtocks lay the equally solid keelson. Men toiled about the half-formed ship, mostly at this stage ship-wrights, their mates and apprentices, drilling holes and driving either copper bolts or wooden pegs, known as trenells, to fasten the rib-like frames to the spinal form of the keel. The smell of pitch, of smoke and steam from the steam chests, the sweet scent of wood shavings mingled in the still summer air. The tonk-tonk of the shipwrights' mallets, the harder ring of steel maul on copper bolt-head, the whinny of a horse drawing a heavily laden cart into the timber yard and the dull rasp of the saws in the saw-pits filled the air. An occasional shouted order broke through the noise of chaffing and conversation among the men at work, while one man whistled tunelessly as he banged away.

On the sheer-hulk Faulkner could see men at a capstan and an over-seer on the rail, one hand extended and motioning for the men to veer, then to stop. He heard faintly the instruction to: 'Engage the pawl!' Then the men at the capstan visibly relaxed their labours. Beyond the ship-yard out on the river the craft moved lazily, their sails barely filled by the wind, driven upstream by the flood-tide. Those bound downstream carried the faint westerly air, their motion pain-fully slow set against the far side of the river. Some had abandoned the attempt and had laid to an anchor until the tide turned and helped them on their way.

Not for the first time Faulkner wondered at how few collisions there were, recalling sailing down this very river when first appointed to command the *King's Whelp*. That had been a long time ago, and he did not like to dwell upon the past, but he could not escape the vivid reality of the dream he had had, even after three days had passed. It was odd, he thought, how a dream, which he knew was a product of nothing more than his own imagination, could nevertheless so unsettle him. He knew he was a fool for thinking of it; even supposing he encountered Katharine Villiers in the street, too much time had passed for either one of them to recognize the other. He threw off the train of thought; he was no love-sick youth, mooning over a lady beyond his reach. There was enough to occupy him in the here-and-now, without reviewing what had long since passed beyond recovery. He turned with a sigh and looked back to Gooding standing at the top of the slipway, patiently waiting for him. There was a good and sound man, Faulkner thought, lifting his hand to him before striding purposefully towards him.

'Come, Nathan,' he said brusquely as he drew alongside his partner. 'We have no time to stand and stare like a pair of loons.'

Used to his partner's poor taste in jest Gooding made no response but fell in step alongside Faulkner as they made for the gate of the yard, passing Sir Henry's large private dwelling known by all who knew of it as his mansion-house.

'He keeps up some style, by God,' Faulkner remarked as they passed the sentry on the gate who saluted their departure. 'Even the guards wear his livery.'

'Johnson is a well-regarded man, as well-regarded as the Petts at Chatham,' added Gooding.

'All those who build ships – whether for the King or we merchant-owners – have a curious reluctance to spend much time in them. They dispose of their business so that the poor mariner has no choice in the matter.'

'If you have any notions it would be as well to voice them.'

'Oh, I shall, I shall.'

Two days later, on the eighteenth of June, Faulkner joined Harrison, Bence and the other Brethren at the old Trinity Hall at Deptford. Here they elected George Monck, Duke of Albemarle, their Master for the year ahead before processing to church to join their alms-people all assembled from the adjacent alms-houses. From there they returned to the Hall and enjoyed a hearty dinner. On their way back upstream in a wherry, Harrison, knowing of Faulkner's intention of building an East Indiaman, asked whether Faulkner had decided where to have her built.

'We have contracted with Johnson's yard at Blackwall,' he replied.

'A good choice,' Harrison conceded. 'You will pay a little above the common price elsewhere but will have little trouble getting the ship taken up by the Company in due course.'

'That is what we supposed,' Faulkner said, nevertheless pleased with Harrison's approval.

Six weeks later Johnson's men laid the keel of the new ship. She was known to be building to the specification laid down by the East India Company, and by the end of ten weeks her frames had begun to rise. The partners were in negotiation with the East India Company's ship's husbands who provided the tonnage required for the company's annual ventures, several of whom were fellow Trinity Brethren of Faulkner's. He knew these men well, and they placed little obstacle in the way of their adding Faulkner and Gooding's new ship to those suitable to tender for the Company's Maritime Service, ventures in which they had previously participated. As the new ship grew upon the stocks, the partners' walk to Blackwall became part of their weekly routine, and although the work slowed as the winter set in, it nevertheless went forward at a steady pace.

They had put down a deposit on the signing of the contract and, despite Faulkner's occasional modification to Johnson's construction, the financing of the new vessel proceeded with equal smoothness.

Christmas came and went, but January brought a sombre event, for on the thirtieth, the anniversary of the late King's execution, the disinterred corpses of Cromwell, Ireton and Bradshaw were dragged to Tyburn, hanged and buried in a deep pit. Although the event was common knowledge, no-one in the family mentioned it and, as far as Faulkner was aware, none of his relatives witnessed the horrid event. Indeed, the building of the new ship introduced an air of optimism, of looking forward and anticipating a promising future.

'The past is past and should be left to rot,' Faulkner was accustomed to growl when any conversation at the dinner-table seemed like growing retrospective.

'Thank God this is a time of peace,' Gooding was fond of pointing out, to which Faulkner came to retort that this circumstance was entirely due to the King's restoration. The word-play became so common a feature of their weekly perambulation that they grew used to laughing at it.

'Johnson has kept to his compounding at eleven pounds to the ton,' Gooding said as they discussed their forthcoming payment which fell due several weeks into the New Year. Faulkner nodded, looking down at the papers over which Gooding toiled. 'We have not decided what to call her,' Gooding added, looking up at him.

'I thought "Wapping" a suitable name.'

'"Wapping",' mused Gooding for a moment before nodding agreement. 'Then "Wapping" it shall be.' He made an entry at the foot of a column of figures before writing *Wapping* across the head of the top-sheet. Laying his quill down, Gooding sanded the wet ink and sat back, wearily rubbing his eyes. 'Great heavens, but my eyes pain me; my sight is not what it was. He looked up at Faulkner. 'Shall you pour a glass that we might drink to the East Indiaman *Wapping*?'

'With all my heart,' responded Faulkner, reaching for the flagon of wine.

It was a bright spring forenoon in mid-May of 1661, and Faulkner and Gooding were ambling back from Blackwall after spending some hours at the yard, as the *Wapping*, nearing completion and being readied for her launch, demanded an increasing amount of their time. They had become familiar with the bustle in the lane, and their faces were known to the regular coster-mongers, carters and itinerant craftsmen that walked hither-and-yon, either in search of work, or proceeding to or from it. The pleasantness of the morning caused them to meander, making intermittent conversation, until Faulkner, keeping a better lookout than his partner, asked, 'Is that young Hargreaves heading our way?'

He had spotted one of the young clerks they employed in their counting-house. The lad, no older than fourteen, was dodging his way through the steady procession of loaded carts and casual labourers seeking work who almost choked the lane leading to the Blackwall ship-yard.

'Good sirs!' the youth cried, stopping in front of them and drawing his breath.

'What on earth is the matter? You sound like an actor declaiming Shakespeare. Has St Paul's tumbled down?' Faulkner asked as the lad recovered his breath.

He shook his head and then announced: 'I am sent to tell you that the Duke of Albemarle attended Goodwife Faulkner, sirs, and is asking for you, Cap'n Faulkner.'

'Good heavens, what doth he want of you, Kit?' Gooding rounded on Faulkner.

'I have no idea. Unless he comes to warn me that the Act of Indemnity and Oblivion has named me as an enemy of the state...'

'I beg you not to jest thus!'

'Oh, for the love of the Lord God, Nathan...' An exasperated and yet half amused Faulkner turned to the lad. 'Have you any idea, Charlie?'

Charles Hargreaves shook his head and shrugged his shoulders. 'No, sir. Only that I was told to tell you that his lordship ought not to be kept waiting and I should run all the way to Blackwall to fetch you as he insisted on speaking with you directly and would leave neither message nor paper.'

'Then we had better assume the guise of Mercury,' said Faulkner. 'Come, Charlie, clear the way for us.'

Honest George had been waiting for over an hour by the time Faulkner reached home; despite his flippancy, Faulkner was embarrassed at keeping Albemarle waiting. He had left Gooding to return to the counting-house with Charlie Hargreaves and come on alone. Now he threw his hat on a chair. 'I am sorry to have detained you, Your Grace,' Faulkner began, but Albemarle waved away his apologies, apparently untroubled by the delay.

Albemarle indicated Hannah who sat opposite to him. 'Your charming daughter has been telling me of a voyage to the East Indies upon which I understand her betrothed is currently embarked in the *Eagle*, East Indiaman.'

'I see...'

'The matter clearly preoccupies her,' Albemarle said with a smile, nodding at Hannah as she bobbed a curtsey and withdrew, her face scarlet with embarrassment and confusion.

'We are, Your Grace, so unsympathetic to the young, even though we know the travail they are under,' remarked Faulkner, pouring two stoups of wine and handing one to Albemarle.

'You are right, but now that I am here I had better discharge my office, which is to require you to join me tomorrow at Court.'

'Court, your Grace? You mean the King's Court, not that of Trinity House?'

'I mean the King's Court, Sir Kit, whither I am bidden to convey you by Clarendon.'

Faulkner felt uneasy. Such a summons followed too hard upon the morning's reverie and his recent dream not to invoke the seaman's superstitious sense that he privately carried within him. His jest about the Act that had been passed by the Parliament and received the Royal Assent had not been made entirely devoid of self-interest.

'Are you aware of why I am thus honoured, your Grace? For I must be so honoured if you have been charged to fetch me and have condescended to—'

'I have not condescended, Captain. I am not risen so far that I would consider you as beyond my regard.' Albemarle chuckled to himself. 'These are curious times, Captain; we are forging a new world. Think you that in the old I should have been a duke? Ha! Never! As for you, you are probably to be preferred in some way. I understand the King and his brother are intent upon some sailing; perhaps you are summoned for this reason. You have a pinnace of your own, I understand.' Albemarle looked at Faulkner. 'Does that satisfy you?'

Faulkner gave a half bow. 'I am at the King's command, your Grace, and at your disposal. Shall you stay to dine with us?'

Albemarle paused to consider the matter. 'What o'clock is it?'

'Shortly before two, I believe. We have a saddle of mutton...'

'I have already divined that, Captain,' said Albemarle, tapping his nose, 'and I find it as irresistible as your daughter.'

After dinner, during which the duke was affability itself, even succeeding in winning both smiles and pleasantries out of Judith, Albemarle showed no desire to hurry away. The two men sat with their pipes and, having discussed some matter relative to the charitable disbursements of the Trinity House and the failure of the state to relieve want and penury among seamen injured in its service, Albemarle remarked upon the debate then in progress through the House of Commons.

'You have heard of the passing of the recent Act of Indemnity and Oblivion?'

'Indeed, Your Grace. I understand that there are many who regard it as providing indemnity for the King's enemies and oblivion for his friends.'

Albemarle chuckled. 'Yes, I had heard that was what the wits were saying, but it restores at a stroke all crown and church lands. Pursuing private claims for recovery of what is rightfully yours will be subject to litigation, but there will be many who lack the deep pockets necessary to go to such an extreme.'

'An injustice for those who have expended their fortunes in the Royalist cause,' added Faulkner.

'There is always a price to progress,' said Albemarle, 'but after the cries of outrage have died away, then I do sincerely hope that the business of government can look to the future. The Dutch are again encroaching upon our trade, and we shall, I'll wager, fight with them again before we are through. 'Tis a pity, for they are much to be admired, but I fear there is no room for both nations without another trial of strength.'

Faulkner nodded. 'I am in perfect harmony with you there, Your Grace. Moreover, I apprehend we shall have difficulties toppling them. They are better financed than ourselves, pay more attention to trade than to other preoccupations, and have withal a readier fleet. I happened to be at Deptford when deciding where to build a new ship and the King's Dockyard there seemed scarcely a model for efficiency.'

'Despite the Petts?' Albemarle asked, raising one eyebrow.

'Perhaps because of the Petts,' Faulkner responded with a smile.

'Wherever the hand of man turns itself to good

employment, it finds itself mired in the stink of corruption. Still, matters are better regulated than in the time of the present King's father, I think, though you would know more of that than I.'

'That is very true.'

'Well, perhaps the Act of Indemnity and Oblivion will draw a much-needed curtain over past misdeeds so that we can move our ravaged country into happier times.'

'If that is its intention, Your Grace; but I hear some vengeance is inevitable.'

Albemarle blew a plume of thick blue smoke at the ceiling and nodded. 'Yes, His Majesty will seek to execute the Regicides still living. The disinterment of Cromwell and his son-in-law was but the beginning.'

'That was a poor thing.'

'But we must bow to the inevitable, Sir Kit, and you would do well not to express yourself with such freedom.'

'I beg Your Grace's pardon...'

'Think nothing of it. You are under your own roof, but I would not have so valuable a sea-officer compromise himself in the hearing of some of the toadies that infest all courts.'

'Your Grace is most considerate.'

Albemarle knocked out his pipe and hove himself to his feet. His leather jack-boots creaked as he stretched himself. 'I shall present you tomorrow. Make yourself known at Whitehall Palace shortly before ten of the clock.'

Faulkner bowed and saw Albemarle to the street door. Here the duke was joined by his two armed servants who had been in Faulkner's kitchen and, by the look of them, had quaffed more of Faulkner's ale than was good for them. Knowing that she would speak of their visitor later when they retired, Faulkner decided not to talk to Judith or to pursue Hannah and tease her on account of Albemarle's flirting; instead he walked down to the counting-house in anticipation of finding Gooding where he had been left on their way back from Blackwall.

He found Gooding ensconced with Captain John Lamont, a Scots master with whom Gooding had insisted they went into a partnership. Lamont owned a small bilander upon which he wished to raise a mortgage in order to marry. It was a matter of a few hundred pounds, and Faulkner had warned that with the fitting-out of the *Wapping* imminent, they ought not to overreach themselves. The matter had raised the temperature between them and had been decided by Judith, who bought into the venture, so that in the end Faulkner had withdrawn his objection. Nevertheless, he considered Gooding owed him a favour.

'What did My Lord Duke of Albemarle want of you?' Gooding asked with an air of mild sarcasm.

'I am to be presented at Court.'

Gooding stared, open-mouthed.

'You will catch flies, Nathan,' Faulkner remarked.

'I wish that you were not,' Gooding said.

'It is a royal command,' Faulkner said shortly, dismissing Gooding's apprehensions. 'But I have had a further thought. I conceive it to be a good idea if we call our new ship "Albemarle"...'

Later, when Faulkner and his wife retired for the night, Judith addressed the problem of the morrow. 'I wish you had not agreed to attend Court,' she said curtly. 'You had said you would lie low and attend to our own affairs, not meddle with the high-born who return from exile only to pretend nothing has happened these last ten years.'

Faulkner suppressed his exasperation. 'I am commanded by the Duke of Albemarle, Judith. He speaks for the King; what would you have me do – spit in Albemarle's eye and tell him to inform the King that I am indisposed?'

'The King would be none the wiser...'

'Indeed not,' Faulkner said, taking the wig from his head, placing it on its stand and scratching his pate. 'He would simply summon me the instant I was on my feet again. And what do you suppose might be the consequences of his learning that only this morning I was discussing a new ship with Sir Henry Johnson? I would say that at the very least His Majesty—'

'*His Majesty*!' Judith spat the words from her like a foul oath, letting her hair down and turning on him so that she made him think of a harpy. 'And as for the noble Duke of Albemarle, he is a triple turncoat, unless, of course, I have lost count. It is a wonder which of you is the greater chameleon.'

'Oh, Judith, desist and give way,' he said wearily, kicking off his shoes and fearing the direction the conversation was taking. 'Thou knowest times have changed and we must change with them.'

'No, the *King* does not acknowledge that; he counts his reign from the death of his father ... Where are you going?'

'Somewhere far from the owl screech that I am subject to.'

Faulkner took his candle up to the attic and unlocked his private room. Through the thin wall he could hear the low and even snore of their kitchen-maid. He sat and stared about him, much as he had done a week or so earlier when he had summoned Henry. He saw the smear of his finger where it had dragged through the rust on his corroding cuirass and encircled the dent driven in by the Dutch ball that had only partially been knocked out.

'I should black that,' he mused to himself. 'God knows but I might yet require it if old George is right about the Dutch. And if he is,' he added thinking of Judith, *'that* would not distress me too much, either.'

Then his eye fell on the portmanteau, and this time he did not resist the temptation to open it and withdraw the telescope. It was in a soft leather bag and, thanks to its origins, possibly his most cherished possession. The feel of it in his hand revived the recollection of the dream wherein the face of Katherine Villiers had so surprised him, appearing at the bow of their proposed new Indiaman. Perhaps, he thought in a moment of pure devilry, he should have the ship named 'Villiers' and adorn her with such a figure-head. It would damn well serve Judith right!

No, that was an ungenerous thought; unfair too. He extended the telescope, noted the faint resistance from lack of use, then closed it with a snap, turning it in his hands. Those distant days when he was a lieutenant aboard the *Prince Royal*, and the exquisitely lovely Mistress Villiers had been attending her grand cousin, George Villiers, Duke of Buckingham, seemed to have played a part in another man's life.

'Who am I?' he asked the chill night air, recalling the wastrel boy who stole apple-cores on the waterfront of Bristol until rescued by Sir Henry Mainwaring. He thought of Katherine and their love-making – and that also seemed too remote to have involved him. 'Who am I?' he repeated.

The metaphysical question hung for a moment until Faulkner's practical spirit dispatched it. 'Bah! What a damned foolish question!' he muttered to himself with some vehemence. 'What man knows? And be he even a king, he is blown by the winds of fate so that one day he is up and the next he is down.' He thought of poor Clarkson, one of his officers aboard the *Union* when they had fought the Dutch. Faulkner had been standing next to him, deep in conversation one moment, and the next Clarkson was dead, his loins shot-out by a ball that severed his trunk from his legs. 'And Nathan speaks of a God,' he muttered almost incredulously, suddenly angry at the dull incomprehension of all those who lived on land.

With a sigh he put the telescope back in its bag, reflecting that it bore witness to the fact that he had indeed been that young man in the *Prince Royal* all those years ago. He returned the relic to its resting place, placated by the instrument's solid existence. He rummaged idly through the rest of the box. It held some manuscript books; some loose papers, all of them long redundant; some nautical instruments and tarpaulin head-gear that the seamen called a sou'-wester; and a large wheel-lock, wrapped in oiled cloth.

Faulkner pulled it out and peeled off the cloth. The pistol was of exquisite German workman-ship and he recalled acquiring it during his exile. Age made him sentimental as well as forgetful. How he now wished that he had given it to Henry. He had thought of it, if the boy had gone to sea as he desired, and now it was too late. He should have done it the moment he thought of it but had hesitated for fear the boy saw it as a crude inducement. No, it was a pity, but such an obvious *douceur* might have wrecked their apparent reconciliation.

Faulkner sighed again. A son with whom he had been at loggerheads, a wife whose politics were likely to encumber them both, and now an imminent meeting with the King, whose lust had utterly destroyed the one true doomed love of Faulkner's life. There was nothing he could do about any of it, he concluded and, moreover, he must get some sleep before Honest George pre-sented him to His Majesty King Charles II.

As instructed Faulkner presented himself at

Whitehall Palace the following forenoon. He was decked out in his best finery, a suit of sober dark blue, the sleeves of his doublet un-slashed with breeches of blue above white silk stockings. The silver buckles on his belt and shoes, and the Dutch lace at his collar and wrists, were the only sign of ostentation. He had bought the outfit on his return home, in spite of Judith's misgivings. He held his plain, wide, curled-brimmed hat along with his grey gloves in his left hand, his sword-stick in the right, looking every inch the successful merchant. He recalled a visit to the Court of the first Charles that he had made years earlier in the company of Sir Henry Mainwaring and looked about him curiously as he was conducted towards the throne room. He cast the recollection of the past aside, for that too contained the memory of Katherine Villiers.

A moment later he was caught up in the bustle as others, keener than he to enjoy the privilege of proximity to the royal personage, hurried forward to secure their place at the assembly. Idly, Faulkner wondered how many had earlier favoured the contrary party and formerly displayed soberer apparel? Did a country need a king to answer some deep-seated desire for general cohesion? He concluded that he rather inclined to the belief that it did.

'Sir? Your stick, sir. I apprehend it contains a sword-blade.'

'What? Oh, of course.' He surrendered the weapon. Clearly, the King was nervous of his subjects. One of the Lord Chamberlain's flunkies took his stick, but he retained his hat and gloves and caught sight of Albemarle waiting for him. 'Good morrow, Your Grace, I have kept you waiting again.'

'Sir Kit, good morrow. It is not to be wondered at; this is like Billingsgate. Come.'

It was unnecessary to force their way through the throng. After the King himself, the imposing figure of Albemarle was the best known in the three kingdoms, whether one knew of him as Monck, 'Honest George' or as Duke of Albemarle. It was said that Honest George was free to enter the King's presence at any time, and to remain there until the King himself specifically asked him to retire.

Having worked his way to the front of the noisy throng, Albemarle took his station, indicating Faulkner should stand on his right. Faulkner had little time to stare about him, though he recognized the hall and knew by which entrance the King would emerge. He felt an attack of nerves, apprehensive at the reception he would receive at the royal hands. Looking sideways he judged there were perhaps two people to whom the King might speak before he came to Albemarle, such was Honest George's standing. Faulkner thought he recognized Clarendon among them, but the other was unfamiliar to him. Then a functionary banged a staff three times on the floor, the babble fell away and a voice cried out: 'His Majesty the King!'

With a scrape of shoes, a sweeping of arms and a susurration of silk skirts, the entire assembly bowed or curtseyed. Those gentlemen, like Albemarle and Faulkner in the front of the crowd, thrust forward their right feet and drew back their left hands, their hat brims gathering the dust of the floor.

As he straightened up, it seemed the King stood before him. 'My Lord Duke,' the King said, smiling and taking Albemarle's hand. Set in the King's strong features, dark eyes – at which Faulkner hardly dare to look – regarded him keenly as Albemarle made a gesture of presentation with his right hand. 'Your Majesty may I have the honour—'

But he got no further, for the King held out his hand. 'Ho! But it is Sir Kit, is it not?'

'Your Majesty,' Faulkner murmured, hardly daring to take the King's finger-tips and bow his head over the perfumed glove of soft leather that concealed them. He remarked the large ring the King wore.

'You taught me to con a vessel, sir, for which I am indebted.'

'Your Majesty is most kind...' He was about to relinquish the royal hand but the King maintained a strong grip.

'I would speak privately with you, Sir Kit,' he murmured and, turning to Albemarle, said in a low voice, 'see to it, Duke.'

A moment later the king was gone; he could be heard discussing the racing at Newmarket with a couple ornately dressed in silks and covered in jewels that stood alongside them.

'What am I to make of this summons, Your Grace?' Faulkner asked Albemarle as they emerged into the rough bustle of Whitehall.

'I have asked that you serve again in the Navy,

Sir Christopher. I imagine His Majesty wishes to commission you directly.' Albemarle paused as Faulkner digested this news, his imagination filling with a myriad of pros and cons. Then Albemarle added, 'He is like to want to test your loyalty for himself. These are still early days for him ... you understand?'

'Of course.' He paused. 'Your Grace, may I ask a favour? May we name our new ship in your honour?'

Honest George chuckled. 'Of course,' he said, his eyes twinkling. 'But I have had enough of titles. On the other hand, if it were to be my wife after whom the ship was to be named, it would please me greatly.'

Faulkner smiled and bowed. 'Then the "Duchess of Albemarle" she shall be, Your Grace.'

Faulkner did not have to wait long. The following day an elegantly clad gentleman arrived at his house at Wapping, commanding him to attend the King the next morning. On his arrival at Whitehall Palace he was immediately conducted by way of several passages into the King's private chambers. Left to kick his heels in an ante-room for half an hour, he was summoned into the royal presence about noon.

The King sat at a table covered with papers. Beside him, to his left, was the man Faulkner had recognized two days previously as Clarendon. The two were conversing over a document and without looking up the King motioned Faulkner to come closer. He stopped a few feet from the table and made a deep bow, keeping his eyes lowered as he came upright. The dull drone of the conference between the King and Clarendon, his Chief Minister and leader of the Privy Council, ceased, and the King sat back, regarding the downcast Faulkner.

'Well, Sir Christopher, we meet again.'

'Your Majesty,' Faulkner responded.

'I have summoned you, Sir Kit, not because of any past love I may have had for your person, notwithstanding your past services, for you were among those who deserted me...' Faulkner made no move, though he felt the colour mounting into his face. The King's pause was pregnant with foreboding, an earnest of his power, and yet Faulkner could not escape the notion that he was being toyed with, as if the King's silence was a lure for him to speak. 'You have nothing to say?'

'No, Your Majesty.'

'Nothing at all?'

'Nothing beyond expressing my desire to serve Your Majesty.'

'Is that all?'

'What would Your Majesty have me say, beyond pledging my allegiance? These have been difficult times, Sire.'

'You served the so-called Protector.'

'I conceived that I served my country, Your Majesty. The Protector had me mewed up in The Tower.'

'Look at me, Captain Faulkner,' the King commanded.

Faulkner raised his eyes and met the King's gaze. Anyone as unlike his father would have been hard to conceive. Where his small-statured parent was haughty, yet halting, a stammerer whose insistence on his divine right to rule his realm without the benefit of a Parliament had sat oddly with his diffidence, the son had a solid, worldly air. Charles's eyes were not only dark, but they were penetrating. His features were strong and his body was that of a powerful man.

'You are an honest fellow, I think,' the King said with a certain heartiness after appraising Faulkner for a moment or two. 'And honourable – perhaps too honourable for your own good.'

Faulkner frowned at the ambiguity, but held his tongue. Was the King referring to...? But no, that was impossible. Charles might condescend a little; but not to the extent that Faulkner perhaps hoped for. He drove the thought from his mind. This was no time to be self-indulgent.

'The Duke of Albemarle speaks well of you. He valued your late services at sea, and I hope, should it become necessary at any time in the future, that I may count upon your exertions on my behalf.'

'I am at Your Majesty's service,' Faulkner responded with a half bow.

The King sighed. 'You are indeed. But there is the matter of your son.'

'My son?' Faulkner was unable to conceal his astonishment.

'You have two sons, do you not?'

'Yes, Your Majesty.'

'And do you know of their whereabouts?'

'One is at sea in command of one of my ships engaged in a voyage to Jamaica—'

'And the other? The one named...' The King's hand passed over one of the papers lying before him.

Faulkner heard Clarendon murmur: 'Henry.'

'Is also at sea, on a voyage in the East Indiaman *Eagle*,' Faulkner said firmly.

'Do you dissemble, Captain Faulkner?' It was Clarendon's voice, speaking to him for the first time. Faulkner shot him a quick glance, before confronting the King. He could feel a rank sweat break out; his breathing seemed difficult, and he felt his face flush. The fact that he was not in command of himself increased his bafflement. 'Sire, I have ... He wrote to me from Gravesend, from the *Eagle*...' The King's eyes transfixed him.

'Did you arrange the voyage, Captain Faulkner?' Clarendon asked.

Faulkner shook his head. 'No, no, My Lord. I was desirous that he went to sea but he would not go upon my own terms...' He paused, shaking his head as if to clear it, before going on. 'I would have had him sail in one of my own vessels, under the supervision of one of my own shipmasters.'

'But he defied you,' Clarendon suggested.

'Indeed, he did, My Lord.'

'And then wrote to you and said he had shipped aboard this Indiaman.' The King set the very obvious facts of Henry's hoax before him.

'But you did not see him board this Indiaman, nor see her sail, nor find out whether any man came ashore at Deal?' Clarendon asked.

'Your Majesty, am I to conclude that you have

83

information that he did not sail in the *Eagle* and that he is here, in London?'

'And keeping dangerous company.'

'Very dangerous company,' added Clarendon. 'You knew nothing of this?'

Faulkner shook his head. He could say little more. A vehement protestation of ignorance would, he felt instinctively, fail to convince either of his interlocutors. 'No,' he breathed in a low voice, 'nothing.'

'Well,' said the King, raising his right hand from its resting place on the papers before him, 'you should look to your son, sir, and mew him up before I am obliged to—' The King brought the palm of his hand down flat upon the papers with a small slap. It was eloquent of royal prerogative.

'You are aware of the Act of Indemnity and Oblivion?' Clarendon asked, as though eager to add his own intimidation to that of the King's.

'I am.' Faulkner paused and then said, 'Your Majesty is most kind but I am at a loss to know where my son is at present.'

'Ask Lady Faulkner, Sir Christopher,' said the King, drawing himself up in his chair and indicating the subject was closed. Faulkner stood stunned for a moment, before bowing again. He would have withdrawn but the King restrained him. 'One moment more. There is another matter,' he said, 'a small service with which you may oblige me.'

Faulkner looked up. 'Your Majesty?'

The King held out his hand; Clarendon lifted a sealed letter which lay on the table, put it into the

King's outstretched hand, whereupon the King extended it to Faulkner. 'Be so kind as to see this is placed into the hand of Lord Craven at Leicester House.'

'You know where that is?' asked Clarendon.

'I do, My Lord.'

Faulkner took the letter directly from the King's hand, sensible of the honour done him. This small errand of trust meant more than that he was expected to convey a missive from the King to a nobleman, but was at odds with the serious charge against Henry.

'Look to your son,' the King repeated as he waved Faulkner away, appearing to resume work on his papers. Then, just as Faulkner was about to make his final bow, the King caught his eye. 'And to your wife, Sir Christopher.'

'Your Majesty.' Stung, Faulkner bowed and, still perspiring heavily, his mind in a turmoil, backed away from the royal presence.

When he found himself in the chaos of Whitehall, Faulkner allowed himself a low but heartfelt oath. The King's reference first to 'Lady Faulkner', a title that Judith never used, conveyed to Faulkner something awful. He was suddenly angry with her; maddened by her refusal to see how the world had changed, and infuriated by her apparent complicity in Henry's outrageous deception, about which the King was so well-informed. He had almost forgotten the King's letter but knew that he must first set it in the hand of Lord Craven.

Leicester House, Lord Craven's London residence, lay within the City of London, and Faulkner, anxious to have matters out with his wife, sped there without much thought about his mission. The house fronted the street, and his over-eager banging of its door-knocker quickly summoned a man-servant.

'I have a personal letter from His Majesty The King for Lord Craven,' he explained.

The man drew back and gestured for Faulkner to enter. Half expecting the servant to request he hand the letter over, he added, 'I am to deliver it personally.'

'Of course.' The man-servant inclined his head. 'But His Lordship iss absent...'

'Absent?' Faulkner was puzzled. 'But I must see ... somebody who...' He got no further. The manservant was not obstructive, only protective of his master.

'Plees, may I haf your name?'

'Captain Sir Christopher Faulkner,' he responded. The man-servant repeated the name and Faulkner nodded.

'*Danke*.' The man's accent was thick and, to Faulkner, sounded like that of a Dutchman. He gathered his wits, pushing all thoughts of Judith and Henry out of his mind for the time being. Of course! The servant was a Bohemian, and this, he recollected, looking about the paved hall in which he had been left to wait, was the residence of Queen Elizabeth of Bohemia, King Charles's aunt. Another monarch dispossessed by war, she was also mother to Prince Rupert of the Rhine, who, he had heard, shared the residence with her.

As the moments of idle waiting ticked by, he

found his thoughts returning to his personal predicament. He would have to confront Judith immediately and locate Henry without delay. The only possible thing to be done was to have the boy put on board a ship by force, removing him from the Kingdom for a few months. He racked his brains to recall which of their ships would next sail for the West Indies, but found himself gripped by some mental paralysis, unable to recollect the detail. He tore off his right glove and rubbed his eyes.

'Damn, damn, damn,' he muttered under his breath.

And then, just when he felt his world had been capsized, it turned over yet again.

'Kit? Can it be you?'

A rapidly approaching murmur of silk came with the waft of a scent that tore at his very sanity. He looked up at a woman standing before him and stepped back hard against the wall.

'Christ Jesus!' he choked, unable to catch his breath after his blasphemy, for he was staring into the still lustrous eyes of Katherine Villiers.

Katherine Villiers

May 1661

As a boy Faulkner had felt faint with hunger; he also knew the weird and debilitating effects of the trauma of a wounding, followed by an effusion of blood. He knew, all too recently, how disarming shocking news could affect a man's composure, but this, this whirl of emotion, of a choking sensation that made the heart trip and then hammer, that set his head in a spin, made his eyes water and his legs fail him: this was something altogether new and terrifying.

He staggered back hard against the wall, feeling preposterous, foolish and yet over-come with shock at the encounter, guilt as the recollection of their parting and yet ... and yet an overwhelming joy. 'Kate,' he breathed as his vision cleared and he held out a hand to her, fearful that he should receive a rebuff.

'Come,' she said simply, taking his hand and drawing him quickly into a side room, the furnishings of which he could never afterwards recall. Still holding hands, they stood stock-still, close enough for each to feel the breath of the other. He could see that time had taken its toll: she was thin and pale, her skin bore the marks of time, but her features – devoid of paste or patches – were as lovely as ever, and he could tell by the heaving of her bosom that she too was in turmoil as they gazed into each other's eyes, almost stupefied.

'I fear we are preposterous,' she said at last, with a smile and an embarrassed little laugh.

'I do not care how we look, only that I can look at nothing else.'

'I am so pleased to see you,' she responded. 'Since I came back to London a week or so ago I have been tempted to seek you out but I could not.'

He shook his head. 'I did not know ... How came you here?'

'In the train of Her Majesty; I am a lady in waiting to the Queen of Bohemia living in exile here, and I am as beholden to Lord Craven for my accommodation as is Her Majesty herself.' He stood looking at her, unable to say anything, digesting the plain facts, and she, awkward herself, ploughed on. 'His Lordship has been a steadfast friend and staunchly loyal servant of The Queen.' She made a little gesture. 'This is his house...'

'Yes, yes, I know,' he said, gathering his wits. 'That is why I am here, to see his Lordship.'

'How so?' she asked, a puzzled look on her face.

He stepped back and drew the King's letter from his doublet. 'I bear him a letter from the hand of the King.'

'Then...' She frowned before continuing: 'But the King knows Lord Craven is in Oxford in hope of turning up papers relating to—'

'Then why...?'

It dawned on both of them simultaneously, breaking the artificial but necessary discourse that had thrust itself upon them in the wake of their mutual shocks. 'He knew you were here,' Faulkner said wonderingly.

'He knew that we parted...'

'Because of him?'

'Because of what you thought of him.'

'He cared that much?'

'You were an outstanding sea-officer. In his opinion you stood second only to his cousin.'

'Prince Rupert of the Rhine?' asked Faulkner, astonished, only half-believing Katherine's explanation.

She nodded. 'Few carried the King's fight to the enemy's doorstep. I heard him say so in those very words.'

'Well.' Faulkner shook his head and looked down. She anticipated him speaking and held her silence, though she took up his hand again and held it to her breast. 'I, er ... I acted infamously then ... both to you and to the King.' He rallied, threw up his head and stared at her. 'But he had proved himself a rake, and I was jealous!'

She put her left hand up and smoothed his cheek. Shaking her head, she said with tears welling in her eyes, 'You were not to blame. The times and our situation was such that...' She paused. 'It was impossible...'

Her upturned face, her half open mouth and the whispered words that trailed off into a desperate longing drew him towards her. They kissed.

Still embracing, their breasts heaving and a hot

desire forcing the blood of both to raise their colour, she asked, 'But what now?'

He opened his mouth to speak and then hesitated. There was so much to think of. Besides this encounter, the King's task and the King's warning galled him with the spur of urgency. He stepped back, holding both her hands and looking at her expectant face. She seemed troubled by his failure to reply.

'You have a wife,' she prompted, 'and children.'

'Yes, but there is much to think of. This letter, I know not what to do with it. If, as you say, it was but a device to bring us together, it may well lie and await his Lordship's return, but His Majesty's express order was that I was to lay it in Lord Craven's hand.'

'I know not what to say of that, unless to advise you to take horse for Oxford, for His Lordship is not expected back until tomorrow.'

'But,' he said with a frown, 'there is another matter more closely attaching to my person...'

'And this troubles you?'

'Aye, my darling, for it involves my wife and children, or at least one of my sons.'

'I do not know what to advise.'

Faulkner suddenly made up his mind. 'Whisht, I am decided. I'll have a horse made ready and leave for Oxford in an hour or so, but first I must return home...'

'But the King's commission, what of that?'

'I think the King, knowing that I had not found Lord Craven here, whither he directed me, would wish me to set other matters in motion before attending to his letter. I can ride all night.'

'If 'tis a matter of horses, I can arrange a relay.' She was all eagerness, and Faulkner felt the balm of forgiveness in her offer.

'You can?'

'You forget who else is resident in this house?' She stared smiling at his puzzlement. 'Prince Rupert.'

'Of course!'

'I can have him order a relay of horses on the Oxford Road within two hours. Indeed, have you a horse yourself?'

'No, I should need to arrange the hire.'

'Forget it. His Highness will oblige me in the King's name. Do you wish to see him?'

'I ... I know not ... I would not importune...'

'Come.' She led him back into the hall, relinquished his hand and led him upstairs, motioning him to wait as she disappeared inside a room from which the sound of an erratically played harpsichord came. He stood for a few moments as two servants passed him, looking at him with undisguised curiosity. Then the door opened and Katherine motioned him into the chamber.

'Sir Christopher. You are most welcome.' The tall and once familiar figure of the Prince rose from behind the instrument.

Faulkner bowed. 'Your Highness is most kind.' He raised his eyes to the smiling Rupert. He too wore his years well; years that Faulkner knew had seen him campaigning on the Continent. His handsome face had lost none of its cool yet pleasant loftiness, the moustache upon his upper lip softened the sharp nose and the intelligent eyes that twinkled with recollection set Faulkner at an ease he had not felt during the entire day.

'The Lady Villiers has explained your predicament, and I shall pass orders for a relay of horses to be ready for you.' He turned to a writing table and seated himself, scribbling a few lines on a paper. Faulkner exchanged a glance with Katherine, who was smiling triumphantly. *There!* she seemed to imply. *That is what I can do for you.*

Rupert scribbled his signature with a flourish, sanded the paper, shook it and handed it unfolded to Faulkner. 'That will secure you the horses. Now, sir, a glass of wine.' He motioned to Katherine, who quickly supplied two glasses of Rhenish from a decanter on a side-board. 'I remember you at Helvoetsluys; a council of war on a winter's day.'

'Indeed, Your Highness.'

'Odd how times change. You are a friend of Albemarle's, are you not?' Rupert enquired in his perfect, if accented English.

'I am honoured to be so acquainted.'

'As one of the Trinity Brethren, I understand.'

'You are well informed, Your Highness.'

Rupert laughed. 'I have to know these matters if I am to live in your country again. Here is a toast to the future: *Prost!*' The Prince tossed off the bumper at a single swallow and Faulkner followed suit as Rupert smiled and sat himself once more at the harpsichord. 'I shall play you a march for the road.' He began thumping out chords as Faulkner bowed and withdrew.

'Your Highness has been most kind.'

Katherine showed him to the street door.

Before opening it she turned to him. A footman was nearby, and she drew Faulkner's face down and, whispering, asked, 'You will come back to see me?'

'Of course,' he responded. Then, with a sudden resolution, he added, 'I shall settle matters, but we must be patient and circumspect.'

'Of course, my darling, of course! But please return – when you are able to.'

'You may depend upon it.'

She indicated to the waiting footman that he should open the door and smiled as Faulkner saw the horse ready saddled for him. Donning his hat and mounting awkwardly, he waved at her before hailing the animal's head round and giving its flanks a kick with his unspurred heels.

His arrival at his home on horseback created a stir. Telling the kitchen boy to walk the horse to an inn, see an ostler had it fed and watered and brought back an hour later, he strode into the house. The events of the day had been so transforming that he felt a strange empowering exhilaration. Weaving through the crowded streets on horseback, he had been somewhat preoccupied by staying in the saddle, for it was years since he had ridden. The knack had come back to him while the congestion of passers-by, vendors, whores, pick-pockets and beggars prevented the spirited horse from running away with him. Nevertheless, it had thrown up its head from time-to-time, throwing froth about, its eyes blazing. He had kept the rein tight and had been able to spare a thought for the turn events had taken. By the time he reached Wapping he had determined upon a course of action.

Having handed the horse over to the boy, he entered the house. Gooding met him, eager to discuss some detail of their business, but Faulkner brushed him aside. 'Not now, Nathan, not now.'

Almost run down by Faulkner's advance, a crest-fallen Gooding stood back until Faulkner, having passed him and set his booted feet upon the stair, suddenly seemed struck by a thought. Turning, he said, 'I am sorry, Nathan, but there is a matter of some delicacy I have first to discuss with my wife and I think it best if you were privy to the affair. Would you call her from the parlour, or wherever she is?'

He turned away and clattered up the stairs. From the landing he could hear Gooding's voice and then Judith's. He did not bother to try to eavesdrop on what passed between them. In the upstairs room Faulkner threw a glance round, then stood facing the empty fire-place, leaning on the over-mantel. Behind him he heard the door open and two sets of footsteps enter.

A short silence was broken by Judith. 'You wished to speak with me, husband?'

He knew immediately from her tone of voice that she knew her treachery had been exposed. He had had time to compose himself and he turned and confronted brother and sister, his face blank of all expression. 'As you know, I have been with His Majesty The King,' he began pleasantly without a hint in his voice of what might follow. 'In consequence I have been charged to convey a message direct from His Majesty to my Lord Craven.'

'What has my Lord Craven to do with me ... us?' Judith asked.

'Very little, my dear, except that I shall be absent over-night; I am taking a relay of horses, for His Lordship lies at Oxford and the King's message is of some importance.'

'Is this to be your future business, Husband?' Judith asked sharply.

'I very much doubt it,' he responded mildly. 'Acting as messenger to the King was but ancillary to His Majesty's purpose in summoning me.'

'Then why did His Majesty summon you?' she asked, clearly emboldened by the apparent allaying of her fears.

Faulkner shot a look at Gooding. He was a better student of his brother-in-law's moods than his sister. His face wore an expression of deep concern; he was almost putting out a hand to restrain her over-confidence whilst simultaneously worrying about what Faulkner was going to say next.

Faulkner smiled. 'His Majesty,' he said with a slow deliberation, 'told me to ask my wife, The Lady Faulkner, where our son Henry is.'

Judith went a deathly pale, and she shot a hand out to steady herself against the heavy table. Gooding swallowed hard and cast his eyes down.

'I see, without pressing for an explanation as to why, that you both know to what I refer. Thanks to the condescension of His Majesty, if I may bring my son swiftly to heel he may escape a hanging, drawing and a quartering.'

'Oh God! No!' Judith cried, before collapsing in a faint. Gooding caught her and settled her down.

Faulkner turned his back on them, walked to the window, opened the casement and let the noise of the street penetrate the room. 'You have five minutes,' he said over his shoulder. 'Then I want water and victuals put in a satchel.'

After a few moments he heard Gooding behind him cough. He closed the window and turned back into the room. Gooding had seated Judith in the chair he habitually used and settled her with a glass of wine. Now he stood behind her.

'Well?' Faulkner said.

The Prince's relay of horses served him well, and he was in Oxford by dawn, though it took him an hour to locate Lord Craven's lodgings near Christchurch College. When he was ushered into Craven's presence, his Lordship was breaking his fast. Learning of Faulkner's over-night journey, he offered his table and a bed, the first of which Faulkner accepted gratefully, the latter he declined on account of having urgent business recalling him back to London.

'Very well, Sir Christopher, but please partake of something.' Craven waved his hand over the breakfast table before taking up a knife and breaking the royal seal.

Faulkner eased himself onto a chair. His legs ached abominably, and he took his mind off his extreme discomfort by observing, with some curiosity, Craven reading the King's letter. He had half expected Charles to have sent a blank sheet, resulting in some ridicule from the noble lord, or perhaps a witty message in which he was to tell the messenger that he had been sent on a fool's errand, though not without purpose. Neither, in fact, proved to be the case. Once, as he read, Craven looked up at Faulkner, smiled, and resumed his perusal of the letter. Then he laid it down upon the table and casually remarked: 'I am here upon private business, Sir Christopher: the matter of recovering lands removed by the Parliament.' Craven blew out his breath, seemingly at the enormity of his task, then added with an air of abstraction, 'I seek certain papers thought to have been left here by the late King. Spending these many last years abroad in the service of the Queen of Bohemia has wrought havoc with much of my life.' He sighed deeply, made a gesture of resignation by shrugging his shoulders and went on. 'No matter; the King advises me of some issues that may clarify my somewhat complicated affairs. Are your affairs complicated, Sir Christopher?'

'Somewhat, My Lord, and chiefly from these late years of strife.'

'And is that why you must return immediately to London?'

'In part, My Lord, though I chiefly return to expedite an affair with which I am charged by His Majesty.'

'I am sorry to have brought you so far out of your way.' Craven picked up the King's letter and turned it over. 'I see that you anticipated finding me at Leicester House.'

98

'That is where I was directed. I believe the superscription to be in Lord Clarendon's hand.'

Craven nodded. 'As is the letter. Ah, well, His Majesty must have thought I had not yet left for Oxford.'

'I am sure, My Lord, that that was the case.'

After easing himself, Faulkner was again in the saddle an hour later. His legs would be red raw by the time he reached London, but leaving his horse at Leicester House meant he could speak with Katherine before walking to Wapping.

If – he thought to himself as his mount moved at a canter and joggled him in the saddle – he was capable of walking.

He was not; dismounting outside the Prince's residence he found that he could hardly stand, let alone walk. The boy who took his bridle called a servant to assist him inside. Helped to a settle in the hall, he waited for some time before Katherine appeared. On learning of his condition her face seemed half-amused, half-concerned.

'We are not as young as once we were,' she said as he struggled to his feet. She put an arm about him and thrust her shoulder under his. 'Come, you must lie here tonight.'

'No, I must get back...'

'No!' she insisted. 'You must rest. I know His Highness to have a receipt for your problem, as any cavalry officer would...'

Twenty minutes later Katherine was laughing at him as he lay face down upon a feather bed, his rump and legs bare as she worked a thick unguent into his bruised and blistered buttocks.

'Watch what thou are about, my lovely Kate,' he said, his voice muffled by swansdown. 'There are parts tenderer for thee than any horse can render them.'

She slapped a buttock with the palm of her hand. 'La, sir,' she cried mockingly, 'there is nothing remarkable here that I have not seen before, though I should not have it tender.'

'Nor will you if you allow a man a moment's dignity...' He groaned with the soreness of her application, aware that – as things stood at that moment – he had just uttered an idle boast.

'I would not have thee incapacitated, but am content until thy vigour is full.'

'You will not have to wait long,' he said, attempting to roll over, but she forced him back.

'I will not play games,' she said, her voice suddenly serious. 'God-willing, there will be time enough for that.'

'Time,' he grunted as she continued to knead him, 'is something we do not have.'

'Maybe not, but what you *do* have is a wife, and I would first determine where she and I stand in your affections.'

'Stop, stop,' he commanded, rolling over and drawing a sheet over his privities. Taking her wrist he drew her to him, kissed her and said, 'Kate, we parted in dreadful circumstances.'

'That does not matter; too much time has passed to—'

'It matters in that I have taken up with my wife,' he interrupted her. 'I have a family and complicated affairs...' He felt her draw away from him. 'No—' He shook his head. 'No, you

100

do not yet understand, I pray thee give me leave to speak without interruption.' She nodded and gave a sniff as he saw her eyes fill. 'I promise that I shall make amends to you, that I shall both love and cherish you notwithstanding any obligation to my wife. As to my regard for her, I can only tell you that no more than an hour before I received the shock of finding you yesterday, I was informed by the King himself that my son is involved with some political matter, possibly a plot against the King's Majesty. He has given me leave to extricate my son and send him out of the country, which I may well do in one of my ships; otherwise he may risk a trial for treason, the consequences of which do not bear contemplation. As I guessed, my wife was party to some of this, though to what extent, I do not know, but I laid the matter before her shortly before leaving for Oxford. I have given her until I return to summon our son, which places both of them at my mercy. I must resolve these and their associated consequences—' He broke off swallowing hard. 'If she gets wind of our encounter...' He faltered again, uncertain of how best to proceed, anxious to return to Wapping. He began again: 'I can only plead that you understand that nothing may pass between us until—'

She placed a finger on his lips. 'I understand. I understand perfectly. Nor is my own situation short of obligations. Her Majesty is demanding–' she shrugged – 'which is perhaps understandable for a Queen who was never a queen above a year and is now both a widow and an exile as I have been. I am thus bound to her.'

'Yes, yes,' he said miserably, 'I left you with nothing.'

'That was, perhaps, partly my own fault, but Charles, when he learned of your defection, quizzed me, and such was the state of my nerves that I confessed. I was not the apple of His Highness's eye – as he then was – and he found me employment in the thread-bare household of his aunt.'

'That was considerate of him.'

Katherine shrugged. 'Perhaps; more like the thought of feeding me filled him with horror. But ever since I have helped Lord Craven attend Her Majesty and have received every kindness both from The Queen and His Lordship.' She watched him for a moment, then added, 'And before you ask, I have never been Lord Craven's bed-fellow, no, nor slept with any man since thee.'

'Katherine...'

'And that is more than I know you can say for yourself, Sir Kit of the red arse!' And smiling, she leaned forward and kissed him.

He walked towards Wapping next morning, his heart light as a bird's so that, had no consequences attached to the act, he might have blithely forgiven Judith her dissembling. Fortunately, his mood darkened, adumbrated by the chafing of his swollen legs so that he rolled worse than any sailor just ashore from a rough passage from Virginia, and he was taken for such by a brace of whores parading along the Ratcliff Highway. With The Tower and the harlots' laughter behind him, his wits had sharpened by the time he came to his own door. He was aware that he had given Judith time to compose herself and hatch a counter-plot; she may even have spirited Henry out of the country in defiance of his order, which, if so, could not be helped.

Entering the house with a deliberate clatter, he summoned bread and wine. He had declined breaking his fast at Leicester House, and when the kitchen-maid brought him a loaf and some cheese he sent her in quest of Judith. The girl bobbed a curtsey and left, her face witness to unpleasantness in the house. A few moments Hannah came in to him.

'Hannah, my dear. Come, kiss your father.'

'Father, what is afoot? All is mystery and whispers, Mother is quite unlike herself and Uncle Nathan got drunk last night. I have never known him to touch more than a glass or two, but he was so drunk that he had to be dragged to bed.'

Faulkner was shocked by this news, but the elation infecting him since his encounter with Katherine compelled him to suppress a smile. 'Your uncle drunk, eh? Then things must be afoot, my darling girl, but you are not to worry about them; they do not touch you, and what does not touch you, you are best to be ignorant of. Come, now, glad as I am to see you, I had called for your mother—' He was about to add Henry's name but stopped himself in time.

'Mother went out last night, before Uncle Nathan began drinking.'

'And where is Uncle Nathan now, pray?'

'Why, still a-bed, I shouldn't wonder.'

'Then I must wake him. The fellow has work

103

to do; we are due at the ship-yard this forenoon,' he said with a business-like air. He turned at the door. 'Daughter, have them boil some water; I have been in the saddle for nigh on twenty hours and reek of the road.'

Faulkner watched her a moment as she scuttled out to the kitchen, then he turned and stiffly ascended the stairs until he reached the upper landing where Gooding's room lay. He threw open the door. Gooding lay fully clothed, though without his shoes and wig, the former having been removed and the latter occupying a place on his pillow like a decapitated wife.

'Well, well,' Faulkner muttered, 'you poor, benighted devil.' He threw open the shutters and flung the casements wide before bending over the prostrate form. 'Brother-in-law!' He spoke directly into Gooding's exposed ear, and the man stirred and came-to, rubbing his eyes and groaning as first the horror of the hang-over, and then the realization of the circumstances to which he woke, invaded his consciousness.

'Come, Nathan, it is not like you to be lying a-bed when work calls. We are due at the ship-yard before noon.'

Faulkner's reasonable tone, telling of mundane commitment, further threw the waking man, who mumbled incomprehensibly. 'What o'clock is it?' he finally managed to ask through a thick and foul mouth.

'Come, sir, you stink so much, I fear you have been drinking, a fact made plain by your apparel. Good God, you look like a cavalier after a night of insensible revelry, or is it a pig rolling in mud?

I cannot decide which you most closely resemble.'

Gooding focussed his eyes with difficulty then frowned. 'Do not mock me, Kit—' he began, but Faulkner cut him short.

'Where is your sister? And where is my son Henry?' Not waiting for a reply, he went on, 'And how much of their devilish and damning folly did you know about?'

Gooding seemed to shrink from this verbal assault, putting up his hand to shield himself, as if from a blow, but in fact from the light that tormented his sore eyes.

'And all the while,' Faulkner went on, pressing his advantage, 'I was walking contentedly up and down Limehouse Lane to the Lea's mouth to take tea with Sir Henry Johnson in the mistaken belief that my partner was an honest man with whom I enjoyed an honest discourse.' Faulkner turned away as Gooding began to drag himself off the bed. He was genuinely troubled by this break-down in trust. 'And do not accuse me of having turned upon you and making war upon you in the past,' he added with an unfeigned vehemence. 'You know I should not have deliberately attacked your ships had I known them to be yours. Such mischances fall out in war when men conceive their duty opposes their friends' interests. I had thought all that faction and heat behind us, but now...' Faulkner drove one gloved fist into the other with a noise like a carter's whip. 'God damn it, Nathan, I even named the one son I can trust after you!'

'Stop, Kit! Stop, I pray you. Give me water

105

from that jug, and I shall confess what I may confess.' After he had poured half the contents of the night-jug down his throat and the remainder down his front, Gooding stood miserably before Faulkner. They made an odd pair, the one still in dusty clothes, the other looking as though he had just swum the Thames.

'I did not know of Henry's deception until about a month ago. He came to the house and I had come home from the counter while you had gone to Blackwall to discuss the fitting of the lower capstan and then aboard the *Arrow*, d'you remember? I expressed my astonishment, but immediately guessed how he had played his trick and that his being in the house meant that some-one here knew too.'

'Hannah?'

Gooding shook his head. 'No, she knows nothing, bless her, though how Henry and Judith kept things from her I do not know.'

'She is trusting and trustworthy,' Faulkner said pointedly. 'She believed Henry had sailed with Edmund Drinkwater, and that association made the lie the more believable. It gulled me, by God!'

'Yes, yes, I daresay. They had concealed the matter from me well enough, but I am not here during the daytime. For all I know they met else-where.' He shrugged. 'To hear Henry talk, the entire city is rife with plots and conspiracies and the King's life hangs by a thread. Ever since the hanging of the first of the Regicides – Thomas Harrison, if I recall aright, though there have been over-many of them for my liking, poor souls – there have been rumours of a revival of the old Army.'

Faulkner scoffed. 'Time passes, Nathan; the New Model has become the Old Army as well as the Royal Army and most get their pay after a fashion, which is more than can be said during Old Nol's reign.'

'That may be, but it does not alter the case in Henry's eyes.'

'Where is the boy, Nathan? And where is his mother? She will burn for a witch if the King has his way, while Henry will be dragged on a hurdle to Tyburn.'

'Don't talk like that about your own son!'

'Don't preach to me, damn you,' Faulkner said in a low voice. 'I set out the plain truth. If that fool of a boy has allied himself with any plot he will hang, and all the rest of the disgusting ritual which has been inflicted on the Regicides will be visited upon him and his co-conspirators.'

'I know, I know.' Gooding was weeping now, the effects of emotion and alcoholic remorse playing havoc with him.

'Where *is* his mother?' Faulkner asked, his voice again low and temperate.

Gooding looked at him miserably and shook his head. 'I don't know, Kit, I truly do not know.'

Faulkner nodded and indicated the stain seeping through Gooding's breeches. 'Very well; you look as though you need a piss-pot. I am going to a bath. I will send up some food.'

'No, don't do that,' said Gooding, his humiliation complete as he rummaged under the bed for the piss-pot. 'I could not bear for anyone else to see me like this.'

'I understand. Come below when you are ready. I will send Hargreaves to Blackwall with a note that we are detained.'

The bath not only refreshed Faulkner, it also gave him time to think. He thought not only of Judith's treachery but of Katherine's pliant hands, for the hot water still stung his wounded flesh, despite the remarkable effects of Prince Rupert's grease. His mood of elation heightened: it was clear that the King entertained some regard for him; he had discovered Katherine and, almost in the same breath, the deception of his wife. Why, the coincidence could not have been more apt! It was astonishing! Despite the dangerous curiosity of his circumstances he felt an extreme pang of sublime happiness...

Until, that is, he recalled that all hinged upon the apprehension and transportation of Henry far from these shores. The recollection threw cold-water on his sudden and infatuated felicity, making him angry again. As he rose from the tub, the water running from him over the paved floor, the absence of Judith only increased his sudden feeling of cold fury.

He was almost dressed when the pallid form of Gooding entered the room. Seeing Faulkner naked, he apologized, but Faulkner insisted he come in, and he called for the kitchen-maid to empty the bath and serve Master Gooding some breakfast. The wan appearance of his brother-in-law had prompted another sudden thought; it occurred to Faulkner that while he had been duped by his wife, Gooding had been used.

Manipulated by a sister who knew well his honest and compliant character, Gooding had been trapped in so unfamiliar a situation that he was quite unable to use his customary moral yardstick. The thought led Faulkner to conclude that Judith's whereabouts were perhaps not so difficult to divine. He looked at Gooding, who had sunk into a chair, leaned his elbows on the table and sat miserably waiting for his bread.

'You say you have no idea of Judith's whereabouts, Nathan?'

Gooding shook his head, the drawn-out monosyllabic groan presumably a negative response. 'Has she been to the counting-house of late?' Again Gooding shook his head. 'And you say you caught Henry here, not at the wharf?'

'Yes, but he would tell me nothing. Nothing about himself, that is.'

Faulkner grunted, then raised his voice and called Hannah's name. The girl came in from the parlour next door. 'You said your mother left last night. Did you see her leave?'

Hannah shook her head. 'No, Father. That is what is so strange; she simply went out.'

'You did not see her go? Did not see whether she carried anything, a satchel or bag?'

'No. She simply left the room and was gone when I sought her out. Molly told me she had left the house.'

'Send Molly in to me and then go immediately to your mother's chamber. See if you can find her keys, and tell me if you think any of her garments have been taken away.'

Hannah did as she was bid, and a moment later

109

Molly stepped into the room carrying bread, cheese and a tankard of small beer for Gooding. 'You sent for me, Sir?' she said after serving Gooding. Her face wore an expression of apprehension as she bobbed dutifully to her master.

'Your mistress left here last night, I understand.'

'Yes, Master.'

'Did she tell you where she was going?'

'No, Master.'

'Did she ask you to pack her a bag, or did she leave with anyone?'

Molly shook her head.

'Has anyone unusual called here in the last fortnight or so? Think, now...'

Molly's none-too-clean brow furrowed. She was a bright enough young woman whom Judith had taken as her maid, but she seemed genuinely at a loss as to offer any credible evidence which would solve the domestic mystery.

'Has she told you anything unusual, offered any hint as to why she might leave in a hurry?'

Molly shook her head with slow deliberation. At that moment Hannah came back into the room. Faulkner turned to her: 'Well?'

'I think there are some clothes gone. Molly, run up and see. The blue gown and the grey cloak. Check the mistress's small clothes and her linen.'

'Aye, Miss.'

After Molly had disappeared, Hannah held up the ring of household keys. 'I found these.'

'I thought as much,' Faulkner said. 'Hannah, my dear, you are in charge of the household and

110

must keep those. Tell me, are you aware of any odd visitors of late?'

Hannah shook her head. 'No, Father, only old Captain Lamont who came to pay his respects ... Something to do with a mortgage...'

'Lamont!' Faulkner thundered in sudden comprehension. 'By all the devils in hell! Lamont!'

'What of Lamont?' said a pained Gooding, turning from the table.

'Where is his damned bilander, Nathan?'

'I don't know.'

'You don't know? You laded him; you *must* know!'

Gooding rubbed his brow. 'I ... he ... I think he was due to clear outwards yesterday or perhaps this morning...' Gooding's mind seemed to clear. 'No,' he said decisively, gathering his wits, 'it was Tuesday, the day before yesterday, but he had not sailed yesterday for I saw his mate with a boat at Wapping stairs.'

'What's the wind been?'

'A light easterly ... That would explain Lamont's still being in the river.'

'The devil it does!' exclaimed Faulkner dismissively, his mind racing. 'Get off your arse, Nathan, at once! D'you hear? Hie you to the counting-house and order Hargreaves to go at once to the Gun Wharf. Tell him to hire a wherry – give him a guinea for his trouble – and get aboard the *Hawk*. Have them make her ready to slip the mooring, then get him back with his wherry to Wapping Stairs. I'll join him within the hour. While he does that, have two barrels of water, some biscuit and a barricoe of beef sent to the Stairs.'

'You are going in chase of Lamont?'

'Of course! Now move, Nathan; you have no idea what hangs upon this.' He turned to his daughter as Gooding hauled himself to his feet and went out. 'Hannah, mind the house. Let no-one unfamiliar across the threshold. No-one, d'you understand?'

Despite her confusion, Hannah nodded. 'Will you be gone long, Father?'

'If I am lucky, no. If not...' He shrugged. 'Who knows?'

Faulkner went upstairs to the room he and Gooding used and sat for a moment considering what he had set afoot. If he was wrong in his guesswork, and it was only guesswork, he would be wasting precious hours. But he was confident that if Henry was as implicated as he feared, he would be making for the Low Countries where, as half of London knew, a handful of the Regicides now lived in exile just as, but ten years earlier, the Royalists had done. What was extraordinary was that Judith had gone with the boy. They were close, it was true, both being of firm Puritan conviction, but for Judith to throw up everything and follow him into exile made no sense to Faulkner. Had his sudden summons to the King's presence had some influence on her thinking? He considered the matter for a moment; it was certainly possible. She was a woman of intelligence, if of little imagination, but – a sudden alliance with Lamont?

He should have asked Gooding whither Lamont's cargo was consigned, and he chid himself for the lack of forethought. It was too late to worry now. Instead, he cudgelled his brain to recall the time of the tides and found himself too out of joint to recollect with confidence. He could not remember the phase of the moon, not even by reference to his recent night's ride to Oxford, for the sky had been cloudy and his mind had been on other things.

Other things! Great heavens, but Katherine was in London! He stood up with an oath, picked up his bag and made for the staircase. Ten minutes later he was at Wapping Stairs, awaiting a sign of Hargreaves and his hired wherry. He looked across the river; it was thick with shipping, most of which was moored, but several were under way: a pair of collier-brigs and a stumpie or two. A few wore ensigns or pendants at their mastheads. The wind, what there was of it, seemed no longer in the east, but appeared to be lifting the bunting from the westwards. Boats crabbed across the stream like so many giant beetles; the tide was ebbing fast. 'Damn,' he muttered under his breath.

'D'you want a boat, Cap'n?' a voice enquired. Faulkner turned round. A couple of seamen lounged at the head of the Stairs. Both men were chewing tobacco, and the man who spoke loosed a squirt of juice into the river.

'I have one coming, I thank you.' He turned away, searching for a wherry heading upstream against the tide. He could see three or four, but none seemed to be heading towards Wapping Stairs and none had a passenger. He could, of course, hire a boat and drop down stream on the ebb in the hope of meeting Hargreaves. In fact it would not matter if he did not meet Hargreaves, only that he got aboard the *Hawk* without delay. He was about to engage one of the loungers, neither of whom was a licensed waterman by the look of them, and would charge him what they liked if they sensed his haste, when he heard a hail.

'Cap'n Faulkner!' A wherry was coming upstream inshore, two boatmen pulling vigorously at their oars. In the stern, waving his battered hat, sat Charlie Hargreaves.

Faulkner lifted his hand in response when a thought struck him. He turned to the two loungers. 'D'you want a day or two's work?'

'What'd you pay?'

'Two sovereigns if you come at once for no more than a week.'

'All found in victuals and a donkey's breakfast if there is anything on board,' said the taller of the two.

'And the sail-maker's locker if there ain't,' said the other.

'Just so.' Faulkner held out his hand. Both men shook it. A moment later Hargreaves and the double-banked wherry pulled in towards the Stairs, the watermen drew in their oars with a clatter and handed the boat alongside. The three men tumbled smartly in, the watermen shoved off and shipped their still-dripping oars. Faulkner settled himself in the stern-sheets alongside Hargreaves. 'Well?'

'I used the money Mr Gooding gave me to engage a double-banked boat, sir. I hope—'

'Yes, yes, that's fine. What of the *Hawk*?'

'She'll be ready. Mr Gooding sent off two extra hands to help old Toshack. He was taking advantage of the wind and tide to dress the mains'l, so she's only to be cast off.'

'Good. Now, tell me. Cap'n Lamont ... what of his bilander?'

'The *Mary*, sir? Why, I know she was on the mooring at noon of yesterday because I saw her, but she is gone this morning.'

'What o'clock was high-water slack?'

'About six, I think, sir.'

'A quarter before seven, Cap'n,' growled the nearer of the two watermen as he leaned forward to make his stroke.

'So, it's after half-ebb, then,' he mused.

'This westerly'll soon pick up,' the waterman added. 'If yer outward-bound you'll likely 'ave a dusting off the Nore by the time yer get there.'

'Very likely.' Faulkner turned again to Hargreaves. 'Charlie, d'you recollect where the *Mary* is loaded for?'

'She's got a part-cargo for Flushing, and part for Leith, including passengers.'

'How many passengers?' The presence of passengers could complicate matters.

'I don't know, sir. Not many though. I heard Lamont say there wouldn't be much baggage to Mr Davey.' Davey was a clerk in the counting-house.

'Were they for Leith, d'you know?'

Hargreaves shrugged. 'Couldn't say for certain, sir, but Davey didn't leave any tally-chits. Usually passengers for Leith leave a dozen tally-chits; not that we see that many passengers, sir, so don't take my word for it.'

'I won't, Charlie,' said Faulkner, unable to restrain a smile despite his preoccupations.

They pulled on in silence and, as they approached Greenwich, Hargreaves, who had been craning his neck to see ahead, exclaimed, 'Old Toshack's got her off the mooring, sir!'

'You'm in an 'urry then, Cap'n,' the waterman observed.

'Just pull, if you please.'

'Sir?'

Faulkner turned to Hargreaves.

'May I come with you sir? To lend a hand; I've never been afloat other than in a wherry or aboard a ship at the moorings.'

'What'd your mother say when you don't arrive home this evening?'

'But we won't be away long, will we, sir?'

'Very well.'

'Thank you, sir.'

Fifteen minutes later they had clambered aboard the little *Hawk* and Faulkner was shaking the hand of the grizzled old seaman who leaned on her tiller. 'Welcome aboard, Cap'n Faulkner. Do I understand we are a-goin' after the *Mary*?'

'Aye. Did you see her going?'

The old seaman shook his head. ''Fraid I don't keep early watches nowadays, sir. Not that I mind getting this little beauty off the buoy now an' again.'

Faulkner smiled. The *Hawk* was the one indulgence he had allowed himself when she had come on the market. Built as a pinnace for a

116

Royalist gentleman who had been killed at Naseby, she had lain in a mud-berth for several years during the dull decade of Puritan rule. Towards the end of Cromwell's Protectorship, Faulkner had heard of her, and she had been knocked down to him at a candle-sale by a penurious widow with four children to support. From time to time she had been useful as a tender to ships waiting for a wind in The Downs. Old Toshack had been engaged as her master on the recommendation of Brian Harrison. An old seaman who had seen service under Blake as a quartermaster, he was a fine skipper of the smart little craft as he proceeded to demonstrate.

'This westerly'll pick up afore sunset, Cap'n.'

Faulkner nodded. Now he was aboard the *Hawk* with time on his hands he began to worry. He paced up and down as the pinnace – her mainsail, staysail and jib gradually filling under the influence of a strengthening breeze – gathered speed. He spared a glance for the *Duchess of Albemarle* on the stocks at Blackwall, but the sight of the new ship, whose revised name had greatly pleased him, now seemed to mock him for his self-satisfaction. If he failed to apprehend Henry and spirit him out of harm's way, he could forget his ambitions where the Honourable East India Company was concerned.

He found himself aft, almost alongside Toshack who was teaching Hargreaves how to steer the pinnace. Faulkner remembered doing the very same thing with the young Prince Charles at his side. Then he rounded on Toshack. 'I can't afford to miss the *Mary* in the dark, Mr Toshack,' he snapped with unnecessary harshness.

'Don' worry, Cap'n. She can't have got far.'

He could not explain to Toshack why they were in pursuit of the *Mary*, but he did not share the old man's confidence. Indeed, now that they were embarked upon this wild goose chase he was beginning to regret starting it. Once darkness fell there was little chance of their sighting the bilander, and while they might sail directly to Flushing and lie-to off the island of Walcheren, the *Mary* could still slip past them in the dark.

Pacing up and down he began to curse the King's summons. His thoughts were in a turmoil; if the King had not sent him to Lord Craven's house only to find that he must needs travel to Oxford, he would have come directly home, confronted his wife and laid the whole matter to rest. By now Henry would have been safe aboard an outward-bound merchantman, even if he, Faulkner, had had to charter one. But then he would never have known Katherine was in London and—

And what?

Failure to catch Judith and Henry meant that he would feel the King's displeasure. All the bright prospects that had been dangled before his eyes in recent hours would be like morning dew. As for Katherine, what possible chance was there for him now?

For one idle moment it seemed as if fate had laid all the advantage in his hand, that Judith had played him false and in doing so gave him the chance – the excuse – to take up again with Katherine as his mistress. Katherine could not leave her confidential position, but she could – damn it! She had as good as said so – *entertain* him at Leicester House.

He turned by the mast and stumped aft again. A grey bank of cloud massed above the smoke hanging over London. On either side the river banks were green, the low land falling back in marsh and creek. He could see a distant church tower, squat and square, on the northern horizon. He supposed it to be Barking, for he had been pacing the deck for some hours. The tide had turned against them, and although the freshening wind set them downstream with a great bone in their teeth, the opposing force slowed their speed over the ground.

Suddenly, Faulkner felt his age and his lack of sleep. He was a pot-bellied old fool! His legs still hurt, his arse ached, he was dog-tired and in no condition to keep the deck later without some rest. He went aft and spoke to Toshack. 'The *Mary* is bound for Flushing,' he said. 'That much I know. Do you go out by the Swin and perhaps we shall sight her. There's a crown to the first man who does. Now I intend to get some sleep.'

'There's blankets below, Cap'n,' said Toshack. 'And a bottle for some comfort,' he added.

Faulkner paused at the companionway and turned to the old man, still with an eager young Hargreaves by his side, leaning on the heavy tiller and trying to look like an old hand. 'Thank you, Mr Toshack. Perhaps, when I come on deck next, you will advise me whether we must make a seaman of young Charlie, or whether we should keep him in the counting-house?'

The Chase

June – July 1661

Faulkner was back in Wapping by early June. After chasing the shadow of the *Mary* out of the Thames estuary and across the North Sea, the *Hawk* had bobbed for a week off the Schelde but seen nothing of her quarry. Faulkner had decided not to enter Flushing or Breskens for fear of involving himself with the Dutch authorities; he had no Jerque Note for leaving London and, even if he pleaded a voyage of pleasure, he knew from past experience that this would result in seemingly endless delay with the authorities. Besides, he knew that Judith and Henry would have landed as soon as possible, to disappear in the safe lodgings of their friends.

If the impromptu voyage yielded anything, it was clarity of mind for Faulkner, though no lessening of his anxiety. True, his wife and son had escaped him and he had failed insofar as the King had advised him; he hoped that the King's agents would know the truth of the matter, or God alone knew the consequences. He resolved to speak of it with Albemarle as soon as convenient, if only to under-write his own liberty. As to the birds which had flown, he had – at least to his own satisfaction – determined why Judith had absconded with their son. The evidence had been plain and might have been plainer had he had a previous whiff of suspicion, but he was now convinced that Judith was deeply implicated in whatever conspiracy Henry had been caught up in. Perhaps, he thought, she may have been the main-spring and inspiration for Henry and if so had played a devilishly subtle game. A woman of strong religious, moral and political opinions, she had never shrunk from expressing them. His fault was not to have taken notice of them, or recognized them for what they were: no mere female railings, but the visible sign of a deeper involvement with the Republicans, forced underground at the restoration of King Charles. The implications of this for himself and his other children made his blood run cold, for both Henry and Judith risked indictment for high treason! No wonder she had fainted at his reminder of the grisly process of execution for such a heinous crime, for she stood already condemned by her own foolish conduct.

And in the tortured conjectures of his mind there wormed an intimate, private and insidious thought that Judith had committed a betrayal that surpassed his own earlier marital infidelity and wiped it clean off the slate. Judith's treason – and whatever consequences it produced – could be construed as leaving him free to consort with Katherine.

Then he checked himself; neither he nor Katherine were young: this required a cool head. The King – while he might tolerate the stupidity of a young man who might be brought to heel by his father – would not look kindly on one of his senior sea-officers whose wife actively pursued a treasonable course intended to culminate in God knew what mischief! Indeed, if he were to maintain his own liberty and not be caught up in the meshes of his wife's outrageous action, he would need all the influence he could muster from Katherine and Craven and, God help him, both Albemarle and Rupert of the Rhine.

The concrete sign of Judith's commitment was the buying into Lamont's bilander, which Faulkner had taken for nothing more than a shrewd piece of business on her part. She had invested on her own account before and he had no objection to the liberty this gave her, but now matters lay under a different light. It was clear that she was, at the very least, a party to all of Henry's clandestine comings and goings; at the very worst their very root and foundation. It called into question his supposed reconciliation with his son, but by now he was prepared to add this to the catalogue of their deception. Perhaps Henry had meant something in it, perhaps not. Either way the pair of them had fooled him.

Of course, Judith had lost control of herself when confronted by Faulkner. Having gulled him for so long, his sudden appearance apparently armed with all the facts *must* have shocked her. He knew that, for all her strength of character, she was afraid of him, and this had overwhelmed her when combined with the stark and awful facts of the process of hanging, drawing and quartering, the stench of which had most recently begun again to drift over London with the execution of Thomas Harrison.

It was not something easily forgotten. On Saturday the thirteenth of October last, Thomas Harrison had been lashed to a hurdle and drawn from Newgate to Charing Cross. He had been hanged by his neck and while dancing the dido of death had been cut down, gasping for breath. Hardly had he gained this than his breeches were cut away prior to his being castrated and disembowelled. While the shock of this ran through what remained of his body, his mind contemplated the outrage perpetrated upon his person as his genitals and intestines had been burned before his very eyes, the stink of it filling his nostrils as his eyes watched the blood pour from his mutilations. Harrison had then been beheaded and his body quartered, his several parts carried away for display in prominent places as a warning to others.

Perhaps it was the prospect of this happening to her darling son that had, quite simply, turned Judith's reason and made her desperate. Whatever her motive, whether in support of Henry or at the root of his involvement, Judith had left her husband in a serious predicament.

She was, Faulkner concluded, so deeply implicated that escape out of the country was her only option. And where else to go, but The Seven United Provinces of The Netherlands? Just as they had been when the Royalists were in exile, the Dutch were prepared to play host to the men whose lives were endangered by Charles II's Restoration. Common gossip told of several of the Regicides threatened by the Act of Indemnity

123

and Oblivion being in The United Provinces, and Faulkner had heard that Sir George Downing, His Majesty's envoy to the States General at The Hague, had caused a near-scandal when he botched an attempt to seize Edward Dendy in Rotterdam. Dendy was one of those exempt from the amnesty granted to most supporters of the Parliament during the late war – the Act of Indemnity and Oblivion. It was Downing's conspicuous bungling that confirmed Faulkner in his decision not to make a landing from the *Hawk*. Given the nervous state of affairs between the two countries, he was reluctantly obliged to abandon his chase and concede defeat.

Unhappily, Faulkner ordered Toshack set the *Hawk*'s head to the west, waving aside the old man's pleadings to allow him to lie off the coast for another few days.

'I thank you, but that will serve no useful purpose. You may land me at Harwich and return to the Thames, where I shall see you and your men well-paid for your diligence.'

At Harwich, Toshack took in much-needed victuals while Faulkner, disembarking with Hargreaves, took a coach for London. He was in a lather, and eager to be at Deptford on the tenth, when the Brethren of Trinity House elected Edward Montague, Earl of Sandwich, as their new Master. As they assembled for dinner on that occasion, Faulkner made a point of speaking with Albemarle who, in standing down after the customary year in office, retained his easy manner and spoke warmly to Faulkner. 'How is your new ship, Sir Christopher?'

'I have not seen her for a week or two, Your Grace,' Faulkner confessed, 'though my partner will have been a model of attentiveness. When I saw her last she was coming on splendidly. With your permission, she will be launched as the "Duchess of Albemarle" and I shall of course invite Your Grace and Her Ladyship to the rout.'

Albemarle smiled. 'My thanks. Let us hope you can profit from your investment before the Dutch come interfering in our affairs – or we in theirs, as I fear must happen by-and-by.'

Faulkner nodded agreement, then lowered his voice. 'Your Grace, may I have a confidential word with you?'

'Now, or shall I offer you a place in my barge after we have eaten?'

'As Your Lordship pleases.'

'I think,' said Albemarle gesturing to the noise of loud chatter that surrounded them, 'that my barge would be better.'

With six oarsmen pulling upstream, Faulkner sat under the canopy of Albemarle's hired barge and explained his situation. When he had laid his case before Albemarle, the Duke rubbed his chin with an ominous rasp.

'It is a difficulty for you, I can see, but if they are both abroad and the King knows that you gave them no warning to escape...'

'That is my anxiety, Your Grace. I do not know that he *does* know that. The errand he sent me on to Oxford delayed my finding out the place where my son was hiding. I did not for a moment think that my wife had any part in any of this. As far as I knew she believed, as I did, that the boy

125

was outward-bound for the East Indies. In fact it seems it was quite to the contrary.'

'I understand. You will be under some measure of suspicion. However, I can explain to His Majesty if the opportunity arises.'

'I would be most grateful. Please assure His Majesty of my deepest sentiments of loyalty.'

'I will do what I may.'

'Thank you, Your Grace.'

It was only then that he felt able to think of Katherine.

During the succeeding weeks, Faulkner attempted to dispel his anxiety by throwing himself whole-heartedly into the final work necessary to complete the *Duchess of Albemarle* for her launching. While it was possible to divert his mind during daylight hours, it was more difficult at night. He slept badly and became accustomed to sitting in the parlour until late with a pipe of tobacco and a glass. Sometimes Hannah would sit with him and, in his preoccupation, he neglected her. One evening, while the two of them sat quietly together, she laid her needle by with a sigh and, in a low voice, asked, 'Father, do you think he will come back?'

Faulkner stirred himself and looked at his daughter, taking the long stem of his pipe from his mouth to say: 'Henry? I hope that if he does he doesn't ask me to seek a pardon of the King.'

'No,' she answered, 'not Henry...'

Faulkner frowned. 'Not Henry? Who then?'

'Why Edmund, Father,' she said, looking at him and his blank, uncomprehending face. 'Edmund Drinkwater.'

The reproach in her eyes smote him like a blow, and he set his pipe and glass down, rose and crossed the room to stand beside her and place his hand on her shoulder. 'Oh, my poor girl, I have been so misanthropic, have I not? So caught up with mine own that I have forgot my child's woes. I am so sorry, Hannah, my dear, but the defection of your mother and brother places me – and, I regret to say, you – in a near intolerable position.'

'I know,' she said with another sigh. 'Many people speak of it, though they say it is not your fault.'

'They do?' Faulkner was astonished.

'These matters cannot be kept quiet, Father.'

'No, I suppose not.' He paused and smiled down at her, patting her reassuringly. 'I shall see what may be done, Hannah. As for your Edmund, he has as fair a chance of returning as any other sea-officer making an eastern voyage. This is not his first and he is not a fool.'

'I pray you are right, Father.'

Squeezing her shoulder gently he was about to return to his chair when Hannah said, 'There is one further matter, Father...'

'And what is that, my dearest?'

She hesitated for a moment before picking up her needle and staring down at her work. 'Uncle Nathan has twice mentioned...' she began before faltering and Faulkner guessed what was coming.

'Had twice mentioned the entanglement of a certain lady, is that what you were about to say?'

127

He eased himself down into his chair with a sigh as she nodded. 'You well know there is a lady, Hannah, a lady who came between your mother and myself many years ago. It is also true that the lady is, even now, in London, and that I have spoken several times with her since I returned from my fruitless pursuit of your mother and brother in the *Hawk*.' He looked at his daughter as she bent diligently over her needle-work, aware that she listened intently to every word he said. 'She is,' he went on, 'Lady-in-Waiting to the Queen of Bohemia, who is old and unwell and demanding, but I am not about to run off with her like some callow youth.'

'Do you love her?' Hannah suddenly asked, looking him straight in the face.

Faulkner sighed again and matched his daughter's gaze. 'Do you love your Edmund?'

'Yes,' she whispered.

Faulkner nodded. 'Then you will understand that I have loved this lady since the first I saw her many years ago. Then there was no prospect of our making a match, for she was high-born and I, I was scarcely worthy of scraping the mud from her shoes, but she loved me, and in the turmoil of the war I—'

'I do not understand you, Father,' Hannah interrupted as he faltered in making his confession. 'But I would not have you unhappy.'

He smiled, his eyes filling with tears, which he dashed away with his hand. 'Life is a difficult business, Hannah, as you are just discovering as you await news of Edmund.'

A profound silence fell between them. Faulkner sensed Hannah wished to say more, but felt constrained; such a conversation with her father was impossible. As for Faulkner, he too wished to explain, to put Hannah in possession of his own experience but, for all his powers of expression, nurtured in his youth by his old mentor, Sir Henry Mainwaring, he found it impossible. Mainwaring's tutelage had not extended to matters of the heart, nor of the complexities of love and lust. Sadly, Faulkner relinquished the imperfect formation of some such explanation and let his mind drift towards the pleasant contemplation of the last stolen afternoon he had spent in Katherine's company at Leicester House while her mistress had dozed. They too had sat like this in companionable silence, as though they had in fact been married for all the years they had been apart. He thought of what Katherine had said to him as he left her after his first visit following his return from the Dutch coast. 'We have waited a long time, my darling; we can – we must – wait a little longer.'

He had been repeating that reassuring phrase over and over in his mind as though it was a talisman to guard him against the malice of his distant, estranged wife and the hostile disposition of the King himself. Looking across the parlour at Hannah, bent again over her needlework, he shivered with apprehension.

One of Faulkner's occasional duties as an Elder Brother of the Trinity House was to inspect the Corporation's Collector of Dues. This individual worked close to the King's Customs Officers,

129

levying the fees ships paid on any ballast they loaded from the Trinity lighters that supplied it. It was in attending this tax-farmer one morning that he noticed the entry of the *Mary*, and the fact that John Lamont, Master, had cleared his bilander inwards in the Port of London. Calling for a boat, Faulkner was soon being pulled downstream in search of the Scotsman. He discovered the *Mary* lying off Rotherhithe and clambered aboard, addressing her mate and asking for the vessel's master.

'He's below,' the man replied, pointing to the companionway.

Faulkner found Lamont sitting in an easy chair talking to another, a gentleman by his dress and another Scotsman by his accent. Lamont rose at the intrusion, but did not seem incommoded by Faulkner's unannounced arrival, nor did he seem moved to concede any priority to his new guest. Instead he introduced the gentleman as a passenger by the name of McNaughten, a merchant from Leith, and invited Faulkner to a glass of Genever.

Faulkner declined the offer. 'I come upon a personal matter, Captain Lamont, touching your late passengers embarked here and carried to Flushing, or thereabouts.' He paused as the Scotsman furrowed his brow in pretended recollection.

'That would be the Mistress Faulkner and her boy? A fine young man, Captain Faulkner.'

'That would indeed, Captain Lamont.' Faulkner looked at McNaughten, who appeared to relish this encounter and may well have been

130

regaled by an account of the scandal during his voyage. 'You will please excuse the directness of my approach, Mr McNaughten, but you will doubtless understand that there are few secrets along the river these days and Captain Lamont is a man, as I know to my cost, who may be relied upon to unravel another's affairs to his advantage.'

'Whisht, Captain, that is a trifle harsh,' put in Lamont. 'The lady appealed to my guid nature, that is all, and since she owned half the *Mary*, who was I to refuse her?' He drew upon his glass and added, 'She seemed somewhat anxious to depart from your company.'

'I presume that you are yourself now entered into a state of matrimony, Captain?'

'Indeed I am, thank ye, Captain, and uncommon happy in the union.'

'I am glad to hear it. I hope that you have chosen wisely in your wife. Now tell me, sir, exactly where you landed mine and what news you have of her. Any intelligence will perhaps put my mind at rest.'

'Well, Captain Faulkner, you being an Elder Brother of the Trinity House could see to it that the *Mary*, should she need to take in a little ballast—'

'Damn you, Lamont! I'll have no truck with that sort of talk! If you want to clear outwards without let or hindrance you'll tell me what I wish to know, otherwise I'll have you mulcted for burning lights after dark, carrying powder above Gravesend and anything else I can find to frustrate you.'

131

'Ach, Mister McNaughten, these English are a touchy lot, to be sure,' Lamont said mildly. He turned to Faulkner with a disarming smile. 'Aye, Captain Faulkner, we landed your wife and that fine boy of yours at Flushing. I carried her at no fee, for she owns half the vessel, and the boy too out of charity. She left me no message, no, nor letter for you, otherwise you would have heard from me long since. That is all I can tell you, alas.'

Faulkner stared at Lamont and decided he was telling the truth. With a curt word of thanks he rose and went on deck. Half an hour later he was ashore at his counting-house.

The Launching

August 1661–February 1662
The summer passed without news from the Low Countries or summons from the King. After the equinox Faulkner's mind eased, though anxiety was apt to keep him awake at nights, following the ineluctable promptings of his bladder. His empty bed irked him, and he longed for Katherine's company but, as they had agreed, they must wait out events, at least for a decent interval. True, the restored King's conduct had a loosening effect upon the morals of his subjects. There were those who pleaded a reaction against the strictures of the Puritan Commonwealth, others

pointed pious fingers at the growing revelations of His Majesty's riotous private life, while most relapsed into the easier ways of their fathers. In such an atmosphere few would have commented much upon Captain Sir Christopher Faulkner taking a 'distant kinswoman' into his household. If she were to grace his bed, those interested enough to ponder on the matter would probably conclude an issue was unlikely, given the age of the bed-fellows, but neither Faulkner nor Katherine were anxious to draw attention to their love. Katherine, busy about her duties to the ailing 'Winter Queen' of Bohemia, was bound to her mistress, while Faulkner remained worried, uncertain of the King's attitude to him.

He was not left long in doubt. Towards the end of September, preparations were made for the launching of the *Duchess of Albemarle* from Sir Henry Johnson's Blackwall ship-yard. Somewhat unwilling to make much of the occasion, Faulkner's obligation to Albemarle compelled him to make the most of it. Exchanges of letters between Albemarle and Faulkner resulted in the presence of the Duchess herself to grace the occasion. So too did the greater part of Faulkner's fellow Brethren of the Trinity House, along with a number of hangers-on, including a pushy young man, recently appointed to some post at the Navy Board who introduced himself as 'Mister Pepys' and another, well-regarded at the Trinity House, named John Evelyn. Aware that Pepys was a creature of the Lord High Admiral, the Duke of York and brother of the King, Faulkner conjectured that he was a spy. Certainly, he drank excessively, which did nothing to enhance him in the watching Faulkner's eyes.

Had there been no clouds on Faulkner's personal horizon that day, it would have been a joyous occasion. Nathan Gooding seemed in sparkling form, which his partner attributed to a desire to redeem himself, while Hannah did duty as the lady of the house, looking radiant enough to attract the attention of young Pepys. Faulkner noticed with satisfaction that she saw him off in fine style. His Grace the Duke of Albemarle arrived in his coach and handed out his Duchess, to introduce her to Faulkner, Gooding and Johnson. She was a large, plain and undistinguished lady named Anne, of whom Albemarle was demonstrably fond, for they had been married when he was plain Mr Monck and neither of their heads had been turned by Honest George's spectacular rise in the world.

The principal party then made their way to the slipway, where a small wooden platform had been raised alongside the ship's bow. It was a dull, autumnal day and the great hull seemed to tower into the grey sky, massive and ponderous. Nevertheless, despite the overcast and lack of sunshine, the fabric of the new ship seemed to gleam, her pale, payed under-body rising to a coating of thick, still slightly sticky varnish above her waterline as her topside turned inwards in a bold tumble-home. Those watching from wherries in the river could observe her fine stern, with its double rows of glazed windows, its garlands of carved acanthus leaves and her quarterdeck gun-ports surrounded by carved wreaths of entwined laurel, man-of-war fashion. Above the principal party that gathered around Albemarle and his Duchess, the gilding and bright-work of her round bow rose to the upwards sweep of her knightheads and figurehead, an ample representation of a grand lady which, when pointed out to her, made the Duchess chuckle.

'Heavens, George,' Hannah heard her whisper to her smiling husband, 'now I *know* I'm a Duchess.'

It was not the image of Katherine Villiers, as Faulkner had imagined in his dream, but in staring up at it, he made a private resolution to himself. If he untangled himself from the mess in which he was presently enmeshed and matters fell out as he desired, he promised himself that his next East Indiaman – and he was optimistic in that moment of hope to think that there would be another such ship – would be named after Katherine. He cast the thought aside; he had no time for such day-dreaming.

Faulkner looked round. Drawn round the platform the Elder Brethren were gathered in their perukes and hats. Harrison gave him a cheerful wave, made a gesture of admiration towards the looming hull on the slip-way and mouthed a compliment. Faulkner's eyes roved out over the assembled workmen and those of their families free to attend the ceremony. He could see several of the men, mostly ship-wrights, with whom he had become familiar in the last months as the *Duchess of Albemarle* neared completion. Looking up he saw the excited mug of Charlie

Hargreaves and the serious be-whiskered face of old Toshack whose duty it was to see the new ship brought to an anchor in mid-stream and then work her down to the sheer-hulk where her lower masts would be stepped prior to moving her to the moorings for her fitting-out.

Looking round the principal party, who had now taken up their appropriate stations at Johnson's behest, Faulkner raised his hat and shouted, several times, until he had achieved some sort of quiet. Then he made his bow to the Duchess of Albemarle. Her Ladyship fulfilled the customary office of pouring a libation of wine down the huge stem of the ship named in her honour and wished the vessel and her people success and long life. At this point Faulkner made a signal and the master ship-wright passed the word to the men stationed along the slipway. In the lull following the Duchess's short bidding, there was a sudden 'tonk-tonk-tonk' as a score of mauls were swung vigorously at wedges, knocking them clear. For a moment everyone present held their breath, and then the great hull began to move along the freshly greased slipway, slowly and majestically gathering momentum as her immense mass was drawn towards the river by gravity. In the river a few wherries were frantically rowed clear as, with a sudden roar of approbation from the crowd, and a sparking grinding, the drag-weights which were tethered to the new ship to prevent her carrying herself right across the river began to follow her down the ways. The stern drove into the water, creating a wave that dwarfed the wavelets chopped up by the south-westerly breeze and higher than the freeboard of the watching boats; for a moment the ship was poised between the upthrust of the Thames and her stabilizing cradle. Then her bow dropped as she became fully buoyant, the cradle fell away, and she slowed as the weights to which she was tethered dragged her to a standstill. A moment or two later she swung round to the tide as Toshack did his duty. At her bow and stern flew the jack and ensign of Great Britain and from her empty mast emplacements tall staffs bore the flags of the Trinity House, the East India Company and, amidships, the standard of the Duke of Albemarle. At that moment, as if a benediction upon the enterprise, the sun made a fleeting appearance, shining on the gleaming bright-work and gilding, on the brilliant heraldry of the silk banners as they lifted to the sharp breeze, and on the new ship as she rode to her anchor in the tideway.

After waving their hats, the cheering crowd began to disperse, the multitude of workmen going in quest of the promised ale. A second and lighter 'tonk-tonk-tonk' could be heard as a dozen casks were tapped. As for the gentry, Sir Henry Johnson led the principal party into his adjacent mansion where a cold collation had been laid out. There was a brief signing of papers, which concluded the successful launch of the new East Indiaman before the Elder Brethren and other guests came in, whereupon the conversation became general and the atmosphere unreservedly convivial. In such circumstances Faulkner avoided any approach to Albemarle regarding his private affairs, though he thanked both the Duke and Duchess for their condescension in attending. It was only as Their Graces called for their coach and made to leave that Albemarle himself raised the matter. As Gooding and Johnson conducted the Duchess to her equipage, the Duke fell into step alongside Faulkner, slowing a moment as if to pass some remark about the ship-yard but dropping his voice to a confidential tone.

'The King is well disposed enough towards you, Sir Christopher, but I fear it comes at a cost.' Albemarle drew a letter from the sleeve of his gauntlet and handed it to Faulkner. 'This is from Clarendon,' he said. 'I would not read it until you are without company.'

Faulkner took the letter and slipped it into his doublet. His heart was hammering with apprehension, Albemarle's words of comfort entirely forgotten. As Albemarle turned to follow his wife, Faulkner stammered his thanks.

At the door of his coach Albemarle turned and smiled. 'Good day, gentlemen.'

'Fifty per centum! Great God that is monstrous!' Gooding stood, his hand on his head, his eyes staring like a madman's, his whole stance that of outrage. 'Fifty per centum!' he repeated in a low voice, subsiding into a chair in the upper room, back in Wapping. 'Fifty per centum for the King...' He could barely be heard now as the shock took him and he buried his face in his hands.

Faulkner stood in silence. He had got over the

shock of the demand an hour ago and had waited for Gooding's return from the counting-house, whither he had gone directly from the ship-yard.

Slowly, Gooding looked up. His face was ashen. 'We are ruined,' he said simply.

'Perhaps, but I doubt it, though we shall need to make certain of our—'

''T'would be best to burn the ship at her moorings,' Gooding went on, disregarding Faulkner's temporization. 'That would serve His Majesty right.'

'I doubt it,' Faulkner said ruefully. He sighed and pulled himself together. 'I scarcely know whether to blame your sister or my wife...'

'Your wife, damnation take her, for I have done nothing!' Gooding said with uncharacteristic warmth.

'There is a way, Nathan, which would ease our troubles.'

'Oh, and what pray is that?'

'That I relinquish my interest. You and the King will share the ship while my name shall remain as joint-owner only for a cover to the King's portion in her.'

It was clear the idea had not occurred to the distraught Gooding and that, for himself, the prospect of Faulkner's self-sacrifice was welcome. He made a mild protest: 'But...' he said, before hesitating.

Faulkner rescued him. He was weary and, if the truth be told, indifferent to the money. Considering the changes that loomed in his life, all this seemed of little consequence.

'But me no buts, Nathan, I am resolved upon

the matter and will respond to Clarendon accordingly, making it certain that the King knows that he has my own share in its entirety. That is what he requires of me.'

Such considerations were beyond Gooding's comprehension. 'You will have to remain as principal managing-owner,' he said.

'Until young Edmund comes home and can be made both commander and part-owner in my place.'

Gooding thought about this solution for a moment. 'He will not like it. Why should he manage the ship for nothing?'

'He will manage it for love of my daughter and his private trade,' Faulkner said curtly. 'Or he may abandon his intention to marry Hannah.' It was bluff, of course. Given his own circumstances, Faulkner had no intention of thwarting a love-match, but Gooding was assuaged.

'Very well,' he said, nodding his agreement. 'Very well.'

Faulkner crossed the room and placed a hand upon his shoulder. 'What is to be done about Judith?' he asked.

Gooding looked up. 'I do not know.'

'Do you think the Lord does?' Faulkner asked.

'I do not know that either.'

Faulkner patted Gooding and crossed the room to stare down into the street, as though the answer lay there, to be divined in the movement of the passers-by.

'When think you the *Eagle* will return?' Gooding asked, after a moment's consideration.

'March or April if they have had a prosperous

voyage, later if not ... Perhaps not at all...'

Gooding ignored Faulkner's last and agreed. 'I thought the spring.'

'By which time we shall have the *Duchess* fitted-out and loading. Young Drinkwater will not have much of a rest if he wishes to command her on her maiden voyage.'

'Maybe he will refuse...'

'Not if he wishes to marry Hannah,' Faulkner said, repeating his threat, finding the reiteration wearing rather thin. 'That we shall arrange immediately he returns. Now, as to the ship, we have covered the costs of construction, and though the fitting-out may leave us at a disadvantage we should not stand more than we can afford. Let Edmund Drinkwater take the usual share after the first voyage.'

'That will be at my expense,' Gooding said.

'I know, but the loss of five per centum is—'

'Very well, you need not labour the point.'

'She is not our only venture, Nathan,' Faulkner said, his temper shortening. 'I can do no more with regard to my wife. You shall play some small part for the blood of familial ties, and five per centum is little enough.'

'You make me sound like Shylock.'

'Who?'

'Shylock the Jew, in Shakespeare's play...'

'What do I know of Shakespeare's plays, Nathan?'

Gooding shrugged and, for the first time since his return from Blackwall, ventured a smile. 'I am sorry, Kit. I am all out of sorts at this news. Must I render accounts to the King?'

141

'No, of course not, but do not think of cheating His Majesty. Keep the accounts and render His Majesty the remittance that is due: fifty per centum of the net profits of each voyage. Clarendon may send for the accounts if he wishes to; he lies somewhere between a lap-dog and a tradesman, so let him do his duty. But mind that you remit the King every farthing to which His Majesty lays claim, or both of us will swing from Tyburn's tree.'

'God help us,' Gooding said.

'The King is in constant want of money. His exchequer is empty, his tax-farmers are resisted, his expenses, especially those of his whores, are endless,' Faulkner went on. 'In that respect Cromwell was a better man, though he too seemed always to be short of money.'

'At least he did not waste it.'

'That depends upon what you think it should be spent.'

'Better the Army than an harlot, surely.'

Faulkner turned towards Gooding. 'Well, Nathan, I am thinking of spending money on a harlot. If I have heard nothing from Judith by Christmas, you will be obliged to welcome the lady Katherine Villiers into this house, at least from time to time. You are not, of course, to ever refer to her as an harlot.'

They heard nothing whatsoever from Judith. The only missive of any consequence that troubled the Christmas of 1661 was Clarendon's letter informing Faulkner that the King acknowledged the transfer to His Royal Personage of his,

Faulkner's, share in the ownership of the *Duchess of Albemarle*. Clarendon had added a note of his own brewing: that His Majesty was contemplating the making of a number of baronetcies and that, for a further sum, Sir Christopher might ensure his title descended to his heir. Faulkner did not reply.

From time to time he waited upon Katherine, delighting in her company, though she was often called away to attend the ailing Elizabeth Stuart. Upon occasion he encountered Prince Rupert, who always greeted him with warmth. Faulkner was not fool enough to think that this constituted any real favour, for he had seen men rise in the esteem of the House of Stuart, only to fall to ugly and untimely deaths soon afterwards. Nevertheless, the son of Frederick V, the Elector Palatine, had no need to show the English sea-captain more than a measure of civility, and the Prince often went further than that. On one occasion, when they met in the hall, the one coming in and the other going out, His Highness smiled and asked after the health of Mistress Villiers, as if he, Faulkner, who was but a visitor, knew more than himself who was – at least to all intents and purposes – virtually resident in the house occupied by his elderly mother. When Faulkner had proclaimed Katherine's health as good, His Highness had said, in an intimate tone, 'You shall take care of that in the future, Sir Kit.'

Faulkner had stood in the street for a moment, left with the impression that Rupert referred to some future arrangement, perhaps not too far distant, when his household would no longer require the services of a lady-in-waiting.

Matters became clear in February when Elizabeth Stuart died. Known to all as the Winter Queen, owing to her late husband's short reign in Prague between November 1619 and November 1620, Queen Elizabeth of Bohemia gave up the ghost in her sixty-sixth year. Faulkner, close to the goings-on at Leicester House, knew Her Majesty's death was imminent, but the note Katherine sent him on the evening of the thirteenth told him the Queen's time had come. Despite the lateness of the hour, he went immediately to Lord Craven's residence and found the streets already strewn with rushes. When he gained entrance he found the hall-way full of men whose age and apparel declared them to have been cavaliers, men who had ridden to war at Rupert's side either in England or on the Continent, or both. These were men who knew defeat, who had sworn allegiance to Frederick V or to Charles I and now came to pay their respects to Charles's sister. There were perhaps no more than fifteen or twenty of them, but they made the hall-way seem crowded, and though many thought their voices muted, the combination of their commiserations had a contrary effect.

It took Faulkner some time to make contact with Katherine, who drew him into a ground-floor pantry to find some privacy. She wept on his shoulder as he held her, for she had come to regard the old woman as a surrogate mother and, as is so often the case with those who dominate our lives, found the end of her drudgery at the poor woman's every whim nevertheless occasioned a deep sense of loss.

Looking up at him through tearful eyes, Katherine shook her head. 'I cannot come yet, my love, there is much to be done.'

Faulkner laid a finger on her lips. 'I know, I did not come to carry you off tonight, only to reassure you that you have only to send word. All is prepared for your reception.'

'What about your wife?'

'I have already explained, I do not have a wife.'

'Your daughter, then? Hannah?'

Faulkner smiled. 'I think that she may be the first to welcome you – after myself, of course.' She went up on tip-toes to kiss him, and he tasted her tears, wiping them away as they drew apart.

'A sennight, perhaps,' she said, 'a fortnight at most...'

But it was not to be. A fortnight passed and Faulkner had heard no word from Katherine who was busy with the funeral arrangements and sent him only a short note urging him to be patient, that it 'would not, could not, now be long'. He went about his business and attended the Trinity House on the fifteenth of February when the pushy young Mr Pepys was sworn in as a Younger Brother. Thereafter Pepys somewhat beguiled the older men by his discourse so that there were those who thought his selection meet enough. Faulkner paid the self-important fellow little heed. Indeed, he remained so withdrawn that Harrison enquired if he was quite well.

145

'Oh, I am out of sorts, Brian, 'tis no fault of yours but all mine.'

So keyed-up with anticipation was he that when, on the last day of February, well towards midnight, a knock came at the door, he roused himself from his fireside reverie – it having become his habit of each night smoking a pipe while the last embers died out. Convinced it was Katherine, who he expected to find on his door-step like some supplicant waif, he was actually smiling and looking down at the level on which he expected to encounter her large and lustrous eyes. Instead he found himself staring at the large buckle of a cloaked and gloved man whose face was partly obscured by a large, feathered hat.

'Sir Christopher Faulkner?'

'Who asks?'

'I do, in the name of the Earl of Clarendon. You are to wait upon him. I have a horse saddled and ready.' The man jerked his head over his shoulder so that a few drops of moisture fell onto Faulkner. 'And rain is coming on.'

'And what does the Earl want with me?'

'He did not tell me, only that I was to bring you to him at once.'

Faulkner swallowed and then nodded. 'Step inside a moment. I will get boots, hat and cloak.' Five minutes later he followed the stranger out of the house. He had taken the precaution of leaving a note for Gooding and of buckling on his sword.

'You will not need the cutlery,' the stranger remarked with a grin.

146

'Let me be the judge of that, sir,' Faulkner responded.

The stranger led through the streets at a canter, shouting out that he rode 'in the King's name!' when a more than usually intrepid night-watch sought to stop them and know their business being out after curfew. At a side-gate of White-hall Palace the stranger threw himself out of the saddle and tossed his reins to a waiting ostler. Faulkner descended from his mount with more caution.

'You do not sit too ill in the saddle, Sir Christopher,' the stranger remarked. 'I have certainly seen worse.'

'I am a sea-officer,' Faulkner replied, some-what irked by the condescension.

Inside the palace the stranger threw off his cloak and hat, handing them to a waiting foot-servant and indicating that Faulkner should follow suit. Then, with a brief, 'Follow me,' he led Faulkner down several corridors through which the latter had never previously traversed. They ascended a narrow twisting stair at the top of which the stranger paused to ensure that his charge still kept up. Then, without further ado, he knocked sharply, waited a moment and then opened a door. Faulkner followed him into a darkened room. Light from a single candelabrum threw soft reflections on the oak panelling and, once the door was closed, the hangings fell back, indicating he had been brought through a clan-destine entrance.

Faulkner stood alongside the stranger, his eyes adjusting. A man he recognized as Clarendon sat at a large table, bent over papers on which he wrote. For a moment Faulkner thought Clarendon to have been alone in the room, but a slight noise, a shift of harness, and the dull gleam of the candle-light on the accoutrements of a gentleman in half-armour sitting on the far side of the table almost made Faulkner start.

'Very well, Miles, you may leave Sir Christopher with us.'

Without a word the stranger bowed and turned, barely flicking a look at Faulkner as he disappeared the way he had come.

'Pray do sit down, Sir Christopher,' Clarendon said, without looking up.

Easing himself into the only other chair in the room, Faulkner stared first at the bent head of the Earl and then at the face of the other man who was studying him. The two men thus measured each other without a word passing between them; the only noises in the room were the quiet creak of leather and the scratch-scratch of Clarendon's pen.

After what seemed an eternity, Faulkner felt the pressure of his bladder defied further procrastination. He stirred uneasily for some moments, casting about for any signs of relief, until he could restrain himself no longer. 'My Lord,' he said, 'I have grave need of a piss-pot...'

'Behind the screen in the far corner, Sir Christopher,' said the man across the table, his face obscured by the shadows.

Faulkner got up and crossed the room. When he had relieved himself he emerged to find Clarendon had set his papers aside. Faulkner did not resume his seat but stood, awaiting whatever business Clarendon had summoned him for.

'Pray do sit down, Sir Christopher,' he said again, turning to the other man. 'Sir George, since you know the room, perhaps you will perform the office.' The other man rose and turned to a side table while Clarendon asked almost kindly, 'A glass, Sir Christopher?'

Taking first his seat and then the glass of wine the unknown Sir George held out to him, Faulkner awaited Clarendon's explanation.

Having sipped his wine, the Earl made a gesture to the third man, who had now resumed his own seat. 'Sir Christopher Faulkner,' Clarendon said, 'may I introduce you to Sir George Downing, His Majesty's Minister at The Hague ... Sir George, Sir Christopher Faulkner, Captain in His Majesty's Navy and a considerable owner of his own tonnage to boot.'

The two men nodded at each other across the table. Downing's face remained in shadow. Faulkner's mind was racing. Setting aside the possible jibe Clarendon had made at his shipowning, Faulkner could only associate this all-but-secret midnight meeting with the ambassador to The Hague with his wife's presence in The Netherlands. Having drawn this conclusion he kept his mouth shut, sipping again on Clarendon's excellent wine.

'Now, Sir Christopher, Sir George is here with certain intelligence, and I have asked you to join us because it is both my intention and the King's will that thou should attend Sir George to The Hague, whither he returns shortly.'

'Forgive me, My Lord, but has Sir George, in his capacity as the King's Minister, need of my attendance?'

The two men exchanged glances and smiled at each other. Clarendon explained. 'From time to time circumstances find Sir George under an obligation to undertake certain tasks that fall beyond the remittance of a Minister Plenipotentiary, Sir Christopher.'

Faulkner recalled hearing at the Trinity House a vague story about a bungled attempt to secure the person of one of the Regicides, Edward Dendy, in Rotterdam. A cold apprehension closed round his heart as he felt the influence of the King. Not content to compel Faulkner to relinquish his share of the profit in his new ship, Faulkner was now to be made to act in a manner that would compromise his honour and make him the King's creature. It flashed across his mind that Judith may have been right – he was indeed the King's chameleon. And it was as quickly followed by a second thought, that Fate was again thwarting him from living with his beloved Katherine. Both Clarendon and Downing were studying him, as if attempting to divine whether or not he understood what was being asked of him.

'Am I to assist Sir George in the seizure of Regicides in The Netherlands, My Lord?'

'You are.'

'And may I ask, Your Lordship, whether this action is—'

'It is clandestine, Sir Christopher,' Downing broke in, thereby avoiding any reference to the legality – or otherwise – or the proposed mission. 'And I am sure you can guess why we have asked you to assist in this delicate matter.'

Faulkner sat back in his chair. 'I assume that my wife lies at the bottom of it.'

'Your wife is proving a deal of a nuisance, Sir Christopher,' Clarendon broke in, his tone mild. 'In fact she and her – *your* – son are known to be caught-up in a plot to kill the King.'

'To kill the King!' Faulkner sat bolt upright. It was not that he had not considered the matter but it was one thing to think the unthinkable in the privacy of his bed, when the black dog had his soul in its teeth, and quite another to have it said to his face by the King's First Minister.

'We have been watching them both for many months, Sir Christopher,' Downing said. 'They are in almost daily contact with three of the Regicides, John Okey, Miles Corbett and John Barkstead. I intend apprehending these men, and I require your assistance in seizing your wife and son. His Majesty has given orders that Lady Faulkner should be placed under your own protection, Sir Christopher...' Downing gave Faulkner a meaningful look.

'You are a most fortunate man,' Clarendon added, 'but His Majesty has an aversion to executing women.'

'And my son?'

'Will submit to the rigour of the law. The evidence suggests the charge will be High Treason.'

'Dear God!'

'Your duty is quite clear,' said Downing, persuasively.

'I do not need to be told my duty, Sir George,' he growled.

'You will take ship at Harwich,' Clarendon said, interrupting in a smooth and conciliatory tone, 'where the *Blackamoor* – Captain, Tobias Sackler – has been withdrawn from the fishery to convey Sir George back to Helvoetsluys. I have made out an order that Sackler is to take all directions regarding the conduct and management of the *Blackamoor* from you, Sir Christopher, as his senior officer.' Clarendon paused, picked up and passed a paper which bore a heavy seal across to Faulkner. The seal and the name scrawled across the top of the paper – *Charles R* – told him what this was: a commission from the King.

'It is dated from the commencement of His Majesty's reign. You are indisputably the senior officer.' Faulkner frowned. The King had dated his reign from that of his father's execution; to be commissioned thus was a mark of singular approval – or something of a bribe.

'His Majesty wished to acknowledge his debt to you. It is a privilege the weight of which—'

'I feel, My Lord. Believe me I feel.' Faulkner nodded and rolled the paper, tucking the seal inside. 'I shall need to gather some personal effects.'

Clarendon and Downing exchanged glances and the former nodded.

'Very well, Sir Christopher,' said Downing. 'Major Miles will attend you and act as escort. My coach will be on Tower Hill at dawn. I shall

Part Two

Contagion

1662–1666

On His Majesty's Secret Service

March 1662

On reaching home Faulkner found Gooding awake, wrapped in a robe and sitting beside the parlour fire which he had made up. Gooding rose wearily, about to speak until he saw the tall figure of Major Miles follow Faulkner into the room.

'This is Major Miles, Nathan; Miles, my partner and brother-in-law, Nathan Gooding.'

Each man made an acknowledgement of the other, and Faulkner bade Miles make himself comfortable in the parlour, asking Gooding to accompany him to the room above.

'Is your brother-in-law...?' Miles asked pointedly, though without finishing the question.

'Is my brother-in-law to be trusted, is that what you were about to ask, Major?' Faulkner said, drawing the rolled commission from his doublet.

'I have my orders, Sir Christopher,' Miles said darkly.

'I have mine too, Major, and this commission–' Faulkner laid the paper on the parlour table – 'which you may read at your leisure whilst I gather a few effects for our journey.'

'What journey?' interrupted Gooding.

'I'll tell you in a moment.' Having silenced Gooding, Faulkner turned back to the cavalry officer who was now sprawling in the chair recently vacated by Gooding, his boots out towards the fire, his feathered hat on the table and his gloved right hand drawing the commission towards him. 'That commission makes it clear that I am, and have been for some time, a Captain in His Majesty's Navy, so I would be obliged, *Major* Miles, for a moment or two to myself.'

Leaving Miles to grin sardonically, he turned and shoved Gooding before him up the stairs. Once in the room above Faulkner bid Gooding remain silent and listen.

'I have no time, Nathan, for lengthy explanations, but the King has thrown me a line and posted me a Captain. I am to go abroad into the Low Countries to smoke out Judith and Henry. If I can get them home I think that we *might* be cleared of trouble, but 'tis a mighty gamble. If not, God alone knows what will happen to us, but I need you to do *exactly* as I say. It is now the end of February. In a week from this night, do you have old Toshack bring the *Hawk* to Harwich. He is to watch for a small man-of-war called the *Blackamoor*. I think her to be a pink, or some such vessel. If he sees her he is to await orders from me. If she does not come by the end of March and he has heard from neither of us, he is to return to his moorings. Is that clear?'

Gooding nodded and Faulkner went on. 'Tomorrow you must send Hannah to wait upon Katherine Villiers at Leicester House. Do you know where that is?'

Gooding had baulked at the mention of Katherine's name, but he nodded and said: 'Near Drury Lane.'

'Yes. Hannah is to present her compliments to Mistress Villiers and introduce herself. She is to explain that Mistress Villiers will be welcome here as soon as she is quit of her responsibilities and duties in settling the affairs of the late Queen of Bohemia–' Gooding looked up as Faulkner drove on – 'to whom she has been principal Lady-in-Waiting. Hannah is to tell Katherine that I have been sent by Lord Clarendon's personal order upon a special service. You know its nature and purpose but it is unnecessary that either Hannah or Katherine is made aware of it at this time. Tell Hannah that I rely upon her to execute this instruction as I do you to ensure all this is accomplished, for I cannot do it myself.'

Gooding nodded. 'I understand ... at least I understand that which you wish me to under-take.' He hesitated, and Faulkner was about to speak when he went on, 'Kit, does this foray into the Low Countries have anything to do with the Regicides there?'

'I cannot tell you that.'

'You already have. Is Judith...? Yes, I see that too. What shall you do? You cannot despatch her in preference for this ... this Villiers woman.'

'I am not without honour, Nathan. I am simply without alternatives. You must trust me to act as best I may. I would not have Judith dead, no, nor

159

Henry ... especially not Henry, but now I must go and gather my effects. Do you go and quiz that fellow below stairs.'

'I would rather walk to Hell on hot coals.'

'I think that is what I am about to do,' Faulkner said, turning his back and making for the small attic room where he threw his precious telescope, his wheel-lock, some powder, balls, his cuirass and a few other useful odds-and-ends into his portmanteau before clattering down the stairs to his bedroom; here he added small clothes. By now the house was roused, and in his haste he was aware of the inquisitive faces of the maids. Then Hannah, wrapped in a blanket, met him at the head of the lower stair.

'Father, what is it? Why all the noise?'

Faulkner lowered the portmanteau and drew Hannah towards him. 'I am called away on state business, my dearest Hannah. I shall be back in a week or two; your uncle will tell you all about it and what you are to do in my absence. I am sorry, but I have no time now and must be off.'

'But where are you going, Father?'

Faulkner did not answer; picking up his traps he drew them downstairs and left them by the front door. Summoning Miles from the parlour, where he picked up his commission and returned it to his doublet, he shook hands with Gooding and went out into the night. Hoisting the portmanteau up behind his saddle, he mounted and an instant later he and Miles had gone.

Captain Tobias Sackler was a thin, pinch-faced man who seemed to feel the cold north-north-easterly wind coming off the North Sea to churn the brown waters of Harwich Harbour into a nasty little chop as a personal assault. A pendulous dew-drop hung from the end of his nose, which was unusually large, as though his Creator, in forming Sackler's proboscis, had drawn most of its substance from his face. Thus his cheeks were drawn and hollow, his jaw pointed and his eye sockets deep-set. Only his round dome of a forehead seemed to have resisted this process, while his eyes reinforced the notion of a man permanently frozen, being of an icy pale-blue. He wore no wig, the lank wisps of hair that protruded under the brim of his plain round hat made a poor attempt at a fringe, shedding a considerable quantity of dried scurf which clung tenaciously to the shoulders of his cloak as he stood to greet his guests upon the wind-swept deck of His Majesty's Pink *Blackamoor*.

Downing suggested they went immediately to the cabin, where if he expected a glass of fortifying wine he was to be disappointed. In the coming days Faulkner would learn that, whatever first-appearances suggested to the contrary, Tobias Sackler was a stickler for doing his duty and had no time for fol-de-rols. He was pure Commonwealth, through-and-through, which made him an odd choice for this mission. If Faulkner foresaw trouble in this assessment it was clear from the start that Sackler was a seaman of competence. Nor did he seem in the least aggravated by Faulkner's presence, the purpose of which Downing made clear as he handed

161

Sackler a written order from the Admiralty Board.

'You will see from your orders, Captain Sackler, that you are required to place yourself and the vessel under your command at the direction of myself and Captain Sir Christopher Faulkner. Sir Christopher has a commission—'

Sackler looked up from his brief scanning of the Admiralty letter. 'Sir Christopher's reputation is well known to me, Sir George,' he interrupted. 'I am perfectly acquainted with my duty. I have the cable hove short and this wind, being in the nor'-nor'-east, will allow us to leave if we do so before it veers.' He paused a moment, and then went on. 'The *Blackamoor* provides but poor accommodation, I fear, but please make yourselves at home. I have ordered dinner, such as it is, for an hour hence, though I have no table-money.'

'I have that if you wish to obtain some provisions,' put in Downing.

'It seems scarcely worth the wait. I can have you off Helvoetsluys by tomorrow evening; until then there is enough. I will gladly accept the money and provide some viands for the homeward passage.'

'Very well,' said Downing, whereupon Sackler left then to attend to his duties on deck. Downing looked about him. 'Looks as though we shall be on short commons gentlemen,' he said to Faulkner and Miles.

Short commons they may have been, but after a sleepless night and a jolting journey from London to Harwich, made at a fast clip thanks to

162

frequent changes of horses, they were sufficient to enable Faulkner to sleep. He woke, uncomfortable and stiff, shortly before the following dawn. The *Blackamoor* had cleared Harwich and doubled Landguard Point before dark. In threading his way out though the sands to the Sunk, before finding deeper water, Sackler proved himself a master of his craft, reacting to the cries of the leadsman in the fore-chains as the pink's head was set for the Herringfleet and the Dutch port of Helvoetsluys.

Sackler was still on deck when Faulkner, wrapped in his cloak, dopey from sleep and stiff beyond remedy, staggered out onto the wet deck. Sheets of spray flew inboard over the weather bow, and at first it seemed to Faulkner that Sackler, a thin figure that seemed part of the *Blackamoor* herself, was the only man on deck. Then he was aware of others hunkered down under the weather rail, out of the wind, and a brace of men at the tiller, their pale faces faintly illuminated by the binnacle lamp.

Faulkner moved uncertainly across the deck, staggering uphill against the heel and grasping the after mizzen shroud.

Sensing his presence, Sackler turned. 'Good morning, Sir Christopher.'

'Captain Sackler,' Faulkner responded shortly. The two stood in silence for a moment, then Faulkner observed, 'I regret I have not my sealegs; it is some time since I was at sea.'

Sackler grunted, but said nothing more, returning his attention to the distant horizon. Faulkner was at a loss to know quite what he was doing on deck, for they were clear of the land and the off-lying shoals and, while half a dozen smacks were in sight to leeward, there seemed nothing pressing that an officer-of-the-watch might not handle.

'You have competent officers, Captain Sackler?' Faulkner said, provoking Sackler to turn round. The first light of dawn fell upon his odd features, causing a skeletal impression, but there was enough light for Faulkner to watch as the dew-drop fell, only to be replaced, a few moments later, by another. Sackler's thin lips drew into a smile; even in the half-light it was a surprisingly warm smile, which struck Faulkner as odd in the extreme, appearing as it did upon the face of a man who might have passed for Jack Frost himself.

'I prefer to remain on deck at night, Sir Christopher. My officers are very good, but young and prone to hiding from the wind. We have been some months on the fishery, and they are best in daylight when their services are most needed. Young men need sleep more than older men so I cat-nap in the daytime and, when on a passage such as this, prefer my own company on deck.' Without any change in tone or pace Sackler added, 'We served under Blake together, Sir Christopher. I was in his flagship off the Kentish Knock and Dungeness.'

'Ahh. I thought you a Commonwealth man.'

Sackler shrugged. 'Times change and a man must earn his bread, if only for his dependants.'

Faulkner thought for a moment and then threw caution to the winds. 'What do you know of your present duty?'

'Why, sir, to convey our Minister to the United Provinces back to his post at The Hague by way of Helvoetsluys.'

Faulkner thought Sackler's response was guarded, and he remarked with an air of casual amusement, 'A most diplomatic reply for a diplomatic mission.'

'I am less sure of your own purpose though, Sir Christopher,' Sackler replied. 'The *Blackamoor* is small enough not to require too many officers of rank, yet you are to direct her. That strikes me as a little odd.'

'Yes, I am to land and assist Sir George. I do not know how long we shall be ashore, but I shall be returning and hope to have company. I shall require you to convey us back to Harwich.'

'And would this company consist of Regicides, Sir Christopher?'

'Not those that I am in quest of,' Faulkner said.

'And what of those that others are in quest of?'

Faulkner considered the matter for a moment and then asked, 'What would be your position if I were to say that it is very likely that they may be Regicides?'

'I should deplore the fact, Sir Christopher, but I should do my duty.'

'As you see it, or as I see it?'

'As you command me, sir,' Sackler responded, his voice cold.

'You see,' Faulkner said, his tone one of reason rather than rank, 'if it went against your conscience, I could order you to put about now and to return to Harwich where, in a day or so, I shall have my own vessel at my own disposal.'

'You mean, Sir Christopher, the matter will happen, whether or not Tobias Sackler has as hand in it?'

'I fear that the affair upon which I am engaged will indeed happen; at least, it will if it lies within my power to accomplish it.'

'I would not survive such a dereliction,' Sackler said shortly. 'I pray you remember this conversation was initiated by yourself. I have already said that I shall do my duty and that I have those who depend upon me.'

Faulkner bit his lip. Who does not? he thought to himself, but this was not at all what he had intended, though he had known his approach might well miscarry. 'I seek only an assurance that we shall not be betrayed and that I may rely upon your presence in the offing when I require it,' he said.

'Needs must, when the devil drives. You may rely upon me.'

'I would have your hand upon it,' Faulkner said, removing his right gauntlet and extending his open fist.

Sackler took it, his own hand dry and frozen. 'You may have my very soul, Sir Christopher.' For all its feeling of bloodlessness, Sackler's hand gripped Faulkner's with a consoling firmness.

'I shall count upon you, sir,' he said. Having relinquished each other's grip they stood a while regarding the scene about them. Then Faulkner remarked, 'She goes well to windward.'

'Aye, she is a weatherly little bird,' said Sackler, patting the rail beside him. 'We shall be off the Herringfleet just after dark. Would you have me heave-to until daylight?'

'Let us see what sea is running at sunset.'

'Very well.'

The wind had dropped at sunset and backed round to the westward so that Sackler stood inshore under easy sail, and he passed word to Faulkner who came on deck after a frustrating day. He had hoped that Downing would have discussed their affairs and how he proposed to manage them after they had landed, but Downing spent the day dozing and Major Miles lay prostrated by sea-sickness, a weakness that proved the only thing to lighten Faulkner's mood during the entire passage.

Having pointed out the failing breeze, Sackler indicated that he was intending to stand as close inshore as he could, a plan attested to by the low, monotonous call of the leadsman in the lee fore-chains as they crept inshore. The Dutch coast lay to leeward, a dark smudge across the darkening horizon, its uniform flatness broken, even in the twilight, by several church spires. Faulkner cast a quick look round then at the ensign at the stern.

'Dutch colours,' Sackler explained briefly.

'Do you have a competent boat's crew?' Faulkner asked.

'The best. And a good young officer to accompany you. If you would indicate a place where you wish to be picked up in due course, please show him. The tides serve this week to give us a flood during the evening, so any rendezvous near midnight will be ideal...'

'And the moon is waning.'

''Twill be new on the twelfth and high water, full and change.'

'That will suit us very well hereabouts if we can accomplish our business. Let us make a rendezvous at the place of my appointment on the twelfth at midnight,' Faulkner said, warming to Sackler's incisive approach. 'What is the name of your officer?'

'Septimus Clarke, my junior lieutenant.' Sackler paused a moment, then added, 'He is a deserving young man, Sir Christopher. If my conduct pleases you, you would oblige me by over-seeing him.'

'Let us not bank too much on what may well miscarry, Captain Sackler.'

'If we prepare for the worst, we may also hope for the best,' Sackler responded sharply, and Faulkner smiled in the gathering darkness. Here was indeed an old Commonwealth man. As if divining Faulkner's thoughts, Sackler said, 'I was never for the execution of the late King, sir. Only his deposition, as indeed many were. You and I both served in the Interregnum.'

'Then I think that we may rely upon each other, Captain Sackler.'

'Indeed.'

An hour later, the *Blackamoor* lay hove-to, her main topsail to the mast as her boat pulled lustily towards the now obscured coastline. Lieutenant Clarke peered occasionally at a small hand-compass and adjusted the boat's course as the tide augmented the efforts of the oarsmen and carried them into the wide, deep channel known to the

English as the Herringfleet. Downing and Miles huddled in the stern sheets alongside Faulkner and Clarke, their light baggage under their feet, awkward and uncomfortable. From time to time both men peered around them, helplessly lost and entirely in the hands of the seamen. A few dim lights indicated the distant location of Brielle, and the banks closed imperceptibly in, though the channel remained wide and exposed. They passed a few boats fishing, and Faulkner summoned his stock of Dutch to call, *'Zoll!'* – meaning that they were customs officers – and, 'Good night,' in his best Dutch as they swept past.

The night was filled with the low grunts of the oarsmen and the gentle knocking of their oar looms against the thole pins. The black water slid by on either side, a faint swishing accompanying its passing. The three passengers huddled in silence until Downing broke it, leaning forward and touching Faulkner's knee to gain his attention. Faulkner lent towards him as he said in a low voice, 'Once we are ashore matters are in my charge. Is that clear?'

There was, in Downing's tone, more than a hint of threat; as though he anticipated some assumption of superiority by Faulkner. Faulkner recalled putting Miles in his place back in Wapping. Was that the root of Downing's anxiety? If so, it was easily quashed.

'I never assumed anything else,' Faulkner replied, his response as bare of courtesy as Downing's own address. 'I am entirely in your hands as regards my own task.'

169

'Quite.'

No further exchange took place as the boat pulled closer inshore.

'Helvoetsluys,' Clarke said eventually, in a low voice, pointing off on the larboard bow.

Faulkner stared into the night. It had grown cold, but this sharpened the air and he could just make out, though his eyes were not what they had once been, the jagged outline of roof tops, a spire and a windmill, dully distinct from the sky and a contrast to the low undulation of the channel's dyked banks. 'Pass above the town,' he said to Clarke, 'about half a mile and you will be able to lie inshore. There is some staithing there, and there may be ships moored...'

'I see it, sir. Two ... three vessels hard under the bank.'

'Run in just below them. I think we may disembark there.' Faulkner recalled the place where what constituted the North Sea squadron of the Royalist fleet had once lain. It almost seemed a happy time in recollection.

They were not challenged as they ran in towards the bank. A few reeds grew at the water's edge, and the boat's bow ran into them with a sibilant hiss, followed by the dull clatter of the crew stowing their oars.

'I'll lead,' Faulkner said, getting to his feet, hitching his sword and working his way forward between the oarsmen. There was a rocking of the boat, a muffled curse as Miles almost lost his balance after so long a period inactive. Faulkner chuckled. The cavalry officer's long legs must be tormenting him now. Downing was more circumspect. An accomplished deceiver, Faulkner concluded. Once the three men were ashore, their traps followed, passed ashore by the boat's crew. Then, somewhat to Faulkner's surprise, he found Clarke at his elbow.

'The staithes will help me get my bearings another time, sir. But if the ships are gone I may need another landmark.' He looked about him from the vantage point of the dyke. 'The church will do very well. May I wish you good fortune, gentlemen.'

Faulkner took the outstretched hand. It struck Faulkner that this man might have been himself a lifetime earlier; the professional interest, the easy courtesy and the desire to please. Odd, he had never thought of himself in that way before.

'Come. We have no time to waste.' Downing touched him on the arm, and Faulkner relinquished Clarke's hand.

'Until we meet again, Mr Clarke.'

'Until then, sir.' Then he was gone, slithering down the bank and into the boat, which was shoved off immediately.

'Come,' Downing repeated peremptorily. 'We must find our horses.'

Faulkner turned. Both Downing and Miles had their saddle-bags over their shoulders, and he hefted the portmanteau. Then, in straightening up, he found Downing confronting him. For a moment the two men faced each other and Faulkner was about to ask what was amiss now, when Downing spun on his heel and led the trio along the dyke. Faulkner was at a loss, especially when Major Miles fell in behind him. He had the uneasy feeling that he was a prisoner.

As they trudged along towards the town, Faulkner consoled himself with the thought that whatever happened was Downing's avowed responsibility. It was a comfort as cold as the night itself but it went some way to reconcile Faulkner to his situation. Within an hour, however, he felt easier, for it was clear that Downing had matters arranged to a nicety.

Although no-one expected the arrival of the three Englishmen, Helvoetsluys was a packet-port, the twin of Harwich on the English shore, and used to the comings-and-goings associated with the transfer of passengers and mails. Notwithstanding the simmering suspicion between the two countries, the inhabitants of both sea-towns continued their business of commercial intercourse. Even in the darkness Faulkner recognized the cobbled streets through which they walked, remembering them from his sojourn in the place years earlier.

Downing led them directly to a post-house where, with the expenditure of some guilders, Miles – who spoke good Dutch – secured three horses. They were of indifferent quality but, before the chimes of midnight had faded behind them, they enabled the travellers to be on the road towards Dordrecht. Here they hoped to cross the River Maas and head north-west towards The Hague.

They stopped and sheltered in the lee of a water-pumping windmill after about three hours, resting men and horses. Dozing fitfully, they woke at dawn to a sleeting drizzle. This set

172

Downing to cursing a country bereft of decent shelter and which seemed, in the bleak light of day, to go on and on without relief to the very edge of the world.

It rained all day, and neither Faulkner nor Miles demurred when Downing announced that they would lay the night at Dordrecht. As they rode into the city Downing led them to an inn and ordered Miles to dispose of the horses while he and Faulkner arranged their lodgings. Downing then proceeded to the burgomaster's house and presented his diplomatic credentials, thus informing the authorities of his presence on Dutch soil. He also begged the burgomaster to arrange for a coach to be made available the following day, confident that the burgomaster would do nothing that day in respect of informing his masters at The Hague of his arrival, but would nevertheless wish to hurry the English ambassador on his way. Then, at table that evening, Downing announced his plan to his two companions.

'Tomorrow we go directly to Delft. 'Tis best this matter is put in train without delay. The partridges we seek will know that I am out of the country and will not expect me to make them my first call on return. I shall then proceed alone to The Hague and muster my forces, leaving you Miles to watch and wait, and you, Sir Christopher, to seize your own quarry. I am ordered to allow you this advantage, which is both against my instinct and all common sense, but I swear to you that if you bungle it and word gets abroad that something is afoot, I shall personally see to

173

it that you hang as you deserve.' Miles grinned his agreement with Downing.

Faulkner bridled at Downing's insulting tone and, recalling the sensation of being a prisoner, rose to the occasion. 'I shall endeavour not to follow your example, Sir George,' he said evenly, referring to Downing's mishandled attempt at the abduction of Edward Dendy.

Downing leaned forward. 'That is precisely why I urge circumspection upon you,' he said, his voice low and insistent. 'We play a low game for high stakes ... *very* high stakes ... and much falls to me. Do you do your part.'

'How may I do my own part?' Faulkner interrupted. 'Particularly when I rely upon you to indicate where my quarry lies.'

'You will be conducted thither when we reach Delft,' Downing said. 'Miles here will keep you company, at least until your quarry is secured. Now,' he said in a changed tone of voice, leaning back and becoming suddenly affable, 'let us have another stoop of ale before retiring.' He added a light-hearted remark upon the day's ordeal as though the intensity of his exchanges with Faulkner had never occurred. An hour later the three men each lay between clean sheets. As Downing had remarked as they bade each other good night, the one thing you could rely upon in Holland was clean sheets.

The Birds Caged

March 1662

They set off at first light, the coach lurching over the wet road, its three passengers wrapped in the silence of their own thoughts. After about an hour Downing leant forward and spoke in a low voice to Miles. It was clear to Faulkner that he was giving the cavalry officer precise instructions, and as he leant back in his seat he said to Faulkner, 'On our arrival at Delft, you will go with Major Miles who has an errand to perform before he accompanies you to your wife's lodgings. Once your wife and son are in your hands he will leave you. You will wait, keeping a close watch on your charges, until you hear from me.'

'I made a rendezvous with Sackler for the twelfth, around midnight,' Faulkner put in.

'I know, but that is of no interest to me. As I said earlier, now we are ashore, matters are in my hands. Sackler has his instructions and will lie off the Herringfleet until he receives further orders. In due course you will get your instructions, either from Miles here, or from a man named Abraham Kick. He is a go-between, familiar to the Regicides but in my pocket. If he brings you a written order signed "Nebuchad-

175

nezzar" you may assume it comes on my authority and act accordingly. You will meet him in Delft. Is that understood?'

'It is.'

'And one further thing: if I find that any laxity, caused by compassion or any other sentiment, results in either your wife or that damnable son of yours escaping your custody, you will answer at your peradventure. Is *that* understood?'

'It is.'

That was the last that was said until they arrived at Delft after a journey during which it seemed that they had crossed at least a dozen wide water-courses on floating bridges or ferries of singular description. Lesser streams had been easier as they passed over by way of the curious draw-bridges of which the Dutch seemed fond. Faulkner lost count of the neat towns, the windmills and the churches, which they half-glimpsed through the curtains of the coach, remembering only the inns at which they stopped to change horses and where he obtained relief for his over-pressed bladder. For as much of the journey as was possible, they dozed, aware that their wits would be best needed after dark. Despite the uncomfortable motion of the crudely sprung vehicle, Faulkner had to be woken from a deep sleep.

'Wake up, Sir Christopher,' said Miles, shaking him to consciousness. 'We are arrived in Delft.'

The coach door was already open, and Miles descended, dragging his saddle-bags and Faulkner's portmanteau after him onto the cobblestones of the yard. Faulkner followed, his sword clattering after him. It was already dark as Faulkner turned and looked back into the coach. Wrapped in his cloak Downing was almost invisible in its unlit interior. He raised a gloved hand in valediction, and Faulkner, gathering his wits, remembered he was going on directly to The Hague.

'Come,' Miles said abruptly, handing Faulkner his portmanteau. The new horses were being put-to, and Miles tossed some coins to the ostlers before leading Faulkner into the bright warmth of the inn. Pinching a passing maid's plump backside, Miles ordered food and beer in his tolerable Dutch – good enough not to raise any suspicions in the girl – before indicating to Faulkner that he should make himself comfortable.

When they had eaten, Miles belched discreetly, finished his stein of beer and leaning forward said, 'Be outside with our traps in half an hour. Wait for me, have a pipe of tobacco and look as though you are taking the air. When I return we will surprise your family.'

Then, having dropped some guilders by Faulkner's hand, Miles left him. Faulkner felt his heart-beat quicken. Within the hour he would confront Judith and Henry. Clearly, Miles, and presumably his master Downing, knew their whereabouts, but beyond that he had little information to go on. He must steel his heart against the inevitable and hysterical excuses, protestations and accusations that his estranged wife would undoubtedly hurl at him. But what of Henry? He realized with a sudden quickening that his son was steeped in treason, *active* treason, not some long ago act of vengeance like the Regicides. He would be desperate, and he was a fit, strong young man. Judith Faulkner he could deal with, but Henry? Henry in this *milieu* was an unknown, a complete and utter unknown.

After an estimated half an hour Faulkner beckoned to the girl, called for a pipe and tobacco and paid the reckoning. Having lit the clay pipe and settled his sword he gathered Miles's saddlebags and his own portmanteau and stepped outside. The yard was empty, though he could smell the adjacent stables, and rain was again falling, turning the isolated horse turds into a mire upon which a single lantern shed an intermittent light. The wind was getting up too. Sackler would be having a none-too-comfortable time of it offshore. Setting the bags down, he drew on the pipe and leaned against the masonry, half concealed by the shadow of a turn in the wall. An ostler crossed the yard at a lope, avoiding the rain and running for shelter.

Faulkner wondered where Miles had gone and concluded he was checking up on the whereabouts of Judith and Henry – *his family*, as they had been emphatically characterized. Well, that was true enough, and he was master of that family. The notion that in order to redeem his honour he must be thus placed began to work upon him as he waited in the wet and windy darkness of the yard. And then he recalled Judith – Judith of the changed name, the purified, puritan Judith – Judith bringing him succour when he had been imprisoned in The Tower.

Faulkner ground his teeth with fury at having been so put-upon and the pipe stem broke in his mouth. Just as he spat the severed mouth-piece to the ground a figure crossed the yard. Miles's long strides were accompanied by a clinking noise the source of which remained unrevealed as the cavalry officer hissed: 'Come!' and turned about to lead him out of the yard. Faulkner dropped the remains of the pipe, picked up their traps and followed.

Faulkner had no idea where they were, nor whither they went. The wind and rain drove into their faces for some yards until they turned down a side street and obtained some shelter. Further turns followed as they passed numerous houses from which chinks of light threw shafts on gleaming rain where candle-light caught the lancing downpour as it escaped the shutters. Noise, laughter and even music came and went as they hurried along, though the over-riding sound was the hiss of the rain, the howl of the wind amid the roof tops and chimneys and the squelching of their un-spurred boots. Then Miles stopped with such abruptness that Faulkner all but ran into him. He was aware of another man, of three other men, who had all been waiting for them in an alley. What little light there was fell upon something gleaming, and Faulkner again heard the chinking sound. Miles had acquired sets of manacles, and as if to confirm his fell intent, he turned to Faulkner and bent his head. The rain accumulated in the wide brim of his hat ran spouting into Faulkner's upturned face.

'We take no chances. These are Kick and a

brace of his men. We'll seize your people before they see who their gaoler is.'

'Watch the boy,' Faulkner said.

'Of course,' Miles responded coldly. 'Leave those things,' he said, indicating the baggage, 'and draw your sword.' There was a dull rasp as Miles's own weapon left its scabbard. Then the men moved forward, turned a corner and within ten yards stood before a door. On either side the windows were shuttered, though a faint gleam escaped one of them. Faulkner was about to edge along and squint into the room but he had no time as Miles, divining what he was intending, grabbed his arm, restraining him and pushing him back against the wall.

Faulkner heard Kick or one of his men knock on the door. It was a light knocking, that of a friend arriving late and unannounced rather than a party of assassins. There was no response, and the knock was repeated. A moment later Faulkner could just make out an enquiry from within. It was a man's voice, speaking in English – and he recognized it.

'Who's there?'

'Abraham Kick, Harry. I've John Barkstead with me. Open up in the Lord's name, 'tis pouring out here!'

Faulkner's heart was racing as he heard the bolts withdrawn. The opening door flooded the wet street with light and then, without a note of protest from the startled Henry, the light faltered, flickered and went out. He would have recognized Kick, whom he presumably trusted, while the presence of Barkstead, one of the Regicides, was pure deceptive fiction. In a rush the men pressed forward, and a moment later Faulkner found himself in a short hall-way and Miles was hissing at him: 'Get the bags inside and close the door!'

Having done as he was bid, Faulkner turned back to the hall-way, which opened onto two rooms. The door on the left-hand side was wide open: within came the dull noise of a moment's confusion; a rustle of struggling bodies, of gasps; and then, as Faulkner passed through the door, silence. He was confronted by his son Henry, pinioned in a chair, his arms behind his back, a silk scarf shoved into his mouth and one of Kick's men kneeling at his feet slipping irons about his ankles. The links dragged on the floor-boards and chinked on each other. Not a word had been said, and the man Faulkner would come to know as Abraham Kick stood behind Henry in his chair, smiling at Major Miles, who stood before the prisoner. Without taking his eyes off Henry he asked Faulkner over his shoulder, 'Is this person Henry Faulkner, Sir Christopher?'

The light of recognition gleamed in Henry's eyes as he saw his father loom over Miles's shoulder.

'He is.'

'Your wife is a-bed. I suggest you go up immediately and apprehend her.' He nodded towards the stairs, and Faulkner turned about. Two men followed him, one carrying the second set of manacles. As they mounted the stairs Faulkner heard behind him the voice of Miles laying the terrible indictment.

'Henry Faulkner, in the name of King Charles the Second, King of Great Britain, Ireland and France, you are charged with High Treason. I bear a warrant with the King's sign manual for your arrest and close confinement...'

Faulkner was on the landing now. Three doors led from it, and he was about to try one when another was cracked open. Instantly, the first of Kick's men raised his leg and booted it open. There was a cry as the door struck the room's occupant in the face as she attempted to peer through the crack. She fell back, and the man was through the door, bestriding her, his sword-point at her throat.

'Not a word, woman!' he snapped as a terrified Judith, on her back, her nightdress half-way up her legs, shuddered with fear. She was gasping for breath but might scream at any moment; Faulkner stepped quickly forward, dropped his sword across her belly, knelt at her side and clapped his gloved right hand over her mouth. The third man grabbed both her twitching ankles and manacled her.

Faulkner looked down at the woman who had caused him so much trouble. For a moment she was too shocked to recognize him, but with his left hand he swept his hat off, throwing rainwater across her face. It was as though the droplets awoke her to the true nature of the living nightmare in which she now found herself. Like her son a moment or two earlier, her eyes opened wide with the dawning of comprehension. She attempted to bawl at him, and he felt the frustrated exhalation hot on the palm of his hand through the leather of his gauntlet, then the attempt to bite him.

In a sudden vicious reaction, he compressed her open mouth between thumb and fingers so that he could feel the bony junction of her upper and lower mandibles. The ferocity of the grip and the pain it caused forced her to subside. He bent towards her. 'I may yet save you if you keep your mouth shut!' he murmured into her ear, retaining his cruel grip upon her face. 'Do you comprehend what I am saying?'

Looking down he saw tears of pain, humiliation and failure well up in her eyes. She closed them and managed, despite the constraint of his fist, to partially nod her head.

'I am going to remove my hand. These men will leave the room and you will dress decently as if to travel. You are forbidden saying a word on pain of instant death. If you refuse my terms I shall have you charged with High Treason, the consequences of which are well known to you. Co-operate, and you will live.' Her eyes were screwed up tightly now. He relaxed his hand, giving her enough room to indicate her agreement when he asked, 'Do you accept my terms?'

Very slowly he withdrew his fist and, never taking his eyes off her, he took up his sword and stood up. 'Thank you,' he said to the others in the room, 'do you please wait below.'

The two men withdrew, and Faulkner stepped back, allowing Judith to struggle to her knees and then, grasping the bed, to her feet. The irons rattled about her ankles. He kept his sword point implacably levelled at her. A mere extension of his arm would pierce her. She staggered, shuffling, her leg-irons chinking, half fainting from her fright. Still he did not trust her.

'Do not think to extinguish the candles,' he said sharply, surprised at his own ruthlessness. She stood, her back to him, half leaning on the bed, both arms straight before her braced against the mattress, her back heaving with the effort to draw breath evenly. 'Do not waste all night in doing as I wish,' he added as she quietly nodded and reached for her gown. He cast his eyes about the bed-room for any sign of a pin or knife. Still with her back to him, she slowly drew the nightdress over her head. She seemed to hesitate indecisively and then turned. She was naked and exposed herself to him in invitation. Once it might have worked, but he had tasted Kate Villiers's lips and knew that nothing sweeter existed under heaven. He was filled with an utter contempt.

'Do you seek now to transform yourself from Judith to Jezebel?' he asked, his mouth in a merciless grin. 'You are wasting your time – for one chameleon knows another. Get you dressed for pity's sake.' He finished with a short upward flick of the sword-point. Judith flinched; he had made his point.

She dressed as he had instructed and when she had finished he ordered her to put into a small bag such necessaries as she would need for a short voyage. This done he drew backwards, opened the door behind him and stepped onto the landing, jerking his head for her to follow. Judith shuffled her feet; the chain links between the iron rings about her ankles were just sufficient to allow her to descend the stairs one at a time if she clung to the bannister. Below men's faces looked up and watched as she came down the staircase and, passing between them, entered the room where her son sat, trussed in his chair.

In Faulkner's absence upstairs, Major Miles, Abraham Kick and his men had refreshed themselves from the house's larder. Miles indicated a platter of cold meat and a pot of beer for Faulkner. He made to shake his head and then decided he needed meat and drink and quaffed what was laid out. Judith, meanwhile, had sat down.

'Back to back,' Faulkner said sharply, his mouth full of ham.

'You learn fast, Sir Christopher,' Miles said approvingly with a lop-sided grin.

'There are some things that I learned before making the acquaintance of you and the Lord Protector's Scoutmaster-General, Major,' he riposted, referring to Downing's former appointment in an attempt to confuse the prisoners.

Miles nodded, unfazed by the mild rebuke, appreciative of Faulkner's dissembling. 'I wonder what Okey will make of it all,' he remarked, turning towards Faulkner, his voice low and confidential.

'Okey? Why so?' Faulkner asked, frowning.

'You do not know?' Miles's tone remained confidential, but his surprise was evident. 'Why, Sir George was regimental chaplain to Colonel Okey's own regiment.'

185

Faulkner raised his eyebrows. And he had thought himself the only chameleon in the King's service; it seemed they were everywhere.

Kick's men had by this time arranged the prisoners' chairs so that they were back to back and separated by a foot or so. Miles introduced Faulkner to Kick, and Faulkner caught the look of pure venom Henry threw at Kick, a man he had thought his friend.

Miles ushered them all out into the hall-way. 'Abraham will leave these two men at your service,' he said. 'They are both English officers who have been in Dutch service and speak the language fluently. I shall leave with Abraham and you must wait here until you hear from "Nebuchadnezzar". You may be here some time but rest assured you *must* remain here in patience, and you *must not* make contact with anyone outside these four walls.'

'I understand.'

'There is enough food in the house for a week. After that one of the officers will obtain more. I hope that it will not be that long – but it may. Only ensure that that pair in there make no noise, nor gull you when they wish to void themselves.'

Faulkner nodded.

'Kick tells me they have few servants: a maid and cook who live out. His men will buy them off when they appear tomorrow.' Miles looked about him. 'They rent this place but I have no idea how they pay. Let us hope that we are out of here before the reckoning is due.'

When Miles and Kick had left them, Faulkner went into the room and faced first Judith. 'You

186

will make no sound,' he said. 'The only thing of which you may speak is to ask for the piss-pot. Nothing else. D'you understand?' She nodded; he noted she seemed calmer.

He then confronted Henry. 'Did you hear what I said to your mother? Nod your head if you did.' Henry remained motionless and without further ado Faulkner removed his glove and struck it across his son's face. Henry gasped with the shock as much as the sting of the leather. 'Do not play with me, boy. Did you hear what I said to your mother?' Faulkner repeated. His eyes filling with tears, Henry nodded miserably.

Faulkner leaned forward and drew the silk from Henry's mouth. The lad swallowed hard, trying to work saliva into his mouth. 'I witnessed your expression when you recognized Kick for a turn-coat,' Faulkner said, almost conversationally. Henry croaked inaudibly, trying to master the sensation of near throttling caused by the silk gag. 'Now,' his father went on, 'you begin to comprehend treachery, and of that I am glad.' Faulkner paused and let all the implications of this sink in. From the sheen of sweat forming on Henry's face he concluded the young man had assimilated some of them. 'Now listen,' Faulkner went on, lowering his voice, 'if I am to do anything for you, you will obey me to the very letter. Do you understand that? To the very letter?'

Henry nodded and swallowed hard. Faulkner watched as tears ran uncontrollably down his cheeks and he began to sob, his body wracked by it. No right-minded man likes to see another weep, least of all his own son; Faulkner turned away.

Long afterwards Faulkner recalled the days that followed as the worst of his life. Men of Faulkner's stamp find charged idleness the worst ordeal that fate can ordain they undergo, for the responsibility they bear while remaining inactive is likely to drive an active fellow mad. Fortunately, he had the staunch and unflinching support of the two Anglo-Dutch officers, who better understood the complications of the situation in which Downing and his fellows must of necessity operate. They knew little of the detail, being mercenaries bound by honour to their current paymaster, but they understood that the extraction of those under the protection of the States General was illegal and impossible, without some form of warrant.

'Your Sir George Downing is as slippery as an eel and as cunning as a fox,' one of them remarked, 'but he will lay out gold and succeed in time.'

Time. That was the trouble. The two Dutch house-servants arrived early the following morning and were met and dismissed – not without a suitable fee to help them delay opening their mouths prematurely. After this brief flurry of excitement, boredom competed with a necessary vigilance, so that it seemed that the five inhabitants of the rented house existed only to watch the motes of dust descend slowly through the air from wherever they came. Faulkner and the two officers set up a roster, one man constantly

188

watching the two prisoners, who were allowed to walk about the room one-at-a-time and were fed twice a day. They were allowed to relieve themselves behind a screen as necessary, and the door to the room was kept locked. It had only one window, which let onto a small courtyard in the rear of the house, and this could be barred. A padlock was applied to the bars. The chief danger was that the guards would fall asleep out of boredom. The two officers could leave the house if they did so discreetly from the rear, but Faulkner was confined like his prisoners, though he had the liberty of more rooms, and unfettered feet. No weapons were kept exposed in the room itself for fear of either Henry or Judith getting hold of them, but each of the three guards carried a dagger in his waistband under his doublet, which would be difficult to extract even if he dozed off. Outside, three bared swords lay ready on a table and three wheel-locks lay alongside them, fully charged. At the slightest noise from inside, those without could enter fully armed and, while one man was on guard inside with the prisoners, another was obliged to sit in a chair in the hall-way, ready to answer a call for help, or investigate a suspicious noise. Each man did four hours within, four without and was allowed four hours in bed. In this way three days passed.

On the fourth morning there came a great knocking on the street door. Faulkner and the English officers were instantly on their feet and the light of hope kindled quickly in the prisoners' eyes. Faulkner, his sword drawn, went in and joined the officer on guard.

'Not a word,' he snarled at the prisoners. The man on stand-by went to the door and laid his ear against it. Faulkner could hear voices outside, but after a further knocking, the voices faded. Their visitors had gone. As Faulkner went out into the hall-way, re-confining the prisoners, the officer at the door turned towards him.

'They've gone,' he said in a low voice. 'From what they seemed to be saying amongst themselves, I gathered that they had come as friends of the others to warn them–' he nodded towards the room with the prisoners – 'that something was afoot.'

'Downing must have picked up the Regicides,' Faulkner remarked.

'It seems so, because I distinctly heard a man say: "Perhaps it was the young Englishman who betrayed them and he and the woman have already gone."'

'It would be a timely irony if they thought that,' Faulkner said.

Something was certainly afoot because a day later more people assembled outside and once again the officers eavesdropped. There was some disturbance in the town, they gathered, and there were those who wished to break into the house until someone reminded them all that it belonged to a Mynheer Maarten de Vliet, a name that seemed to deter them from further action. Who or what Mynheer de Vliet was, Faulkner never knew, though knowing their landlord's name made the threat of his sudden appearance more of a reality. No-one apparently alerted de Vliet to the probability that his tenants had vanished, or

190

at least not for the period that Faulkner and his associates occupied his premises.

'He probably resides in Amsterdam,' one of his companions advised him unconcernedly. 'Or perhaps Sir George has rendered him inactive with a sweetener of King Charles's gold.'

After that they continued to watch the dust fall by day and listen to the mice at night. In the event, it was four days before a man the Anglo-Dutch officers knew as Captain Armerer arrived with a letter signed *Nebuchadnezzar*.

Rendition

March 1662
After withdrawing with Armerer out of his prisoners' hearing, Faulkner read Downing's letter. Although Sir George said nothing of his other victims, it was implicit that although he had succeeded in securing the Regicides, this had been far from easy. Faulkner was ordered to 'accompany the bearer of this letter and discover in the port of Delft a craft capable of conveying the assembled cargo to the place of our disembarkation'. He was to charter such a craft – 'the suitability of which I leave to your charge' – and follow Armerer's directions as to where it was to lie to embark its reluctant passengers. His own prisoners were by that time to be confined on board.

Having read Downing's missive, Faulkner looked at Armerer. 'Do you know the contents of this letter?' he asked.

Armerer nodded. 'I am jointly responsible with you for getting these people aboard your man-of-war.' His English was so perfect that Faulkner concluded he too was English-born, a dispossessed cavalier, perhaps, who had wound up in the Dutch service and settled here with a buxom and satisfactory Dutch wife.

Faulkner nodded. 'Have you any idea of a merchant house willing to charter me a suitable vessel, or is that a test of my own initiative?'

'I have the money,' Armerer replied. 'As for the knowledge of who to approach...' He shrugged and left the sentence unfinished.

'It strikes me that this is unplanned. I had wondered how the miracle was to be conjured. Tell me, what has transpired with the others?'

'Kick and Miles met in the Oude Kerke and made the necessary arrangements while Downing was at The Hague. He managed to wrest an arrest warrant out of the Stadtholder – do not ask me how he did it but your use of the word miracle is not inapt, though I think he concealed his victims' whereabouts to frustrate any later complications. The three Regicides were at Kick's own house in the Nieuwe Langendijk where they had been drinking beer and smoking their pipes. Corbet was on the point of leaving his companions; they had his lantern prepared when Downing and his men, Miles, Kick, myself and a number of other English officers arrived. Downing served the warrant and restrained the

192

three men in irons, but could only get them into the Steen, the prison within the Rathaus...'

'*What*?' Faulkner showed his surprise. This rodomontade indicated an unravelling of catastrophic proportion. 'This is a repeat of the Dendy fiasco,' he said curtly.

'Certainly the diplomatic consequences may be profound,' Armerer agreed. 'Already, the local magistrates view the affair as breaching the integrity of Dutch sovereignty. Downing is obliged to keep a constant watch on the prisoners, consisting of his own servants. Several of the burgers, having visited the men in their cells, have got up petitions on their behalf. There have been some disturbances in the city...'

'Yes, we heard something of that. But surely we now have a stalemate.' Faulkner's tone was one of disappointment, if not desperation. His own family was one thing, but he was unwilling to lend himself to so egregious an act as springing the Regicides from a Dutch city gaol.

Armerer shrugged his shoulders again. 'I will give Sir George Downing the laurels for his audacity. Despite the burgers' protests to The Hague, he himself secured an order to the Bailiff of Delft from the hand of de Witt himself...'

'The Stadtholder?' Faulkner could hardly believe what he was hearing.

'So I understand. The Bailiff is now compelled to handover the indicted men. The Stadtholder, or one of his secretaries at the very least, outflanked the magistrates. Now Downing, having spread more gold than I can carry in my hat and both saddle-bags, is ready to move, while the

193

Bailiff fears a riot if he does so. Ergo, sir, you and I must conjure a vessel, bring it to the narrow canal behind the Rathaus and – abracadabra – the deed is done.'

'Abracadabra indeed...' Faulkner, his mind in a whirl, considered the state of affairs. Clearly, he could not alter what Downing had done, howsoever he reprobated it. He dismissed the horrid implications of the night's work and made up his mind. The sooner he did what was required, the better their chances of extricating themselves. He nodded to Armerer. 'Thank you for your candour. Let us make ourselves less martial. We have three or four hours before darkness, by which time my eye and your Dutch must have secured us a suitable craft. Come, I must inform your companions.'

Fifteen minutes later Faulkner and Armerer were casually walking along the quayside. The sensation of suppressed action troubled Faulkner's belly; he found the lax deception difficult to accomplish, but fell in step with Armerer who had the knack of pretence. Faulkner concluded that such insouciance must be one consequence of mercenary service, for Armerer and his Anglo-English colleagues had been exemplary in their obedience and efficiency.

A number of small vessels lay alongside the quay, several desultorily working cargo. They were all single-masted and cutter-rigged, broad of beam, bluff of bow and stern, with massively heavy leeboards on either side. Gay pendants flew from their thick masts, their huge rudders curled over their sterns, often decorated with

194

carved heads of mythical beasts and long, curling tillers. Some of their stem-posts were curved, others straight and raked. Most were well cared for with thickly rosined timbers and gaily painted iron-work. They each betrayed their origins and their purpose by their build, which the Dutch could interpret with far greater skill than Faulkner. His own cursory knowledge identified them imperfectly as *schuyts*, *tjalks*, *botters*, or *boiers*, though he knew they ran to a dozen types. What he was looking for was one which most closely resembled the Dutch yachts which, in a generous moment which would be sadly defiled by the present enterprise, the States General had given to the restored King Charles and his brother James, the Duke of York.

Towards the end of the quay lay a likely looking vessel. No-one was on deck but a curl of smoke rose from the chimney of the after cabin and a skylight showed a light was burning below. 'That one,' he said pointing her out to his companion. 'Do you go aboard and throw your gold about. Tell them there's an English gentleman and his family anxious to charter him. Half the money now...'

'And half when we reach Harwich,' Armerer said a little testily. 'You, I take it, are His Lordship.'

'Not a Lord, Captain Armerer, but a common knight. The nobility of the gold will testify to my own proof.'

'Ha!' Armerer grinned and made his way down the single, swaying gang-plank while Faulkner, watched by some curious by-standers and three or four boys, affected an air of nonchalance as best he could. He was far from feeling detached because it struck him that the King was spending his, Faulkner's, money. He was torn between a cool fury and admiration that the impecunious Charles had secured half the profits on the *Duchess of Albemarle* not least to fund this present, desperate and egregious act. Not only was Faulkner being made to pay for securing the Regicides for the King, but also his own wife and son too. It began to rain as he turned this notion over in his mind, but it did occur to him that such a payment might, if he could obtain audience with the King, buy Henry his freedom. He had not forgotten the terrifying words with which Major Miles had apprehended the foolish boy.

Armerer had boarded the Dutch vessel, causing a curious crew-member to apprehend him. Faulkner had watched him taken aft and disappear into the after cabin. A few minutes later he re-emerged, accompanied by a stocky man in baggy trousers, wooden clogs and a short blue jacket. Armerer indicated Faulkner's figure, and the man pulled a narrow-brimmed hat over his head, looked up at the clouds and hurried up the gang-plank. Faulkner had no doubt that this was the skipper. Armerer followed gingerly as the Dutchman approached him, uttering an incomprehensible torrent of a Dutch dialect which only afterwards Faulkner knew as Frisian, but which ended with the intelligible word 'Koom' which was accompanied by a beckoning motion.

'He wishes us to follow, to the house of his principal owner. He is the skipper and part-owner...'

'Sir Christopher,' Faulkner muttered under his breath.

'Sir Christopher,' Armerer added in a louder voice for the benefit of the idlers. Faulkner heard some unfavourable remarks about the English, and Armerer jerked his head with an air or urgency.

'We are not popular in Delft, Sir Christopher,' he remarked somewhat archly. 'Let us not tarry for fear they make two and two into four.'

They followed the skipper as he led them to a house some way back from the quay and a few moments later found themselves ushered into a comfortable parlour in which a man and a woman were sitting.

An exchange of greeting followed, and Faulkner learned that he was dealing with Jacobus Goedhart. The skipper had explained why he was troubling his partner, and Armerer answered a series of questions as to who wanted to charter the *tjalk*. Armerer's explanation was inventive enough, for Faulkner grasped much of it. He winced inwardly at the use of his real name, but Armerer's flourished use of his title had an impact, even on the stolid Dutch republican.

'He says you know a good craft when you see one, Sir Christopher.'

'Thank him, and tell him I admired the Dutch yachts that the States General presented to His Majesty King Charles and the Duke of York.'

The exchange took place, then Armerer asked, his face bland, 'Are you acquainted with the King?'

197

'Tell him I am, though I have not made the acquaintance of the Duke of York. Tell him I have been in His Majesty's private service.'

Once again Faulkner waited while this was passed to the old man. 'Our friend wishes to know if you have anything to do with the scandalous arrest of some other Englishmen in their city.'

'Tell him no, but I have heard of it and I am anxious to get to England with my family, having been travelling only to get here and find all in turmoil. I require a boat from Delft because it is important that I get to London in order to explain the grave insult now being offered to the Seven United Provinces.'

Armerer passed this on, then turned back to Faulkner. 'D'you mean to tell the King himself?'

Faulkner nodded emphatically. 'It is my duty to inform His Majesty exactly what is going on,' he said, the irony inescapable.

Again Faulkner waited; then Armerer said, 'That went down well, Sir Christopher. He offered you a roof for tonight, but I pleaded the urgency of your mission.'

'Then be so kind as to settle the reckoning.'

There followed a haggling which Faulkner affected not to watch, smiling instead at Vrouw Goedhart. He heard the chink of coin and the involuntarily indrawn breath of the old skipper, whose name they learned was Cornelius Bouws. 'Pray ensure you make it clear that the skipper will receive a personal bonus from me when we reach Harwich,' he loftily ordered Armerer. Old Bouws recognized the word 'skipper' and pricked up his ears.

'Of course, Sir Christopher,' Armerer answered with a wry deference. 'There; all is done,' he added after a few moments of further argument.

Faulkner was aware that the others were all smiling. He smiled too, then said, 'See to it that the boat is brought to my lodgings beside the Rathaus immediately. I would get my family aboard and under way before the night is upon us.'

'Of course, Sir Christopher.' Armerer gave a mock bow and passed the instruction.

Mynheer Goedhart chivvied Bouws, and the skipper almost ran out of the house to do the bidding of his twin masters. Faulkner made a courtly bow to the happy couple and withdrew, with Armerer following as a pretty maid let them out of the house and secured the door behind them.

'You to the *tjalk*,' Faulkner said sharply. 'The minute she is in the correct spot come directly to me and I shall have all ready. As soon as we leave our house to join her, you to the Steen prison and Sir George.'

'Very well.' Armerer hurried back to the boat while Faulkner made for the house, re-entering by the rear door. The relief at his return was palpable.

'We think that you may have been seen leaving here,' he was told by the guard on stand-by. 'There were some noises in the street and again, knocking on the door. We think they may come back, possibly with a warrant...'

'Very well. We must move with absolute

199

caution, for we are to go tonight. I will need you two until our prisoners are secured on board a vessel which I have hired. We will embark near the Rathaus. Do you know where that is?' The Anglo-Dutch officer nodded. 'Good. I need now to talk to them and gull them if necessary. I will relieve your companion while you brief him and make yourselves ready. Understood?'

'Yes, of course.'

Once Faulkner was alone in the room he addressed Judith and Henry. 'In a moment I am going to knock off your leg-irons. You will both get up and walk slowly round and round the room to restore yourselves. In a little while we shall leave this place and go aboard a small vessel on our way to England. Hold your tongue, Henry, at least while you still command it yourself.'

Judith gave a huge sob. 'Husband...' she began in a tone of miserable contrition.

'Be quiet! Listen to what I have to say. I can save your mother's life, Henry, of that I am sure, for the King wants no revenge upon a woman. As for you, despite the charge of High Treason at your arrest I am convinced that the King, in his mercy, may well be pleased to spare you upon the rightful pleading of your father. The King is obligated to me, the manner of which is private but to be relied upon. If you value your life, you must trust me on this, and I must needs trust both of you to accompany me in your rightful condition as my wife and son when we embark. Everything is contingent on this; *everything*. If either one or both of you think to raise the alarm, you will feel the point of my dagger.'

He had been walking round and round, alternately catching the eye of each of them, impressing upon them the desperate sincerity of his plan.

'Now, should we be apprehended, this is what you must remember. We are returned from Hamburg and are on our way to Helvoetsluys to take passage to Harwich. I heard of the arrests of Englishmen and, as a former Commonwealth commander, I seek to sail directly from here in order to remonstrate with the King. That is the story that covers our movement. You may talk in low voices about that as we walk to the boat; nothing else. The minute we are on board you will be confined until we are at sea. Do you both understand?' He looked from one to another. 'Henry?'

'Yes.'

'Judith?'

'I do.'

'Believe me,' Faulkner said, moving towards the door, 'I have undertaken none of this lightly. Its personal cost to me is immense, remember that. Immense. Neither of you have another soul under heaven that you may trust. Do exactly as I say and we may yet win through. Now, when the time comes – and it should not now be long – act with boldness and resolution. Remember our sentiments of righteous indignation; they at least can be Puritan.'

Almost immediately after this confident address, Faulkner was beset by doubts. As he stood silently watching Judith and Henry, their shackles knocked off, first relieve themselves and then stagger round and round the room until their dizziness and unsteadiness had passed, he felt the cold grip of terror seize him. The risk they ran was breath-taking; at any moment the watch, armed with a warrant from the Bailiff, could break down the door and apprehend them. The forthcoming walk through the street would be after curfew, and while they might plead their English nationality and offer a bribe or two, nothing could be relied upon. And at the bottom of his anxiety lay his real fear – could he trust Judith and Henry?

The call took longer to come than he had imagined, until he considered, realistically, the task of moving the *tjalk* under her sweeps to the waterside of the Rathaus. It was about eight of the clock when Armerer's cautious tap-tap could be heard on the rear door.

'All is ready,' he said simply.

To Faulkner's astonishment and relief their progress through the darkened streets went unchallenged. The night was cloudy, rain threatened and a brisk wind funnelled down the narrow alleyways so that he was unclear of its direction and had no idea of his bearings. He was equally relieved that neither Judith nor Henry disobeyed him. Four days of enforced silence and immobility seemed to have conditioned them in some way, robbed them of independence and stunned their initiative. They had been kept well-fed and adequately watered, but Faulkner's strictures on silence had been enforced ruthlessly. Consequently, they did not even attempt to feign any discussion as they were hastened along. One of the two officers preceded them, leading the way, the other followed, walking immediately behind Henry. Faulkner marched just ahead of his son, his left arm tightly linked with his wife's right and his pace such that she, only recently liberated from her hobbled state, could scarcely keep up. Armerer had, in accordance with his instructions, returned immediately to Downing at the Rathaus.

The officer leading them acted faultlessly, and they did not have far to go. Faulkner caught sight of the huge towering spire of a church and a glimpse down a side-street of the open space of a market-square. He assumed the Rathaus must lie somewhere close, central, complimentary to the great church. They turned a corner, and he smelt water. The canal was narrow but the pale streak of it opened up the road home and his heart leapt at the prospect. Although still consumed by anxiety, Faulkner felt that at least the first hurdle had been jumped when he came in sight of the *tjalk*. Bouws had lowered her mast to pass under a bridge and had moored her as close to the Rathaus as possible.

They hastened aboard, and Faulkner had to remind himself of the fiction of their voyage. Bouws grunted a courteous greeting and led them aft, to the cabin which he had vacated under the terms of the charter. Faulkner bundled his entourage below, the two officers standing on deck as their prisoners left the deck. Faulkner followed and cast a quick look round the cabin.

203

It was cosily domestic, the brass lamp glowing warmly, and in other circumstances it would have filled him with delight, but he must now await the arrival of others and hoped they would not be long in coming. 'Sit down,' he instructed his charges, 'and remain silent.'

The English officer who had led the way to the canal, and who Faulkner knew simply as Captain Brown, remained on deck, explaining to Bouws that the English gentleman's secretary and three servants should already have been aboard and that they would have to wait for them. Bouws made some reply that a man did not need such an entourage and that he was keen to start since as soon as this escapade was over he had a serious living to make. Captain Brown joshed him that he would make more tonight by cozening up to an English gentleman, such as his passenger was, than in a month of Sundays otherwise. Bouws grunted, spat over the side, lit his pipe and shouted something in Frisian to his men standing by on deck.

To Faulkner waiting below, his eyes on his prisoners, his ears trying to divine what was going on on deck, these were moments of re-newed tension. He hated the passivity and the reliance upon others. He heard a shouted exchange; was this Downing and the Regicides, or someone else? It was the night-watch, and Faulkner felt his heart lurch, noticing the sudden change of expression on Judith's face. Henry too had undergone a transformation as the awaken-ing of hope came to him.

'I'm watching you both,' Faulkner said balefully, his hand on the butt of his wheel-lock. He drew the heavy weapon and cocked it, pointing its brutal muzzle at first Henry and then his wife. 'Move beside each other,' he said.

On deck the leader of the watchmen was demanding to know what was afoot at this late hour and why Bouws intended moving his *tjalk* after dark. Bouws launched into a complex explanation in which the skipper adopted a sudden change of face, extolling the importance of his mission and the riches and virtues of his passenger. 'He threw them three guilders to drink to his own health and to be off and leave him to his affairs,' Brown said when he told Faulkner of the incident next morning as they sailed south towards the River Maas. 'My, 'tis wonderful what may be wrought with a little gold; it was his own money he ventured. At that point I knew you had chosen well!'

Ignorant of all this at the time, Faulkner kept his eyes on his two prisoners. Eventually, the tone of conversation on deck fell away to a desultory exchange of comments between Brown and Bouws. Then, after what seemed an eternity but was in reality no more than three or four minutes, Faulkner heard Brown's voice raised, speaking in English.

'Come on, damn you, you are keeping His Lordship waiting. He expects his servants to precede him, not lag behind like camp-followers.' Brown switched to Dutch, instructing Bouws to get under way at once, distracting him from noticing anything odd about the new arrivals.

Faulkner heard footfalls on the deck then the knocking sound of hatch-boards being lifted; then came the noise of more steps. It was clear the Regicides were being accommodated in the hold immediately forward of the cosy after-cabin. That would be understandable, though the precipitate manner of their descent might raise suspicions; but the gold – or at least the prospect of it – had done its work. Bouws had cast off and was occupied in the business of getting sweeps out to work astern, out into the main canal. Faulkner felt a gentle movement under his feet and noticed that both Judith and Henry were equally aware that they were under way. They sat thus side by side, confronting Faulkner, the cabin table between them, the barrel of the wheel-lock an accusation of the prisoners' past conduct and an augury of their future fate.

'You scum,' Judith said quietly.

Faulkner was saved the necessity of a response for, with a thud, the companionway slid open and a pair of muddied boots descended. Sir George Downing came below and stared at Judith and Henry. Without taking his eyes off them he said, 'Well done, Sir Christopher. Our other friends are trussed in the hold. I shall dis-embark as we turn the corner into the main canal.' Downing withdrew his right hand from his glove and held it out to Faulkner. 'Until we meet again,' he said.

Faulkner was watching the effect Downing's arrival had on Judith and Henry. He had no idea whether or not they knew who he was, but his confident presence was tangible evidence that they had been caught by an efficient network from which escape was impossible. He shook Downing's hand, and Downing clambered up on deck. They felt the slight bump as the *tjalk* scraped the canal bank, presumably as Downing disembarked. A moment later they received a second visitor; it was Armerer, and he carried leg-irons.

He too looked at Faulkner's prisoners and slowly expelled his breath. Faulkner felt the easing of tension but dared not drop his own guard. Armerer moved round the table, knelt and snapped the leg-irons on each prisoner in turn, padlocking them securely. Then he sat down alongside Faulkner.

'Our Anglo-Dutch friends have left with Downing,' he said quite deliberately in front of Judith and Henry, 'but Sir George has kindly left four of his personal body-servants to act as guards. In an hour or so I shall send one of them down to relieve you. He looks somewhat like an ogre. Now I am going to get something to eat. We have some cold meat and beer with us, and there will be enough for you too. I suggest we leave these people to go hungry for a while. By the way,' he added conversationally, 'you have chosen a fine little ship, Sir Christopher.'

Left alone again Faulkner regarded his two charges. 'You may talk if you wish, but you will oblige me by keeping a civil tongue in your heads,' he said simply.

'You scum,' Judith repeated.

Faulkner affected not to listen. He laid the wheel-lock down on a locker behind him, stood, took off his gloves and hat and scratched his pate vigorously. It was the act of a relaxed man.

'You scum,' Judith said yet again.

In one movement Faulkner picked up his gloves, leaned across the table and flicked them in Judith's face. Her head jerked back and they barely touched her, but her arms flew up and she grabbed at his extended wrist. Faulkner twisted free but Henry had stood and lunged at him only to discover that Armerer had not merely secured his ankles, but had run the chain links through an eye-bolt secured to the deck to restrain the chair upon which he sat. The sudden, unexpected restraint caused him to fall forward, and Faulkner, perceiving him losing his balance, shoved his head hard down against the table with his left hand. His right, meanwhile, savagely twisted Judith's wrist, all but breaking it as he relinquished his grip and stood back. Henry slowly raised his bruised head from the table and fell back into his chair while Judith slumped into her own.

Faulkner hefted the wheel-lock. 'Next time...' he said significantly.

Half an hour later he was on deck, drinking in the cold night air. It had rained, for Bouws stood at the tiller in oiled tarpaulin and the decks were wet, but it had eased and the wind was blowing the sky clear of clouds. Bouws said something like, *'Goot vind,'* nodding forward where the dark shapes of men were clustered round the foot of the mast, now swung vertical again in its large, solid tabernacle. The great mainsail went creaking up into the sky, its short curved gaff

uppermost, its foot stretched along a massive boom the thickness of man's thigh – of the ogre's thigh, in fact.

Armerer's description of Downing's servant had not been inaccurate. The man was huge, went by the name of Hendricks, and had grinned at his charges as Faulkner had handed them over. He spoke heavily accented and faulty English that, combined with his bulk, sufficiently intimidated both Judith and Henry, who appeared cowed.

Faulkner looked at the mainsail as it caught the stiff breeze that blew over the flat landscape. Although they were now running south under sail, Faulkner grasped the complexities of moving a small craft in and out of the canal system – complexities which would have occupied Bouws for that long period during which Faulkner waited impatiently for news of the *tjalk*'s arrival at the rendezvous. Bouws and his crew would have had to use long oars, or sweeps, combined with warping, a tedious business of carrying out a long line, making it fast and then hauling the *tjalk* along by heaving it in. Longer legs were made by passing a line ashore and man-hauling it, for which task old Bouws had to rely upon the muscular power of his small crew, just as he did now in the hoisting of sail.

They were well clear of Delft now, and the wind, Faulkner guessed, was from the west, broad enough on the bow to allow them to sail on a narrow reach along the canal. In places trees screened them, but these fell back as they scudded south-south-westward towards Vlaardingen.

Armerer joined him on deck and drew him out of earshot of Bouws at the helm. 'D'you think this wind will hold?' he asked.

Faulkner looked at the sky; it was much clearer now. He could see stars and a hint of moonlight from the new moon, though that still lay behind thinning cloud. 'I don't see why not,' he said. 'In fact it may chop round to the nor'-west, which would improve our position. You are concerned that once daylight arrives the alarm will be raised?'

Armerer nodded. 'Just so. The Dutch were not happy with Sir George; my guess is that legal processes had been started in order to thwart him. The only reason we escaped so easily was that we moved when we did, before the lawyers and advocates woke to our machinations. A relay of horsemen could—'

'But they think we are for Harwich,' interrupted Faulkner. 'If they seek to detain us at Maasluis or The Hook, they will wait all day. It is time we told our friend Bouws that he is not going to Harwich, but to Helvoetsluys. Come, let us deal with the matter at once. Tell him I don't fancy a crossing of the North Sea in this tub. Have you any more guilders to sweeten him if necessary?'

'Downing left me some,' Armerer replied.

'Good.' Faulkner led Armerer to the stern where the skipper leaned nonchalantly against his huge curved iron tiller and serenely smoked his pipe.

'Sir Christopher, my master,' began Armerer, 'wishes to change his mind. He does not want to

go to Harwich, Mynheer, he wishes to go to Helvoetsluys.' Faulkner watched as Bouws's weathered brow furrowed. Armerer affected to look over his shoulder at Faulkner before lowering his voice. 'He is scared of crossing the North Sea in so small a craft.'

Faulkner heard the recognizable nouns 'Noord Zee' and watched as Bouws cast him a glance, removed his pipe and spat to leeward. 'Helvoetsluys,' he said slowly.

Armerer nodded. 'There will be money for you Mynheer,' he said, adding: 'A private arrangement.'

Bouws nodded, considered the matter, spat again, then responded. Faulkner recognized several of the words and the names of towns before Armerer turned to him and translated. 'He doesn't appear to mind. Perhaps he is as scared of the North Sea as I pretend you to be. He says that the ebb will be running in the Maas and he could run down, double Voorne to get into the Haringvliet that way, but he would rather cross the Maas and use the canal system to reach the Haringvliet.'

Faulkner nodded. 'That suits our purposes admirably. Do you think he has smoked us?'

'Hmm. I think he may suspect something, but he isn't certain.' Armerer smiled. 'As long as we are not stopped, I think we may rely upon the persuasive power of gold.'

Faulkner nodded. As long as they were not stopped. 'It will be daylight in two hours or so. I will breathe easier when we are south of the Maas.'

The dawn lit up the east behind the rooftops and spires of Vlaadingen. The canal had swung towards the south, and they entered the locks in the town before passing into the tidal waters of the River Maas. Bouws said something to Armerer, who remarked that it were best that they went below and left the skipper and his men to handle the lock-keeper.

'There are tolls to pay and papers to be seen.'

'Does he have papers?' Faulkner asked, suddenly alarmed.

'I doubt it, but he may have obtained clearance for Harwich, though we left him little time for it. Anyway, I doubt he'll have a problem; he's a shrewd old bird. Let's go below and ensure our own birds do not sing too loudly. Come and see the Regicides.'

Faulkner followed Armerer through the open hatch-board and under the corner of the tarpaulin that had been drawn across to keep out the dim light of a half-shuttered lantern. The after end of the hold was occupied by Downing's servants, the forward end by the Regicides. The three men lay on some loose straw, the remains of an earlier cargo, for it was sparse enough. They were bound, hand and foot, and gagged. Faulkner regarded the restraint overly cruel but held his peace.

'Here they are,' said Armerer, 'John Okey, Miles Corbett and John Barkstead. They do not seem so very terrible, do they, and yet their continued existence threatens the peace of England and the foundations of our King's throne.'

Armerer spoke with that simple direct conviction that these three Roundheads had once known well. Faulkner, schooled by Sir Henry Mainwaring, and living close to the complexities of first court and later state life, found such dogmatism naive and immature. Would that the world could be regulated like the child's nursery he had once seen in London at one of the Trinity Brethren's houses; a small world where everything had its place and all was joyous and happy. But the world was not inhabited by children, unless it was these men with their honest straightforwardness who were the world's innocents. If so, the world, with its insatiable appetites, was about to consume them.

Faulkner regarded the three wretches. They were trussed like piglets on their way to market. No, they did not look like a threat to King Charles II but, like the other two persons confined abaft the bulkhead in the *tjalk*'s cabin, they could make mischief enough. One man – Okey, Faulkner thought him to be – seemed asleep, at least his eyes were closed, though how one could sleep in so cramped and awkward a state puzzled Faulkner. The other two regarded him with a burning hatred. Whether or not they knew his identity seemed irrelevant; that he was among their gaolers was sufficient to earn their visceral contempt. He was, he realized, one of the engines moving them inexorably towards the most terrible end.

He would never forget the look in their eyes.

Faulkner slept in his cloak on deck for an hour as they crossed the Maas and entered that complicated system of waterways that wound southwards, past Spijkenisse and Oud-Beijerland to debouche at last into the Haringsvliet – that Herringfleet of the English jack's Anglicization. The winding nature of the waterway, the now contrary tide and a falling and backing wind confounded Faulkner's predictions, delaying them. But no horsemen raised any alarm, and the sun was already westering behind low banks of cloud by the time the near-open water of the Herringfleet – bounded on the far side by the low land of Over-Flakke – lay before them.

It would be a hard beat downstream before either the town of Helvoetsluys or the *Blackamoor* came in sight. Faulkner made periodic visits to the cabin but largely left the duty of guarding Judith and Henry to Downing's men. It lessened the risk of the prisoners taking advantage of any weakness; besides, he was weary, the strain of the last weeks telling upon him. He was, he told himself, the oldest person involved in this horrid affair.

Once the few light of Helvoetsluys were in sight Faulkner went forward. His eyes, the eyes of an old man and none too certain of what they saw, scanned the darkness until he saw what he was looking for. 'The next tack will do very nicely,' he murmured to himself as he turned aft and went to rouse Armerer. 'Tell our skipper that he may forget about Helvoetsluys; he is to lay us alongside the man-of-war on his larboard bow.'

'I don't know the Dutch for "larboard bow",' Armerer complained.

'Try *"backboard* bow" – but he'll see her soon enough ... Point over there.' Armerer hurried off, and Faulkner heard the old man expostulating. He strode aft and drew his wheel-lock. Bouws saw the dull glint of starlight on gun-metal and fell silent. 'Tell him to rig fenders and get mooring lines ready. If he wishes, I will take the helm.'

Armerer translated, and Bouws shook his head vigorously, making conciliatory gestures to Faulkner. 'He'll comply,' Armerer said shortly. 'Downing's gold will see to that.'

Faulkner went forward, leaned against the *tjalk*'s larboard rigging and cupped his hands about his mouth. '*Blackamoor*, hoy!' he bellowed, repeating the hail after a moment. He did not have to wait any longer for a response. Tobias Sackler was aware of his duty.

'Who goes there?' came the answer.

'Captain Sir Christopher Faulkner with diplomatic packages for London!'

'Come alongside!'

'We shall need a whip and net at the main yardarm!'

'Aye, aye!'

There was a nasty chop running in the Herringfleet, and Bouws's fenders were needed, even against the ample tumblehome of the pink, but the Dutch skipper laid his little craft alongside the man-of-war with accomplished flair while his crew dropped the mainsail and then hurried fore and aft to make fast. From the low whistle which he emitted, Faulkner knew Bouws was enjoying himself. At least he did not have to entangle himself with the authorities at Helvoetsluys; as a packet-port they were likely to be far more efficient than those at Delft. By the time double head and stern ropes had been secured, and springs from bow and stern had been made fast to the *Blackamoor*'s main and fore chains, three lanterns hung over the pink's side and a rope net dangled over the broad hatchway, suspended from a line rove at the pink's main yardarm. Bouws's men swiftly ran a lanyard round the lowered mainsail to prevent it flogging over the open corner of the hatchway.

Faulkner looked up at the pink's gun-whale. He could see Sackler. 'We have five prisoners, Captain Sackler,' he called out. 'Four men and one woman!'

'We are fully prepared, sir,' Sackler called back. 'Send 'em up!'

The three Regicides were brought on deck one at a time by Downing's servants. None of them could walk or help themselves. Making a motion for the net to be lowered, Faulkner unhooked it. 'Spread that canvas,' he told Armerer, indicating a sheet of sail-cloth thrown into the loose net. Armerer swiftly did as he was bid. The *tjalk* was bouncing up and down the *Blackamoor*'s side, occasionally thumping against the little man-of-war, which was herself moving and snubbing at her cable as wind and tide competed with each other as the dominant force ruling the Herring-fleet that blustery evening. The man Faulkner thought of as Okey was laid on the canvas.

'Hoist away,' he called, and the seamen aboard the *Blackamoor* ran away with the whip. The net drew tight and, with its inert human cargo, shot into the air; a second line plucked it inboard and,

216

as the seamen slacked back on the whip, John Okey was laid on the deck of His Majesty's Pink *Blackamoor*. The operation was repeated twice more before the ogre brought Henry up from the after cabin. Henry was more mobile than the Regicides, but the ogre had not removed the leg-irons and Henry was pushed roughly into the net on the hatch-tarpaulin. Then he too was snatched up, into the custody of King Charles's Royal Navy.

Armerer had gone below for Judith. Faulkner called out for Sackler to wait and, after Downing's men had forced Judith into a crouched position on the canvas, he drew Armerer aside. 'What shall you do now? Get Bouws to carry you back to Delft?'

'Yes, that was my intention. I shall settle with him then.'

'Give him my thanks, and ask him the name of his *tjalk*.'

Armerer called aft and repeated the name Bouws had said. 'She's the *Velsa*,' Armerer told him. He held out his hand, and Faulkner briefly clasped it. Perhaps he sensed something of Faulkner's repugnance at the task in which they had been jointly engaged; perhaps he was offering sympathy to a man whose future was uncertain, given the conduct of his wife and son. 'Downing's gold maketh all smooth, Sir Christopher,' Armerer said. 'Besides that, the end so often justifies the means.'

Faulkner bit his lip, burning to say that both Sir George Downing and King Charles were actually spending money mulcted from Sir Christopher

Faulkner, but he forbore the peevish indignity. 'Give Sir George my compliments,' he said with a curt courtesy. A moment later he stuck the toes of his boots in the net, grasped the four loops that secured it to the whip's hook and waved for the seamen to take it up.

He landed awkwardly, but on his feet, bent and handed Judith to hers. He could feel her shaking.

Sackler approached him, one hand at the brim of his hat, the other extended in greeting. 'A desperate business, sir,' he said succinctly, regarding Judith with a cold eye. Faulkner guessed it was only partly made up of curiosity; there was a strong prejudice among seamen of all classes against women on board ship. It was only to be expected that this would find an extreme form in a Puritan like Sackler.

Taking Judith's arm and drawing her close to him, he introduced her. 'This is my wife, Captain Sackler.'

Even in the fitful light thrown by the lanterns, Sackler's astonishment was obvious, his eyes gleaming briefly in their cadaverous sockets. He mastered his surprise in a second, with a slight inclination of his head in Judith's direction. 'Madam ... I have made no arrangements for passengers,' he said, addressing Faulkner, 'but you had better have my cabin, Sir Christopher. And now, if you'll excuse me, I'll get the vessel under way.' He made to turn away and then swung back, adding in a low voice, 'Arrangements have been made to secure the others, I can assure you.' The last gleam of the lanterns hung over the side caught the sincerity of Sackler's eyes as they were hauled inboard and extinguished. 'You have my word on it, Sir Christopher.'

'Very well.' With the deck plunged into darkness, it took a moment for Faulkner to adjust to his new circumstances. He walked a reluctant Judith to the rail and peered over the side. The *Velsa* was being cast off. He could make out the faint glow of Bouws's pipe and heard him bellow his orders as the men at the foot of the mast began work on the halliards. Armerer, Downing's assortment of thugs and body-servants clustered about him, waved, and Faulkner returned the compliment. Then the wind caught the sail, the main-sheet was paid out and Bouws leaned against his huge tiller. The tide caught the *Velsa*, she swung away as the foresail drove her head round and she faded into the night.

Aboard the *Blackamoor* the hands were already tramping round the capstan, the topmen were aloft loosening the topsails and Sackler had taken his post beside the helm. He would have a hard beat out of the Herringfleet, but the tide would soon serve and, in any case, that was Sackler's problem. Faulkner led Judith below.

The Home-Coming

March 1662
During the passage of the *Velsa*, Faulkner had consoled himself that his troubles would be over when they boarded the *Blackamoor*, but the presence of Judith redoubled his woes, bereft as he now was of the assistance of Armerer and his colleagues. Once the cabin door closed behind them Judith exerted all her strength and withdrew her arm with such ferocity that the release sent her reeling across the cabin. It was a confined, tapering and narrow space, sparsely furnished, as one would expect of an impecunious commander like Sackler. A small, lightly-partitioned sleeping-space led off on the starboard side, the small windows were shuttered and a dim lantern threw more shadows than light. As Judith recovered her balance the *Blackamoor* heeled to the wind: they were under-way. The sensation of movement released a flood of relief throughout Faulkner's body. Sackler might consider that the older a man was, the less sleep he needed, but Faulkner was dog-weary. He would have injudiciously tossed off a pint of wine had one been to hand, its ownership notwithstanding, but no such supply was visible. Must he sit guard over his wife for the hours it

would take to reach Harwich? Were they going to Harwich, or directly to London? He chid himself; he should have asked Sackler. And had he not ordered old Toshack to meet them at Harwich? He expelled his breath in a sigh of utter exhaustion, slumped into a chair, and withdrew the wheel-lock from his belt, placing it beside him and regarded his wife.

Judith stood, one hand against the bulkhead, the other to her mouth. The sight almost brought a smile to his face: Judith was going to be sea-sick! A moment later the *Blackamoor* came to his assistance and lurched to leeward before coming upright. They were in the process of going about, Faulkner realized; the pink hovered 'in-stays' for a short while and then obligingly lay down on the opposite tack. A thin stream of vomit escaped Judith, who gave a short cry of mortification and slumped back into Sackler's sleeping-space and fell into the crude bunk. Faulkner got to his feet, discovered a pewter bowl and shoved it into her hands. Pulling the curtain across the entrance he resumed his chair. Ten minutes later he was fast asleep.

Faulkner awoke with a start. The lantern had gone out or been extinguished and light filtered through the window shutters. There was a light knocking at the cabin door. His first thought was for Judith. He leapt to his feet, moved swiftly to the sleeping-space and drew the curtain back. She lay asleep, one hand across her mouth, the bowl beside her. She had fouled Sackler's bed-linen, and the air stank of vomit. The knock came again at the door, and he went to open it. A small man in a serge jacket and frock confronted him.

'Cap'n Sackler's compliments, sir, we have made a fast passage. We're approaching the Sunk, and would you an' her leddyship require some breakfast?'

Faulkner shook his head to clear it. 'That would be most kind,' he said.

'We've some eggs and burgoo, sir.'

It proved a capital breakfast, and Judith stirred as Sackler's servant brought it into the cabin. It was followed by Sackler himself; his proboscis wrinkled at the smell of vomit.

'I give you a good morning, Sir Christopher. I trust Her Ladyship's night was not too uncomfortable.' Faulkner explained his wife's plight, but Sackler waved his apologies aside. 'No matter, I regret your distress, ma'am,' he said in Judith's direction before returning his attention to Faulkner. 'As you probably guessed I am making for Harwich, where I shall land Lieutenant Clarke with despatches as my orders require. I shall then await orders. If the wind serves I am to proceed directly to Deptford, otherwise I am to discharge three of my passengers at Harwich, whither, I am given to understand, a squadron of cavalry will shortly arrive. As I am also expected to serve under your direction, Sir Christopher, perhaps you will tell me what you expect of me.'

'Of course. I regret that you have been placed in so awkward a position. The fourth man is my own prisoner, a charge I am laid under by the highest authority. As I told you, I have my own vessel at Harwich and should wish to transfer into her on arrival.' He paused, weighing up Sackler, who thus far had behaved with impeccable propriety. However, it occurred to Faulkner that if he wished, once he had gone, Sackler could weigh anchor and do as he wished with the three Regicides. Both men's eyes met, and it was clear that Sackler divined Faulkner's train of thought for he smiled that curiously attractive smile of his and said, 'I gave you my word, Sir Christopher.'

Faulkner nodded. 'Yes, you did, but...' He glanced at Judith. He had once trusted her. She stared back at him, her face pale from her discomfiture. It was clear she had withdrawn into herself, biding her time, Faulkner suspected, until she was ashore and could determine which way the wind blew. 'Well, no matter. I shall remember Septimus Clarke, Captain Sackler, as I shall remember you.'

Sackler nodded and made his excuses. 'I am needed on deck, as you will understand.'

To the surprise of both Faulkner and Sackler, a troop of cavalry was already awaiting their arrival in Harwich; so too was the *Hawk*. By the end of that day the three Regicides had been placed inside a locked coach, surrounded by the troopers, and had left Harwich by the town gate on the Colchester Road. Faulkner, Henry and Judith had been pulled across to the *Hawk* in the *Blackamoor*'s boat, and the little pink had slipped out to sea, to resume her duty of protecting the fisheries.

As Faulkner had taken his departure from Sackler, the latter had asked, 'Who is the fourth man, Sir Christopher?' Faulkner had looked at him, and Sackler had added, 'Forgive my curiosity.'

Faulkner had expelled a long sigh. 'He is my son, Captain Sackler; as to his condition as a prisoner, I beg you not to press me. I recall you too have dependants; sometimes they are a mixed blessing.'

'They are certainly a burden,' Sackler had observed drily. 'I apologize for asking.'

'Not at all.' They had shaken hands and taken their leave of one another.

Once aboard the *Hawk*, where to his annoyance Faulkner found the lively and expectant figure of Charlie Hargreaves, he addressed Toshack without any greeting. 'Have my son confined amidships, Mr Toshack, and ask me no damned questions.' He turned to Judith. 'You are to settle in the after cabin. I will be down shortly.' He lowered his voice. 'Do not try to be clever, Judith. Save all your arguments for later, when we are ashore. I would not have your linen washed in public.'

He watched as she involuntarily bit her lip, the very picture of chagrin.

'There's a gale brewing,' Toshack offered. 'A good 'un from the sou'-west.'

Faulkner looked up at the western sky. It was full of dark clouds while overhead streamed the harbingers of wind, long white and curling mare's tails. He cursed under his breath. 'Watch for the shifting of the wind; the instant it veers I want us under canvas. Why did you bring the lad?'

'Mr Gooding ordered it, sir.'

The wind veered into the north-west at noon the following day after a twelve-hour blow from the south-west. It came with a clearing of the sky, and Toshack wasted no time; by noon the following day they lay off Blackwall. As they secured to a mooring-buoy Faulkner thought of his splendid Indiaman. Toshack had told him her masts were in and the business of fully rigging her was in hand. He looked upstream for her then postponed the matter.

'Time enough for that tomorrow,' he muttered to himself; there were more pressing matters. As he gathered his wits it occurred to him that he had no idea where his wheel-lock was. A visceral fear constricted him as a suspicion formed in his mind: Judith!

He tumbled below into the cabin, his face flushed. She rose at the intrusion and saw the look on his face. 'I think you left it aboard the *Blackamoor*,' she said coolly, guessing exactly what was worrying him.

Faulkner thought for a few moments and then nodded. 'Perhaps,' he said. He needed her explanation to be correct. 'A boat is being made ready. It is time to go on deck, but before we do, I must speak to you and have your agreement.' He paused, staring at her intently. She remained stubbornly quiescent. 'You will find things changed at home. Hannah has been mistress of the house since you left. I wish that matters remain so arranged. I shall not restrain you once we are ashore, but your continued freedom rests entirely upon your conforming to my wishes. Your liberty is assured but is conditional upon your obedience. As you are aware, the King has a long arm and I am bound to it. So too are you, if you wish to live in liberty. You have it in your power still to ruin me, but I promise you that I will not submit without a fight. As to Henry, the best I can offer you is that I shall plead that his youthful enthusiasm and indiscretion were regretted ... Judith?'

She made no reply, merely making a gesture as of resignation. Faulkner stared at her a moment, willing her to commit to his intention, but there was no sign of compromise, still less of good-will. 'Very well, then,' he said, turning away. He picked his sword and baldric, then glanced at his portmanteau. 'Hargreaves can follow with my traps,' he mumbled to himself, then to Judith: 'Let us go on deck.'

He scrambled up the steep companionway steps and, at the top, laid his sword down, turned about, offering Judith his hand. She seemed to hesitate deliberately, and as the worm of suspicion suddenly uncoiled in his belly, Faulkner felt the ball before he heard the explosion of the wheel-lock's detonation. He roared with pain and fury, spinning round as the shattered glass of the amidships sky-light fell tinkling to the deck, sparkling in the sunlight. Through the shattered glass Faulkner saw Henry, lowering the wheel-lock. He turned and bent over it, as though re-loading it. Faulkner swung round, Toshack, Hargreaves and the *Hawk*'s crew staring at him, shocked at the incident. The shock of the sharp pain had passed, and Faulkner felt the onset of the deep throbbing that would require the services of a surgeon to dig the wheel-lock's large projectile out of his buttock. He could feel the blood streaming down his leg but ignored it. 'Toshack! Hargreaves! A boat-hook!' He snatched up his sword and stabbed it down through the skylight. Below, Henry had almost completed reloading and priming the wheel-lock but was out of Faulkner's reach. Having completed his task, Henry turned, the loaded wheel-lock in his right hand. Instinctively, Faulkner drew back, out of Henry's line of sight; a split-second later the loud bang of the weapon's second discharge was ringing in their ears – then there was complete silence.

Cautiously, Faulkner peered down the skylight. A faint coil of smoke rose through the broken glass, the interior of which was splattered by blood. What remained of Henry lay slumped below, and Faulkner could see his brains.

The house in Wapping was an unhappy place for some weeks. Hannah's welcoming smile froze on her face when she saw her mother and had learned of Henry's suicide. Judith, expressionless, made no sign of greeting Hannah or of even recognizing her, retiring to her room, while Faulkner had stood awkwardly in the parlour, whither both Hannah and Gooding attended him in the hope of understanding what had happened. He waved their questions aside to demand a surgeon, calling out that Hannah should: 'Boil

227

water before the rogue touches me with a knife.'

When the man arrived, Faulkner insisted the barber-surgeon washed his instruments before he laid a finger upon his person and then, the others having withdrawn, he dropped his breeches and submitted to the humiliating probing and extraction of the lead ball.

'You are lucky, Sir Christopher,' the man remarked as he suppressed his patient's groans with professional commentary. 'Both that your muscles are strong, preventing the ball from going deep, and that the ball does not seem to have found its mark very effectively.' It did not feel like a ricochet to Faulkner, though he thought of the route it had travelled and told the man to look for glass. After a further debasing struggle, the barber-surgeon straightened up, holding a piece of glass in his forceps. 'But a single shard, Sir Christopher,' he said triumphantly. 'Now, you will likely have a fever for a few days, but if you keep warm, drink regularly and pray that the Almighty will favour you, I have no doubt of your recovery.'

His wound plugged and the surgeon dismissed with yet more money, Faulkner slumped awkwardly into his chair. Hannah came in and slid a cushion under him, for which he kissed her and fondled her hair.

'Do not cry for Henry, my dearest,' he said sadly. 'He is in a far better place and sent there by his own hand before the King's butchers got to work upon him.' If his words were meant to comfort Henry's sister they failed, for Hannah withdrew weeping inconsolably as Faulkner waved aside her demand that he should go to bed. Instead, in defiance of his surgeon and his daughter, Faulkner sat staring into the fire. He would have done what he could for the boy, but the matter had never been certain, a matter of the King's whimsy. But that was not the King's fault: Henry had made his own bed and must, perforce, lie upon it.

Except that Judith had made that bed up for her son in every detail, of that Faulkner was now convinced. Judith was obviously caught up in the conspiracy, and whatever she had done herself or persuaded Henry to do, only Judith herself could have possibly seized the wheel-lock, which she must have accomplished when he slept aboard the *Blackamoor*, assuming she was prostrated by sea-sickness. How she passed it to Henry was as yet a mystery, but she had managed it, as the puncture in his buttocks bore painful testimony.

Thus night fell upon the unhappy house.

It was in the small hours that Faulkner, still in his chair, cold and cramped, woke to a full comprehension of the previous day's events. He was furious with Judith for betraying him and placing in Henry's hands the means to destroy her husband and, that having failed, kill himself. Despite his discomfort and pain, his mind seemed to see things with the utmost clarity. He did not recognize in this the onset of fever, the consequence of infection in his wound, but he said his farewells to Henry, regretting much – as fathers of wayward boys do – but consumed with a fiery hatred of his meddling wife. As his temperature rose, his fury kept pace, so that when an anxious Hannah came down at daylight, she found her father writhing in a delirium on the floor, mired in ash from the extinguished fire.

Henry was buried in unhallowed ground. Only Hannah and Gooding attended him as Faulkner still lay in bed, feverish and too weak to leave it. In an adjacent chamber the dead man's mother lay prostrated in a world of her own fashioning.

Of Faulkner's kin it was Hannah who came best out of the events of the month of March 1662, for she had risen to the challenge of the sudden burden of responsibility for the house. Hannah displayed that spirit of swift resolution that had made Faulkner's inactivity in the house in Delft so irksome, and that Henry possessed in perverted form. Too like his mother in his inflexible acceptance of dogma, of his insistence upon 'right' and 'justice', among other philosophical forms, *his* version of Faulkner's resolve had led him into a death-trap.

Hannah had too practical a turn of mind to be ensnared so easily. Besides, her father had not only left her the house to manage, but an uncle whose sense of moral self had received a body-blow, together with a curious mission to contact her own father's lover. It was this last which had proved the true challenge. At first she had recoiled from the task, constantly postponing the decision until her sense of equivocation, and a horror of addressing a scarlet-woman, had been replaced by curiosity.

When at last she had walked to Leicester House and asked for a letter to be placed in the hands of Mistress Villiers, she had plucked up courage to inform the footman that she would await a reply. This bold initiative had aroused a reciprocal curiosity in Katherine, who had ushered Hannah into the same chamber into which she had shown her father. Alone, she had immediately seized Hannah's hands and, drawing back and smiling, had looked her up and down.

'I am charmed, Mistress, charmed,' she had said regardless of Hannah's blushes. 'I can see why your father speaks so highly of you. Now, tell me what news you have of him.'

A beguiled and confused Hannah had left an hour later, the taste of sweetmeats still in her mouth, mixed with the tang of Bohea tea. Her ears had rung with the delightful invitation to come again and Katherine's advice that, insofar as the future was concerned, 'Matters may rest where they presently lie until your father is returned from foreign service.'

As Hannah had lain in bed that night, thinking over the day's excitement, the words 'foreign service' had come back to her. They seemed extraordinarily powerful, a window on the world inhabited by such powerful figures as Katherine Villiers, whose very importance was confirmed by her position as confidential lady-in-waiting to the late Queen Elizabeth of Bohemia. That the legendary Prince Rupert of the Rhine also occupied Leicester House, along with its owner Lord Craven – neither of whom she had seen, but the presence of footmen clearly guaranteed – only added a frisson to the day.

Katherine had so completely won Hannah over

that she saw beyond her father's occupation with his ships and the Brethren of Trinity House – all things which, though acknowledged to be men's affairs, had impinged upon Hannah's life – another, grander world, associated in Hannah's young mind with the stirring events of national upheaval to which she was heir, but in which her father had been, and still was, immersed. From her encounter with Katherine Villiers she caught again the tremendous excitement of life, an excitement that she had known when Edmund Drinkwater first declared his love for her but which, in the months since his departure, had withered and shrunk her soul.

During the absence of her father, Hannah had twice returned to Leicester House. On both occasions Katherine had received her warmly and they had retired to Katherine's own modest chamber. The affairs of the late Queen were complicated and, while much of the work was in the hands of Lord Craven, Katherine found herself involved, not least with Elizabeth's correspondence. All took time, so Hannah's occasional visits, though they interrupted Katherine's duties, proved welcome diversions for them both.

Katherine's interest in Hannah was unfeigned and swiftly grew into affection so that when she saw off her visitor at the end of her second visit, Katherine was able to ask that Hannah let her know as soon as her father returned home. 'I know there will be difficulties with your mother,' she had said, 'but I beg of you not to let that conceal his arrival, my dear.'

Hannah had acquiesced, though on her homeward journey she feared Katherine's charm and apparent friendship might have seduced her from her duty to her mother. In the succeeding days this troubled her but, in regarding the state in which she found her father that morning and with her mother apparently gone mad, she had little hesitation in writing to Katherine, explaining the situation, once she found the leisure to do so.

Thus it was that after Faulkner's fever had broken, he woke, weak and sweat-soaked, to find Katherine sitting beside his bed.

'Where am I?' he asked, confused.

'At home, my love,' she said gently, taking his hand.

'At home..? But you ... Judith ... Oh, God, Henry...' The events of the recent past flooded back to him in all their horror. He moved, the pain of his wound making him wince, then he realized fully who it was who held his hand.

'How is that *you* are here?' His voice was full of wonder; her face seemed to wash away something of his fears.

'I am here at your daughter's invitation. Hannah and I are friends, and your wife is in the next room. I fear she has lost her reason, or is in some form of deep catalepsy, though I have not seen her. You must rest and get better.'

'And you?'

'I am still resident at Lord Craven's pleasure. The late Queen's affairs are taking time to conclude and His Lordship has offered me accommodation; permanently, if I wish.'

'Do you wish it?'

'I must live somewhere.'

'You *must* live here.'

'We shall see.'

They remained gazing at each other in silence for some time, then Katherine laughed.

'What amuses you?'

'I was thinking that the last time you lay in bed in my company, it was to attend your arse!'

Faulkner chuckled. 'To be shot in one's posterior is an indignity not to be borne. I would it had not been my troubled boy, though.' The humour had drained from him, though she said nothing, allowing him time to recover. 'He was, alas, corrupted by his mother.'

Silence fell again between them, this time less comfortable, as though the presence in the adjacent room thrust its dire influence through the very wall. 'She is a witch,' Faulkner said, his voice low and accusatory.

Katherine leaned forward and placed a cool finger across his lips. 'Perhaps,' she said. 'Who knows? Though I doubt it. What is more certain is that if your surgeon had been better acquainted with his business, he would have inserted a bristle into your wound and allowed the poison to escape. Your fever would have been less malevolent too. As it was we had to reopen the wound and drain it, after which you improved quickly.'

'*We*?'

'Hannah and I.'

'And how do you know these things better than my surgeon?'

'You forget, I followed the drum.' Katherine cut short her explanation for at that moment they heard urgent footfalls upon the stair. A second later Hannah burst into the room. She was waving a letter, her face a picture of happiness.

'Father! Oh, Father ... Katherine, news of Edmund!'

'My, my; I have not seen you so light-hearted in an age, my dearest,' Faulkner said, patting the bed beside him. As Hannah settled herself, Faulkner turned to Katherine. 'Edmund Drinkwater is—'

'I know, my dear. Hannah has told me all about him. Come, tell us, Hannah, what exactly is this news?'

'This letter,' she said, almost waving it with delight, 'is from Portsmouth. The *Eagle* will be in the Thames within the week, and it has been a most successful voyage! He will be home soon!' Her face glowed with delight as she smiled at them both.

Faulkner looked from his daughter to Katherine and said, as though it was the most natural thing in the world for the three of them to discuss, 'Then we have a wedding to arrange, banns to be called and you two had better discuss a suitable day.'

The Deodand

April 1662–September 1664

Hannah was married to Edmund Drinkwater at St Dunstan's church, Stepney, in early April when a spring breeze lifted the heads of the last of the daffodils that grew among the headstones in the church-yard as the guests assembled.

The bride's mother did not attend, a scandal augmented by the presence of the bride's father's mistress, neither of which circumstances prevented a goodly attendance of family friends, chiefly seafaring gentlemen with their wives. These were mostly Brethren of the Trinity House, but included the commander, mates, surgeon and purser of the Honourable East India Company's ship *Eagle*, and some of their professional colleagues from others of the Company's ships. Opinion was divided as to whether the condescension of His Highness Prince Rupert of the Rhine in attending as escort to Mistress Katherine Villiers excused the impropriety of her presence, or compounded it. More certainly popular among the gossips of east London was the sight of Honest George Monck and his homely duchess, whose obvious pleasure at being present made up in greater part – or so a portion of social opinion opined – for the awkwardness attaching to the bride's father's moral turpitude. Not that this troubled many, most enjoying a whiff of scandal, aware that a certain louche conduct was now licensed, particularly by the King and his Court if all that was rumoured was true. Nevertheless, it did not go unremarked that the Faulkner family had but recently buried a son – a suicide, nonetheless, and a man rumoured to have been plotting against the King – and had effectively buried the unwanted wife who was said to be chained to her bed. Such ill-informed rumours gained a certain currency, buttressed by Captain Faulkner's unconventional conduct which, it was said, had never been properly explained to the wretched groom.

Happily oblivious to all this, Faulkner, splendid in dark blue silk and a new full-bottomed wig of chestnut, gave his daughter away. He deeply regretted that neither Judith nor Henry were present but, he told himself, Henry had taken his own life and Judith might have attended her own daughter's wedding, had she not chosen otherwise. Thus his only real sorrow was the absence of Hannah's surviving brother, Nathaniel, who was at sea.

After the wedding breakfast and the toasts, Faulkner introduced Edmund Drinkwater to the Duke and Duchess of Albemarle as 'the newly appointed commander of the ship named in Your Grace's honour'. This further delighted the duchess who expressed herself as being 'tickled'.

In the days that followed the departure of

Hannah on a brief honeymoon, a sense of normality began to settle upon the house in Wapping. In Drinkwater's absence Faulkner took in hand the final stages of the preparation of the *Duchess of Albemarle* for her maiden voyage, acutely aware that Hannah's ecstasy would be short-lived when her husband assumed command and sailed once again for the Malabar coast, Bengal and China.

Of course, the past hung like a shadow over them all, for Judith remained in her room, attended by Molly, her maid, who took in her food, helped her wash and dress and saw to her daily needs. The only other member of the family she would countenance admitting was her brother Nathan. She reserved all intercourse for him. Gooding thus occupied the equivocal status of go-between. It was contrary to his honest nature and distracted him from what he did best – run the partners' business.

The morning after Faulkner had left his bed, he had called Gooding in to brief him on the current state of affairs. Having ascertained that no message had been received from Lord Clarendon, it was only then, his personal anxieties set aside for the time being, that Faulkner had looked properly at Gooding. In asking about their ships, and in particular the *Duchess of Albemarle*, he had noticed Gooding's changed appearance. For a moment, with his wits still dimmed by his fever, he could not identify the detail but then it had come to him. Nathan was less kempt and looked far older than his years. It seemed to Faulkner that he had been absent for many, many months, so intense had been the experience of his Dutch 'adventure' and the mental wanderings of an over-heated brain, but when reality had dawned it had been clear that his brother-in-law was in some distress. As Gooding's voice had concluded his summary it seemed to fade, as though all the energy had been drained from him; he had stared through lacklustre eyes into the middle-distance.

'What's amiss, Nathan? You look like death.'

Gooding had stirred, regarding Faulkner abstractedly; then he had gradually gathered himself, finally shaking his head. 'Forgive me, Kit,' he had said, at last, 'but I ... I am...'

'You are what?' Faulkner had prompted.

Gooding had shaken himself, like a dog emerging from water, before his pent-up feelings had burst from him in a torrent of words. 'I am all out of sorts. Ever since that evil day when I fell in the beastliness of drink, the world had changed around me. Now Henry is dead by his own hand, Judith is mad, and you, you are changed and brought near death. Nothing, it seems, is the same, and that upon which I depended is shifted like the ground under-foot when the earth moves.' He had run his hand over his head, through his now unfashionably cropped hair, his expression a mixture of fear and desperation. 'We have a woman who comes and goes, and has been like an angel to you and Hannah, who Hannah clearly worships yet bears with her the reputation of ... of...' He had paused, glancing at Faulkner almost as though expecting a blow.

Faulkner had said quietly, 'Of a whore, d'you mean?'

'Of a scarlet woman ... *your* scarlet woman,' Gooding went on. 'And if such domestic troubles were not enough I have the business to run in your protracted absence, occupied in God alone knows what evil, evil in which my sister—' Here Gooding had choked back a sob, his affection for Judith clear and unambiguous, before repeating himself as he laboured on. 'In which my sister has been caught up and her son, my nephew, has become a suicide!'

'He was my son, too, Nathan,' Faulkner had said in a low voice.

'I know. I know.' Gooding had shaken his head as tears flowed freely down his be-stubbled cheeks. 'But what, Kit, what shall become of Judith? She is in no mind to come to her senses and berates me for continuing my association with you. But what am I to do? We must maintain our association if only for her sake, for she is past handling her own affairs, so envenomed is she with the world, the King, the Parliament – but mostly, it seems, with you.' He had leaned forward and put his head in his hands, giving way to great wracking sobs. Unnoticed by Gooding, the parlour door had opened, and Katherine appeared. Distracted by the movement and embarrassed at Gooding's breakdown, Faulkner had looked up. Placing his finger to his lips he had motioned for her to come into the room, which she had done, quietly closing the door behind her to lean against it. The impropriety of inviting her to witness his brother-in-law's humiliation had not immediately struck Faulkner. His action had been instinctive, as though Katherine was now so close a confidante that the intimacy with Gooding had been of no account.

After a few moments, and oblivious of Katherine's presence behind him, Gooding had drawn himself upright, dashing the tears from his eyes. He had cleared his throat before he could speak, but it had been clear that he had mastered himself. He was still oblivious to Katherine's presence, though Faulkner could smell the warmth of her body and her perfume. Gooding began to speak again. His voice had recovered its old timbre.

'I cannot ... cannot deny that my sister is not the women she once was. Much of what she has told me troubles me, but the matters of which she speaks cannot be laid upon my own soul...'

'Except?' Faulkner had ventured.

Gooding had stared at him. 'You know?'

'I guessed. She has confessed something to you, something to bind you in and use to drive a wedge between us. She is clever, cunning and determined, Nathan.'

'She is the woman ... She is Eve ... She is either Eve or a *witch*!'

Faulkner forbore looking at Katherine, fixing Gooding with his eyes. 'What did she confess, Nathan?' he had asked quietly.

Gooding had hesitated before he had again lowered his voice so that it had been almost inaudible. 'How she almost had you killed.'

'*What?*'

'How she passed to Henry the weapon with

241

which he tried to kill you.'

Faulkner had hardly heard the end of the sentence. He had realized that Judith had stolen the wheel-lock from him aboard the *Blackamoor* while he had slept. Later, aboard the *Hawk*, she had somehow managed to slip it to Henry, mewed up amidships, that much was clear. Faulkner had frowned, his heart beating as it came to him: she could only have accomplished the transfer through the treachery of a third party.

'Who was it who helped her, Nathan?' he asked quietly.

Gooding had shaken his head, burying it in his hands.

'Who, Nathan?' Faulkner persisted.

'I cannot tell you ... You will exact a price, take revenge.'

'Perhaps,' Faulkner had admitted, 'but does the secret lie happily with you, or shall you feel the cold stirring of conscience every time this person, or persons, is near you ... or near to me, for that matter?' Faulkner had paused, then prompted Gooding, 'Was it Toshack? I can hardly believe it, but...' He had been about to say that Judith had charms and beauty, but forbore. Would she have attempted the seduction of Toshack? And how could she when surely he would have been aware the old seaman had entered the cabin? But someone had come in and taken the wheel-lock from her.

Gooding had shaken his head again. 'No, not Toshack.'

'One of his crew then?' Faulkner had stared at Gooding and had then realized who it had been.

'It was the lad, wasn't it? It was Hargreaves.'
Faulkner had risen, had felt his head spin and
had sunk back into his chair. Katherine had rushed forward in a rustle of grey silk, to kneel at his
feet and chafe his hands.

Gooding had looked up. 'How long has she
been in the room?' he had asked.

Katherine had turned to Gooding. 'I am not a
tell-tale, Mr Gooding,' she had said simply.

'What are you then, Mistress?'

'A whore, as you suppose, but also a woman
who finds the world wearying at times, as I
perceive you do. We have that in common, sir.'

'Such treachery,' Faulkner had muttered, wrapped in his own thoughts. 'How did she do it?' he
had asked of Gooding.

'Apparently, the boy had come below to see if
either of you required anything. She must have
been awake, and you, you were fast asleep again.
She engaged him in conversation, discovered he
had a widowed mother and told him that she
would see that he had, I don't know, ten, twenty
sovereigns if he would do something for her. She
tricked him into agreement before revealing
what his task was – she prides herself on that;
out-Heroding Herod, she said, referring to you.
No-one need ever know, she told him, and it was
important that Master Henry had the means to
defend himself. Master Henry had always been
good to him, hadn't he? All that impressionable
nonsense.' Gooding had shrugged. 'The boy fell
for it, and the deed was done in the darkness. I do
not think Toshack understood the need to keep
Henry confined or out of touch with anyone. You

cannot have explained that properly. In truth I do not know the details but likely he was implicated through ignorance.'

'And the boy still waits for his money,' Faulkner had observed drily.

'Judith has asked me to pay him.'

'Good Christ!' Gooding winced at Faulkner's blasphemy. 'And what of Hargreaves? Has he shown himself at the counting-house?'

'Yes.'

'And?'

'I paid him to stay silent.'

The last words ought to have shocked him, Faulkner had thought afterwards, but they did not. After a moment's consideration he had said, 'Leave Hargreaves to me. Katherine, my dear, would you pass us that wine and join us in a glass. Now, Nathan, you and I are going to drink to the future, then you are going to shave, I am going to do likewise and we shall take a walk.' He had brushed aside Katherine's protestations that he was not yet well. 'We have ships to attend, a wedding to arrange.'

Some sort of normality had then settled upon them, in the days leading up to the wedding, gradually embedding itself as day succeeded day and routine gathered its own momentum. There was no escaping the past, of course, for Judith's presence made its own demands upon the household and, in conformity with the law, the wheel-lock was surrendered as a deodand to the crown officers. In due course, Faulkner was obliged to buy it back again as an expiatory act to God for his son's suicide, the fee being directed to

244

charity. He had walked down to the river at Wapping Stairs and tossed the thing into the grey Thames, watched by several incredulous watermen. He had no doubt that one or other of them had fished it out later, for the sunlight had caught it as it spun from his hand, revealing itself not merely as a hand-gun, but a weapon of great expense.

As Faulkner had watched the waters close over the pistol and the annular rings of disturbed water dissipate amongst the wavelets lapping the stairs, it struck him that the extraction of the fee by the coroner was a further irony associated with the events of the last weeks: he had been made to pay for everything that had occurred, even his son's death. Now, in a final act, he discarded the beautifully wrought wheel-lock.

Good-riddance, he had thought as he walked home.

As the day of the wedding approached Hannah's happiness seemed to purge the house of gloom. Judith's presence in her chamber became an inconvenience, not a reproach. Word circulated of its own volition that she was mad. The national mood played in their favour: Puritan solemnity and virtue were things of the past. Life was to be enjoyed as the Merry Monarch and his court so ably demonstrated. Faulkner was regarded as an unfortunate man whose admittance of a beautiful woman into his house was but a manifestation of his vigour. In a very short space of time, if not admired, he was absolved of moral turpitude.

Two days before the wedding both Faulkner

and Gooding were in the counting-house in-specting their ledgers, their clerks about them, when, in accordance with an arrangement, Edmund Drinkwater waited upon them. He was tall and tanned, his features regular with a wide, engaging smile that made his grey eyes twinkle. Faulkner regarded him with approval; Hannah had chosen well, though he could less easily perceive what the young officer saw in her.

The interview went well, and further arrangements were made to have Drinkwater sworn-in as both a Younger Brother of the Trinity House and a sworn officer in the East India Company's service. These formalities having been attended to, Faulkner took the young man aboard the *Duchess of Albemarle*. The two men spent four hours touring the ship as she neared completion, agreeing on some late modifications that Drinkwater thought useful. As they regained the shore Drinkwater informed his future father-in-law that he had purchased a house in Stepney and, at the end of the day, they shook hands like old friends.

The day after the wedding Faulkner had walk-ed to the counting-house alone and sought out Hargreaves. 'I want you to attend me tomorrow morning,' he told the lad. 'We shall be gone all day.' He did not bother to read the youth's face. It was possible that some apprehension filled his mind, but youth has a short memory and Mrs Hargreaves's delight at her son's cleverness in so pleasing Captain Sir Christopher Faulkner that he had been given seven sovereigns was suffi-cient to wipe from Charlie's mind any sense of wrong-doing.

Hargreaves was on the doorstep at daylight, eager to please. 'Perhaps the Good Sir Christopher will be generous again,' his mother had said as he left her. 'You keep working for him and be a good lad.'

'Good morning, Sir Christopher,' Hargreaves had greeted his master. Faulkner responded civilly, encouraging Charlie to enquire, 'Pray, where are we bound today, sir?'

Faulkner looked at the lad; his face was open, his use of the nautical term far from disingenuous as they began to walk westwards. 'Do you know what happens when people incur the King's wrath, Master Hargreaves?' he asked conversationally.

'They hang, sir.'

'Have you ever seen a hanging?'

'Oh, yes, sir.'

'Well, you are going to see something a little different today. Hanging is what happens to common felons, thieves, murderers, pirates and so forth. Today you are going to see three executions, not simple hangings but the choking, disembowelling, castration and quartering of three men who were party to the execution of King Charles I. Not only that, Charlie, but they were planning to kill His Present Majesty.'

Hargreaves frowned. 'Castration ... isn't that...' He made a twisting gesture towards his loins, making a wry face.

'That is exactly what it is.'

'Oh.' Hargreaves digested the intelligence. 'What are these men's names, sir?'

'John Okey, John Barkstead and Miles Corbett. They were among those who had the King's father executed.'

It was only when they were walking home that Faulkner addressed Hargreaves's ill-judged conduct aboard the *Hawk*. 'You did wrong when Mistress Faulkner paid you to pass my wheel-lock to Master Henry, Charlie, for she and he were both trying to kill me.'

Hargreaves stood stock still, his face losing its colour, his brow furrowed by incomprehension. 'To *kill* you sir? But why?' Then, seeing his master made no move to answer, and realizing the impropriety of his question, put up his defence: 'But sir, Master Gooding paid me...'

'I know, Charlie, I know, but you should forget that. Master Gooding did not know what the money was for, only that he had been told to pay you.'

They resumed their walk in silence for some time, then Hargreaves said, his voice small and anxious, 'But Master Henry did not kill *you*, sir ... He killed himself.'

'He put a ball the size of a chestnut into my arse before he turned the gun on himself,' Faulkner said.

Another long silence followed before Hargreaves asked, 'Are you angry with me, sir?'

'Yes, Charlie, I am, but I am angrier with others and I do not think you knew what you were doing.' Hargreaves had the sense to remain quiet until Faulkner resumed. 'I will tell you one thing, Charlie, one thing I was not entirely displeased with in your conduct.'

'What is that, sir?' Hargreaves asked, eagerly.

'You saw what they did to those Regicides today, didn't you?'

Hargreaves shuddered in recollection and nodded. 'I *smelled* it, sir,' he said.

'Well, had Henry not shot himself it is very likely that they would have done that to him, for he had threatened the King's life.' The lad stopped again, his mouth and eyes open wide. 'Come,' Faulkner said, placing his hand on the lad's shoulder, 'let us go home now.'

After the wedding, the departure of Hannah for her new house, and the executions of the nineteenth of April, Faulkner's household truly settled into new ways. Nathaniel came home from another voyage to the West Indies and announced he was to marry a young woman who had travelled as a passenger aboard his ship. In due course, Hannah Drinkwater bade her new husband farewell and the East Indiaman *Duchess of Albemarle* slipped her moorings and made her way downstream, beginning her long passage to India under the command of Captain Edmund Drinkwater. On the ship's departure Faulkner wrote to Lord Clarendon, informing him of the fact, along with a summary of the manifest. He received neither reply nor acknowledgement but late in August a letter arrived from the Lord Chamberlain inviting 'Captain Sir Christopher Faulkner to match his sailing yacht against those of His Majesty The King and His Royal Highness The Duke of York, to which may be added the Personal Yachts of several other Gentlemen of the Court'.

The match began abreast of The Tower of London at eight in the morning, taking the ebb down the Thames to Gravesend. One of the King's several Royal Yachts was moored off Shorncliffe as a turning mark, and the little fleet doubled this and began their passage upstream just as the tide turned. The running was close, and in several reaches it was necessary to tack, the boats criss-crossing each other's tracks, their helmsmen exchanging challenges and wise-cracks with a waving of wine-bottles and capon's legs as they wove recklessly in and out of the shipping busy in the waterway.

With Toshack and his crew, Faulkner took Gooding and his son Nathaniel, young Hargreaves making up the numbers and as eager and active as a monkey. Gooding commented on the lad's ability and asked what Faulkner made of him. Faulkner smiled. 'He is too good to waste, Nathan. Now do you give that sheet a good haul and let us see if we can beat the Duke to the Kent shore and take his wind.'

It was late when the yachts crossed the finish and lay-to off The Tower where their owners were to disembark at Tower-wharf. Faulkner handed over to Toshack and shook Gooding's hand before tumbling into the *Hawk*'s little shallop, which was pulled to the shore by Hargreaves. Stepping ashore Faulkner settled his dress and bade Hargreaves farewell, then he turned and nodded at a fellow competitor, Roger North, landing in his own shallop. The two men walked up to join the ladies. These included

250

Queen Catherine of Braganza, the King's newly wedded consort, and the Duchess of York, Clarendon's daughter Anne. With their ladies-in-waiting and attendant gentlemen, they made a glittering company, withdrawing to The Tower where the Constable had been obliged to lay out wine and a cold collation for the King's pleasure.

Katherine was among the wives of the three other yachtsmen, apparently accepted by them, though the risk of a public rebuffing was not inconsiderable. These ladies greeted their respective heroes with as much enthusiasm as the Courtiers applauded the King and his brother, following the procession as the royal siblings led through the Lion Gate towards Tower Green. The King was in high good humour and summoned his fellow contestants to take wine with him, toasting first the winner.

'To my Royal Brother!' They raised their glasses with a ragged hurrah and then the King walked among them, coming last to Faulkner. 'Ah ha! Sir Kit and – of course – Mistress Villiers.'

Faulkner footed a low bow, and Katherine, on his arm, dropped a low curtsey. The King reminded them of an old joke. He passed a quick glance at Katherine and then detached his competitor with the command: 'A word with you, Sir Kit, if you please.'

Faulkner felt Katherine remove her arm and back away, her eyes cast down. As Faulkner's publicly acknowledged mistress, the King could not properly acknowledge her and might, had he been so minded, have ignored her altogether, especially as it was said he had reformed his morals on his marriage. No-one thought this would last, but Faulkner had refused to leave Katherine at home. 'You faithfully served Her Majesty of Bohemia,' he said when she remonstrated, 'and it is well-known that I have a mad wife.'

'Now, sir,' said the King as they strolled towards the Royal Menagerie in the shadow of the Conqueror's pale and massive keep, 'had I not done so long since, I should have been pleased to have dubbed you this day, for you conceded the ground in tacking off Tilbury.' The King wagged a finger at him. 'No, don't deny it, I noted it, and again when off Deptford. You might have beaten both my Royal Brother and Myself; you have a fine boat in the ... What is her name?'

'*Hawk*, Your Majesty.'

'Ah, yes, just so.'

'I assure Your Majesty that we near missed stays off Tilbury...'

'Pah! I do not believe Sir Kit missed stays any more than he missed his target in Delft.'

'Your Majesty?'

'We have deeply angered the Dutch,' the King confided, 'and were it not for Sir George's skill in getting de Witt's signature on his warrant – God knows by what means – we would likely be at war with them today.'

'It was a tricky business, Your Majesty.'

'But ended most satisfactorily for all of us, you included, Sir Christopher.'

'As Your Majesty pleases.'

'How is your wife?'

'She is quite out of reason, sir.'

'How so?'

'She is turned in upon herself; keeps to her room, speaks to no man but her brother and that but occasionally.'

The King stopped and looked about him at the grim ramparts that surrounded them. 'You were confined here once, I understand,' he remarked, changing the subject.

'I was, Your Majesty.'

'Hmm.' The King's grunt was equivocal; Faulkner had been mewed in The Tower at the point of his defection from the King's service to that of the Commonwealth. 'Freedom has its price, they say,' the King remarked, 'and, like exile, changes a man's view of the world, do you not agree, sir?' Then, without waiting for a response, he went on: 'Now, tell me, have you news of your new ship? Damn me, I forget her name too. No! Wait, she is named for Monck's duchess, is she not? The *Duchess of Albemarle*.'

'No news since she sailed from St Helen's Roads, Your Majesty, but I am anticipating a profitable voyage, providing, of course, we do not go to war with the Dutch.'

'*Touché*, Sir Kit, *touché*.' The King laughed. They were walking back towards the company now, and Faulkner knew the unofficial audience was ending. Faulkner could see Katherine cast him an anxious glance; so too did the King. 'How is she, Sir Kit, *your* Villiers wench? She looks well for her years.'

Faulkner recognized the intimacy and the reference to his own Villiers connection. He remembered, too, his suspicions of the King when he had been the Prince of Wales exiled in The Netherlands. It was now said that was when he had first encountered Barbara Villiers, a distant cousin of Katherine's, when she had been used as courier to pass him money. Married, with a compliant husband who had been ennobled at the King's Restoration, the former Mrs Palmer currently enjoyed the title of Lady Castlemaine along with the pleasures of the King's bed. It was gossiped abroad that His Majesty had been supping at her house when the news was brought to him that Princess Catherine of Braganza, his affianced, had arrived at Portsmouth from Lisbon.

'Well, sir, has the cat got your tongue? Does the lady please you?'

'She delights my heart, Your Majesty,' Faulkner stammered, aware that the King, shrewd and observant as he was, had noted his hesitation. The two men were now being stared at by the entire assembly. Someone, probably the Duke of York, must have remarked at the interest His Majesty was showing in Sir Christopher Faulkner.

'Count yourself a lucky man, sir,' said the King, before nodding his dismissal, turning aside and walking swiftly back towards his new Portuguese Queen. Faulkner made an elegant bow at his retreating figure. As he straightened up, aware that all eyes now followed the King as he re-joined them, Faulkner was flooded with a profound relief, and it took him a moment to set his legs in motion and return to Katherine's side.

Later, when they lay in bed together, he told her what had passed between them.

'All is well then, between the King and you, my darling,' she said, rousing herself to look down on him.

'And he approves of us too,' Faulkner breathed, drawing her mouth down to his own.

'Now perhaps we can be happy.'

The *Duchess of Albemarle* took up her mooring off Blackwall in early January 1663. Having laid his logs and accounts before the Directors of the East India Company and spent a night with his happy wife, Captain Edmund Drinkwater paid his respects to his ship's owners. Bronzed from his travels, he apologized that his duty required him as a sworn Company commander to report first to the Company's Court before appearing before his owners. Faulkner waved his excuses aside. 'I hope you also did your duty by your wife, sir,' he said, making the young man blush. Hannah had not conceived in their post-marital intimacies, and Faulkner, increasingly aware of his own mortality, was anxious for grand-children.

'It is enough that my portion goes to the King,' he remarked to Katherine as they prepared for bed that night. 'Still, Edmund made a substantial sum from his private trade, so if I starve, he and Hannah will be well enough.'

'I doubt you will starve,' Katherine said drily.

Captain Drinkwater sailed again in July. He had pronounced the *Duchess of Albemarle* a good ship, and Gooding had filled with cargo those spaces the Company could not. Meanwhile, Faulkner did not starve. On the contrary, his and Gooding's business throve, though the market was not an easy one, with Dutch shipping constantly under-cutting the costs of their English competitors.

Her husband absent in the Indian seas, Hannah gave birth to a fine boy that December. He was christened Edmund in his father's honour and Christopher in his grand-father's. Hannah refused to allow her mother to see the baby for fear of the evil-eye. When Faulkner informed Judith she had a grand-child, she stared at him. 'What is that to me? I know nothing of the father while the mother abandons me, so the child might as well be a bastard.'

Faulkner walked out without a word.

Nathaniel, whose voyages to the West Indies were shorter that those of his brother-in-law, had meanwhile married well and was, besides being captain of one vessel, part-owner in three other ships in the West India trade. He cherished his independence, making his own way in the world, and it came as a terrible shock when his ship went missing, presumed lost in a West Indian hurricane.

When a grieving Faulkner dragged himself upstairs to inform Judith, she smiled at the news. She laid her Bible down and said, 'Hannah's bastard may carry your seed, but no-one shall carry your name, Husband. That is the Lord's judgement upon you.'

Looking at her expression, Faulkner had the

unpleasant thought that she had had something to do with the loss of their son. He dismissed the evil assumption immediately. That night Katherine held her lover in her arms. It seemed to her that he was inconsolable, for she knew that it was not merely Nathaniel for whom he wept.

On morning in mid-September 1665, Faulkner sat in the parlour drinking tea with Katherine and Hannah, who had come a-calling with her young son. Despite the absence of her beloved husband, Hannah was radiant with good health and delight at the toddling Edmund playing at their feet. A shaft of autumn sunlight illuminated the tableware, all of which set them in good humour as they chatted companionably, chiefly about the boy. They were disturbed by a knock at the door announcing Hargreaves, who brought a message that Gooding wished to speak with his partner in the counting-house.

'I shall be down this afternoon, Charlie—' Faulkner began.

'Beg pardon, Sir Christopher,' interrupted Hargreaves who, since witnessing the executions of the Regicides, had proved a model of punctiliousness, 'but Mister Gooding said it was urgent and brooked no delay. Something about pratique, sir.'

'Pratique, eh?' Faulkner made a face at the ladies and begged to be excused. Puzzled at this unusual summons, Faulkner knew at once that something was wrong when he saw Gooding's face as he met Faulkner at the entrance to his office. Without a word Gooding made way for him, ushering him into the room where a familiar figure sat, eyes cast down.

'Captain Lamont! By God, I am astonished you dare show your face here!'

'I think you should hear the Captain's news from his own mouth. We need to cease handling all cargoes from The Netherlands, Kit.'

'Why so? That would be throwing away valuable agency money,' he said, looking at Gooding, his eyes asking the question he could not air before Lamont, for all his part in the flight of Judith.

Gooding, sharp as ever after his temporary breakdown, shook his head. Turning to Lamont, Gooding said: 'Tell Sir Christopher what is rife in Amsterdam, Captain.'

Lamont looked up. 'Plague, sir. Plague, and 'tis bad ... *Virulent*, they are saying.'

The Plague

October 1664–April 1666

Throughout Faulkner's near sixty years of life, plagues had paid intermittent visits to the ports of Europe, and it was known that the plague was as surely spread by ships as the news of its coming. No-one knew how, though many said that if the contagion was not spread by the seamen then it must come by that other roving population – rats. Others, particularly the Breth-

258

ren of Trinity House whose business in shipping and the professional instincts engendered therein, also considered that the rapid dispersal of the disease could only be explained by the dispersal of cargo; how else – if it arrived by ship – did the plague appear in places distant from the ports of discharge? Indeed, in an outbreak some years earlier, one among their number had what he considered conclusive proof, tracing a consignment of cloth to a small town in Bedfordshire from its landing in London. Forwarded from Rotherhithe, where an outbreak of the plague followed the discharge of a ship from a plague-ridden Antwerp, a fortnight later five people were infected in Bedfordshire. Two had handled the consignment of cotton, the three others were members of their families; in all fifty people had died before the disease had run its course. Despite this conclusive proof, few heeded the warning outside the Fraternity.

Both Faulkner and Gooding took Lamont's warning seriously, not least because he convinced them of the seriousness with which the ever-practical Dutch city-fathers of Amsterdam were taking it, and the fact that both of Lamont's own mates were sick.

'Buboes,' he explained succinctly as both Faulkner and Gooding instinctively drew away from him. The case of Lamont and his bilander *Mary* were indeed a matter of pratique. When the old master-mariner had withdrawn, to report his case to the Custom-House officers, Faulkner undertook to notify Trinity House, responsible for the governance of the shipping in the Thames.

His mind was in a turmoil, not least occasioned by his proximity to Lamont and the thought of conveying the infection to his home, and he was picking up his hat when Gooding said something indistinguishable.

'What's that you say?' he asked, looking at his brother-in-law. Gooding stood transfixed, his eyes almost wild, though whether from fear, as seemed likely, or some terrible visitation it was impossible to say. 'Come; what's amiss? Surely you cannot have taken the contagion that quickly...'

'It's *her*,' Gooding said, still half-talking to himself.

'Her? What the devil do you mean, *her*? Whom do you mean?' Faulkner was frowning, eager to be off and spread the word so that some sort of precaution might be taken and that herbs, tobacco and brimstone might be obtained to fumigate his house.

'Judith,' said Gooding, his expression one of fervent conviction. 'She has bewitched us all, damn her.'

'Don't be ridiculous, Nathan...'

Gooding closed the distance between them and nailed Faulkner to the spot. 'Don't you understand?' he said insistently, 'Lamont's vessel, the *Mary* – Judith half-owns her; she has conjured this, summoned God-knows what demons to destroy! Now I know what she has been conniving in that chamber of hers! She wishes to destroy us all – King, Parliament, you, me, all of us...'

'But that is impossible!'

260

'Is it? Cannot you hear the arguments in her favour? The corruption of the Court, the unholy vengeance taken upon the exhumed corpses of Cromwell, Ireton and the others, the martyrdoms of the Regicides, the frustration of her divinely appointed mission and the death of her son. Why, Kit, I could find you more detail if I wished. God knows she has preached her venom at me for weeks now, but surely you must see what has been accomplished under our roof ... under our very noses ... or under mine, at least.'

Faulkner shook his head. Gooding was in distress; all his old Puritan instincts had been stirred up, conflated and confused. 'No, no, Nathan, there is no logic in your argument. Vengeance is God's, not Judith's. She is as small a grain of sand in God's world as are we all ... This is just coincidence; another ship could have brought the same news into the river; the *Mary* will not be only vessel arriving from Amsterdam this week.'

'No, no, Kit,' Gooding said frantically, button-holing Faulkner in his eagerness to convince his partner. 'That is true, but the *Mary* DID bring the news and, Almighty God help us, perhaps the plague itself. To say that the plague is sent to chastise us is no conjuration of my imagination; it will thunder from every pulpit the first Sunday the news gets abroad.'

'Yes, yes, I know the prating priests will say that before they decant themselves into the country or lock themselves in their priest-holes, or wherever they secrete themselves, but that at least is an argument few can rebuff. Vengeance is, as I say, attributable to God...'

'But Almighty God took possession of it. As the Lord sayeth in the Book of Deuteronomy, Chapter Thirty-two, Verse Thirty-five, "To Me belongeth vengeance and recompense." Thus did Almighty God lay his claim, but He did not wrest evil from the Devil or his agents. Why else would war, the plague, malice and all sundry evils stalk the world still? God's words were a rebuke; an order to desist from such acts. *That* is why Judith is a witch! She is aware of, but defies, God's commands. She is an active agent of Satan!'

'But—'

'To argue as you do is to deny evil and, in particular, to deny witchcraft. Surely you do not deny witchcraft?'

Faulkner gently pushed Gooding's plucking hands from his person. There was a distinct wildness in Gooding's eyes that he had never seen before; this was not Puritan zeal, or, if it was, it was a perverse form, such as had troubled Judith and Henry. Were they all mad? The thought revived his fears for Hannah and her children, born and unborn. No, Hannah was not mad. 'Nathan,' he said firmly, 'you must stop. Now. You are in danger of derangement. Judith is no witch but a deeply troubled woman who has perhaps a contagion of the mind and for that I must bear my part. Lamont has brought us news, bad news, but that is enough. We – you and I – are not fools to be gulled by superstition. Let us not take fright like those infected by the moon. This pestilence may overwhelm us all but I for one am reluctant to attribute it entirely to God or

262

the Devil.'

Gooding shook his head, turning aside, murmuring that he was convinced of his argument and nothing could, or would, shake him from it.

Reluctantly, Faulkner left Gooding and hurried off. Later in the day he returned home, his mind made up, and at dinner that evening, having acquainted Katherine with the dreadful news, he told both her and Gooding what he had decided. 'We will put such personal belongings as we require aboard the *Hawk* and take her down-Channel. We may land somewhere in the West Country, Falmouth, perhaps, or even,' he said, turning to Katherine, 'the Isles of Scilly.'

She responded, at his reminder of their encounter there many years earlier, 'I can think of no lovelier place, and it would be well to take Hannah with us.'

'Of course. We can shut the house up...'

'You cannot,' said Gooding with a sharp finality, as though the matter was put beyond argument.

'Why, pray?' asked Katherine, before Faulkner could interject.

'Because my sister cannot be removed.'

Gooding had calmed himself since Faulkner had left him, but his present mood was unfamiliar to Faulkner – and deeply troubling. 'Cannot or will not, brother-in-law?' He paused, then went on, 'If she will not come, then she must be commanded. I am still her husband.'

Gooding dropped his eyes and bit his lip. 'But you are not mine,' he murmured.

'We shall go...'

'I shall stay,' said Gooding, his head held high, his tone accusatory. 'Someone must look after our affairs.'

Faulkner took Katherine's hand, squeezing it reassuringly. 'And Judith?' he asked Faulkner. 'What of her?'

'I cannot see you insisting upon taking her,' Gooding said, looking with deliberation at Katherine.

The sudden tension in the room was utterly foreign. Katherine was now clenching her hand, and he sensed her holding her breath. This was a truly awful moment. Faulkner knew things would never again be the same between them. Picking his words carefully, he said, 'I shall do my duty, Nathan, as you very well know.'

'She is a witch,' Gooding said in a low and level tone. Katherine drew her breath in sharply and in that moment, Faulkner divined his unholy purpose.

'You cannot condemn your sister, but you wish her to remain here, to become infected and to perish.'

Gooding made no response for a moment, then he said, 'God's will be done,' and rose from the table. As he withdrew he began intoning the ninety-fourth psalm: 'O Lord God, to whom vengeance belongeth; O Lord God, to whom vengeance belongeth, shew thyself. Lift up thyself, thou judge of the earth...'

The door closed behind him, and Katherine turned to Faulkner. 'He's mad.'

'They are all mad.'

* * *

In the weeks that followed no-one died of the plague and Gooding behaved as though nothing particularly unusual had occurred. Only once did he refer to earlier disputes between himself and Faulkner – disputes and arguments that had attended their first acquaintance when Gooding and his sister were so obviously Puritan and Faulkner, then an ingénue in such matters, had seemed to them to embrace the opposing argument. The allusion, so Faulkner supposed, went by way of excusing Gooding's extreme behaviour. As for the conduct of their business and daily life, it fell again back into its comfortable rut; more or less.

Lamont's *Mary* was quarantined and one of his two mates died. The cause of death was attributed to the pox. The other recovered and, in due course, the *Mary* discharged her mixed cargo. True, occasional intermittent reports of the plague in Amsterdam reached them, but London dismissed the rumours of its arrival in England; there was simply no evidence. Faulkner laid aside his plans for an evacuation of his house in Wapping.

Then, in early December, two men, said to be French, died in a house in Long Acre. The deaths were concealed, but word got abroad. Two physicians and a surgeon were despatched by the Secretaries of State to examine the bodies and their conclusions were duly printed in the Weekly Bill of Mortality, in the usual way: two men had died of the plague. Before the month was out another death was declared to be due to the plague; it too was near Drury Lane. From then on, although the death-toll mounted, this was attributed to the season. There had been no mention of the plague as a cause of death, and in this atmosphere of increasing hope, the *Duchess of Albemarle* returned home. The voyage had not been as successful as Edmund had hoped. He had lost money in his private investment and was now perturbed for his own economic future.

It was not until April that deaths of the plague and spotted-fever, held to be one and the same thing, reappeared. The number of its victims thereafter rose inexorably, and once again Faulkner grew alarmed. Edmund had already expressed his anxiety for his family's health, and Faulkner had reassured him, floating his intention to leave the city if necessary. As for the *Duchess of Albemarle*, Faulkner and Gooding agreed not to submit her for lading by the Company that year, for if the plague took hold there would be an embargo and more money would be lost. Gooding could find a cargo for her; there were goods enough stacked in the warehouses as trade slowed for fear of the plague and in anticipation of an embargo. In May Edmund left for Jamaica, taking up the slack left by the absence of his late brother-in-law. In such threatening and uncertain circumstances, Edmund's departure was painful, especially for Hannah, but it was generally agreed that it was the best possible course of action. Faulkner took some comfort from the arrangement, though anxiety ate at his guts as he lay unsleeping with worry.

By mid-summer, war had again broken out with the Dutch. This last news filled Faulkner with dread, for he feared a summons to command a man-of-war which would take him away from tending his household. Nevertheless, his conscience prompted him sufficiently to make known his willingness to serve, but his offer was not taken up.

'I think,' he told Katherine, 'that Mister Pepys has taken against me. He is now high in the Lord High Admiral's favour, and I imagine he considers me among the older and duller Brethren of the Trinity House. I suppose it to be a mixed blessing.'

'Perhaps the Duke of York considers you have done enough, or that if you were to fall into Dutch hands they might regard your person as beyond the law. You are not unknown to them,' she added pointedly.

'Perhaps,' he agreed. 'Anyway, I would not wish to be absent from your side now, for I fear we must leave London or risk our lives. I have already lost one child, I cannot countenance anything happening to Hannah, and Edmund expects me to act in his stead.'

'Of course.'

These considerations did not stop him reading, with mixed feelings, the accounts of the defeat of Obdam van Wassenaer off Lowestoft in early June. The powder-magazine of the unfortunate Dutchman's flagship, the *Eendracht*, had exploded, killing all but five of her company of eight score men. The English Commander-in-Chief, James, Duke of York, had himself had a lucky escape aboard his own flagship, the *Royal Charles*. A chain shot had flown inboard, killing half the officers at the Duke's side. What troubled Faulkner was the fact that of the other flag-officers, Admiral Penn, with York in the *Royal Charles*, and the Earl of Sandwich, commanding the rear squadron, were Elder Brethren of the Trinity House. Besides these two, Prince Rupert had also hoisted his flag in command of the English van. Consequently, a sense of chagrin that none of these men had thought fit to include him in their line of battle was, despite his anxieties for his family, a bitter pill to swallow.

And there was the *Duchess of Albemarle* to fret over. He was confident that news of hostilities would be better transmitted to the West Indies than the eastern seas, but still if Edmund failed to find a convoy, guarded by a man-of-war, all was at hazard to the enemy and a hostage to fortune. Since the loss of Nathaniel, Faulkner's confidence had ebbed, as though he sensed his star was on the wane. He shuddered; it was not a grey goose flying over his grave, but the cold consideration that behind his losses, past and future, lay Judith's spells.

However, such fears grew most terrible at night. In daylight he derived some comfort from the fact that the war, like trade, was affected by the plague. Following the battle off Lowestoft no further reports of anything other than scuffles reached London, suggesting the war might simply fizzle out.

While death in battle was the seaman's lot off the Suffolk shore, the plague raged unabated in London. By late-July, with only the briefest of discussions and an assumption of Gooding's earlier declaration on the matter being his final word, Faulkner announced himself satisfied that Gooding should manage the business as he had done during his, Faulkner's, exile. On news of the King and the Court leaving London for Salisbury, Faulkner gave orders that his household should embark in the *Hawk*. Faulkner ordered Hargreaves to join them, adding his mother to the little vessel's company on the lad's pleading. By August they had taken up lodgings in Falmouth from where Faulkner made an occasional long and tedious journey up to London, meeting Gooding at the counting-house. He was careful of his person and, on Katherine's insistence, with whom he came in contact.

It was not now difficult to keep Gooding at arm's length when they met, for their relationship had become strained. Besides, Faulkner had convinced himself that the disturbed Gooding wanted himself infected in order that he might carry the disease home to his sister and in so doing dispose of her and martyr himself.

The business of travelling, a matter of indiscriminate propinquity, was another matter. Claiming some knowledge of avoiding contagion thanks to her indigent existence as a camp-follower, Katherine insisted that his small clothes were removed immediately upon his homecoming and he himself took a hot bath.

However, Faulkner eventually gave up these ventures. The plague had such a strong grip upon London that all trade was suspended, as he had predicted. Still unrequired by the Admiralty, he bent his energies elsewhere, purchasing a small vessel by the candle, putting Toshack in command and sending Hargreaves aboard by way of supercargo. Despatching her across the Channel, he was soon doing a lively trade with the Channel Islands and the Breton coast, better, in fact, than Gooding languishing in London.

Hannah delighted in her son, whose every achievement she considered quite remarkable. As for Katherine, she became adopted aunt to little Edmund, while Mistress Hargreaves insisted on cooking for the household. In retrospect Faulkner regarded the months they spent in Falmouth an idyll, despite his worries. Privately, he continued to be torn by mixed feelings regarding the war. Disappointment at not being given a command competed with the delight he felt amid the beautiful countryside and the society of Katherine, Hannah and the boy. From time to time he took the *Hawk* to sea, or up the lovely Helford River, discovering in the lazier occupation of yacht-cruising something infinitely more pleasurable than the charged and competitive racing he had been obliged to undergo on the Thames in order that the King or his brother might have the opportunity to win.

Even the autumnal gales – worse in Cornwall than in London – followed by the icy blasts of winter – which were less so – failed to disturb the idyll. At Christmas Faulkner and Katherine duly attended the parish church of St Charles The Martyr; Faulkner reflected that he never expected to have spoken to a saint, recalling to Katherine their own first meeting aboard the *Prince Royal* on her voyage to Spain to embark

the young Charles I – then himself Prince of
Wales – and Katherine's infamous if distant kinsman George, Duke of Buckingham. On the way
home they recalled the unhappy events of the
voyage, which had precipitated the first of their
long separations.

In January came the news that the plague had
abated, and that the better-off were returning to
London where the shops were reopening. At the
same time they learned that France had joined
the Dutch in their war against the English, cur-
tailing Faulkner's new venture of trading with
Brittany. Selling his ship by the candle, as he had
bought her, he paid his bills and, leaving the
Hawk in the charge of Hargreaves until the
weather improved, Faulkner, Katherine, Hannah
and young Edmund began the long trip home.

Though less people were abroad than was
usual they found Wapping unaltered. Gooding
was absent, but the maid Molly greeted them
with delight. 'How is the mistress?' Faulkner
asked her, almost dreading the reply, but the girl
bobbed cheerfully enough and declared all was
as it had been when the master left.

Before the others settled in, Faulkner decided
to see for himself, ascended the familiar staircase
and paused before the door to Judith's chamber.
He had not ventured into the room for many
months but now he did so, abruptly pushing the
door open, stepping inside and closing it behind
him. He had not known what to expect but it was
certainly not what he found. Her brother's long
mental decline combined with his wild declara-
tions about Judith's intentions, her madness and

her witchery had led him to expect a wildly deranged creature, unkempt, her hair in disorder, raving, even chained to her bed. Instead he found her cool, elegant, groomed to perfection, a figure in perfect possession of both her person and her mind. Faulkner suddenly understood why her brother had been convinced of her being a witch; certainly she seemed possessed of some supernatural qualities.

She had been sitting beside the window when he entered, and she turned, apparently unsurprised at his intrusion.

'You are returned, Husband.' She inclined her head as he bowed.

'You look well, Madam,' he said with icy formality, on his guard.

'I do not have the plague, if that is what you mean. I hope that does not disappoint you,' she added wryly.

'It was always my hope that you would not catch the contagion.'

'Was it?' she arched an eyebrow. 'It was not your brother-in-law's.'

'Whatever his motives, Madam, your brother was always assiduous in your welfare.'

'The welfare of my soul, perhaps; otherwise...'

'Madam,' Faulkner interrupted, unwilling to drag the conversation down its present road, 'do you not think it is time for you to forsake this mode of life? We have lost a son, we have acquired a grandson...'

'But we live in a corrupt land, under a corrupt King and I find myself shackled – that is, I think, the word you mariners use – to a corrupt

husband.'

'Madam, the world's corruption is much as it always has been.'

'It was not so under the Commonwealth.'

'Pah! Was the court of Cromwell less corrupt than that of King Charles? Folly and prejudice stalked about in solemn apparel. True, Charles flaunts his coxcomb, but it is arguable as to whether this is less pleasing to God than the sanctified cant and sober vice that put the money of the poor into the pockets of the indifferent gentlemen that held their military commands as tight as their purses.'

'You become quite eloquent in your old age, Husband, but nothing will dissuade me from the righteousness of my cause.'

'Not even Henry's death?'

'No, only that I failed him and, thank God, he had the courage to give his life to God's cause, rather than allow the Great Malignant's spawn to order his body be butchered.'

'But, Judith, he lies in unhallowed ground, a mortal sinner.'

'He lies in the Lord's good earth. That it is unsanctified by the Established Church does not mean it is unhallowed by Almighty God; did not God look upon the earth as His creation and call it good?'

'Enough. I have had enough of this endless cant! I would have done all in my power to save Henry—'

'But you could not guarantee it, and you knew in your heart that not all of your pleadings, no, nor the abject grovelling that you Royalists seem

not to find demeaning, would have saved Henry. The King was determined to root out all opposition, and Henry would have faced execution – you know that, and do not try and persuade me otherwise.'

'Then you *had* set him on the path of assassination.'

'Inexorably.'

'God, you are evil. Nathan is right.'

'What? That I am a witch?' She was smiling. 'Is that woman with whom you share your bed – *our* bed – not a witch? Certainly she is a whore and you, my precious husband, are a whoremaster; you have corrupted my daughter by association...'

'Damn you! 'Twas you abandoned Hannah! Kate has shown her nothing but kindness!'

'Hah! Kate, eh! Kit and Kate again! I'll lay money that pleases your licentious King and his covey of poxy whores. Why, they shall yet burn in Hell-fire, devil take them all!'

'Why, Madam, you swear with the ease of a cavalier trooper.' Faulkner was incredulous. He stared at her for a moment and, realizing there was nothing more to be said, withdrew. Outside, on the landing, the door closed behind him, he sighed. He was almost convinced that she was a witch.

Once again an uneasy peace settled on Faulkner's household. Slowly, trade picked up, and Edmund returned from the West Indies, having employed the *Duchess of Albemarle* in some local trading between Jamaica and the American

colonies. He was much pleased with their profits and with his son. Only Faulkner rued the sum he remitted to Clarendon with a letter of explanation as to why the *Duchess of Albemarle* had been taken out of the East India Company's service. Fortunately, no-one blamed Faulkner for doing so; indeed, there were those who marvelled at his shrewdness. Although the East India Company now considered her too old for further eastern voyages, the Company's Court of Directors intimated that were Sir Christopher Faulkner to build a new ship, they would be happy to consider her for their service.

'I shall,' he told Katherine, 'realize an old ambition and name a new vessel after you.'

'Before you make such a declaration,' she riposted, 'you had better ensure you have sufficient funds. These last months cannot have been easy.'

'No, indeed, they have not.'

Nevertheless, Faulkner resolved to consult Gooding on the matter until, a week later, all such thoughts were driven out of his head when he received a private letter. It was followed the following day by one bearing the Admiralty seal.

'What is it?' Katherine asked.

'I am called to take command of the *Albion*,' he said.

Part Three

Conflagration

1666–1667

Battle

May – July 1666
'Your Grace.'

Introduced into the great cabin of the Duke of Albemarle's flagship, Faulkner swept off his hat and footed a bow. He could not deny the thrill he had felt as the pipes had shrilled their harsh salute as he had ascended the battered tumble-home of the *Royal Charles*, to be greeted on the quarterdeck by the officer-of-the-watch and Albemarle's secretary. He had looked about him for a moment, recalling the ship as the *Naseby*, Blake's flagship, flying the Cross and Harp colours of the Commonwealth.

'You have despatches for the Admiral?' the latter asked.

A moment later and Faulkner was ushered in to the great cabin of the flagship. Albemarle looked up from the papers on his desk and, with an expression of genuine pleasure of his weather-beaten face, jumped to his feet, came round the table and seized Faulkner's hand. 'My dear Sir Kit, how glad I am to see you!' Albemarle motioned to a man-servant to bring wine. 'Take off your cloak, please do...'

'Most kind, Your Grace.' Faulkner laid aside his hat and cloak on the admiral's secretary's vacant chair. Albemarle was smiling at him. He hitched the satchel that he wore beneath the cloak.

'How's that Indiaman of yours?' Albemarle asked conversationally as he took the proffered sealed packet from Faulkner, who briefly explained the fortunes of the *Duchess of Albemarle*. The admiral looked up from the packet, half un-opened in his gnarled hand. 'I cannot comprehend why you have been left on shore so long.'

'I did apply to serve.'

'Huh! I cannot think you did otherwise. Still, you are here now and I am much in need of you.' Albemarle motioned to a hovering man-servant and wine was served. 'Pray take some wine,' he said cordially to Faulkner as he riffled through the crackling pages. 'Just give me a moment to digest the contents of these despatches.'

'They are from the Admiralty but include one from the King,' Faulkner said, sipping his glass of wine. Albemarle, meanwhile, shuffled through the papers, occasionally clucking his tongue. Then he laid them down, picked up his wine and joined Faulkner.

'How d'you find the *Albion*?' Albemarle asked conversationally. The two men stood side by side, each with his glass of wine, staring out through the stern windows of the *Royal Charles*. All around them Albemarle's squadron lay anchored in The Downs.

'Knocked about somewhat, but sound enough I think, Your Grace, though I see you too have had a fair share of it.' Faulkner indicated the patched,

280

shattered panes, and the damaged wood-work about the flagship's stern windows.

'Indeed. It's been warm work, and there is more to do – more than I wish to contemplate.' Albemarle sighed, cast a rueful glance at his littered desk and sipped his wine for a moment. 'Pity about young Verney,' Albemarle went on, referring to the *Albion*'s late captain who had died suddenly. 'He handled himself well off Lowestoft,' he said with a sigh. 'That's the pity of it, and now, my dear Sir Kit, it is left to us old men to fend off these God-damned Dutchmen. They fight like the Devil, as you well know, and they are most ably commanded.'

'As are we, Your Grace.'

Albemarle turned towards him, a wry smile crossing his face like a sword-slash. 'Damn it, Sir Kit, you have been too long ashore and picked up courtier's ways. The truth is I am at my wit's end. The King has sent Rupert to the westwards, having heard that the French fleet is ordered into the Channel from the Mediterranean. I have scarce fifty men-o'-war, and now the wind lies in the east.' There was a note of exasperation in Albemarle's tone. 'De Ruyter will not miss the trick, and he has van Tromp and Evertsen with him; their strength must exceed eighty sail, and the Thames lies open but for us...' He waved his wine glass in an encompassing sweep, taking in the ships lying at their anchors, their colours and flags waving gallantly in the breeze, their boats plying between them with the punts of the Deal hovellers hanging in wait, like the gulls themselves, in case anything

281

fell to their advantage. 'I am in want of powder, shot...'

'I am to tell you several hoys are coming from the Medway with powder, wads and shot.'

'Good. Will they be here before nightfall?'

'I should hope so.'

'What about men?'

'Nothing, I'm afraid. At least none that I know of.'

'Odd, is it not,' Albemarle observed with a dry resignation, 'that when one wants men to put to sea the government is in want of them, yet when the poor devils are wounded in the state's service and put ashore to lick their wounds, that is about all that they can do, for the government complains there are too many of them and does nothing. Then, of course, it is the responsibility of the Trinity Brethren to help them, the King's ministers washing their hands of it all.'

'I can only say that I agree with you, Your Grace.'

Albemarle sighed and looked at Faulkner with a sad smile. 'I wish you could say otherwise.'

'As do I.'

'I wrote to the King,' Albemarle confided, 'and said that if I met the Dutch, then honour bound me to fight, notwithstanding the odds against us. The point of my plight seems lost on him, pleasure boating making him an expert in these matters. Now he requires me to weigh anchor at once and cruise between the Longsand Head and the Galloper, in order that de Ruyter does not pen me here.'

'I understand he has recalled Prince Rupert.'

'Yes, he tells me Rupert is to reinforce me at once. I should have sent a cruiser to watch the Dutch, but I am so damnably short...' The admiral's voice tailed off. There was no doubt that he should have sent a cruiser; certainly not in Faulkner's mind. 'You used to do the job rather well, I recall,' he added, turning to Faulkner. 'Truth is, Kit, I am grown old...'

'Well, Your Grace, we may still give a good account of ourselves.'

'I hope so,' Albemarle said with a grim laugh. 'I suppose one may as well die in action as in a bed.'

'I'd prefer the bed, Your Grace,' Faulkner said drily, finishing his wine, 'and preferably not alone.'

He made to take his leave, but Albemarle stopped him and asked: 'How is your wife?'

Faulkner bridled at the awkward question, especially following his facetious remark. Talking of death, he had thought not of Judith, but of Katherine, glad that in his absence she had moved to live with Hannah. The poisonous intrusion of Judith, even if by way of Honest George's enquiry, was disconcerting. Something of this train of thought must have crossed his face, for the admiral added quickly, 'I ask as a friend.'

'Your Grace is very kind,' Faulkner said hurriedly. 'You have likely heard she is deranged, or some such thing.'

Albemarle dodged the implied query. 'I had merely wondered if her condition was what had prevented your coming to sea.'

'No,' Faulkner replied shortly, then unbent. 'To tell truth, Your Grace, she confines herself to her room, sees no-one but her brother and blames me for the loss of our son.'

'Who took his own life...'

'Who took his own life after she had embroiled him in a plot against the King, as you may recall.'

'Yes, yes, I spoke to the King in your interest.'

Faulkner inclined his head. 'For which I am most grateful.'

'Huh,' Albemarle said ruefully. 'I don't doubt but that our Royal Master made you pay for it.'

'Indeed he did, your Grace,' Faulkner said, finding that he could laugh at the imposition in Honest George's company.

'One sometimes wishes more could share the burden of service to the state,' Albemarle remarked. He was in confidential mood. 'It seems sometimes that it falls hard upon the shoulders of a few men while others openly offer their wives and lay them before his Majesty's ever-quivering sceptre. That rogue Palmer, for example, who is to become Lord Cleveland and that whore of a wife – the Villiers woman – will be his Duchess! Pah!'

'True,' Faulkner said, grinning, 'but there are those poor seamen who bear a heavier load...'

'And their families, who bear the heaviest.' Albemarle sighed again, then bestirred himself. 'Come, Sir Kit, we had better be about our business or we shall both be hanged for treason. Who's your first lieutenant in *Albion*?'

'Septimus Clarke, your Grace.'

'Clarke, Clarke...? No, I do not know him. Is he a good fellow?'

'He seems so. I have made his acquaintance before. He was with Sackler in the *Blackamoor* when we brought the Regicides out of Holland.'

'I would ask you to dine with me but these orders...' He gestured at the papers on his desk.

'Not at all, Your Grace, I have my own preparations.'

'The tide turns to the north at first light; I shall give the signal to weigh then.'

Faulkner put on his cloak and picked up his hat. 'Your servant, Your Grace.'

As if on cue there came a knock at the cabin door and the admiral's secretary peeped anxiously into the great cabin. Albemarle beckoned him inside. Albemarle and Faulkner exchanged glances. 'You have the knack of timing, Sir Christopher,' Albemarle said grimly. 'Until we shake hands again here, or in Hell!'

As Faulkner stepped out onto the quarterdeck, he could hear Albemarle already dictating orders. He cast a quick look aloft at the main masthead of the *Royal Charles* where Albemarle's flag rippled in the breeze.

'It's still in the east, Sir Christopher,' the officer-of-the-watch remarked. 'De Ruyter will be on the move by now.'

'De Ruyter will have been on the move ere now,' Faulkner said, adding matter-of-factly, 'would you be so kind as to call my boat.'

During the night the wind changed, and at dawn on the last day of May it was blowing fresh from

285

the south-west. Albemarle's fleet weighed from The Downs, avoiding the trap the King feared, coming in sight of the Dutch the next morning, the first of June, when off the Longsand Head, some ten miles south-east of Harwich. It seemed to Faulkner, in the days of furious fighting and manoeuvring that followed, that if he ever met Albemarle again, it would undoubtedly be in Hell. For, apart from the brief hours of darkness of the summer nights, the two fleets were embattled upon its very threshold. In after years, Faulkner's recollection of those subsequent days were confused, far less distinct than his memories of any other action in which he had fought. This was due in part to exhaustion, to the effect of the deafening noise; of the need to assess the constantly shifting situation, interpret Albemarle's signals and handle the *Albion*, all of which taxed him mentally and physically. But it was also because of the confusion inherent in a battle that went on for four days, so that one recollection ran into another and the conflation of memories served no purpose other than to confuse a mind already disturbed by the relentless thunder of the guns, the shrieks of the wounded and the imperative necessity of *thinking*, of dealing with the present moment with no capacity for past or future. Younger men, unwounded, and for whom this was their first fleet action, emerged claiming they had never felt so *alive*, such was the potency and excitement of the instant. If they too escaped wounds, older and experienced men were more likely to find the prolonged noise and strain simply wore them out. Irrespective of age, however, at the end of each day's action, as the fleets broke away and moved out of range of each other, no-one left standing on deck could escape the deafness accompanied by tinnitus, the hunger, the thirst or the bone-weariness that engendered an overwhelming desire to sink down where they stood and seek the arms of Morpheus.

What no man forgot was the smell: the stink that gradually overcame the tang of sea-air as each day advanced and left behind the luminous innocence of the dawn. Yet both bore the hint of salt; the morning breeze carried it as did the reek of blood which, compounded with its ferrous smell and the choking salts of sulphur and potassium emanating from the muzzles of the hundreds of belching cannon, filled the lungs of all. Thousands died in the action and, in later life, it was only necessary to discharge a shotgun after game, or pass a butchers' shambles, for the olfactory nerve to produce the most poignant recollection.

Despite the nightmarish amalgamation of Faulkner's memories, one or two moments stood out, imprinting themselves vividly on his mind's eye, though he was afterwards confused as to their chronological order. When first sighted, the Dutch fleet had been at anchor off the Galloper shoal and Albemarle threw out the signal to attack. Led by the van squadron under Vice Admiral Sir William Berkeley, the English fleet bore down upon the enemy, which was swiftly got under way and fell into line, heading southeast led by Tromp. Ayscue led round to run parallel with the Dutch, the entire English fleet following, battering Tromp's squadron before de Ruyter could come up to his assistance about mid-day. However, although Albemarle's ships held the weather gauge, such was the strength of the wind and the heeling of his ships that many could not open their lower gun-ports, adding another disadvantage to being out-numbered.

In the years that had passed since the First Dutch War, Johann de Witt, the Dutch Stadt-holder, had permitted the building of larger Dutch men-of-war, able to compete with the English ships in weight of metal. These bore more ballast than their opponents, making them stiffer, and thus they fought from leeward to advantage over the English, throwing their shot from all their gun-ports. Among these was de Ruyter's magnificent new flagship, *De Seven Provinciën*, mounting eighty guns. During the day the two fleets hammered away at one another relentlessly, each seeking a weakness in their opponent so that some confusion broke the regularity of the twin lines of battle. From time to time, the English found themselves working both broadsides as the rear Dutch squadron under Cornelius Evertsen bore up and crossed to take the windward position. During the long afternoon, Albemarle's centre squadron – in which lay Faulkner in the *Albion* – followed by Allin's rear squadron, was heavily engaged by de Ruyter and Evertsen. As the hours passed, they drew ever closer to the banks of shoals that lay parallel to the Flanders shore, and Albemarle, whose ships were in general of deeper draught than the Dutch, was forced to bear up.

De Ruyter and Evertsen fell upon the turning English men-of-war with deadly effect, particularly the van under Berkeley. Sir William Berkeley was killed, and his flagship, the sixty-four-gun *Swiftsure*, surrendered, while Berkeley's rear admiral, Sir John Harman in the *Henry*, fought his way through Evertsen's squadron and evaded three fireships sent towards him. Such was the ferocity of his action that with the *Henry* on fire, Evertsen ranged up alongside and called upon Harman to surrender. Harman refused, his next broadside killing Evertsen and others about him.

Faulkner recalled seeing the *Henry* on fire and being astonished later that she was still afloat and still fighting. The *Loyal George* was not so lucky, for she was also lost. As darkness fell and the two fleets drew apart, Faulkner called for the butcher's bill; he had lost eighteen men, and of the forty-one wounded upwards of a dozen were mortally so. To this number he could, with confidence, add another twenty who would not survive their surgery, though they might languish some weeks yet.

The following dawn was fine and clear, promising a hot June day, as it proved. By now the two fleets were east of the Galloper as they formed line ahead and passed and re-passed on opposing tacks, individual ships, and even squadrons at times, passing through the enemy's line. It was a long day of ceaseless gun-fire, of station-keeping on the ship ahead, of watching and waiting for the signal to tack and then of carrying out the manoeuvre and falling into station before re-engaging the enemy. As a mark of his faith, Albemarle had ordered *Albion* into a leading position of the centre division of the fleet, just ahead of the flag-ship. Thus Faulkner had to keep an eye on the ships ahead of him, thereby maintaining the cohesion of the line, yet watch for any signals the Commander-in-Chief might make for tactical reasons. This task was made all the more difficult by the clouds of gun-smoke that obscured the *Royal Charles*, even though she was but a few hundred yards astern of the *Albion*.

But it was the Dutch that out-classed the English that day, for when Tromp appeared cut off, de Ruyter came to his rescue and put Albemarle's ships under increasing pressure. One by one many of the English warships were beaten out of the line of battle and fell back towards the English coast, licking their wounds. So it went on during the third day until, towards the evening, Albemarle's fleet was reduced to almost half its full strength. Forming fifteen of his heaviest remaining ships in line abreast, he withdrew to the west-north-westwards, his stern chasers holding off the damaged but pursuing Dutch and covering the retreat of his damaged fleet. By this time the manoeuvring of the two fleets, driven hither and thither by the inexorable thrust of the tide, had rendered their reckoning uncertain. The pall of smoke that lay on the surface of the sea, the preoccupations of war and the effect these had on routine, sealed the fate of one of the finest ships in the English navy.

290

From the *Albion*, lying in Albemarle's defensive line, Faulkner was a witness to what turned out to be an incident which touched him personally. This ensured it was among those few vignettes of the long struggle that remained indelibly imprinted on his mind. He recalled the sails of the pursuing Dutch extending from north to south as they chased what they thought was a defeated enemy until, at about five o'clock in the afternoon, unbeknown to Faulkner at the time, distant sails were seen to the south-west. Were they the French ... or Rupert?

Faulkner then had little appreciation of this development, his own attention being occupied by the plight of the *Royal Prince* which, under Sir George Ayscue, had driven hard upon the Galloper Shoal. He bore away in the *Albion*, intending to assist Ayscue, but anxious to avoid the tail of the Galloper. In his desire to succour Sir George he was too late: de Ruyter was approaching, igniting and sending fire-ships towards the casualty, so terrifying her crew, as was discovered afterwards, that with their fighting spirit in doubt, Ayscue surrendered. Faulkner afterwards recalled this moment poignantly, for not only was the *Royal Prince* one of the noblest ships in the English fleet, but she had once been the *Prince Royal*, the ship in which he had served as a lieutenant, had been honoured by the man who would become the ill-fated King Charles I, and had met and fallen in love with Katherine Villiers. The ship had been reconstructed several times at great expense; she had suffered a name-change under the Commonwealth, becoming the *Resolution*; but she was, nevertheless, a reminder of his own long career. It had almost choked him to see her colours struck and the Dutch boats pull towards her to take possession.

In the face of over-whelming force and the close proximity of a fire-ship to the *Albion* herself, Faulkner had been obliged to run, but the smoke pall that marked the burning of the *Royal Prince* had hung over the horizon long after the flames had dropped below it, deeply affecting him. De Ruyter's act of setting the *Royal Prince* on fire angered his own men, for they were thereby deprived of a rich prize, but its effect upon the English, particularly when word was later passed that her crew had behaved badly, produced a remarkable consequence.

De Ruyter did not press his pursuit; the arrival of English reinforcements persuaded him to gather his forces and await the morrow. He still possessed the advantage in numbers, by some seventeen serviceable men-of-war, and was in a sanguine frame of mind. He spent the remaining hours of daylight repairing damage, redistributing powder and shot, and tending the wounded. On the English side Albemarle and Rupert conferred, determining to fight on, despite the odds, the damage to the serviceable ships, the exhaustion of commanders and crews, the mounting list of casualties and the falling reserves of powder and shot.

Faulkner could remember little about the fourth of June beyond an utter confusion of noise and weariness, of fear and horror and an increasing anxiety over the expenditure of ammunition. When, days earlier, the *Albion* had withdrawn from Albemarle's fleet to land the dead Verney at Sheerness and where Faulkner had joined her, Septimus Clarke had diligently ensured that the opportunity had been taken to refill the ship's magazines with the regulation forty rounds per gun. Remarkably – the dock-yard officers usually resenting any requisition in excess of the bare minimum – an Admiralty order had been received to increase this allow-ance by an additional ten rounds if a man-of-war had sufficient capacity to safely stow the extra powder and shot. Lieutenant Clarke had con-sulted with the *Albion*'s Master, and they had duly taken the extra munitions on board.

But after four days of action, even this gener-ous allowance was looking inadequate as the two fleets, neither doing much in the way of keeping station, engaged in a confused mêlée. With con-siderable skill, de Ruyter mustered enough ships round his flag to mount an attack upon the main body of what was left of the English fleet, but Rupert's flagship, the *Royal James*, was dis-masted late in the day, and Albemarle's *Royal Charles* was severely damaged. Sir Christopher Myngs, one of the junior admirals, was mortally wounded in the *Victory*, and the *Albion* had her fore topmast shattered, her knightheads shot to pieces, her upper gun-deck pierced in three places and eight of her guns dismounted. Faulk-ner had lost about one third of his ship's com-pany, killed or badly wounded. Like most of the other men-of-war, the *Albion* was able to work up to Sheerness, where the fleet recovered its breath, aware that it had suffered a defeat.

But while de Ruyter withdrew – his captains, officers and crews, cock-a-hoop with their success, and convinced that they had beaten their enemy into submission – the Dutch admiral was less euphoric. He was wise not to be; his superiority of numbers had told in his favour, but the more prescient of the observers had noted the discipline in the English fleet and that, for the most part, the English had revealed the power in the relatively new tactic of men-of-war sailing head to tail in line ahead. The Dutch had met them with the same method, but now, as the ships began their repairs, and after Rupert and Albemarle had consulted their commanders, they drew up revised Fighting Instructions. The loss of the *Royal Prince*, the smell of which still haunted Sir Christopher Faulkner as he regarded his shattered battle-ship and discussed her repairs with her officers, was a potent spur to revenge.

But there were also grave political issues at stake, issues with which Faulkner himself was all too familiar. He was almost unique among the post-captains who had assembled in the great cabin of the flag-ship the night they anchored in the Medway in not belonging to either of the two factions that divided his colleagues. In general there were those who favoured Prince Rupert and deprecated Albemarle, and those for whom Rupert was a cavalry commander of indifferent talent who owed his position entirely to his high birth. Faulkner was therefore almost alone among the assembled company who stood well in the opinion of both admirals. Although there were those who saw it their duty to disgrace Albemarle and intrigue for his removal after the recent defeat, both Rupert and Albemarle, being supremely fitted for their office, spoke with one voice. Like every other captain in that glittering if battered company, Faulkner was aware of the schism, but he was the only one privy to Albemarle's personal opinion.

'Well, we have avoided Hell, Your Grace,' Faulkner had said, taking Albemarle's hand with a smile as he entered the great cabin.

'Thus far,' responded the Duke confidentially, his face grim. 'They will roast me alive for this,' he said. 'We lost *sixteen* men-of-war besides the *Royal Prince*, and gained but a paltry handful.'

For a month the combined squadrons of Rupert and Albemarle lay in the Medway repairing damage, recruiting their crews, recharging their magazines and landing their wounded. Of the last there were many hundreds, almost past the reckoning. Although the flag officers left their flag-ships, few captains did, all being intent on readying the fleet for further service. Sorely tempted to travel to London to see Katherine, Faulkner drove himself and his crew to their work. Young Clarke proved his worth; slightly wounded in his shoulder, which temporarily disabled his right arm, the *Albion*'s first lieutenant laboured as hard as his commander, inspired by the older man's example. Having been badly damaged by cannon-shot, the main-mast required replacement, as did the fore top-mast, the long yard on the mizzen, the bowsprit and four upper yards. Of their sails, four had to be unbent, sent down and replaced. There were a score of shot-holes to be properly plugged, and the sections of the upper hull, in way of the upper gun-deck, needed extensive repairs, requiring the services of the dockyard ship-wrights from Chatham. In securing their services, Faulkner was not alone; his fellow commanders of almost every sur-viving ship in the fleet were clamouring for shipwrights, so that much of his time was taken up pleading, begging, cajoling and threaten-ing the Master Attendant and the Master Ship-wright.

In such circumstances, a visit to London was out of the question and, had he attempted such an adventure, it would have proved impracticable. Such was the demand for coaches, or any other suitable conveyance, that few were to be found, while the recollection of the state of his arse after his ride to and from Oxford put any thoughts of riding on horseback out of Faulkner's mind. He did, however, find time to write to Katherine, explaining the urgency of the situation, pleading the sense of revenge transfusing the fleet and making particular reference to the loss of the *Royal Prince*. In this he reminded her that she had once been the *Prince Royal*. Ignoring the fact that he had in fact suffered several super-ficial wounds, he reassured her that – in his opinion quite miraculously – he was unwounded. Only one of his four wounds, a laceration from an oak splinter across his left thigh, caused any concern, until he ordered his surgeon to wash out the wound with the contents of a half-empty bottle of wine, roaring at the pain but urging the over-taxed man to: 'Scour the damn thing out!' Having then ensured that, instead of a bristle, a waxed thread was left to drain out the excess of 'yellow bile', he improved rapidly. This wound, along with a bodily stiffness and mental lassitude occasioned by four days' near continuous exertion, added to his reluctance to mount a horse, though this last could not affect the repair of the *Albion*.

Within a week he had a reply from Katherine.

My Dearest, she wrote from Hannah's house.

We have Good Intelligence that Edmund and the East India fleet is at St Helen's Road, awaiting Convoy into the River of Thames when your Present Business is Resolved. God grant my Prayers that this may be Soon and to the Advantage of the King's Majesty. Edmund speaks of a Fever, but his Letter to Hannah was Reassuring, from which we Suppose him to be Recovered.

Hannah is well, as is the Boy. She would Dearly Desire Another and sends you her Duty and Love, saying she will Write soon. Knowing you would rather have News I have not detained this Letter in order to await her Pleasure.

I have heard but twice from Nathan, on both Occasions it seems that Your Wife Troubled him. He spoke of Her leaving the House, which thing She has not done in my Recollection. And of her being a Witch, which I think very Foolish, She having a Distortion of Mind more Dangerous

297

unto Herself, than unto Others. Hannah is Concerned that She may attempt to Harm the Boy but I have Calmed Her in that Prospect.

As for Your Kate, She is well and Awaits only Your Safe Return...

Faulkner sniffed and rubbed the unmanly tears that had, unbidden, filled his eyes. He re-read the letter, hearing Katherine's voice in the words, and her tone in the idiosyncrasy of her handwriting. It was good to know that the *Duchess of Albemarle* lay off Portsmouth in company with the other East Indiamen. That sharpened the urgency of his present task. As for the news of Judith, that was of some concern. Why had she taken to leaving the house? Where did she go, and to what purpose? Of course, there was nothing essentially wrong with her going abroad, Faulkner knew. He had promised not to lay any restrictions upon her, but the sudden change of habit, occurring in his absence, bothered him. While Katherine sensibly dismissed wild talk of witchcraft, there lingered in Faulkner's mind a less-enlightened point-of-view. Such women may have been incapable of the magic they had once been thought to practise, but Judith had already demonstrated her headstrong beliefs, and her willingness to accomplish her fell plans. Who knew what she might have precipitated had she not been thwarted? What else did you call such waywardness in a mature woman but witch-craft? Faulkner asked himself.

He shook his head over Nathan. Although he had seemed to recover his wits after his drunken breakdown, it had long been clear that his sister's conduct had affected him deeply. He was a man accustomed to a steady routine, used to the vicissitudes of commerce, to be sure, but not a man to meet the unexpected with that resolution expected of a sea-officer. He had been willing enough to leave such matters to the likes of Faulkner, just as Faulkner left the book-keeping, the tallying, the supervision of clearances inwards and outwards, the levying of agency commission and the payment of dues and other impositions to Gooding. Until Judith's murderous politics had intervened, their partnership had worked well.

Lying in the Medway, surrounded by the disorder of his repairing ship, he was impotent. There was nothing he could do but rely upon Katherine's good sense; that, at least, was a certainty in this shifting world. He went out on deck, to be met by Clarke.

'I was on my way to see you, Sir Christopher. An officer from the *Royal Charles* brought this.' He handed Faulkner a sealed letter. Looking over the rail, Faulkner could see the flagship's boat being pulled to their nearest neighbour, the frigate *Sweepstakes*, with orders for her captain, Francis Sanders. Beckoning Clarke to follow him, Faulkner led him to the great cabin, unsealed and read the letter.

He looked up at Clarke. 'The Dutch are said to be at sea again, and His Highness and the Duke are of the opinion they mean to attempt a landing near Harwich. They express a desire for the fleet to be ready for sea by the twentieth. I see no reason why we cannot comply. Do you?'

Clarke shook his head. 'Not at all. Water is my only concern at the moment; the Master is fretting over it and asks if you could use your influence...'

'Huh!' Faulkner expostulated. 'I have precious little left of that hereabouts! Have you not noticed I need a new pair of breeches every time I go ashore, so worn are the knees out of my others?'

Clarke grinned. 'I had not noticed, sir, only that you were sprouting wings in imitation of an angel. The men are much impressed with your ability to conjure spars and cordage out of the dockyard's chief misers.'

Faulkner smiled. 'If they only knew the truth. Now, tell me, our sails ... have we made good the damages in full?'

'Not quite; the mizzen is still in the sail loft but I am myself going ashore this afternoon to chivvy them. I have three seamen working with the dockyard but so too has *Sweepstakes* and *Old James*...'

'And all the rest of them, I'll warrant.' Faulkner finished the sentence for Clarke. 'Now what about men?'

They went on to discuss the most troublesome matter of all, recruiting their ship's company.

The fleet did not weigh anchor on the twentieth, but not because the *Albion* kept it waiting. In the event it was the following day that the signal, emphasized by a gun, was made aboard Rupert and Albemarle's joint flag-ship, the *Royal Charles*. The westerly wind was steady – 'a topsail breeze' – as the fleet sailed downstream in its order of battle. In the van lay the White Squadron, commanded by Admiral Sir Thomas Allin in the *Royal James*, and itself led by Allin's vice admiral, Sir Thomas Teddiman in the *Royal Katherine*. Faulkner's *Albion* lay in the centre division, the Red Squadron under Rupert and Albemarle. This was led by Vice Admiral Sir Joseph Jordan in the *Royal Oak*, with the *Albion* next astern of her, ahead of the *Warspite*. Ship after ship passed Sheerness, cleared the Nore and followed her next ahead down the King's Channel, eighty-seven sail, mostly men-of-war but with eight armed merchantmen and a score of fire-ships. From Teddiman's flag-ship, the *Royal Katherine*, to the armed merchantman *Loyal Merchant*, latter-most ship of Admiral Sir Jeremy Smyth's Blue Squadron forming the rear division of the fleet, the line was some nine miles long.

By the evening of the twenty-second of July this immense fleet lay anchored off the Gunfleet Sand. It was soon bruited abroad that de Ruyter and his fleet lay a score of miles away, just east of the Galloper Sand. That evening Faulkner called his officers in to dine with him.

The evening passed convivially enough, though Faulkner noticed that he was not the only one to cup a hand behind an ear to hear what his neighbour was saying, for they were all suffering from the debilitating irritation of a hissing and ringing tinnitus.

'We can expect to sight the Dutch tomorrow,' he said, looking round at them. 'With our last

301

encounter in mind, I suggest you try and get a good night's sleep.'

They came in sight of the Dutch fleet the next morning, and for two days the long lines of ships passed and re-passed at a distance, out of range, each trying to obtain the advantage. For hour after hour Faulkner paced up and down the *Albion*'s quarterdeck, leaving the ship-handling to the master and his lieutenants. Nothing more was necessary than to keep station, something the English fleet did with more precision than ever before. From time to time Faulkner would study the Dutch, throwing the odd remark at the master, an elderly man named Dixon.

'I don't know whether he has been counting, or not,' he remarked impatiently at one point, 'but de Ruyter shows no sign of acknowledging the fact that he has fewer ships than we do.'

'No, sir,' responded Dixon, 'but he cannot think that we have an appetite for battle after the drubbing he gave us last month.'

'You think that he considers our manoeuvrings as vacillation, do you, Mr Dixon?'

'It would seem so, Sir Christopher. My guess is that he is trying to weary us.'

'He could certainly achieve that!' Faulkner remarked, drily.

'Except that he wears himself out in the doing thereof.' Dixon spoke with a conviction that Faulkner considered entirely misplaced.

'Hmm. That doesn't seem to be the case,' Faulkner mused, studying the Dutch through the telescope the late King had given him.

'I beg your pardon, Sir Christopher, but the

admiral's signalling,' interrupted the second lieutenant, then on duty on the quarterdeck.

And so it went on until, at about ten o'clock on the forenoon of St James's Day, the twenty-fifth, de Ruyter laid his fleet of seventy-two men-of-war on the same tack as the English. As the two parallel fleets converged, heading east, the thunder of the guns broke out again, and the men, standing easy by their cannon in anticipation of being called, were summoned to stand-to. A quarter of an hour later, her ship's company at their battle-stations, her officers at their posts, the fifty-gun *Albion* again went into action.

They say that you see the ball that is going to kill you – if, that is, you happen to be looking in the right direction. Certainly, before noon that day three balls had passed so close to Faulkner that, had he been aware of their coming, he might have observed this curiosity. The first sucked his hat off, the second spun him round like young Edmund's red spinning-top and the third took the telescope clean out of his hands, its eye-piece goring his nose, damage mitigated only because he was in the act of lowering it as the ball passed. The first and last of these projectiles were light-weight, from swivel-guns or arquebuses, pos-sibly deliberately aimed at him from a height, for he was conspicuously the *Albion*'s commander in his scarlet sash. The second was a ball from a great gun; it too spun him, but it also tore the air from his lungs and flung him to the deck, so that he collapsed and lay as though dead, until his reflexes dragged air back into his respiratory system and he gasped his shuddering way back to consciousness.

Directed by the ever-watchful Dixon, two seamen dragged him to the foot of the mizzen mast and propped him against it until he fully recovered his wits.

'The *Gouden Draaken*,' Dixon remarked and waved his hand in the direction of the nearest Dutch ship in a brief lull when his voice could be heard, indicating the source of Faulkner's near miss.

Faulkner wanted to say that he could not care less from where the shot came; only that he wished all aboard the enemy vessel in Hell and he himself allowed to go home. At that moment, as he hovered between animal recovery and sentient thought, the idea of dandling little Edmund on his knee, while Hannah and Katherine looked on, seemed like a vision of Paradise.

But Paradise, or the other place, lay closer to hand. He struggled to his feet and steadied himself against the adjacent mizzen fire-rail. He accepted his precious telescope from Dixon, who had picked it up, remarking that it appeared to have suffered no damage. 'It must have been the suction in the air,' he remarked conversationally.

'No doubt,' responded Faulkner. He needed no glass to see the *Gouden Draaken*, close to their starboard side, her topsails looming against the sky. He would be a lucky man if he survived the day.

As they lay in their allotted place in the long line of battle and exchanged broadsides with their opponent, the *Albion*'s men, weakened by their losses in the Four Days' Battle, stood to their guns with a furious determination. Even the weakest-minded among them appreciated the humiliation they had suffered in June, and the lower-deck chatter had been of little more than bloodying 'the square-heads' noses' – a joke which translated rather well in the sailors' argot. Having a square head, a Dutchman had no need of a nose!

The rage which these men brought to the serving of their brutal artillery was enthusiastically harnessed by the young lieutenants commanding the upper- and lower-deck batteries. Nevertheless, in the noise, confusion, smoke and howl of constant imprecations to, 'Hull 'em!' or to, 'Aim high, my lads, and knock the sticks out of the bastards!' – depending upon the prevailing point of view of the officers – few could properly see their target.

Faulkner had learned to leave the station-keeping to Dixon. The master gave his orders to the quartermasters at the helm with cool efficiency, constantly and apparently simultaneously trimming sail to maintain their position, a puppet-master to the top-men and seamen detailed to leave their guns and tend the braces when called upon to do so. Faulkner's task was to press the enemy, to oversee the effort his people made in serving the guns and, with one officer detailed to do so, ensure than any signal made by any of the admirals – but chiefly the two flag-officers commanding the central Red Squadron – was conformed with.

Not that Rupert and Albemarle had much

opportunity to do anything other than stand helplessly side by side on the *Royal Charles*'s quarterdeck, for as long as the ships of war lay head to tail in the line of battle they had jointly determined upon, neither could do very much. Indeed they barely knew what was happening ahead, still less astern, where Smyth's Blue Squadron had fallen back and become detached, inducing the Dutch rear admiral, van Tromp, to break his own line and turn to fall upon the English rear. They could just make out that extensive damage had been inflicted upon de Ruyter's flag-ship, *De Zeven Provinciën*, for she had lost much of her top-hamper, falling out of the line as de Ruyter's men exerted themselves in emergency repairs.

Faulkner saw none of this, only the bulk of the *Gouden Draaken* and the ships ahead and astern of her, each of which was engaged with her opposite number in the English line. Towards four o'clock in the afternoon someone forward shouted that the Dutch line was breaking. Faulkner and Dixon peered ahead through the smoke, but could see nothing.

'They've haven't maintained their battle-line with the same precision as we have all day,' Dixon remarked, adding: 'It don't signify.'

Nor did it seem to for some few minutes more. Faulkner turned to look astern, and when he swung forward again, it was to see Dixon cut in half, the ball passing before his eyes like a dark line, to smash into the opposite bulwark in a shower of splinters. He tore his appalled gaze away, looked to starboard at the loom of the

Gouden Draaken. Her silhouette had changed! She was turning, breaking off the action!

Up and down the English line the noise of cheering could be heard; the gunfire slackened and slowly the gun-smoke cleared as the two fleets drew apart. Instinctively, the English fleet dressed its line under reduced sail until, as the sun westered, Rupert and Albemarle decided to finish their enemy off.

'Signal from the flag-ship, sir,' one of the master's mates reported, looking at the signal-book. 'General chase in line abreast, sir!'

'Very well. Mr Dixon's dead...'

'I knows sir.' The younger man, whose name Faulkner knew, but could not for the life of him remember, spoke solemnly, his eyes alighting on the two distinct parts of what had, but a short while earlier, been a man to whom he was beholden.

'Can you take the conning?' Faulkner asked him sharply.

'Why, yes, Sir Christopher.' Faulkner observed enthusiasm kindle in the younger man's eyes. It was that easy, he thought sadly, for one's fate to make another's reputation.

'Then do so. Lay the ship on a course of...' Faulkner crossed the deck and stared into the binnacle. 'Of south-east by east.'

'Sou'-east by east, aye, aye, sir.'

The fighting went on, but was less savage as de Ruyter began a masterly retreat. As had the English after the Four Days' Battle, the Dutch played their guns to good effect, holding the pursuing English at bay. Far to the west, Smyth likewise drove Tromp into conducting a clever withdrawal, and both elements of the Dutch fleet made for the shelter of the extensive shoals off their native coast.

As night came on the English withdrew to deeper water, attempting to re-engage next day but without success, de Ruyter passing his ships into the shelter of the Schelde and under the fortifications of Vlissingen. Captain Sir Christopher Faulkner knew little of this for not long after he had given the order to chase, he fell to the deck, blood pouring from one leg. Clarke was summoned to take over as Faulkner was carried below. Half an hour later, when the surgeon had conducted his inspection of Faulkner's wound, he reported to Clarke. 'I fear for his life, Mr Clarke. He has lost a quantity of blood; his boot was full of it!'

Holmes's Bonfire

July – October 1666
'We have conjured dawn early, Sir Christopher,' Clarke remarked. Both men stood at the larboard mizzen stays, their glasses levelled at the red glow that showed beyond the low silhouette of Vlieland. A spire and the regular ridges of dwelling-houses broke the low, extended hummock of the Frisian island. Night was coming on, and the red glow showed like a premature sunrise, a

308

mirror of the sunset suffusing the western horizon with lurid hues of scarlet.

'Damn!' Clarke swore, nearly dropping his telescope as he lowered it, still incommoded by the sling he wore to ease his wounded shoulder.

Faulkner looked round at the younger man, concerned. 'Are you all right?'

'Yes, thank you, sir. It's this damned shoulder.' Clarke's tone was one of exasperation. The wound was taking some time to heal, and Faulkner feared an infection. The disability had prevented Clarke from commanding the *Albion*'s boats, which had been sent in with those from the rest of the squadron to burn the Dutch merchant shipping lying at anchor inside the shelter of Vlieland.

Clarke stuffed the collapsed telescope in his tail-pocket and smiled at Faulkner. 'And how are you, Sir Christopher? You had us all a-feared, particularly after we all thought you had a fever.'

''Twas only a loss of blood. That damned ball that threw me on the deck reopened my wound. I had no idea I was bleeding ... Still, it prevented the saw-bones from bleeding me further.'

The two chuckled companionably, their chatter idle as they watched, at a distance, the result of the raid on Dutch commerce. 'We must have burned a score or two of their ships,' Clarke remarked.

'Perhaps more,' Faulkner offered. 'At all events, let us hope it brings the Dutch to the table to discuss terms.' Clarke agreed.

After the Battle of St James's Day, while Faulkner had lain in his cot, weakened and recovering from the effusion of blood that followed the reopening of his leg wound, Clarke had temporarily assumed command of the *Albion*. Rupert and Albemarle had cruised off the Dutch coast behind the dykes of which de Ruyter had skilfully retired with the loss of only two of his ships. However, four Dutch admirals had been killed during the battle, including a second of the Evertsen family from Zealand, signalling to the States General that de Ruyter had been beaten by a fleet thought to have been brought its knees a few weeks earlier. Although the English did not yet know of it, a vicious dispute had arisen following accusations by de Ruyter that Maarten van Tromp had deserted him, a row that would result in van Tromp's dismissal.

Determined to press their advantage, Rupert and Albemarle had ordered Rear Admiral Sir John Holmes, the junior flag-officer of the Red Squadron, to shift his flag into the *Tiger*. When Clarke had received the order for *Albion* to join Holmes, he had gone below to confer with Faulkner, uncertain whether or not to notify the joint commander-in-chief of Faulkner's incapacity.

'You are competent, are you not, Septimus?' Faulkner had asked from his cot.

'If you are content with my retaining command, sir.'

'There is no point in troubling His Highness or the Duke. Do you conform. I am able to prop myself up on deck, if the need be. Here, let me sign the acknowledgement...'

With the *Advice*, *Hampshire*, *Dragon*, *Albion*,

Assurance, *Fountain*, *Sweepstakes*, *Garland* and *Pembroke*, together with the fire-ships *Lizard*, *Richard*, *Fox*, *Bryar* and *Samuel*, and the yacht *Fanfan*, Holmes sailed north. The squadron proceeded up the coast of Holland until, on the eighth of August, it reached the channel between the off-lying Frisian islands of Vlieland and Terschelling. Here, in what they thought was a safe and sheltered anchorage, tucked away among the tortuous sandbanks that seamed the shallows between the Frisian Islands and the mainland, lay a large number of laden Dutch merchant ships of all sizes, fearful of proceeding further south with the English fleet at sea and no news of a convincing Dutch victory. This was Holmes's quarry. On the late afternoon of the ninth, Holmes sent in his fire-ships, accompanied by his smaller men-of-war. His own flagship, along with *Albion* and the other larger men-of-war guarded the approaches, sent in their boats, each equipped with combustibles and enlarged crews of men as eager as schoolboys to set fire to the enemy's shipping.

The raid was a success, doing immense damage to Dutch trade by burning not two score of merchantmen, but over one hundred and sixty. Unsurprisingly, the cock-a-hoop seamen named their exploit 'Holmes's Bonfire', their only regret that the Dutchmen had been destroyed and not brought out of the anchorage as prizes. It was, nonetheless, a spectacular raid, its impact upon the Dutch economy greater than any other exploit during the Dutch Wars. After Holmes rejoined the main fleet, Rupert and Albemarle

311

cruised in the southern North Sea. The annual return of the ships of the powerful Dutch East India Company was imminent; to seize even a portion of that would bring the Dutch to their knees at a stroke, and the two English commanders were anxious to crown the campaign with such a brilliant *coup de main*.

De Ruyter succeeded in foiling the English after several weeks of manoeuvring; mostly out of sight of each other, the Dutch interposed their battle-fleet between the hovering English and the homeward-bound Indiamen. These all passed through the Zeegat van Texel and into the Zuider Zee; with de Ruyter bringing up the rear, they were now beyond English reach. By the end of September, Rupert and Albemarle decided nothing further could be done and ordered the fleet into the Medway, a short voyage marred by the loss of another ship on the Galloper. By this time it was common knowledge that a great disaster had overtaken the country.

London had been burned. Fresh from their triumphs in Vlieland, it seemed to the home-coming fleet like an act of God. Faulkner recalled his argument with Gooding. 'To me belongeth vengeance and recompense,' he muttered uneasily, the illogical, guilt-ridden supposition that Judith had some part in the dreadful event entered his head unbidden – and lodged itself there.

It was a month after the fateful event of early September that, in company with the fleet, the *Albion* picked up a mooring in the Medway. Here a short letter from Katherine awaited him:

it did nothing for his peace of mind, though it was clear that the house in Wapping was unaffected, as was Hannah's in neighbouring Stepney, from which Katherine wrote. Almost conversationally Katherine told him that among the buildings consumed by the great fire was the Trinity House, before proceeding to write a phrase that from the evidence of two deletions, she had had trouble formulating.

We are at a Loss, she wrote at the third attempt, *to Explain the Whereabouts of Your Wife or Brother-in-Law. Master Hargreaves says that Nathan was at the Warehouse then the Counting-House, from which he went Home on the Afternoon of the 2nd Instant. Enquiries of Molly have also Proved Useless.*

Dashing off a letter to inform Katherine and Hannah that he would be with them as soon as was possible, Faulkner fretted and fumed for a week while the *Albion* was decommissioned and laid up in the charge of her standing officers. One of these being the master, the necessity of finding a replacement for the dead Dixon delayed his departure.

In the days that Faulkner, assisted by his officers, tended his ship, sending her masts down and her guns ashore, it became known that there was little money to pay the seamen. The King's excesses had near ruined the Treasury, and what the King had not pilfered the fire had consumed, for all economic life in the city was at a standstill. In addition, the loss of credit from London had effectively compromised much trade elsewhere, while the destruction wrought by the flames had ruined markets, destroyed quantities of stock, and burned contracts, letters of credit and promissory notes.

Thus when he finally left his ship, Faulkner did so without a backward glance. Even the dinner he had given his officers had smelled of ashes, for anxiety was writ large on every face. In the last days of de-commissioning the men had been near-mutinous, and who could blame them? The following morning Faulkner took his leave of Clarke. The younger man looked pale and ill, his arm still in its sling. Faulkner thought of Katherine and how her ministrations had cured his own infected wound. He was on the point of offering to take Clarke to London and place him in her care, but Clarke gave him a wan smile and bade him farewell. A month later Faulkner heard that he was dead.

For his own part, Faulkner went directly to Hannah's house, to be met by her husband. Edmund's face looked drawn, but brightened when he saw who was at the door.

'Edmund! I had forgot you were home, forgive me.' They took each other's hands.

'I have not been here long, Sir Christopher, no more than a fortnight. The *Duchess* is safe on her mooring, and the voyage, though not without incident, has turned a merry profit.'

'A *merry* profit. Well, well, that at least is good news...'

He got no further; Katherine was in his arms, and Hannah hovered with his grandson, a fine boy who stood higher than his father's knee.

After the euphoria of greeting they sat in Hannah's neat parlour, supping fresh tea, and broached the two subjects that hung in the air.

'What of the fire?' Faulkner asked Edmund. 'Have you seen the Trinity House?'

Edmund nodded. 'Oh, yes. Most of the Brethren now in London have. Fortunately, the Clerk escaped with some at least of our papers, but much had been lost.' He shrugged resignedly, the awesome aftermath almost too great to express in words. 'It is as though we had just emerged from the Garden of Eden, innocent yet laden with sin, and all our work to do again.'

After a moment of profound silence, Faulkner enquired, 'Have you any news of Judith?'

Edmund shook his head, and Katherine did likewise. 'No, nothing, my dear,' she said. 'We did hear that Nathan had been seen; a chandler who knew him and had done business with him saw him after the fire in a wherry heading downstream.'

'Where was this?'

'Off Tower-wharf.'

'So he could have been heading home, or to the counting-house.'

'Yes, but young Charlie would have told us if he had done so, as we have asked him to keep us informed.'

'And nothing of Molly?'

'No.'

Faulkner was deeply troubled. His presentiment seemed increasingly possible. Nevertheless, he found the question difficult to frame. 'Might she have been caught and burned in the

315

fire?' he asked after a pause.

Katherine nodded. 'It is possible, indeed likely, if she went west when she left Wapping, although, thanks be to God, relatively few people are thought to have been consumed in the flames.'

Faulkner nodded and rose to his feet. 'I had better go to Wapping and see for myself.'

'Must you go now, Father?' Hannah asked. 'You have been travelling all day, and it is already growing dark. Go tomorrow.'

'Do, sir,' added Edmund.

Faulkner shook his head. 'No, 't'were better done now.'

'Then at least let me come with you,' Edmund volunteered.

Faulkner shook his head and put out a restraining hand. 'That will not be necessary, Edmund, though I thank you for your kindness. I shall be back in two hours.'

The house was unlocked, which surprised Faulkner, making him angry. Had Judith compounded her folly in leaving with imprudence by leaving the house unlocked? Then he stood in the gloom, reproaching himself. If she had deliberately left with no intention of returning, why should she lock the doors? He recalled giving the keys to Hannah, though he knew them to have been returned to Gooding when she married. Nevertheless, it was possible to perceive, in the act of leaving the door unlocked, some ulterior motive.

He looked about him, moving through the other rooms on the ground floor. Though things had been moved, this was consonant with daily life and nothing was obviously missing, which was unlikely in the circumstances, not least because the burnt-out homeless were desperate, many wandering the streets in despair.

There was something odd, though. He felt the kitchen hearth; it was cold but showed signs of recent use. He peered about him. The utensils in the kitchen hung from their hooks, but several had been left unwashed beside the sink and mould grew in some of them. There were the remains of some food, and dirty platters lay in the sink, which bore a line of grease where it had not been scoured after its last use. Indeed, there was a general air of squalor about the kitchen that was new. Leaving the kitchen he ascended to the first floor, initially entering the large room where he and Gooding had conducted their business. He opened the closed shutters to let the last of the daylight in. The degree of disorder among the papers on the table seemed normal. Pen, ink-well and sealing wax lay where a man might have laid them down. He removed his glove and wiped his finger over the table. A thick layer of dust covered it; no-one had been here for days, if not weeks.

Then he noticed that the light showed a slight rotational movement of one of the ledgers had scuffed the layer of dust. He peered at the book; it was not familiar. He realized that it was new. He searched for and found flint and steel. A moment later he had a lit candle and was holding it over the ledger. Opening it, it was instantly recognizable as their daily *Proceedings*. Cursing failing eye-sight he peered at the last entry. It bore the date of the previous day. Faulkner felt an uncomfortable sensation of foreboding. He ran his finger down the page; it bore only a few lines of script in Gooding's hand. Gooding's hand-writing showed signs of age, for it had once been a model of legibility, but the entry gave no clue, other than marking two ships entered inwards at the Custom House. He thought it incomplete, but that signified nothing, for the *Proceedings* book was inevitably retrospective, and often written up the next day. But the next day was nearly over.

Instinctively, Faulkner extinguished the candle and stood stock-still in the darkness, seized by the conviction that he was not alone in the house.

It was impossible to move across any floor in the house in silence, even in stockinged feet. In boots he must have announced his arrival as with a fanfare of trumpets, but he still moved as quietly as possible as he edged out to the stair leading to the upper chambers. He pushed open the door of Nathan's chamber. The room was empty and the bed was made. He found the same thing in Judith's, though it struck him that he could smell the scent of her. True, she had spent months and months there alone and must have impregnated every hanging with her odour, but still...

As he moved towards the upper staircase his right hand went for his sword, only to find that he had left it at Hannah's. Not that a sword was of much use to him in such a confined space, but he thought he knew where he might now find Judith, and he paused a moment to consider what he should do. She was undoubtedly aware of a presence in the house, but it was inconceivable that she actually knew it was him. On the other hand, if Gooding was right and she possessed the second sight, or had cast a spell to draw him hither, she would be awaiting him. If so, it was entirely possible that she remained afraid of his physical superiority, though he was inclined not to rely upon such a hunch. It seemed to him, in that lonely moment in the darkness at the foot of the upper stairs, that Judith had indeed lured him to the house alone, unarmed and unaware of her new powers.

Was the presentiment that he knew where she was no insight at all, but the very fabric of her witchery, binding him and inexorably attracting him to her? He felt his heart hammering and a feeling of incipient sickness fill his belly. This was unmanly; he was not himself; he must think clearly, for it struck him now that she wished to kill him. Drawing his breath steadily he calmed himself. What was he thinking of? He did not believe in supernatural powers; a cunning and malicious woman, yes, but that was all.

She was luring him upstairs, of that he was certain, but only by playing on logic and knowledge of her quarry. But if so, how did she know it was him and not some opportunist thief? He thought again and something occurred to him. Was it possible that Nathan had gone downstream, not to the counting-house, but to gain intelligence of the fleet? If so he was no longer trustworthy and Judith had him in her power, but if not, if she thought the intruder an opportunist thief, then whatever she had planned for her husband, she could equally apply to any man.

The process of thinking steadied him and he began to descend the stairs. She wanted him to go up, of that he was sure, so he would go down and sit in the parlour in the dark until she came to determine what had gone wrong – or to lock the door for the night. That she would wait in an upper room under the eaves all night was not consonant with Judith's character.

He retired to the parlour, relieved himself and sat, determined to draw Judith downstairs. He fretted that he had told Katherine and the others that he would be home in two hours. For some time he sat upright and alert, his every sense straining to catch any indication of movement in the house; from time to time he thought he heard something, or caught Judith's scent. As time passed, however, he felt weary; he had been up early, had travelled from Chatham and now found it difficult to keep his eyes open in the thickening darkness. He strove not to fall asleep as he waited upon events, but fell into a light doze from which he jerked awake, disturbed by a sudden noise.

His heart accelerated to a thumping so strong that he thought it would sound throughout the house like a drum. Anticipating a step upon the stair as a frustrated Judith descended to see what had gone awry with her plan – so had he argued the train of events that would ensue – he was confounded when he realized it was the lifting clink of the door-latch that had bestirred him. He felt relieved that his ordeal was over, but equally

320

annoyed that Edmund had come to look for him. He half rose from his chair until he realized that whoever was opening the door bore a sword, for the pale gleam of it preceded its bearer. It was followed by a figure he recognized instantly.

The Triangle

October 1666–May 1667

Faulkner was rooted to the spot, for the sword-bearer was none other than Nathan Gooding. It was clear that Faulkner's brother-in-law was in a high state of nervous tension, for his movements were furtive, he was muttering to himself under his breath and his entire being seemed intent upon watching the stairs. Without looking round, Gooding closed the door with his foot and it shut with a dull thud and a second clink of the door-latch. Faulkner, whose poor eyes had long become accustomed to the dark, could just discern Gooding's form. He watched as Gooding, holding the sword with some awkwardness, begin to ascend the stair. It came to Faulkner that Judith was indeed upstairs: she was not awaiting her husband, but her brother.

Judith lay in wait to entrap Nathan while he was intent on ... on what? Killing her? What else was the sword for?

And what should he, Faulkner, do? He sat perplexed for a moment, transfixed by Gooding's cautious ascent of the stairs. As his brother-in-law passed from sight on the lower landing Faulkner slowly rose to his feet. He was stiff with inaction and waited a moment for his circulation to restore itself, then he began to move across the flags of the parlour. The instant he set his foot upon the stair he heard Gooding, his voice so keyed up he thought for a moment he had made a terrible mistake in his identification.

'Who's there?'

Faulkner drew in his breath and ran up the stairs, spinning round the newel post at the top. He lunged across the landing. Gooding was already half-way up the attic staircase, his upper body half-turned to see who was behind him.

'Who's there?' Gooding's voice bordered the hysterical. 'Is that you, Kit?' In a flurry of desperation at this unexpected pursuit, Gooding threw a glance upwards and resumed his ascent, his feet clattering on the steps. All pretence at furtiveness had gone. With a cry of, 'Don't stop me!' Nathan rushed up the last of the stairs. Now all was noise and confusion.

Concentrating on not missing his footing as he thundered upwards in Gooding's wake, Faulkner did not see what happened, for when he reached the attic Gooding had vanished in the gloom. Faulkner heard a cry, followed by a screech and the sound of a struggle. Instinctively, Faulkner put his shoulder to the door to his own private room. Inside it was quite dark, but it was clear two bodies were wrestling on the floor.

The grunts, the thuds against the floor-boards

and the few sticks of furniture, the flurry of clothing and the harsh drag of heavy breathing told of the violence of the encounter.

'Stop it!' he commanded, but the struggle went on until, a few seconds later, there was a yelp of pain. Faulkner heard more than saw the sword strike the floor but he slammed his boot on the sword-blade's faint gleam, swiftly bent down and seized it. As he straightened up he was aware that Gooding had pulled back and was crouched whimpering in a corner; Judith lay at his feet, struggling to draw breath. Faulkner withdrew, shut the door and hurried down stairs. Finding flint and steel where he had left it, he struck a light, ignited a candle and reached for the sword again. There was blood on the blade, he noted as he made to return upstairs.

On the attic landing the door remained closed. Kicking it open he stood in the doorway and held up the candle-stick. Judith had drawn herself into the opposite corner and was still recovering her breath. Her eyes were closed and her pallor hinted at extreme nausea. She appeared unlikely to pose any threat, at least for a few moments, though Faulkner did not trust her one whit. A glance at Gooding showed him nursing a wounded hand. From the dark flow of blood Faulkner guessed it was deeply gashed; he was in a deal of pain.

'We must bind that up,' Faulkner said practically, but Gooding twisted his body away in a curiously childish movement. It was as if he deliberately denied Faulkner the chance of assisting him. 'Come, Nathan, we must staunch that bleeding.'

Gooding looked up, his expression at once angry and anguished, pain and fury distorting his smooth features in equal measure as the candle-light danced across his twisted features. 'No! Run that damned sword through her, for the love of God, Kit! Do it now! Now, before she casts another spell!'

'Don't talk nonsense,' Faulkner snapped, feeling a rising anger himself.

'I talk no nonsense. Why else are you here now, tonight of all nights, if not by incantation?'

'I am here by chance. I arrived from Chatham this afternoon. Now let us—'

'No, you came here because that *witch*–' Gooding spat the word in Judith's direction with a transcendent venom – 'enmeshed you by a spell in order that she could invoke Satan against a Godly justice.'

'You came to kill her?' Faulkner asked, abandoning his attempt to staunch Gooding's haemorrhage. 'You came to kill your own *sister*?'

Gooding nodded. 'Aye, I did. The Book of Exodus, Chapter Twenty-two, Verse Eighteen: "Thou shalt not suffer a witch to live."'

'Great God, Nathan, even if she were a witch she must first be condemned as one! It is not for you to take on the work of the executioner.'

'I would not have the disgrace upon my name.'

'Had you succeeded, the hangman would have seen to that,' Faulkner said shortly, casting a glance at Judith. Her eyes were open and she was staring at Faulkner.

'I should have followed Henry's example,'

324

Gooding said, adding, 'see, she wakes and fixes her eyes on you.' He chuckled, an other-worldly noise that made Faulkner's blood run cold as he looked from brother to sister and back again.

'He is mad, Husband. Quite mad.' Judith twisted round and drew her legs up, crossing her arms on her knees and putting her chin on her arms. 'He came here to murder me.'

'You are a witch,' Gooding repeated his accusation, then turned to Faulkner. 'Ask her whither she went on Sunday, September the second. Go on, ask her!'

'You are deranged.' Judith's voice was cool and measured. 'So what are you to do about this pleasant home-coming, Husband?'

A silence fell between the three of them. It crossed Faulkner's mind that he had formerly been close to both these people and yet he felt nothing towards them in that bleak moment.

'What is the significance of September...?'

'Why,' cried Gooding, interrupting, ''twas the night the fire started! *She* went into the city intent upon arson! *She* is the architect of all our troubles, the bitch of Satan!' Gooding was panting when he finished, the sheen of sweat across his face.

Faulkner turned to Judith. 'You had better answer his question,' he said.

'I went for a walk. Molly and I often went for walks. The rest of you were in ignorance of the fact, but that is what we did. That fool thinks I walked at night to consult the Devil. The fact that I went for a walk on the night in question was as much a coincidence as your arrival here now, Husband – though you might have made your intervention earlier.'

'Where is Molly?' he asked, ignoring her irony.

'Molly has a man. I let her go to him from time to time. Knowing Nathan would come tonight with murder in his heart...'

'You see!' Gooding screeched. 'She confesses! How could she know when I would come, still less how I came intending to put an end to her evil ways, if not by sorcery? Eh? Eh? Tell me that, Kit!'

'Because, you fool,' Judith said coldly, 'you said as much yourself, only this morning as you muttered and mumbled in the chamber below when you were making up your books. I heard you. 'Tis not I that am a witch but that you, brother, are losing your senses.'

The page of the ledger marked *Proceedings* and Gooding's muttering as he entered the house attested to the probability of Judith's evidence. Faulkner sighed. 'We had better go below and dress Nathan's hand,' he said flatly. 'Can you stand up?' Faulkner offered Gooding a hand, and Judith rose to her feet.

'Don't let her touch me!' Gooding cried.

'Be quiet, Nathan, you do your case no good.'

'She shall not touch me, she shall not touch me...' Gooding repeatedly muttered to himself as he waved aside any assistance and struggled to his feet. The bleeding on his clenched hand seemed to have eased.

They were in the act of coming down stairs when a loud knocking was heard at the door. Gooding, who led the way, stopped abruptly, then swung round to stare at Faulkner, his eyes wild. Behind him Faulkner urged him to continue, and a moment later Faulkner opened the door to Edmund Drinkwater; behind him, wrapped in a cloak, stood Katherine.

'We were concerned about you,' he said, looking at the three of them, his mouth open, his face incredulous. It struck Faulkner that what Edmund and Katherine saw was incriminating: Gooding was injured, and he, Faulkner, held a sword. 'Well,' Edmund said, 'I see you have found your wife.' He raised an interrogative eyebrow.

'It was necessary that I disarmed Nathan here,' Faulkner explained, his voice flat, his eyes on Katherine's. 'He is out of his mind and attacked his sister.'

'She is a witch, a witch...' Gooding banged his wounded right hand on the table for emphasis, opening the wound with a cry and falling into the chair so lately occupied by Faulkner.

'I will start a fire,' Judith said, adding, 'let us have more light. Perhaps Captain Drinkwater might bring some sea-coal in from the yard.' She threw a glance at Katherine and bent to the hearth.

'Don't do it, Edmund,' Gooding urged through clenched teeth. 'She is bewitching you...'

'Hold your tongue, Nathan. You have done enough damage for one night,' Faulkner ordered.

It was late by the time Gooding's wound had been dressed and he had been put in his own bed. Molly had returned to find the house bewilderingly full and lights burning everywhere; she had made herself useful warming Gooding's bed, but Faulkner found her appearance grubbier than ever. From the mode of her address to Judith it was clear that since his own absence and the removing of Katherine to Hannah's house, the relationship between the two women had changed. Molly had become more of a companion and confidante, adding credibility to Judith's revelation that they had both gone on nocturnal walks. Such things were not easily accomplished after dark, and a degree of close complicity would have been necessary. It was entirely in character that Molly would have neglected her household duties in proportion, and he recalled the mould in the unwashed kitchen utensils, the general squalid air of the kitchen and the thick layer of dust on the upper chamber table.

Such neglect would have annoyed and perhaps cumulatively unhinged the increasingly unstable but fastidious Gooding, Faulkner thought sadly as he left the poor man in his bed and returned to the parlour.

Edmund had found some wine and was pouring it into four beakers. He was alone. 'Some wine, Sir Christopher?'

'Where are...?' He got no further; Edmund indicated with a jerk of his head that the women were in the kitchen.

Faulkner went to the door, moved along the short passage and peered in. Two lanterns had been lit and placed upon the large kitchen table. Their light disguised the lack of cleanliness, but it was the three women who gave the domestic scene its air of normality. They worked in complete silence. Molly was fanning a crackling fire beneath the griddle, Judith was beating eggs and Katherine was cutting and buttering bread.

Faulkner went back and joined Edmund. They sat a moment in silence, and then Edmund asked, 'And what will you do now?'

'I don't know. Nathan is, indeed, out of his mind. 'Tis a pity, for he was a good man and a solid partner. I trusted him implicitly in affairs of business.'

'You have clerks of competence. Can you not bring one of them on?'

Faulkner shrugged. 'Perhaps. But I must first look to Nathan. He may get better in time.'

'I doubt it. He is an old Puritan. Their world has passed, and the present drives them to desperation.'

'That is equally true of his sister.'

'Yes, Hannah has told me of her mother's creed.'

'And what about you?'

'Me? Why, I have a ship to command.'

'You could come ashore; you have made enough of a fortune to become a ship's husband. I have a conceit to build another Indiaman and I should name her for Katherine.'

'After your...' Edmund lowered his voice and flushed. 'I beg your pardon, Sir Christopher, I did not mean anything disrespectful.'

Faulkner waved aside his son-in-law's apology. 'She is my mistress, but also the love of my life. I married Hannah's mother thinking that Katherine was beyond my reach. She was a kinswoman to the ill-fated Duke of Buckingham.

Before Felton's knife robbed him of his life, no man stood higher in the King's favour, nor wielded greater influence. She might have been a Duchess now.'

'She is a remarkable woman,' Edmund said, 'and Hannah is very fond of her.'

'That pleases me, but–' he made a gesture of deprecation – 'I have a wife.'

'It is ironic, but had you not ventured here tonight, you might not have done.'

Faulkner looked at his son-in-law and nodded. 'I have enough on my conscience not to lay that speculation upon it.'

'Katherine is part of your household. If your wife—'

'My dear Edmund, the happiness of hundreds of thousands of men and women would be agreeably enhanced *if*. But, alas, *if* is just wishful thinking.'

They committed Nathan Gooding to Bethlem Hospital. He remained obdurate, convinced his sister was a witch, and he might have been believed had he not constantly compromised his accusations by his own behaviour. The slow degeneration that had begun by that bout of drunkenness had created such a sense of self-loathing, engendered though it was by the way-ward behaviour of his sister and the suicide of his nephew, that it nevertheless consumed him utterly. Before a month was out his ravings had him chained to the wall, and he became a popu-lar object of curiosity to those minded to spend a leisurely hour in the company of the insane.

On the afternoon that Faulkner had taken Gooding into the custody of the hospital, he returned home to Wapping.

Judith was awaiting him. 'So,' she said, 'he is gone.'

'No, Judith, he is not gone; he is in Bethlem Hospital near Moorfields, a pathetic and broken man. You cannot dismiss him so easily, for not only was he your own brother, but your conduct made him what he became.'

Surprisingly, Judith remained silent. After a while she said: 'I did what I believed in. There is no sin in that.'

'Not in itself, perhaps, but in its consequences much wrong was done. Oh–' he held up his hand – 'I take responsibility myself, do not fear. And for you. How was I to know that the tranquillity of our lives was to be disrupted by civil war and in the ensuing turmoil I should again encounter Katherine, or that the fire should be so fierce?'

They both became lost in their own thoughts. There were tears in Judith's eyes, and Faulkner said, 'I shall never forget your coming to me in The Tower.'

She nodded and cleared her throat. 'Is that why you did not do what my brother so clumsily attempted when you had his sword in your hand? You might so easily have taken my life for...' She began to sob and fell forward on her knees, staring up at him, the tears coursing down her face. With a tremendous effort she spat out the words, as though determined to void the thought from her system: 'Taken my life ... for Henry's?'

He regarded her with suspicion. She still

possessed the power to attract, and in this posture of submissive helplessness he perceived the dangers of misplaced sympathy. He shook his head in denial, embarrassed at her abasement. Gesturing Judith to get up, he handed her a handkerchief which he pulled from his sleeve. 'Come, Judith, this is no answer. What is done is done, you know that.'

Again silence fell between them. Faulkner's patience was running thin. He felt the awkwardness of his own position acutely and wished himself for the solution suggested by those speculative *ifs*. She must have divined something of this, for she asked: 'We are none of us any longer young. What shall become of us?'

'What would you have become of us?' Faulkner asked. He hesitated a moment and then threw caution to the winds. 'You are not without means,' he went on before she could prevent him embarking on the logic of separation, 'for I have never argued, as the law does, that you should not have property. Your shares in Lorimer's *Mary* and the other vessels would make you a woman of independence. I would see that you lived free of encumbrance...'

'By putting me in your alms-houses in Deptford?'

'Of course not! Why would I do a thing like that? Besides, the Brethren would determine you had no need of such charity. No, we could find you somewhere pleasant enough to live with Molly, after which we could arrange an estrangement.'

'Or I could turn a blind eye like the cuckolded

fools that surrender their wives to the Royal bed and accept a title in return. What would my title be, Husband? *You* cannot make me Duchess of anything – but you could give up your whore!'

'She must live somewhere too,' he said quietly, ignoring Judith's outburst.

'But not here! Not under my roof!'

Faulkner regarded Judith for some time. She met his gaze with steady eyes, as determined as ever. The brief hope that had kindled in his foolish heart when he had seen her and Katherine working in such apparent amity in the kitchen that night had been, he now realized, nothing more than an illusion. Judith might have been affected by the events of that night, but she had had no Damascene moment and was, as he supposed he was himself, still herself.

They were, as Judith had pointed out, none of them any longer young. Whatever motive Judith had had for reminding him that he might forsake Katherine's bed, it had no effect upon Faulkner. In the weeks that followed he strove to recover his business and introduce Edmund into its complexities. They received generous and enthusiastic help from a surprising quarter. Under their noses Charlie Hargreaves had matured and grown in intellectual and physical stature. When Faulkner summoned his head-clerk and offered him a rise in pay and the prospect of an offer of partnership if all went well, the old man shook his head.

'Ten years ago, I would have thanked you for it, sir, but my eyes are failing. While I can sit at my desk in your interest, Sir Christopher, I shall do so and that as diligently as I may be capable of so doing. As for a new partner, for that is what you need in the...' The old man coughed with a deferential distaste. 'In the, er, absence of Master Gooding, I should recommend young Hargreaves. He will need a year, to be sure, but I can see to that, for an increase in my emolument, of course. I do not think that you will be disappointed. He is an active and able young fellow, though his elevation will doubtless annoy others in the counting-house. But I should not trouble myself over them, Sir Christopher; not if I were you, that is.'

By the spring, with the change of the year, the shipping enterprise established by Faulkner and Gooding entered a new phase. Captain Edmund Drinkwater became the new ship's husband and with his father-in-law negotiated a new contract at Blackwall. By May 1667 a new East Indiaman had been laid down, and while Faulkner left the ship's supervision to Edmund, he took particular interest in the carving of her figurehead, for it was soon known that the ship was to be called the *Katherine Villiers*.

'I would it were *Lady Katherine* and that you were my lawful wedded wife,' he said to Katherine one evening as they sat in Hannah's new withdrawing room. She looked up from her needle-work, her eyes still lustrous, her face as beautiful as ever to his old eyes.

'La, sir,' she said mockingly, 'I hear marriage is vastly over-rated at the Court and held to be of little account. I should not trouble yourself on

334

the matter.'

'But I do. I am being serious Kate. I am grown old and increasingly helpless.'

She laid aside her point-work to kneel beside him. Taking his hands in hers, she rubbed their backs with her thumbs. 'You are not old, my love, not to me. Do you not think that following all the tribulations of my life, all the changes of fortune that I have seen in others and undergone myself, I give a fig for the forms that so often bind men and women in fetters stronger and more repulsive than steel. I understand that you cannot abandon Judith; you would not be the man whom I adore had you done so. I am content; it is you who is not.'

He looked at her, his heart full. He found it difficult to speak for a moment, and she smiled as she saw his eyes fill with tears. He smiled back and gave a mighty sniff. 'The fire of love is unassuaged, my dearest,' he said, bending towards her.

'That,' she breathed in his ear, 'is as it should be.'

Disaster and Disgrace

June 1667

While youth considers itself eternal and maturity recognizes mortality, old age trembles in fear of death. While youth embraces change, and maturity knows it for the chimera it is, old age fears it and seeks its days of constant quietude. In those months, though Judith remained in the house at Wapping and he and Katherine were a burden upon an uncomplaining Edmund and Hannah, Faulkner sought his own days of restful idleness, pottering about the garden with his grandchildren – Hannah and Edmund had added a second boy to their first. True, he called regularly at the counting-house and made his forays to Blackwall to watch the *Katherine Villiers* rising on the stocks, but these were leisurely in their character. In the summer, he had promised Edmund, they would take a sea-cruise down to Harwich in the *Hawk*. Old Toshack was dead, but Faulkner thought himself fit enough to command the little ship and relished the prospect. At Edmund's suggestion, early in June, he and Faulkner had gone to look over the *Hawk*, to survey the repairs they had put in hand and admire the repainting undertaken by Shish's yard at Rotherhithe. As they stood in the sunshine,

Faulkner was delighted at the *Hawk*'s handsome appearance, congratulating himself on his wise purchase all those years earlier. Beside him, Edmund was full of admiration for the little vessel that had been matched against those of the King and a Prince of the blood.

'I suppose we must now follow the fashion and call her a yacht,' he remarked.

Faulkner grunted. 'That's a damned Dutchman's description,' he grumbled.

Their business done, Mister Shish had been called away; the two men lingered, idly regarding the movements of boats, barges and vessels in the river. A fresh north-easterly breeze lifted the flags and pendants of several vessels moored in the stream. They watched with professional interest as a collier worked her way up, through the press of shipping. The direction of the breeze and Edmund's remark touched an instinctual response in Faulkner, making him think of the Dutch and the risk of de Ruyter putting to sea; he felt a quickening heartbeat before recalling that the war was as good as over and he could rest easy. Thank God the King's ministers were conferring in Breda with a view to ending the bloody and expensive conflict between the two rival Protestant states. Not that the present condition of the Navy would admit further fighting, by God!

Since its triumphs the previous year, lack of money had resulted in few proper repairs of battle-damage being under-taken, the ships being virtually abandoned at their moorings off Chatham in the River Medway, exactly as their crews had left them. Almost none had been taken into the dock-yard where work had all but ceased and he had heard by word of mouth at the Trinity House that Pett, the Dockyard Commissioner, was being deliberately dilatory in bringing the *Royal Charles* upstream for repairs. Faulkner chuckled to himself: the Trinity Brethren did not like the Petts, regarding the whole pack of them as troublesome, ill-informed and, worst of all, busybodies, whose interference with their own advice to the Admiralty was an outrage.

Such arguments were amusing enough and should not be taken too seriously, Faulkner mused, but if the neglect of the ships was a cause for concern then that of the seamen was a far worse and more consequential one. Matters stood as badly as they had years earlier, long before the Civil War, when Faulkner had been in the employ of Sir Henry Mainwaring and the dockyard labourers and craftsmen had laid down their tools. It was rumoured, or so Faulkner had again heard at the Trinity House, that large numbers of seamen had offered their services to the Dutch, a horror he did not dare think about. Young Sam Pepys had mentioned it, railing against the practice of paying the seamen off after service with promissory notes instead of hard cash. Once again, as in the bad days of the King's father and grand-father, and even on occasion in those of Oliver, when the men presented their 'tickets' the authorities declined to pay them, pointing to the ravages of the great fire, the dearth of trade and the consequent loss of this most essential mother of wages. Such events undoubtedly had their effect, but the obvious and licentious excesses of the Court seemed equally to blame. No belt-tightening was in evidence in that quarter.

In desperation the seamen who had so lately beaten off a determined enemy were driven to seek out usurers and sell their tickets at a shameful discount. Treated thus, it was hardly surprising that many took boats and slipped out of the country; some of them would make good pilots, if the Dutch or the French decided to send a force against London and its river.

These were sombre thoughts for a lovely, early summer day. He looked at Edmund, who appeared happy and content as he watched the collier take the bend in the river with a half-smile of appreciation on his face. Faulkner consoled himself. What was the Navy to him now? Though he still held his commission, he would never serve at sea again for he was far too old. Besides, the future lay with the merchant shipping moving in the river; and they operated without the interference of the Lords of the Admiralty, aye, and turned in a handsome profit for their owners.

'At what do you laugh?' Edmund asked.

Faulkner was unaware that the cheering thought had so altered his mood. 'Oh, I was just thinking of these ships out here, yours and mine, and the vessels of others of our acquaintance.'

'And what of them?'

'Why, that they are of vastly more value to the lives of men and women than are the King's men-of-war.'

'Well, that is generally true, but consider the necessity of the man-of-war to the fleet of richly laden Indiamen cowering under the cliffs of the Wight awaiting convoy up-Channel for fear of the Dutch – or the French for that matter. Under such circumstances a man-of-war is a welcome sight and one would gladly pay for her comforting presence.'

'Ah, but you talk of war...'

'But we are still at war, Sir Christopher. Peace has not yet been signed.'

'Pah! It will be, it will be. Come, let us go home. Hannah promised some of last year's honey.'

Heading for Stepney they fell into step, Edmund matching his own long stride to the less active movements of his father-in-law. Conversation had drifted away from the new ship and the proposed cruise in the *Hawk*. In consideration of his age, Faulkner had intended speaking to Edmund about the future but in doing so their talk brought a remembrance of Nathaniel to mind.

'I never really mourned him,' Faulkner confessed. 'The death of Henry by his own hand loomed large, and Nathaniel's own end, being a distant event and a hazard of seafaring, seemed both final and yet incomprehensible. I did not bury him.' He paused and then went on in a lower tone of voice, 'I am still persuaded that some day I will hear of his arrival in the river and find him smiling on my threshold.' He threw up his head and caught Edmund's eye. 'Huh! How the old deceive themselves and allow their minds to play tricks upon them.'

'Hannah speaks of him often,' Edmund offered. 'She was very fond of him.'

'Hannah is a good woman. Perhaps, had life and her husband treated her better, Judith would have been like her.' He sighed. 'I have been a great sinner, Edmund ... Edmund? What is it?'

Edmund had stopped, and his head was cocked, as if listening to something, something faint and far away. 'Do you not hear it?' he said, his right index-finger halfway to his lips.

'Hear it? Hear what? All I can hear is a damned ringing in my ears!'

'Shush! There it is again. Surely you can hear it now?'

Faulkner shook his head, and then he thought he caught something, something borne on the fresh wind very like the faint rumbling of distant thunder. 'Gunfire,' he said, his voice low. 'Gunfire off Harwich or in the Wallett. By God, Edmund, the Dutch are at sea!'

The two men stood still, taking stock. 'Thank God the *Duchess* is on her mooring,' Edmund said.

Faulkner nodded, but his face wore an expression of concern. 'But the *Martha*, the *Speedwell* and the *Concord* are all at sea, and the *Judith* is expected daily. We thought ... no, *I* thought there would be no further hostilities!'

'They are not yet lost to the enemy, Sir Christopher,' Edmund said. 'Let us wait upon events, at least in respect of the ships at sea. I shall go to the counting-house; we must at least prevent anyone sailing, and we have two agency vessels almost complete in their lading.'

'Do you do that, Edmund, and I must to the Trinity House.'

The two men separated, agreeing to meet at Stepney that evening with as much news as each could glean. Instead of Water Lane, where lay the blackened ruins of the Trinity House, Faulkner hurried to Ratcliffe, where the Brethren had temporarily installed their Secretary and Ballast Clerks in leased premises. He found the place a-buzz with excitement, news just having come in that a Dutch squadron had been sighted from the Naze of Essex. He sought the familiar face of Brian Harrison until he recalled that Harrison had died. Among the score or so of milling Brethren John Prowd caught his eye; they had become acquainted after Harrison had introduced them and now Prowd was their Deputy Master.

'They are probably after the new men-of-war Sir Anthony Deane has under construction at Harwich,' Prowd said to Faulkner. 'The *Rupert* is already fitted-out, I hear.' He showed Faulkner a letter he had clearly only just received.

'But I thought the King's ministers were negotiating at Breda,' Faulkner said, frowning.

'They are saying that the King, so pleased with the late actions of the fleet, has placed too high a price of peace. As for the Dutch, who would blame them for not conceding? Our last victory was a narrow one, they out-fought us for four days, and after Holmes burnt those merchantmen off Vlieland, why would they not regret agreeing to negotiate in the face of the King's demands?

Damnation, Sir Kit, their best negotiator is de Ruyter and his fleet!'

'I wish I found reason to argue against you, John,' Faulkner conceded hopelessly. 'This could be a bloody business with our own fleet laid up in the Medway.'

Prowd's eyes widened. 'Why of course! That's it!' Prowd drove his right fist into his left palm to emphasize his conviction. 'They'll make for Chatham and requite Holmes's Bonfire with one of their own, by God!'

Faulkner needed no time to consider the accuracy of this prediction. 'You are right! By God, a descent in force on the Medway would be an unmitigated disaster!'

The realization of this seemed simultaneous, passing like dry wind through grass. In an instant 'the Medway' was on the lips of the entire assembly of old sea-officers.

'There is no doubt but that we must attend to our duty, Sir Kit,' said Prowd, assuming his office and calling them all to order. 'In the absence of Admiral Penn, our Master,' he said formally, 'I must request that you recall your obligation to serve. If the Dutch land, then the King will take up all his subjects' properties that may be seen to save the Kingdom. I need not remind you that, as for us this day, it seems that our chief task must be to arm those ships that lie within our compass in the Pool. Mr Pepys has sent word that he and Sir William Batten have gone to Deptford to meet Admiral Penn. They are preparing fire-ships and we might with advantage send any such suitable vessel thither for conversion. There is no general summons, Brethren, so I advise all those of you not immediately employed to go home, make what preparations you need and to hold yourselves available for sea-service according to your oaths.'

Prowd ended his oration by naming half a dozen Brethren required to assist immediately while the others made their way to the street. Faulkner shook hands with several of his colleagues. 'And I had thought us too old for all these alarums,' Faulkner remarked with a grim smile.

'One is never too old to defend one's country,' someone responded as a score of weather-beaten old seamen stepped out into the Highway.

'There's an odd comfort in that,' Faulkner murmured to himself, pulling his hat down hard. 'But I don't like that damned wind.'

He was hardly inside the door of the Drink-waters' house when Katherine approached, her eyes alight with alarm. For a moment Faulkner thought it was something about Judith, for she could know nothing about the news of the Dutch, and a quick enquiry revealed that Edmund had not yet come home. However, the letter Katherine pressed into his hand came from an unexpected quarter.

'You know the contents of this?' he asked, hunting round for his new-fangled spectacles.

She nodded. 'Yes, the bearer was Albemarle's man. He was quite open about it: the Dutch are out.'

'I have heard the same thing.'

'The King, it appears, places the Kingdom in the Duke's hands.'

'Well, he could do no better.' Faulkner found his spectacles, settled them on his nose and scrutinized Albemarle's letter. It appeared to be in the Duke's own hand and the haste and ferocity of the writer's sentiments showed in the urgent angular scrawl. Albemarle's pen nib had torn at the paper, thrown small drops of ink ahead of the words, like the thoughts that must have been tumbling out of the old admiral's head as he summoned help.

Sir Christopher, it read,

Rec'd this day a Report that D'Ruyter is at sea with upwards three score of Sail. Do you repair at once to Chatham with whatever Men you may Muster. Our Fleet is in the gravest Danger. I must leave Powder and Shot to your judgement, likewise Small Arms. I rely upon Y'r Diligence.

Albemarle.

'What can I do?' Katherine asked, and Faulkner requested she pack his necessaries.

'I shall look to my weapons and money.' He gave up a few moments to gathering his wits.

Hannah came into the room. 'Katherine has told me; you will need some food before you go.'

'Bless you, Hannah ... Ah! There is Edmund returned.'

The younger man strode into the room. 'There is a summons out for all available barges to work down to the Lower Hope. They are intending to

345

throw a bridge over the river for the passage of troops.'

'What troops?'

'The trained bands are called out on pain of death for failing to muster.'

'Huh! They will be as useless as they were in Elizabeth's day,' Faulkner said contemptuously. He handed Edmund Albemarle's letter.

Edmund cast his eyes over it; looking up he said, 'I shall come with you.'

'No, Edmund, I cannot allow that.'

'Who else can you muster?' Edmund asked drily. 'Six clerks, a few bargemen, a score of watermen and a lumper and ballastmen or two. Come, sir, judging from His Grace's tone there is little time. I'll organize horses, Kate will help you muster what small arms and personal effects we shall require while Hannah will provide us with some pies, some wine and any other tit-bits she may shake up – maybe some honey!'

'The women-folk of this house have anticipated you, Edmund,' Katherine said, coming back into the room to ask something of Faulkner, who was unable to repress a smile, in spite of the seriousness of the hour.

'I must gather my effects,' Edmund said, leaving the room.

Katherine and Faulkner exchanged glances. 'The enthusiasm of the young for war,' Faulkner remarked, shaking his head.

''Tis what takes our best, both in blood and character,' she said, her eyes tearful. 'Hannah will not like it if Edmund goes.'

'I would rather Edmund remained here. God

knows how this affair will turn out if it is left to the trained bands to defend us.'

'But my Lords Oxford, Douglass and Albemarle himself all have standing troops under their command...'

'But they need to be in the correct place at the correct time, Kate. That is why this country is best defended at sea...' He paused. Advancing such arguments at such a time was a fruitless occupation when there was much to be done. Nevertheless, it seemed impossible to leave Katherine for a moment, for neither wished for another separation. Faulkner sighed. 'I'm told the King extended his demands at Breda.'

'Where the Peace terms were being discussed?'

'Aye. It seems the Dutch lost patience.' He lowered his voice. 'What is *wrong* with the Princes of the House of Stuart, Kate?'

She shook her head. 'Vain and silly,' she said, as if discussing children. 'Both Princes *and* Princesses.'

He took her in his arms. 'God help us,' he murmured against the fragrance of her hair, feeling the fierce clutch of her embrace. 'Alas, though I wish this moment never to end, I must go.'

'You must promise to take care of yourself,' she said, pulling away from him and looking him straight in the eye. 'Promise me you will take no foolish risks. I could not bear to lose you now, when we have the prospect of some peaceful years ahead of us.'

Faulkner smiled down at her. She seemed to him as lovely as she had the day he had first set eyes upon her, and he told her so.

She pulled away from him, making a face. 'Don't be an old fool. You don't have your spectacles upon your nose. You might look at a melon and think it me without them.'

'Bah! Nonsense!'

She gripped him firmly by the upper arms and stared at him, her eyes as fierce as a falcon's. 'You have not promised.'

'How can I promise and mean what I say? The vicissitudes of life are not such that I—'

'Promise me you will take every care, every precaution; that you will not hazard your person for honour or whatever folly tempts you ... *Promise me!*'

'Very well, I promise you.'

If Faulkner's ride to Oxford was bad, that to Chatham was worse. Edmund's horse cast its first shoe shortly after they had crossed the Thames at London Bridge and the second before they were half-way to Maidstone, where they intended crossing the River Medway. On the second occasion the delay in first finding and then knocking up a blacksmith cost them dear, for the hour was late. They reached Maidstone at dawn and broke their fast, giving their mounts and themselves two hours' rest before pressing-on. The inn was full of people on the move and full too of news, some of which seemed incredible.

The Dutch had burned Harwich. The Dutch were in the Thames. The Dutch were attacking Sheerness. The Dutch had captured Sheerness and were already in the Medway. Chatham was under siege and expected to fall at any moment. The banks had shut their doors. There was daylight robbery on every highway. The King had fled London, and all depended upon Honest George Monck.

Faulkner listened to this flood of hysteria, attempting the impossible task of sifting its reliability. What seemed plausible when uttered by one sounded ridiculous when stated by another. What was one to make of it all? Edmund expressed himself equally confused as they fought their way into the inn parlour and ordered oatmeal and eggs.

'You'll have to wait, gennelmen,' they were told, to which they wearily acquiesced. Faulkner threw his hat on a table, took off his sword and baldric and contemplated removing his boots, but decided against it. The bother of putting them on again dissuaded him. Instead he leaned back and called for a pipe of tobacco.

'I do not often take the weed nowadays,' he said conversationally, easing his sore arse, 'though I used to habitually when in Holland.' They sat listening to the uproar all about them. Occasionally, someone would sit suddenly beside them and deliver some item of news which, or so they claimed, they had had from a man on the Dover Road who had seen it for himself. As abruptly as they had come, they would be gone, eager to spread the gloom to another group of travellers. A woman was led in screeching with fear, crying out for her daughters' safety in the face of a rapacious soldiery. The daughters, who followed in her wake, seemed both confused and too young to excite the most brutal Dutchman, while the husband – and presumably the father – consoled his wife while exchanging looks of embarrassment with the men looking on, inviting their solicitude for his circumstances.

'What would *you* do?' Edmund suddenly asked, leaning forward across the table.

'Me? Why, what do you mean?'

'I mean, what would you do if you were de Ruyter?'

Faulkner shrugged. 'Why, there is little argument against a direct attack upon the Medway. All our power lies there so, destroy that and you have rendered the Kingdom impotent. By the time we have mustered another fleet, and we have the ships, it will be too late, for a want of seamen would prejudice it.'

'Just the Medway, Sir Christopher?' asked Edmund insistently. 'Tell me why, with sixty men-of-war, would you not also poke your snout into the River of Thames?' He paused before running on. 'You fight fire with fire, except that the fire you bring to your enemy is larger, burns fiercer and has more effect than that which he brought to you. Holmes burned your merchant shipping off Vlie; why not return the compliment and add the King's ships to your own bonfire? Why would de Ruyter, with sixty odd ships and a nor'-easterly at his back, not carry the flood up the Thames and burn our merchant shipping with half his fleet whilst at the same time sending the other half into the Medway? The latter has a fort at Sheerness; the Thames has a few guns at Tilbury...'

Faulkner had slowly sat up as Edmund delivered himself of his argument and at this point
brought a fist crashing down on the table. 'You
are right, Edmund!'

'If they get into the Thames...'

'The *Duchess*...'

'And the other ships! We must part company.
Do you ride directly to Gravesend. Take a boat
upstream and, if necessary, move the *Duchess*
further upstream.'

'And if I find the Dutch already at Gravesend?'

'Ride on to Deptford.'

'Very well. But breakfast first, for the horses
deserve a rest.'

Faulkner reached Rochester alone late that
evening. He had suffered further delay by his
horse going lame, and he soundly cursed the
livery stable whence Edmund had hired the two
mounts. If he had had his own horses, even his
own coach, none of this would have happened,
but he would have been several hundred pounds
the poorer.

Finding a remount took two hours, for the
stream of fleeing gentry choked the roads, not to
mention the inn-yards. The chorus of gloom and
doom increased at every halt so that, half-dead
with exhaustion, his arse as sore as he ever
recollected it to be on the Oxford ride, he decided to put up in the town for the night. If he was
at neighbouring Chatham, Albemarle must wait
for the morrow. Calling for food Faulkner
supped, pulled off his boots and outer garments
and lay down on a hard bed in a flea-ridden

chamber which promised him little more than a miserable night.

He woke to hear a church-bell strike one. No other noise could be heard beyond the scratching of mice behind the skirting board, even when he concentrated, trying to suppress the tinnitus in his ears. He lay back and fell into an uneasy sleep, his back sore and his arse red-raw. The light of dawn peeped through the shutters when he next awoke. The day was still young, for it was early June, but he could hear a noise now and he knew it for what it was: gunfire. A second later there came a louder detonation, as of a great explosion.

A sudden and uncharacteristic panic filled his belly. He was too late! Albemarle had charged him to raise men, to muster powder and shot aboard the *Albion*, and here he was lying in a bed with a stinking mattress in Rochester. He washed, shaved and dressed hurriedly, waving aside offers of breakfast, only insisting that an ostler be chivvied to prepare his horse. An hour later he was in Chatham, asking for the Duke of Albemarle.

He found the Duke on horseback, a little below the dockyard at Chatham on a low ridge of rising ground overlooking the estuary of the Medway. He was furiously waving a cane and cursing with all the ripe vocabulary of the army subaltern he had once been. A small suite, consisting largely of over-dressed and fashionable cavaliers, followed him up and down as he cast a furious gaze over the wide expanse of tidal water that was part uncovered mud-flat and part navigable channel. Galloping up to Albemarle, Faulkner saluted him. The Duke reined in his charger and Faulkner pulled up alongside him.

'No dispatches for me this time, eh, Sir Kit?' Albemarle asked bitterly as he chewed a quid of tobacco with a vigour eloquent of his inner feelings.

'None, Your Grace. Nor men, nor powder, nor shot, I fear.'

'Just two old men on their horses, by God!' It was clear Albemarle was furious, a mood reflected by his horse, which shook its head with a jingle of harness, champed at its bit and threw flecks of foam flying. 'See there!' Albemarle pointed with his cane. In the distance Faulkner could see a press of sails beyond which a pall of smoke hung over distant Sheerness. 'They have broken the boom and attacked the fort, God damn it! If they force the block-ships, the whole river is theirs!' He waved his cane across the sweep of land below them. 'I dare not take my guardsmen downstream and reinforce the fort at Sheerness, for fear the Dutch will attack Chatham and get among the ships there.' He pointed to the twin trots of moorings that extended down the Medway where most of the line-of-battle-ships of the English fleet lay. 'Laid-up in ordinary', the phrase had it, but it signified only that they were disarmed and all but defenceless.

'My God, but we have *buggered* ourselves and no mistake,' the old man swore, his face em-purpled with rage. He turned his head, surveyed his suite and ejected a squirt of tobacco juice. '*They* are no God-damned use except to be killed,' he said, referring to the young men, several of whom regarded the Duke's expectoration with affected disgust. 'Look at them,' Albemarle said confidentially, 'milksops the lot of them.' He waved his hand along the river bank. 'Where are the guns the King's council ordered along the river to defend the dockyard, eh?' Having delivered himself of his outburst, Albemarle returned to the present. 'Douglas and Middleton are on their way, but I know not when they will arrive. Did you see anything of their troops upon the road?'

'No, Your Grace.'

'No ... And Oxford has gone up to Harwich with two regiments in the hope of mustering the trained bands at Colchester. By the time he gets there, all the damage will be done *here*!' Albemarle pointed his cane to the long line of men-of-war laid-up in twos-and-threes at the heavy mooring buoys, the *Albion* and Albemarle's old flag-ship the *Royal Charles* among them. 'I rue the day that I allowed the King to acquiesce to the laying up of the fleet as others advised, but such was the lack of money—' Albemarle broke off his confession before flinging the accusations elsewhere. 'That scoundrel Pett should have had the flag-ship in the dockyard long since, but there they lie, with hardly a round of cartridge and ball between them. By heaven he should hang for his negligence!'

Faulkner attempted to quieten his own steed which he felt increasingly nervous alongside Albemarle's excited charger. The thought of getting off his horse's back led him to suggest to

Albemarle that he should get a boat and try and organize a defence.

'I have already sent others to attend the matter. No, do you hold yourself here, with me. When Douglas and Middleton arrive with men and artillery, I shall decide whether to move in support of Sheerness. In the meantime I shall remain close to my boys, who shall remain where they are, down there.'

Faulkner could see infantrymen loosely formed on the low land he knew as St Mary's Island, linked by a bridge of boats to the mainland. His 'boys' were Albemarle's old regiment, with which seven years earlier he had marched south to hold London – and hence England – for a restored monarch. Like Oxford's Regiment of Horse, Albemarle's troops were now among the King's guards.

'My Coldstreamers will decide the fate of Chatham and possibly, once again, the whole damned Kingdom. I've thrown half of them into Upnor Castle yonder.' Albemarle pointed to the grey battlements opposite them on the north bank. 'And while I fear for the shipping in the river,' he went on, pointing again at the moored men-of-war, 'I fear more for the dockyard.' He paused, looked round then said: 'I've posted the gallopers down there,' he said, referring to four light field-guns attached to his guards, 'no more than mere peashooters, damn it, and no match for the Dutchmen's artillery, but, if Douglas comes in time, we might trap de Ruyter by closing the river against him at Sheerness...'

Both men transferred their attention to the east.

'I ordered block-ships sunk in the channel but they forced the boom at first light.'

'I heard the explosion in Rochester.'

'It will depend upon their luck in the channel. They have the flood tide to help them, but perhaps the block-ships ... Well, it was all I could do! Damn de Ruyter and his Dutchmen!'

Something occurred to Faulkner. 'Where is His Highness, Your Grace?'

'Rupert? I'm damned if I know, though he was supposed to be establishing a battery at Woolwich.' Albemarle lowered his voice. 'I cannot think Rupert is hunting the moth with My Lady Cleveland like his Royal Cousin.'

Despite himself, Faulkner smiled. 'Not at this hour, surely, Your Grace.'

Albemarle caught his mood and mellowed. 'Hmm, perhaps not, but at this hour His Majesty will be reaching for a piss-pot in Milady's bedchamber before tupping the whore again as a prelude to breaking his fast.'

'And the Lord High Admiral?' Faulkner persisted. 'Where is he?'

'I know not. He may at least be relied upon to do *something*, if only to ride up and down!'

They sat their horses for ten minutes in silence, watching the distant sails of the Dutch warships. 'They say there are English seamen aboard those ships,' Albemarle growled beside him. 'Defected for want of pay.'

'So I had heard.'

'If there are any among them who know their lodes manage to add to de Ruyter's native courage and cunning, they will have little trouble negotiating the block-ships.' Albemarle fell silent for a while. 'I fear the King's Majesty has lost its lustre ... Damn me, I've changed my mind, Sir Kit,' Albemarle said, suddenly resolute. 'Take six of my suite...' He called out names, and the officers walked their horses forward. Albemarle looked them over and squirted another stream of tobacco juice at their horses' feet. One reacted, throwing itself on its haunches, its front hooves pawing the air as its rider fought to master it and retain his seat. Several of the other horses jigged aside and grew restless. 'Do you ride towards Sheerness with Sir Christopher here,' Albemarle ordered. 'Reconnoitre the enemy and determine his strength and intentions at Sheerness.' He turned to Faulkner. 'It must not be said of us that we did nothing. If the Dutch take the fort I'll move Douglas against the place the instant he arrives. Do you seek out the best approach. 'Tis all marsh there, I think.'

Faulkner's heart sank. Another hour in the saddle and he would have not a shred of skin on his arse, but he touched the wide brim of his feathered hat and tugged his horse's head around to canter off, six officers in his rear. He had long since forgotten his promise to Katherine.

The ride towards Sheerness was agonizing, both physically and mentally, for as they rode eastwards along the roads bordering the river they could see the Dutch fleet debouching into the river through the narrow entrance between Sheerness and the Isle of Grain. Whatever the merits of the block-ships, they appeared to offer no obstacle, and the Dutch advance was inexorably westwards. Leading their fleet Faulkner could see the smaller fire-ships; there was no need to speculate on their objectives.

They rode on, crossing the Swale by commandeering the ferry at Harty. On the far bank they encountered demoralized soldiers who, it turned out, were part of the garrison of Sheerness. Faulkner rode into the milling mass of men. 'Who commands you?' Faulkner asked as they rode up to the soldiers. 'Where are your officers?'

No-one seemed to know. Some thought they had gone to Minster, others were convinced they had crossed the Swale to the mainland, all were agreed that they had gone somewhere. Seeing one man with the red sash of rank and supposing him at least a sergeant, Faulkner summoned him to rally the men. The response was reluctant. Handing this extemporized force over to two of his companions with orders to follow, Faulkner urged the remainder forward, barely registering the fact that, with the garrison ejected from the fort, Sheerness was already lost to the enemy.

Coming in sight of the new fort of Sheerness, Faulkner saw first a huge Dutch ensign flying above the low ramparts. He reined in to a stop, fished in his pistol holster and withdrew the small pocket glass he had stowed there and swept the horizon. Behind him his escort sat their horses, which snickered and blew through their nostrils. As he studied the situation Faulkner ignored their impatience. 'Time spent in reconnaissance, gentlemen,' he said without lowering his glass, 'is seldom wasted.' He was unaware that in his rear, the young cavaliers were, to a man, judging him as great an old fool as their Captain-General, his Grace the Duke of Albemarle.

Far beyond the fort he could see along the northern horizon the low Essex shore. Between that distant blue line lay the buoy of the Nore where a few of the larger Dutch men-of-war lay at anchor. Here, he recognized de Ruyter's magnificent flag-ship, *De Zeven Provinciën*, but to the eastwards there came a score of ships, their topsails filled by the easterly breeze and borne along by the flood tide.

Just to the left of the fort a pair of Dutch yachts, de Ruyter's despatch vessels, slipped past what had been the defences commanding the narrow entrance of the Medway. They were followed by a man-of-war of perhaps sixty guns. A smaller forty-gun warship lay at anchor off the fort, presumably that which had landed the storming party that had taken the place that morning.

Below them he could see the remains of the boom which, once blown apart and divided, had washed back along the shore under the impetus of the tide. From his low eminence he could also see the English vessels hurriedly sunk as block-ships in the navigable channel. They had served little purpose: once the chain-boom had been destroyed, the Dutch fleet had begun its passage into the Medway with impunity. To the west-wards the river opened up as, with every minute, the flood tide rapidly covered the mud-flats. Even as he watched, the vast estuary seemed full of de Ruyter's ships, some already at anchor, some ghosting up stream, as if waiting for the right moment to press home their attack in the wake of the fire-ships. In another hour or so the majority of the fleet would have passed the outer defences and, Faulkner had no doubt, the Dutch would soon thereafter make their bold move, for there was nothing now to stop them.

It was a shameful moment for Faulkner. He recalled all the admonitions of old Sir Henry Mainwaring who had recruited him to become a naval officer, so concerned had he been to improve the quality of the English navy. Had all that work been thrown away? If it had been Mainwaring's life's work, it had been the greater part of Faulkner's too. He felt the hot tears of angry frustration start in his eyes. But no, it was the wind, that easterly breeze that yet persisted. See how it caused the Dutch flag to snap and flaunt under its influence.

He was suddenly aware that behind him his gilded escort had become restless. One of their number rode alongside him, a jingle of polished harness, his long ostrich plume nodding in the sunshine.

The young man drew his sword. 'With your permission, Sir Christopher,' the cavalier said languidly, clearly intending to ask permission as a mere sop to convention, 'my friends and I cannot *tolerate* the sight of foreign colours on English soil. Such is our infuriation that we are determined to show those fellows our mettle.' The young officer could not have been more than eighteen or twenty years of age. But for his soft moustache, one could have taken him for a girl of pleasing looks. Without awaiting a reply, he asked as he drew his sword: 'Shall you come with us, Sir Christopher?'

Faulkner put out a hand. 'Stay, sir. The fort is in enemy hands. You can achieve nothing except make your mothers weep for loss of your lives...'

The young man drew himself up in his saddle. 'Sir,' he declared pretentiously, 'I cannot *bear* to look upon that flag!'

'I forbid it,' Faulkner began, but the rasp of swords leaving their scabbards reassured the young cavalier of support as he dug his heels into his horse's flanks. A moment later Faulkner, caught off guard, still holding his telescope and with his reins slack, felt his mount jerk forward, excited by the onrush of the others. In an instant he had dropped the glass, grabbed the reins to restrain his horse and found himself galloping in the wake of his escort.

The slope of the island was gentle as it descended to a shoreline of marsh, but the ground was firm on the fort's approach as the horses got their heads, unrestrained by their riders who stood in their stirrups whooping and waving their swords. Following on his bolting steed Faulkner was aware that they passed a group of armed men hidden in a ditch who looked up with astonished expressions, hollering a warning to them as they swept past.

Ahead of them the gate of the fort was closed, and a head or two could be seen above on the ramparts. Their charge was an utterly futile gesture, Faulkner realized, a piece of stupid bravado in which he had been involuntarily caught up despite his inexpert attempts to master his horse, his endeavours thwarted by the necessity of retaining his seat. He was no practised horseman, unlike the young bloods in whose wake he was dragged. In his struggle to rein in his mount he had failed to draw his sword, but the sight of the men in the ditch, soldiers by the look of them, had persuaded him that what he was about was potentially disastrous.

By now he was some yards behind the hotheads and his horse was slowing, though the foam flew from its mouth in its fury at being thwarted. It was almost at a standstill when a volley of arquebus balls flew about them. One of the dolts ahead of Faulkner cried out and fell sideways. Another rode alongside and put out an arm to support him as they all tugged at their reins, pulling their horses' heads round whence they had come. An instant later they were cantering past Faulkner, who was at that moment struck. His hat was whipped from his head and he felt stung. He did not see one of the cavaliers cleverly catch his spinning hat, but he followed their retreat, which did not slacken until they drew rein alongside the armed men in the ditch.

Faulkner's first thought was for the disobedience that had caused the injury of one of his escort. 'You should be cashiered, sir!' he said to the young man who had precipitated the escapade. His voice was cold with fury.

'Come, come, Sir Christopher, no harm is done and the horses have had good exercise...'

'No harm? No harm you say? Why you have a

wounded officer there!' He pointed.

''Tis nothing. He'll be fine.' The young man was grinning and nodding at his companion.

Faulkner looked round and the young man, though pale, smiled back and stared down at his thigh. His breeches were torn, and a red slash in the flesh of his leg showed where a ball had gouged but not penetrated the muscle. Meanwhile, the men in the ditch had all clambered out, covered in mud, some wounded and all of them in obviously low spirits, but their incredulity at what they had just witnessed was plain to see.

'And who may you bold fellows be?' one of them asked, half amused despite his scarecrow appearance. Faulkner introduced himself and acknowledged that of the other.

'I am, alas, the late commander of the Sheerness garrison,' the officer explained. 'Most of my men have run after receiving a drubbing from an over-whelming force landed by the Dutch who forced the gate at dawn.' Faulkner sensed the man had no case to answer and would risk death at his court-martial. 'You are lucky to have escaped with your lives,' he added, 'for there are Englishmen in that place, under one of Cromwell's colonels, a man named Dolmen. Do you bruit his traitorous name abroad and, if you have any influence, have him share the fate of all traitors.'

Faulkner inclined his head non-committally, but the officer who had led the charge asked for the name to be repeated. 'I have a little influence,' he said, smiling, 'and my sister has the, er,

363

ear of the King.' His fellows sniggered as the hapless garrison commander looked quizzically at Faulkner.

Embarrassed by this unpleasant exchange, Faulkner bethought himself of his duty. Shaken by both what he had seen of the Dutch and the captured fort, and the folly of the last few minutes, he gestured to the passing men-of-war. 'Is this the entire Dutch strength?' he asked.

'No,' the garrison commander explained. 'Another squadron passed north of the Isle of Grain bound up the Thames.'

Faulkner nodded and thought of Edmund; their worst fears were confirmed. 'Your men are by the ferry,' Faulkner said. 'They were in want of discipline. Some of My Lord Duke of Albemarle's officers have rallied them. I suggest you march with me and join His Grace at Chatham. He will welcome reinforcements.'

'Even from so unwelcome an origin as ours?' the officer responded bitterly.

'There is no dishonour in defeat; it is what one does afterwards that signifies,' Faulkner answered curtly. He looked about him. The cavaliers looked as if butter would not melt in their mouths, and he was struck by this contrived innocence. Just before they set off one of them rode up holding out Faulkner's hat.

'You stopped to pick it up?' Faulkner asked, astonished.

The young man grinned. 'I caught it, Sir Christopher,' he said, emphasizing his adroitness with a flourish of the hat. 'By the way you have been clipped. Your ear is bleeding.'

'It is?' Faulkner put his hand up and found his right ear gored, a small slice of it missing. 'Good heavens, I had no idea.'

'Your hat blew towards me,' the fellow said lightly. ''Twas fair bowling along in the wind.'

Faulkner took the proffered hat and slapped it against his thigh, which caused his horse to twitch. It had gipped alongside Albemarle's large gelding; no wonder it had reacted in company with the spirited mounts his companions sat. He set the creature's head towards the ferry and, as the officers from the fort followed, settled down to a walking pace, much relieved in his nether parts that he no longer had need to move any faster. His ear was stinging now, and it came to him that he had broken his promise to Katherine: more than that, his lug would betray him. Behind them the number of Dutch ships in the estuary increased.

It was dark by the time they re-joined Albemarle's headquarters in a cottage on the outskirts of Chatham. Faulkner left the wretched garrison commander to make his peace with the Duke and went in search of something to eat. When he returned from an inn about a mile away he could see reddened smoke rising from the moored fleet as the first ships began to burn. By midnight, as Faulkner accompanied Albemarle and his suite along the low ridge of rising ground they had occupied that morning, it seemed as if the entire river was on fire. The wind still blew fresh from the north-east, fanning the flames and bringing the roar of the conflagration to their ears. Even without a glass they could see sparks rising from the burning ships, accompanied by the occasional small explosion as the flames found some combustible material.

'Are we to stand here all night and watch this disastrous humiliation?' Albemarle growled. 'All our work ... All our blood and treasure wasted and gone for nothing, damn my eyes.'

'What must be said of us, Your Grace? That we went to bed while the fleet burned?'

'That is exactly what His Majesty will do this night, my dear Sir Christopher,' Albemarle said, his tone viciously sardonic, leaning from his horse towards Faulkner and lowering his voice. 'And aren't these *His* ships?'

The following morning the Dutch remained in the river, reluctant to leave, though their work was done. A new pall of smoke rose over the distant fort at Sheerness. Those who saw it reported that pin-pricks of bright light had been followed some seconds later by the thunder of explosions. Even at a distance they could see, amid the smoke and flashes, debris flung sky-wards as the Dutch destroyed the fortification itself. Faulkner thought of the foolish exploit he had been caught up in the previous day. 'There is,' he muttered in self-reproach, recalling his broken promise to Katherine, 'no fool like an old fool.' He shuddered at the thought of how close he had come to death, putting a tentative finger up to his right ear, where a hard crust of scab had formed.

'You have a scratch,' Albemarle had said, noticing the damaged ear. 'That is truly a mark of honour, Sir Kit,' he remarked wryly, 'and more than most will have gotten in defence of our fleet.'

'We came too close to the enemy, Your Grace.' There was no need to say more, though Faulkner glared at the young jackanapes who was now grinning at him behind the Captain-General's shoulder.

During the attack during the night, Albemarle's guards had stood to their arms, and the Captain-General had gone down to the water's edge, dismounted, and with a cane in his hand, walked up and down roaring obscenities at the enemy. There were those among his officers that declared his intention was to stop a Dutch ball and die reproaching others but with his own honour intact. Whatever his motives, Albemarle's mood was foul as he surveyed what was left of the fleet he had so gallantly commanded.

More news came in that morning. Lords Douglas and Middleton had arrived with their forces. They had passed through Rochester in some disorder and there were reports of rape and plundering by Douglas's soldiers. Similar complaints came from Chatham, and a deputation of the local councillors, led by the Mayor of Rochester, came to express their outrage to 'Honest George'.

It seemed to Faulkner, kicking his heels among the Duke's staff, that no further infamy could possibly be visited on his country. It was clear from Albemarle's face when he came in from meeting the citizens' representatives that he felt the same.

Later that morning, Albemarle ordered Faulkner to take a preliminary inventory of the damage, and he spent most of the day in the saddle, pocket-book in hand, as he catalogued the disaster. Late in the afternoon he returned to the Duke's headquarters, shifted now to the dockyard, where Commissioner Pett hovered obsequiously rubbing his hands in his anxiety at being in some way culpable. Calling for pen, ink and paper, Faulkner paced up-and-down impatiently until Pett, now in a fluster, chivvied his clerks with an activity he might better have expended in moving the King's ships, in accordance with his written instructions.

'Sir Christopher...' he said at last, indicating a table, chair and the requisite writing materials. Without a word Faulkner sat down, opened his pocket-book, drew a blank sheet before him and took the quill Pett offered him. He paused before putting pen to paper, recalling the hours in the saddle, then, sighing, he began to write. After a brief account of the forcing of the chain-boom and capture of the fort at Sheerness, he recorded that 'the land forces were being led, it is said, by Colonel Dolmen late of the Army of the Commonwealth'. After mentioning the advance of the Dutch fire-ships, Faulkner listed the large ships of war which had been either seized or burnt by the Dutch.

Burnt – *Royal James*, *Loyal London*, *Royal Oak*, *Vanguard*, *Charles V*, *Matthias*, *Marmaduke*, *Maria Sancta*.

Captured and borne off by the Enemy – *Royal Charles* & *Unity* – this last formerly the Dutch

Eendracht taken a prize by the *Diamond* and *Yarmouth* in the North Sea, April 1665.

He added the details of the *Eendracht* out of a desire to mitigate the disaster; somehow it made not a scrap of difference. Presenting the result to Albemarle he waited while the Duke looked it over.

'I desire that you remain here for a few days, Sir Christopher,' he said, 'in order to accompany Mister Pett, visit all the vessels once the fires are all dead and to survey the damage in detail. If you have private correspondence to convey to London regarding the delay in your return, I shall be happy to see it delivered.'

Part Four

Redemption

1667–1672

Rupert

June 1667–January 1670

Edmund, hearing of his father-in-law being detained at Chatham, joined him a few days later and assisted in the tedious and depressing task Albemarle had assigned Faulkner and Pett. In an attempt to win over the man with whom he must, perforce spend the next few days, Commissioner Peter Pett, son of the famous Phineas, offered Faulkner hospitality, extending this to Edmund when he, enquiring for Faulkner and being directed to the Commissioner's house, turned up on his doorstep.

Thus the three of them dined together that evening, being joined by Mistress Pett until she withdrew, leaving the men to talk of the present calamity. They discussed the disgraceful conduct of Lord Douglas's men and remarked upon the arrival of Lord Middleton with more troops, and the futility of their raising defensive works along the river's bank.

'Everything done too late,' Faulkner growled, an oblique accusation thrown in the embarrassed Pett's direction.

'Believe me, Sir Christopher,' Pett defended himself, 'I share your sentiments but the fault does not lie with me. You will doubtless charge me for not having moved the *Royal Charles* as ordered, but the lack of money with which to pay the labourers has led to indiscipline among them. Without the means to pay their rents, their landlords expel them; the same is true of many seamen who reside hereabouts. They mustered last night in great numbers once they saw with their own eyes what was afoot but, as you say, too late ... too late.' He lowered the palm of his hand on the table in a gesture of despair and shook his head. 'Besides, the orders to fit out only half a dozen small frigates this spring, and to leave the ships above forty guns laid up in ordinary, *must* be the cause of their all lying here supine, must it not? The Chancellor and Lord Treasurer are said to have persuaded the King that it was unnecessary: the one said our last victory would dissuade the Dutch from further mischief; the other insisted that no matter what might be desirable, the Exchequer was devoid of funds. Ergo, the thing was impossible and there would be no Summer Guard!' Pett paused to let the implication of his privileged information sink in. 'As for His Grace the Duke of Albemarle...' Pett shrugged. 'I have heard both that he added his weight to the prevailing opinion and that he did not. I am inclined to believe he said little and abided by the conclusion. I did hear,' he added confidentially, 'that His Highness the Lord High Admiral dissented strongly, but his was a minority view within the Council of State, and even Rupert's opinion, which coincided with the Duke of York's, carried no weight. In short we were left without a naval force at sea and de

374

Ruyter even now lies anchored off the Nore.' He shrugged, looking directly at Faulkner. 'Thus ends my exculpation, Sir Christopher.'

Faulkner nodded. 'I apologize if I spoke too hastily, Mister Pett,' he said. 'At the root of it lies a lack of money. Indeed, only yesterday, His Grace mentioned his regret at not compelling the King to over-rule the other members of the council.' He paused, adding, 'Their judgement might have been worth the hazard were it not for the fact that de Ruyter is a formidable opponent. Indeed, all the Dutch admirals are able men; one does not rise to high station in The United Provinces without ability, but de Ruyter is a giant among them.'

Eventually, they turned to Edmund, who thus far had had nothing to contribute to the discussion, asking what he knew of events in the Thames.

'All I can tell you is that de Ruyter's second, Admiral Willem van Ghent, attempted to force the river. His ships carried the flood tide as high as they could, intending to take the Indiamen at Gravesend, but we got them shifted in time. Then the ebb came away in our favour so that van Ghent withdrew, the wind then falling light. I saw nothing of this beyond a few sails in the distance, but the King and Duke of York had made their appearance, and ordered ships down from Woolwich and Deptford to be sunk at Barking, which was all done but too late. I heard too that Prince Rupert was at Woolwich and Deptford, very active in placing artillery to cover the upper reaches and protect the Pool, which was well enough done in its way but...' Edmund shrugged and left his sentence unfinished. These measures seemed not to have impressed the populace who dwelt by and on the River of Thames.

For the next two days the three men took the Commissioner's barge and went from ship to ship. Truth to tell there was little to cheer; the burnt-out hulks had most of them broken free of their moorings, some from the burning of their bitts where the mooring chains were secured, others cast adrift by their skeleton crews in order to avoid the approaching fire-ships. Those few whose crews had attempted to save them in this manner had been attacked and set ablaze by armed parties of Dutchmen in their boats, putting off from their men-of-war with combustibles. The burning ships had drifted, to run aground on the copious mud-flats which were exposed at low water. Among them were the *Loyal London* and the *Royal James*, their huge hulls reduced to a residual skeleton of massive oak futtocks that smouldered yet as they lay like decomposing whales, heeled over, dead.

'All the pride of the state reduced to this,' Pett remarked as their oarsmen lay on their oars and the barge glided towards the *Royal Oak*, the three gentlemen in her stern regarding the sad wreckage. As they pulled away over the calm waters of a river unruffled by the slightest breeze and running like molten copper over the hot sunlight of the June day, a lone herring gull landed on what was left of the great ship's beak-head. Opening its gape it let out its cry.

'I never heard anything more like a great laugh

of derision,' Faulkner said.

Before they left Chatham, Edmund and Faulkner mounted their horses and rode downstream, towards Sheerness, to observe what was left of the fort. Faulkner had some hopes of finding his lost telescope. It was not the long-glass presented to him by the late King, but it was a useful item and he was annoyed at having lost it in such circumstances.

On their way they passed Lord Middleton's encampment and, in paying their respects, encountered John Evelyn in conversation with the general. Evelyn seemed keen to know what Faulkner had seen of the Dutch attack and, learning that they were proposing shortly to return to London, advised them that the roads were bad.

'The country is in an uproar, having heard that the Dutch have landed, and there are those among the soldiery busy robbing and looting. As for the populace, many run like rats in fear of their lives, abandoning their property and clutching their chattels. They achieve little thereby except to create disorder to add to our disgrace.'

''Tis my Lord Douglas's men who do the looting,' Edmund remarked sardonically. 'I saw some of their handiwork. I have little doubt but it is they who put the word about that it is others.'

Having passed the time of day and commiserated on the state of affairs, the two continued their ride to the fort – or what remained of it. The Dutch had done an efficient job in its demolition. Its embrasures had been destroyed, its guns tipped into the fosse and those parts of the structure made of wood burned. Faulkner thought of his madcap charge with a sense of shame; he thought better of regaling Edmund with a narration. Instead he picked at his scabby ear and began a half-hearted hunt for his lost glass. Finally, he gave up.

Edmund had walked his horse down to the shore to investigate the shipping lying in the distant channel. Reluctantly, Faulkner followed. By the time he drew rein alongside Edmund, the younger man had scanned the horizon and turned to his father-in-law.

'Look!' Edmund exclaimed, sweeping his right hand from left to right. 'As far as one can see the Dutch fleet lies at anchor on our doorstep as though it were their own – which I suppose it is for the time being.' From the faint speck of the buoy of the Nore, eastwards as far as the keen eye could see, lay a long line of men-of-war. Every one of them within sight bore the red, white and blue colours of the Seven United Provinces. 'You did not find your glass?'

'No.' The two men sat for a moment side by side. 'De Witt has had his revenge,' said Faulkner resignedly. 'Revenge for Downing's outrage on his country's integrity, revenge for de Ruyter's late defeat and revenge for Holmes's Bonfire. We are laid low, Edmund, as low as it is possible to be, and I recall how low we were in King James's day, aye, and that of the first Charles. I was myself adopted, brought up and nurtured to help end that state of affairs, and now look at us: back where we began. It is as though my life has meant nothing.' He paused, aware

378

that Edmund was looking at him, ignorant of what he spoke. He smiled. 'I will tell you some time, Edmund, of old Sir Henry Mainwaring, of the late King presenting me with a long-glass, of meeting and losing Katherine, of marrying Hannah's mother, of raiding the coast of Morocco to root out the Sallee pirates from their lair, of teaching the present King how to sail, of civil war and exile and much more, but now–' he tugged his horse's head round a second time – 'now we shall go home.'

If Faulkner thought that he might be allowed a life of retired ease, he was mistaken. Although a peace treaty was signed at Breda in July, there was a growing appetite for revenge upon the Dutch. It was whispered that there were secret negotiations in train between King Charles and King Louis of France, the latter eager to extend his kingdom's borders to the Rhine and over-run Flanders.

In the immediate wake of the Dutch raid the Duke of York, in his capacity as Lord High Admiral, ordered Faulkner to join other senior commanders as a commissioner to investigate the best way to restore the Royal Navy to its former power. Only one fleet flag-ship, the *Royal Sovereign*, had escaped destruction through being at Portsmouth, but it was the lack of money that doomed the commissioners' recommendations from being carried out in the months that followed. There were also political dimensions: a Committee of Miscarriages set up by the House of Commons, in an unholy union of Royalist and

Republican members, sought to discover where the two and a half million pounds sterling voted by Parliament for the war had gone.

This in turn engendered a seeking of scapegoats, though the King's mistresses were exempt. Among those who lost their posts in the wake of de Ruyter's final retreat from his anchorage along the coast of north Kent was Peter Pett at Chatham. Dismissed with obloquy, his dilatoriness was unjustly held to have been the chief cause of the Dutch success. Clarendon also fell from grace, dismissed as the architect of disaster and subject to impeachment. Albemarle too faded from public notice from this time, age and infirmity taking their toll.

Although Sir George Downing, sometime earlier recalled from The Hague and appointed Secretary to the Treasury, skilfully reconstructed the King's finances, they waited upon time for the effect of taxation to pay its dividend. Nevertheless, the Admiralty and the Navy Board underwent reform, driven by the Duke of York and largely put into effect by that same Samuel Pepys who Faulkner had first noted at the Trinity House as a pushy young fellow. Meanwhile poor Evelyn toiled to ease the burden of the sick, the wounded and the unpaid seamen, supported as far as they were able, by the Trinity Brethren.

Against this background the optimism in which Faulkner and his fellow commissioners first met withered quickly and had little effect. The commission was quietly wound up and, in the end, Faulkner's contribution to the rebuilding of the King's navy was to answer some questions put to him at Trinity House by Master Pepys. This grew into a modest correspondence in which Faulkner gave of his experience, remarking to Katherine that he considered Master Pepys would reserve to himself any credit accruing to his suggestions.

'That is the way of the world,' Katherine replied, smiling. 'The young push out the old when they can, thinking the old know little and what little they know is made better use of by the young.'

Faulkner chuckled, reaching for his spectacles. 'He'll learn, and one day likely suffer the indignities of old age.' Faulkner rubbed his eyes before clamping the spectacles on the bridge of his nose. 'Now I have Edmund's report on the new ship to read.'

'Oh, and a missive came for you today from Bethlem Hospital.' Katherine rose and found the letter, passing it to him. He broke the seal and read it, Katherine watching him. 'What is it?' she asked.

'It is to inform me that since it is not the practice of the Hospital to retain patients for longer than necessary Nathan Gooding is to be released, and I am invited to collect him.' He laid the letter down, removed his spectacles and stared at Katherine.

'What shall you do?'

'I have no idea. I must speak with Judith.'

'You may surely leave that until tomorrow.'

It took a vigorous knocking to summon Molly to the street door of the house in Wapping. She led

381

him upstairs to where Judith lay a-bed; the air in the room was stale, the bed-sheets filthy and Molly's air was proprietorial. Judith looked dreadful; her eyes were closed, her face was pale and waxy, her hair lank and undressed, her nightgown stained. A tray of half-eaten food lay neglected upon a bedside table and the chamber stank of fetid air.

'She's a-fevered,' Molly offered, by way of explanation.

Without a word Faulkner crossed the room and laid his hand on Judith's forehead. It was cold to the touch, and he noticed her respiration was weak. Bent over her he looked down the length of the bed at Molly, standing at its foot.

'There's no fever,' he said shortly and then noticed an odd protuberance under the bed clothes. Lifting the bedding he saw her swollen belly and gently replaced the sheets and blankets. 'Do you know what that is?' he asked Molly. She shook her head.

'I do, Husband.'

He turned his head and stared into Judith's eyes. They were yellow, and her breath stank.

'So, you have come back to me. Is your harlot taken by the French pox?' Her voice was weak, but her thoughts were lucid.

He said nothing, unable to do so, and waved Molly from the room. She flounced out, pouting.

'I knew nothing of this,' he said, 'or I should have come sooner.' Judith stared at him. 'Do you have a physician?'

'No ... There is no point, Husband,' she said with difficulty. 'You will be rid of me soon, and

I will have passed to a better place.'

'I will have a physician come,' he said suddenly, straightening up, 'and I will see to it that you have better care than that slut gives you.'

'No!' He felt her hand on his wrist; it was like a claw. 'She is the only one to remain loyal to me. She has brought me what I wanted, and that is enough.'

'And what was that?'

'An attorney. I have dictated and signed a testament in defiance of your rights and wish that some portion is left to her. The rest, Husband, is yours as the Law and God require.'

He bit off an unkind remark that he cared not a fig for her money, at the same time realizing that he could not concern her for her brother. 'Is there nothing I can do?'

'Nothing, unless it is to see my remains properly interred.'

'Of course.'

'And that the loyal Molly receives her due.'

'Yes.'

She turned her head away from him but, as he rose to leave the room, she asked, 'Where is my brother?' She was frowning and seemed puzzled, uncertain, as though her grasp of reality was slipping away from her.

'He is in a safe place.'

'He has bewitched me, you know.' She made a pathetic gesture towards her swollen belly. 'You saw what he had done.'

Faulkner stood a moment. He had nothing to say, but as he watched, she closed her eyes. He waited a moment then said, half to himself,

383

'Goodbye, Julia.' It was only after he had sent Molly back into his wife's chamber that he recollected he had used the name she had been Christened with. For a moment he thought of the perversion induced by Puritan radicalism; of the invocation of God, the importance of outward forms and that troubling business of witchcraft. Not, he thought to himself as he left the house, that witchery did not trouble people other than Puritans. Had not the King's grand-father, King James, written a book on the subject? Still, aside from the irony that Judith considered her brother the satanic agent of her disease, her condition was appalling.

He returned to Katherine a much sobered man. Explaining to her, and later to Hannah and Edmund, they all agreed that some amelioration of Judith's plight was indispensable. The details they left until the morning, but as they got into bed that night Katherine offered a solution.

'My dearest, I think we should remove ourselves from this house, where we are an encumbrance, and return to Wapping. We could nurse Judith until her time comes, which, if you are correct, will not be long. Moreover, there we may also comfortably accommodate her brother. We have the means to hire help, and the house is large enough.'

Faulkner looked at Katherine. 'You would do that?'

'If I did not do it alone – yes.'

Faulkner feared Judith's reaction when she encountered Katherine. Molly's insolence was quickly stifled by Faulkner threatening her loss of immediate employment. She was bright enough to see where her future lay and, after a week of peevishness, she resumed her previous station without protest. Whether or not she was aware that her mistress had made provision for her, Faulkner neither knew nor cared. As long as his wife lived, he was determined that she should not lie in filth and squalor.

Katherine worked her charm and, as a result, Molly's appearance was considerably improved. At the end of a fortnight, with the efforts of Molly and Katherine, with some supplementary assistance from Faulkner and two men brought in from the wharf to attend to some repairs, order and cleanliness had been re-established.

Nathan was released from Bethlem Hospital a month after they returned to Wapping. He too was much altered. Thin and withdrawn, the learned doctors declared him harmless, suggesting that he be given some book-work to attend to, declaring him to be 'an excellent clerk'. Gooding had smiled at the condescension and nodded his head slowly. Before they left the hospital, Faulkner looked Nathan straight in the face and asked if he was recognized.

'Of course, Kit.' Gooding's voice was low, measured, reasonable.

'And could you live in harmony with your sister?' Gooding nodded. 'She is very ill, and not expected to live long.'

'If she could live with me,' he said, apparently untroubled with the news of her disease.

When led into Judith's chamber, Gooding took

one look and sank to his knees beside his sister's bed, putting his head in his hands. Katherine, who had been tending the invalid, motioned Faulkner to withdraw. Leaving brother and sister together, Katherine and Faulkner stood on the landing outside, half expecting some outburst from Judith.

Aware of his poor hearing, Faulkner asked: 'Can you hear anything?'

Katherine put a finger to her lips, bending towards the door, which stood ajar. 'They are talking,' she said after a moment in a low voice, 'or praying. I cannot quite determine.'

After several minutes Katherine knocked and, leaving Faulkner on the landing, went in.

'You would never have known anything but a state of perfect amity had existed between them for their entire lives,' she advised him later. 'He was reading The Bible to her, or had been when I entered.'

'Does one presume that this state of mind is set, or do I have to lock him up at High Water, Full and Change?'

'What *do* you mean?'

'I mean when the moon is full and new.'

'Oh!' Katherine shrugged. 'But I suppose we must watch him.'

They never discovered what influence the moon might have upon Gooding, for Judith died of her cancer eight days later and Nathan Gooding conducted her to her grave in his sober black, a Puritan gentleman to the last, and the chief mourner of his sister Julia, latterly known as Judith.

386

'I am widowed,' Faulkner remarked that night to Katherine, 'and free to marry again, my darling Kate.'

'After a proper interval, perhaps.'

'Perhaps? What mean you by *perhaps*? Is the matter not a certainty? We have braved scandal...'

Katherine pulled a face. 'Braved scandal? Come, sir, the times do not care for a scandal such as ours, not as they might have done in the recent past. Whatever we decide we must wait. Some propriety is called for.'

'I suppose so,' Faulkner grunted in response.

'Do you not feel grief for her? She bore you children; you must have loved her once.'

'Once, perhaps, and yes, she bore me children. I feel more remorse than grief, but life is such a trifling thing that I cannot pretend to more than that.'

Katherine frowned. 'A trifling thing?'

'Not to each individual,' he said, thinking of those slaughtered about him in action. 'But I have seen it too oft snuffed out like a candle to hold it as anything more than a small thing. Something of the instant. D'you see?'

She nodded, thinking of the vicissitudes of their two, twin, lives, of the separations and the entanglements, and of Judith's part. 'For you and I, knowing death and battle and exile, perhaps that is so. For Judith and her brother there were expectations. They lived their lives...' She sought for a metaphor, and he came to her aid.

'Less close to the abyss?' She nodded and smiled at him. The thought contented them as

387

they settled in bed. As they lay in each other's arms on the verge of sleep he whispered, 'Nevertheless, you *shall* be Lady Faulkner.'

The philosophical conclusions arrived at by Faulkner and Katherine were rudely shaken the following morning when Gooding came downstairs for breakfast. Faulkner was on the point of leaving the house, intending to visit Johnson at Blackwall before going aboard the *Hawk*, when Gooding made a remark that caused Katherine to place a restraining hand on Faulkner's arm. Gooding's voice had been low, and Katherine rightly guessed that Faulkner had not heard what he had said, and Faulkner turned, looking first at Katherine and then, seeing the look on her face, at Gooding.

There was nothing immediately remarkable about Gooding. They had become accustomed to his pale face, his withdrawn, almost other-worldly appearance. He seemed to move through life as if untroubled by his surroundings, a man who would wander out in the pouring rain without taking regard for the deluge. He had that vacant look about him now, and Faulkner was puzzled as to why Katherine called his attention to him.

'What did you say, Nathan?' she asked quietly.

'I said, I had defeated Satan and prayed triumphantly for my sister's death.'

Faulkner frowned. It was clear that Katherine had divined something more serious in Gooding's revelation, but he felt imbued with a faint sense of exasperation and was eager to be about his business. Faulkner sighed. He did not share Katherine's concern. 'I'm sure you did, Nathan,' he said soothingly. 'Judith was a very sick woman and we all wished that her end was swift and with as little pain as God in his mercy...' Faulkner's voice tailed off, aware that his words were deeply troubling to Gooding, whose eyes had suddenly taken on a wild look. He began to make defiant, jerky motions with his hands.

'What do you mean, Nathan?' Katherine asked, stepping forward and catching one gesticulating hand.

'I *tricked* Satan,' he said, his tone insistent, each word enunciated emphatically. 'I,' he repeated, 'deceived Beelzebub ... the Devil...' His voice rose. '*Now* do you understand?'

'You prayed for a swift end?' Faulkner queried.

'No! I prayed that she should *die*!'

Katherine understood. Keeping her eyes on Gooding, she explained: 'He means, I think, that Judith's affliction, her illness, not the coming of her end, was entirely due to his prayers and supplications.'

Gooding was nodding. 'Yes. Yes ... my supplications ... I prayed constantly when I was in ... in that place...' His reference to Bethlem Hospital seemed to calm him. He closed his eyes for a moment. Opening them again he had resumed his detached air. Looking from Katherine to Faulkner he smiled. 'She *was* a witch,' he said simply, 'and one must not suffer a witch to live.'

Gooding sat at the table and called for some eggs as Faulkner exchanged a glance with Katherine. 'I cannot leave you alone.'

'Do not be so foolish. He is harmless ... now.'

Faulkner regarded Gooding. He did not believe

for a moment that Gooding's prayers had had the slightest influence on Judith's cancer and saw him only as a man who did not behave rationally.

Feeling Faulkner's eyes upon him, Gooding looked up and smiled again. 'Do you wait upon Sir Henry Johnson, Kit?' he asked blithely.

'That is ... was my intention.'

Gooding looked at the summer sunshine streaming through the window and nodded happily. 'I think that I shall accompany you. Yes, I shall, if you have no objection.'

The thought of having Gooding under his supervision rather than left in the house with Katherine and the servants weighed more heavily than having to explain the presence and behaviour of a lunatic to Johnson. Fifteen minutes later they stepped out and set their faces towards Blackwall just as they had done years earlier when they had been building the *Duchess of Albemarle*.

The summer passed like a dream. With peace finally concluded at Breda in July, almost the entire household embarked in the *Hawk* and sailed for Harwich. They anchored in the Blackwater before reaching the Naze of Essex and, as they made their approach to the harbour at Harwich, Faulkner pointed out, to those interested, the fort at Landguard Point where the Dutch had landed before their descent upon the Medway. 'You will recall you heard the guns,' he reminded Edmund.

'Good heavens, so I did,' said Edmund, beaming at his boys.

As for Gooding – though it required a certain legerdemain on the part of Faulkner and Edmund – he had been allowed to think that he had resumed his old role as a partner. In fact they gave him the most complex book-keeping tasks and requested he audit the accounts for some years, checking especially how much money had been remitted to the King. Apparently contended enough, Gooding took on these tasks willingly, asking nothing more than his daily bread and the opportunity to join a dissenting congregation. For the most part, once it had been established, he was left to his routine, though he accompanied them to Harwich, along with Edmund, Hannah and her two boys.

The *Hawk* was crowded, especially so, it seemed, for Hannah was expecting again.

'Hannah thinks she is carrying twins,' Katherine confided as they lay in their cots in their tiny cabin, 'for she is so exceedingly large.'

After visiting Harwich and Ipswich they sailed about the rivers Stour and Orwell, whose confluence forms the harbour, before returning to London. It proved a hard beat to windward, helped by the tide but discommoded by the short, sharp sea this induced. The young Drinkwater boys thought it a great lark; their expectant mother was less enthusiastic as the *Hawk* scooped buckets of sparkling spray over her weather bow. As they beat up the Thames, Gooding took it upon himself to point out to the ladies all the ships for which they were responsible, either as owners in part or in full, or for which they acted as agents. To this he added a babble of sundry details of a recondite nature attaching to the business of ship-owning and ship-broking. By the time they approached their moorings off Wapping the ladies professed themselves exhausted by the encyclopedic catalogue displayed by Gooding. Even the boys found Uncle Nathan a source of the most amazing tales, Gooding having mixed in his narrative a sufficient stock of yarns about the adventures enjoyed by the sailors they saw on the scores of ships past which they sailed.

As they stepped ashore they were met by Charlie Hargreaves, who had been left in charge and was shaping up well, entirely answering the expectations of his employers. Hargreaves bowed to the ladies, ignored the two boys and briefed Edmund and Faulkner on the latest news from Fort St David. Gravely, Gooding stood close to the other three men, for all the world a party to their deliberations.

Noting this, Katherine smiled, discreetly remarking to Hannah that, 'One would never guess.'

'Indeed not,' agreed Hannah, more anxious for her two scallywags whose proximity to the water's edge and their fascination with a filthy old man in a stinking Peter boat promised undesirable consequences.

The cold of winter brought Hannah to bed. The birth was difficult and the services of the midwife proved inadequate. A barber-surgeon was summoned and was as swiftly kicked out of the house by Edmund, desperate as his wife lay bleeding. Only one of the twins, an undersized girl, survived. Hannah lived for nine days before puerperal fever killed her; the little girl, though put to a wet-nurse, was buried with her mother. Edmund was distraught and withdrawn, raging against fate and the barber-surgeon who, he maintained, had condemned his beautiful wife to an early death. Faulkner found him inconsolable, and it was many months before Edmund could be induced to take more than a passing interest in affairs, both public and private. Oddly, Gooding filled some of the vacuum, diligently working at his books and unwilling to be distracted from what he was apt to call his 'essential labours'. The importance of these tasks he gave as his excuse for declining an invitation to the wedding of Faulkner and Katherine the following year. The nuptials were quiet, attended by those few of the Trinity Brethren with whom he had been long acquainted.

A fortnight after the wedding a recovering Edmund brought the news that the *Duchess of Albemarle* was no longer fit for any service. ''Tis the ravages of the ship-worm,' Edmund explained.

'What would you have done with her?' Faulkner asked. 'The old order changeth, and all things must pass.'

'That is for you to decide, for Nathan explained to me that she has some entailment.'

Faulkner smiled. 'Nathan remembered that, eh? Well, well.'

'To the letter. I understand the King has personally enjoyed the profits of her voyages.'

393

'You knew that, surely? You commanded her.'

'I do not recall you ever telling me.'

'Did I not? Oh, well, perhaps tomorrow you will ask Nathan to be good enough to draft me a letter to the King explaining her condition and her end. In the circumstances it will be best that she is broken up.'

Edmund smiled. 'That is sufficiently important for Nathan's attention,' he said.

'Quite so,' Faulkner agreed with the mild irony.

In the months that followed Gooding regarded the importance of his work undiminished, but he accomplished less and less, his intellectual grasp failing with a sharp decline in his health. For some months he lay a-bed and died five days before Christmas 1669.

Death now seemed Faulkner's constant companion. He long mourned the loss of Brian Harrison, his old friend and neighbour at Wapping. They had served together on the raid on Sallee. Then, less than a fortnight after Gooding's death, on a freezing January day, Honest George Monck, First Duke of Albemarle, died sitting in a chair at his lodgings in Whitehall Palace. He had been unwell for many months and had a year earlier retired to his country seat at New Hall, in Essex. Afflicted by the dropsy, breathing with difficulty, he had been expected to die. The country braced itself, for Honest George was regarded as a prop without which Charles's throne would topple. Taking some pills made for him by an old companion-in-arms turned quack, Albemarle's oedema lessened and he was again to be seen in London. Men and women breathed easily again. But this remission did not last for long. Allowed privileged access at any time to the King's chamber, the old man who had saved the throne, who had remained in London throughout the plague and there nipped in the bud a conspiracy against the king, whose ruthlessness had made enemies and whose courage compelled admiration, gasped his last surrounded by officers from the army as though on the field of battle.

Anne, his home-spun duchess, died within days of her husband, but while his widow was laid to rest in Westminster Abbey, Albemarle's funeral was delayed. Although laid in state caparisoned for war, he was unburied for lack of sufficient money to provide his obsequies with sufficient pomp. Eventually, four months after his death, he followed his wife to his grave in the great Abbey, attended by the King in a procession of almost regal grandeur.

Accompanied by Katherine, Faulkner attended the crowded funeral. As they emerged from the Abbey, Faulkner found himself close to Prince Rupert, who immediately paid his respects to Katherine, congratulating the pair on their marriage. He discreetly drew the couple to one side and asked, 'Sir Christopher, if I had need of advice could I rely upon you?'

Faulkner was non-plussed. 'You can rely upon me, Your Highness, but as to what advice I might—'

Rupert cut him off. 'Albemarle thought highly of you, mentioned you several times and commended you to me. I know enough of you myself to heed the old fellow's words and there may come a time...' Rupert smiled and cast his gaze over the milling congregation debouching from the Abbey in the wake of the King. 'This is not it, however.' He took Katherine's hand and raised it to his lips. 'Your devoted servant, Lady Faulkner. Your services and devotion to my mother can never be requited.'

She dropped her elegant curtsey, and beside her Faulkner footed a bow as Rupert, surrounded by a group of ladies and gentlemen, withdrew to his coach and escort. Faulkner turned to his wife, only to see her face flushed.

'You are angry?'

'What does he mean by that?' she asked shortly. 'Surely he does not wish you to go to sea again at your age!'

'I have no idea what he means,' he temporized. 'He mentioned advice, not a seagoing post; I have served on a commission before; perhaps he means something similar.'

Katherine bit her lip, thought for a moment and then said in a low voice as she took his arm and led them to where their own hired carriage awaited them, 'There is talk again of war, and I know these Stuarts, they take no consideration of those they command.'

'Kate, you of all people know that if he commands, I must obey.' He spoke in a low voice, embarrassed by Katherine's uncharacteristic and public outburst, aware that they were within a few feet of a company of guards drawn up after escorting Albemarle's body from Whitehall.

Their officers were taking post to move them off, and an order was barked close to them. But Katherine had not yet finished with him.

She stopped, disengaged his arm and confronted him for all the world to see. 'I would ask you to promise that you will refuse to serve at sea; others have done the same, even Albemarle – but I know that you do not keep your promises.' As she cast the last words at him she nodded at his ear. She had never previously mentioned the minor blemish to his looks. Faulkner stood stock-still, his face flushed, lost for words. Katherine was about to turn and resume her walk when a voice spoke close behind Faulkner.

'Milady, you seem to have dropped your handkerchief.' They turned to find a handsome young officer of the guards who, removing his plumed hat and making a most elegant bow, offered Katherine the embroidered silk with a flourish.

'You are most kind, sir,' Katherine took the handkerchief with a ravishing smile and twinkling eyes that Faulkner knew was intended to incite jealousy in himself. 'May I ask your name, sir?' Katherine went on.

'Churchill, Milady, Ensign John Churchill of His Majesty's Guards.'

'Thank you, Mister Churchill.'

They went home in silence.

The King's Chameleon

January 1670–August 1672

In the eight years since they had been together following the death of Elizabeth of Bohemia, Faulkner and Katherine had not exchanged a cross word. It was as if the pain of the past, the misunderstandings and the separations had combined with advancing years to remove causes for disagreement, but Katherine's conduct outside the Abbey, although far less conspicuous than Faulkner supposed, had deeply galled him. He sat silent on that homeward journey fulminating, alternately dismissing the notion that Katherine had deliberately dropped her handkerchief and then admitting the possibility. He knew the gossip about young Churchill and suspected Katherine also did. If so her flirtation was as deliberate as it was ridiculous, for he was known to be close to the Duchess of Cleveland, Katherine's distant kinswoman and the King's most influential mistress.

Casting the occasional glance across the coach in Katherine's direction he could see her face was pale, except for two points of colour high on her cheeks, marking her anger. She remained fixed, staring at the street scene as they rumbled and jolted eastwards. He handed her down and into the house with neither word nor thanks and, once inside, went directly to the upper room he continued to use as an office. Here he sat for an hour, listening to the house creak quietly about him, the street-noises muted by the ring of tinnitus in his ears. His body creaked like the house and he felt tired, exhausted by the long ceremony, confused by the mixture of liturgy, pomp, politics and plain hypocrisy that attended Albemarle's ritualized end. Faulkner remember-ed the old warrior defying the Dutch, eager to stop a Dutch ball and end his association with the humiliation of a country whose fate he had assiduously guided, only to watch it frittered away by the King's thoughtless lust and luxury. And now it seemed to an anxious Faulkner that Katherine had fallen into the louche ways of the Court; at her age it was ridiculous. No – despite her inherent beauty – it was grotesque.

At the same time he could not believe it. Surely, he thought, he had got it all wrong. It was all so uncharacteristic. He sat thus musing for some time until he was driven to ease himself at the piss-pot. He rose, crossed the room and stood confronting the effects of age, when a knocking came at the door. It began to open, and Katherine entered, averting her gaze until he had finished. 'I would speak with you,' she began. He remain-ed silent, bereft of comment. They stood, con-fronting each other across the table on which lay the ledgers, the pens and ink-pots, the scattered papers, sealing wax and accoutrements of his trade. 'It was not what you think, Kit,' she said softly. 'I was not such a fool as to think I might flirt with young Churchill, nor did I do so to make you jealous.'

'Then why?'

'Because I was angry.'

'Angry?'

'Yes, angry. With you and with the Prince.'

'What had I done? What had Rupert done?'

Katherine sighed, as though the explanation was too complex and Faulkner nothing but a child and difficult to persuade. 'He says come, and thou cometh, and he says go, and thou goest,' she quoted, at last. 'He commands and you are obedient unto death.'

'But Kate, he is a Prince, an Admiral, and I am a commissioned Captain in His Majesty's Navy. It is for him to command and for me to obey, just as it is for an officer under me to obey my commands. That is the authority that compels order out of anarchy.'

'But you are *old*, Kit, *old* ... The affairs of this world must pass to younger men, men like John Churchill.'

'You do not understand; there is too much at stake. There are too many factions in the fleet, in the army, in Parliament. Old Albemarle understood, as does Rupert. Their respective coteries hated each other, intrigued the one against the other, yet Rupert and Albemarle stood above such factions, riding those half-hearted rogues who resented fighting the Dutch as fellow Protestants, fighting tooth-and-nail to have the seamen fed and paid, despite the King's wanton excesses, for fear of what a want of willing men would cause. Albemarle died not in Whitehall, but on the banks of the Medway three years ago. Rupert knows, as Albemarle knew, that we must fight the Dutch yet again. Ask Edmund, our trade depends upon it.'

'But why you?' she broke in. 'Why such an old man as yourself who are near Albemarle's age; why *you*?'

'Because,' he said, 'like Albemarle, like Rupert and perhaps like a dozen other men of near my age and experience, the vicissitudes of our lives have taught us some wisdom.' He paused, choosing his words carefully, the spectre of old Sir Henry Mainwaring at his side. 'There are those who say that Albemarle was a murderer, a bigamist, a turncoat. He was ruthless in war yet once said he bore no man malice beyond the necessity of war. He detested extremes in religion, saw the legitimacy of a proper Parliament and the dangers in an army with a mind of its own. In consequence he maintained discipline with an iron hand, yet was laughed at for his parsimony at table, the coarseness of his Duchess and the ordinariness of his manners. Despite all this, he was approved of by Rupert, the embodiment of the opposition, who perceived his solid virtue and sought him out. Both men knew that weakness in the state's government, whether Royal or Republican, made fertile ground for dissension, and that civil division and strife are the worst misfortune to befall a people.

'Oh, to be sure there were those, even those of staunch principle, who considered them as slippery as lizards, or as able to turn their coats as a chameleon does. Such men, it is believed by

401

many, have no principle but that of cynicism which combines with so overwhelming a lust for power that they must be resisted. Such men stand in the second rank, unfit for high-office, or the understanding of it. They place their moral judgements above the necessity of keeping the peace of the nation, confusing it with God's business – which in my eyes is best left to God. Those of us who see the virtue in these few chameleons must of necessity support them, or all will again descend into anarchy. Young men, especially young men brought up in the licentiousness of the present age, lack this knowledge ... this wisdom.'

She shook her head. 'That is all very well, and selfless and noble, but not my point. You forget my own experience of life's vicissitudes, of my years of exile...'

'Kate, how could I forget—'

'Be silent! Hear me out. You have no knowledge of my years of servitude, *none at all*. From the earliest days until but a few years ago when I was bound hand and foot to Rupert's mother. A tragic figure to be sure, but a tyrannical old woman, every inch of her a Stuart: demanding, unforgiving, entitled by her high station, but with not a bone of compassion or thought for others in her entire body.' She had silenced him now. 'Oh, I was pleased enough with the billet, to be sure, for I had no other, and on the occasions we went abroad my station as a lady-in-waiting might persuade me, at least for an hour or two, that I was not a drudge. But I was like the prentice boy, bound to my mistress body

402

and soul, night and day, year in year out. That is the price the House of Stuart levies for its protection and condescension. Rupert, though full of charm, is his mother's son.' She paused again then, catching his eye, she concluded. 'When he summons, refuse ... Refuse on grounds of ill-health, but refuse. I no longer ask you to promise me, but I shall not expect to hear otherwise.'

She glared at him for a moment and then withdrew. After she had gone, Faulkner expelled his breath. There was an undoubted attraction in what she was demanding; there was no avoiding the passage of time, or of its corroding effect upon his body. He knew, too, that Anne, Duchess of Albemarle, had berated her husband time after time for his constant return to his duty, even though the King increasingly spurned his advice. When her husband had died, she had relinquished her own hold on life, given up and died within days.

Sighing, he stared into the corners of the room for the shadow of old Sir Henry. He too had died disappointed, in penury, forgotten by those he had served. Was that the fate of all men who lived beyond their own time? But it was Judith's ghost who came to him. In the heat of his diatribe to Katherine, he had forgotten it was she who had described him as 'the King's chameleon'.

A fortnight later, Faulkner received a letter. It was from the private secretary to the Duke of York and acknowledged the news that the East Indiaman *Duchess of Albemarle* was to be broken up. Invoking the King's name, it thanked

Sir Christopher Faulkner for his loyalty, advising him that it was His Majesty's wish that, on the construction of a replacement placed in the service of the Honourable East India Company, the monies profiting the owner be remitted to His Royal Highness, James, Duke of York, Lord High Admiral, etc, etc, etc.

In consideration of this, Faulkner read, *His Majesty wishes to confer the Honour of a Baronetcy upon Sir Christopher Faulkner, an Honour which would, His Royal Highness felt Certain, and of which His Majesty was Confident, also be Pleasing to Lady Faulkner, in Recognition of her many Services to the House of Stuart and for which His Highness Prince Rupert of the Rhine had particularly Solicited the King's Majesty.*

Faulkner read the letter several times before taking it to show Katherine. They had put the incident outside Westminster Abbey behind them, but this resurrected it with uncanny precision. He handed it to her in silence and watched her face grow pale and the twin patches of colour appear again on her cheekbones. Her hands were shaking as she looked up at him.

'I shall of course, refuse it,' he began hurriedly. 'Besides, I have no sons. As for the profits of a new ship...'

'Do not build one.'

'But I *am* building one.'

'But no longer for the East India trade,' she said defiantly. 'Send it to the West Indies, or the Guinea coast.' He shrugged and remained silent.

404

'*Not* for the Company,' she said emphatically.

He shook his head. 'No, we cannot do that; it is not in the interest of Edmund's boys, and they are all that is left to me.'

'Then let Edmund build her in his own name. The King has no demands upon Edmund.'

'Except the lien every monarch has upon his subjects. He will make the demand of Edmund, and Edmund dare not refuse.'

'That would be outrageous.'

'Not to His Majesty, nor to his Secretary of the Treasury, Downing. The King understands that he can mulct only part of the profit otherwise the enterprise is doomed to fail. He is so impecunious and so profligate that he will not wish to kill off a goose capable of laying a golden egg. Charles is no fool ... At least it is only be the *principal* owner's share. Edmund must find others ... You, perhaps.'

Katherine sighed and bit her lower lip. 'So we must do it,' she said.

'He sayeth come and we cometh...'

In the spring of 1671 Letters Patent were issued and Faulkner became a baronet. He and Katherine were received at Court, singled out by the King and subjected to his considerable charm. The ladies and gentlemen of the Court reminded Faulkner of the bevy of young officers who had provided his escort to Sheerness that infamous day he lost a portion of his ear and when he better deserved to have lost his life. The Faulkners made their dutiful obeisance to Their Majesties, Queen Catherine, the King's Portuguese consort, receiving Lady Faulkner most graciously. Although present, Barbara Villiers, Lady Castlemaine and Duchess of Cleveland, paid no heed to her distant kinswoman, and the facile frivolity of the Court engendered in both Faulkner and Katherine a vague sense of distaste.

Afterwards Faulkner remarked to his wife that the experience was 'rather like sleeping with a whore – momentary pleasure leavened with longer-term disgust'.

That summer Sir Christopher and Lady Faulkner removed their modest household into the countryside of Essex, buying a house in Walthamstow. The house in Wapping was sold, and Faulkner's appearances in London grew infrequent. He was only occasionally to be found at the Trinity House, though he attended the annual convening of the Court at Deptford, staying with Edmund in Stepney. Edmund's two boys visited their grand-father on several occasions, bringing a lively cheerfulness to the ageing couple, and they joined him when, with Charlie Hargreaves at the helm, Faulkner made several excursions down the Thames in the *Hawk*. On one occasion they doubled the buoy of the Nore, entering the Medway and venturing as far upstream as Chatham itself so that he might show his grandsons the place where England's pride was laid low in disgrace.

'But if the fleet was all burned,' young Nathaniel had asked, 'why are there so many ships here now?'

It was a good question, and Faulkner was heartened by the number of men-of-war lying at

406

the trots. Much had been made good since those days of infamy.

'Because to keep old England safe, my boy,' he had replied, 'we have to keep our fleet strong. Some of these ships have been built in recent years.'

'Are any of these your ships, Grandpapa?'

'No. These are the King's.'

'But you're a Captain ... a King's Captain, aren't you? Father says you fought in the old days.'

'Yes. In the old days,' responded Faulkner with a smile. 'Now do you look to the sheets, boys, and stand-by the running backstays as we must go about.'

Faulkner's fading interest in the politics of the day meant that he took little notice of the talk about the King's secret conversion to Catholicism. He considered that the Duke of York might compromise himself as a Papist, but Charles was not such a fool. He heard of negotiations with the French and assumed the King was seeking to pawn something for pecuniary advantage, unaware that an alliance with Louis XIV was a preliminary manoeuvre to a new war with the Dutch, or a secret concord between two Catholic kings. When, in the spring of 1672, war again broke out, Faulkner spent a fortnight anxiously fearing a summons from Rupert, but it was James, Duke of York, who commanded the English fleet, now allied to French squadrons under D'Estrées.

Towards the end of May the allied fleets had

been at anchor in Sole Bay, off Southwold, revictualling by boat from the Suffolk town. Almost caught at anchor on a lee shore, with many of his seamen ashore collecting stores, the Lord High Admiral sustained a near drubbing in another furiously contested battle. Sending his second-in-command, Banckerts, to engage and cut off D'Estrées, de Ruyter and his main body fell upon the Duke of York's men-of-war.

Katherine had rejoiced in her husband being ignored when the appointments were made on the fleet's commissioning, but when Faulkner received the details of the battle in Sole Bay, he was furious, glad that Honest George did not live to see the day. The action had proved long, bloody and furious. York's vice admiral, the Earl of Sandwich, was dead, drowned escaping from his blazing flag-ship. Thanks to severe damage to his own ship, York himself had been compelled to shift his flag twice during the course of the long day, first to the *St Michael* and later to the *Loyal London*.

Although the English had lost four ships and the French one, the Dutch had lost two in action and a third from an explosion in the hours of darkness after the action. Among the many dead lay Admiral van Ghent, and both fleets were almost out of powder and shot. The consequent battle-damage was enormous, while, in the aftermath, the recriminations on both sides were vicious. To the discerning, however, the result was clear: despite the bravery of the English seamen, and pyrrhic though the Dutch victory was, there had been a lack of decisive leadership, and the French squadron had played little part in the main action.

'What did I tell you?' Faulkner said to Katherine when he read the bulletin to her as they sat in their withdrawing-room. 'York is competent enough, but he lacks the *weight* of old Albemarle. He is one of those younger men of whom I spoke, has too much to learn and no time in which to learn it. And why? Because he was up against de Ruyter, and yet old de Ruyter must be sixty-five years of age if he is a day!'

In the weeks that followed, more news filtered through. Although de Ruyter's action had frustrated allied plans to invade Zealand, the French army had taken four of the Seven United Provinces and the Dutch had flooded the countryside surrounding their great commercial city of Amsterdam. Other cities now followed suit in inundating their hinterlands, but French success had induced a political crisis, ousting the Republicans and elevating the House of Orange. Prince William of Orange now became Stadtholder, but in a savage breakdown of civil order, a mob had soon afterwards barbarously murdered the deposed Stadtholder, Johann de Witt, and his brother Cornelis, architect and political director of the Medway raid.

At home, the Duke of York was forbidden to hoist his flag at sea on the grounds that he was henceforth debarred by the Test Act from holding public office as an openly avowed Catholic. Indifferent to public opinion, having lost his first wife, Clarendon's daughter Anne, he recklessly married a Catholic Princess, Mary of Modena.

Having garnered this news on one of his infrequent forays to London and a meeting of the Brethren of Trinity House, Faulkner had been eager to pass the information on to Katherine. It was already late, and he found her sitting alone in a darkening room. Calling for candles and a servant to help him with his boots, he flung his hat and cloak on a chair, sat and began impatiently tugging at his boots, all the while relating the news of York's folly.

'No good will come of this,' Faulkner declared, getting the first boots off with a grunt, but she made no reply. After a moment he looked up; Katherine appeared withdrawn, unusually pale and something about her expression alarmed him. He leapt to his feet, hobbled across the room and knelt at her side. 'What is it, Kate?'

Her breathing was laboured, she was unable to speak and there was terror in her eyes.

Destiny

August 1672–August 1673

In the physician's opinion Faulkner's wife was suffering a malignant fever. She was bled, and an anxious Faulkner was advised that rest in a darkened room would bring on the crisis.

'The disease must culminate, Sir Christopher,' the physician explained. 'She is of strong constitution and will likely survive.'

'But the onset...' Faulkner choked on the words. 'It was so swift.'

'These maladies afflict the body when the humours are out of balance. Was there something that may have upset her sensibilities?'

Faulkner shook his head; he could think of nothing. 'She seemed in good health when I left for London this morning.'

'I suspect a miasma; you lived long by the river, and an insidious infection may have laid hold of her for some time since; such things are difficult to attribute. Besides that, there may be an excess of black bile, not uncommon in women of her age. Has she complained of sharp, shooting pains?'

'She has complained of nothing.'

'But she has been on the river? In that yacht of yours?'

'Not for some months.'

'Ah! But it is proximity, Sir Christopher, proximity. She is a lady of breeding, of sensibility; such creatures possess a delicacy unimaginable to men of your condition. You have survived at sea; those that do so – and there are many that do not – most usually have bovine constitutions.'

Faulkner's shock was fading, and he was increasingly tempted to do as Edmund had done with Hannah's quack, kick the knave from his house. The man was prating, gulling him with pure sophistry. The physician must have noticed some change in Faulkner's demeanour, for he picked up his hat, decided to settle his bill on the morrow and fired his Parthian shot.

'Keep her warm. A little brandy too. If she will

411

not take it, dab it on her lips. No water; let her sweat out the fever. It is best to bring on the crisis while the body remains substantially vigorous, so that inducement aids a rapid return to health, d'you see? I give you good night, Sir Christopher. I shall, with your permission, call again tomorrow.'

When he had gone, Faulkner sat at Katherine's bedside. Her eyes remained closed and her breathing was shallow, though not laboured as it had been at first. Sweat bedewed her, and he wiped her brow. Her forehead felt on fire, yet her hands, lying outside the sheets, were cold and pallid, reminiscent of those of a corpse.

All that day and into the following night he sat beside her. From time to time he wet her lips with brandy and wine, wiped her face and held her unresponsive hand. From time to time he prayed too, as best an unbeliever might, but he knew the worst was upon him and that the crisis Katherine confronted was not one she would surmount. Towards dawn he fell asleep, his old head falling forward on the bed, his wig awry, exposing his bald pate. Afterwards, though he had dreamed, he could not recall the spectres – except that he thought he remembered them walking, hand in hand, upon the island of St Mary's in the Scillies.

He woke suddenly, unable to move and stiff with cramps, to the cold realization of reality. He lay a moment immobile, his neck seized, until he felt a strange sensation, light as a bird's wing, upon his bare head. With an effort he raised himself; Katherine's hand fell back upon her covers

412

but he found himself looking into her eyes. They were large and liquid, and full of some inner fire; perhaps more beautiful than at any other time in her life.

Disregarding the agony of sudden movement, he bent over her, for she seemed anxious to speak, though nothing more than a barely perceptible breath escaped her dry lips. He took her hand and stared into her eyes, sensing she wanted water. The physician's proscription of this meant that he reached for wine and, in holding her up and encouraging her to sip, he achieved little more than ensure it dribbled down her chin. What she had consumed seemed nevertheless to have rallied her. He heard her whisper something and bent again to hear, damning the accursed eternal ringing in his ears. He was never quite certain but always believed her to have said: 'Farewell, my love.'

He had kissed her and held her, his own body wracked with sobs of such magnitude that he never heard the final death-rattle. It was only after some minutes that, watching her eyes, he realized that the fire in them was extinguished and the liquid depths had grown cloudy. Slowly, he leant forward and kissed her again, then he drew down her eye-lids, slowly rose to his feet. Crossing the room, he opened the casement to allow Katherine's soul to fly free.

Rupert's summons came in the following March, wrenching Faulkner from his grief and his daily pilgrimage to Katherine's grave. His sense of relief was immense; rescuing him from his piteous state. While His Highness's orders transformed his situation, His Highness's words transformed his spirit.

I rely, Rupert had written privately in his own hand, *upon those Talents that only Sea-officers of your own wide experience can Muster: besides your skills, a lack of Faction, an understanding of our Wants, and of the Enemy's weaknesses...*

Faulkner's blood ran a little faster. He felt the years slip away, masked by a grim determination. He went once more to Katherine's grave and then came home to gather his accoutrements, have his armour and harness polished, his sword sharpened and his portmanteau packed. He wrote several long letters, one to Edmund, one each to his grandsons, and another to Hargreaves. Then he sent for a coach.

'What *is* to be done, gentlemen? Can none of you tell me?' Rupert strode up and down the great cabin of his flag-ship, the magnificent *Royal Sovereign*. Before him a large table was littered with papers, a Waggoner, and two large Dutch charts of the estuary of the Schelde. 'We have achieved nothing but a vast expenditure of blood and treasure, powder and shot.' He paused, staring round at the assembled senior officers, his expression one of weary resignation, for none among them could be charged as not having done his utmost. They remained silent, their eyes downcast, as tired and bereft of ideas as their commander-in-chief.

Faulkner stood at one end of the table in his capacity of Captain-of-the-Fleet, Rupert's chief-of-staff. He had a good view of the assembly of battle-hardened sea-warriors, some in their half-armour, some soberly dressed, others more colourfully, their sleeves slashed, lace at their throats and wrists. Rupert's second-in-command, Sir Edward Spragge, tugged at his chin and shook his head. He was flanked by the two admirals commanding the van and rear squadrons of his division: Sir John Kempthorne, whose flag-ship was the *St Andrew*, and Sir John Butler, the Earl of Ossory, whose flag flew in the *St Michael*. Next to them stood Rupert's own squadron commanders: Sir John Harman of the *London* and Sir John Chicheley of the *Charles*. Besides Faulkner himself, the only two post-captains present were the *Royal Sovereign*'s own first and second captains, Sir William Reeves and the curiously named John Wetwang. None seemed able to assist their chief.

Rupert ceased his restless pacing and leaned upon the table, attempting a gentler, more persuasive tone: 'Ned?' He looked up at his vice admiral, Sir Edward Spragge.

Spragge sighed. 'Your Highness, the Dutch possess rare talents in their flag-officers, and they all know their business. It seems to me that one must cut off the head, to kill the body.'

'Single out their flag officers, d'you mean?'

'Aye, Your Highness.'

'But they are Hydra-headed, Ned,' Rupert said. 'Kill one and another immediately springs up in his place.'

Spragge shrugged. 'Our men are equal in valour, our guns as worthily served as theirs, our ships as staunch – better, some say. We have fought them in two actions off their own coast and, though they have been inferior in numbers, they have driven us off, thwarted our intention to land troops and yet neither they nor we have lost a ship. Another push, perhaps...' Spragge ran out of wind and shook his head.

Rupert looked from Spragge to his other admirals, 'Sir John? Sir John?' All four were knights and all bore the same Christian name so that the repetition brought slow smiles to their hitherto grim features. They all shook their heads. Rupert turned to Faulkner. 'Sir Kit?'

'Sir Edward is right, Your Highness. They defend their own shore and escaped us after the first action off Schooneveld by hiding amongst their own shoals. When the wind next favoured them they again came out and drove us nigh back to Sole Bay. Their direction is always competent in the hands of their admirals and is most assiduously followed by their captains. De Ruyter is, of course, pre-eminent. I was not present off Southwold but from what I have gleaned he separated us from D'Estrées then, and he has done so ever since...'

'Or D'Estrées has separated himself from us!' Spragge put in.

'Quite so. As for Sir Edward's advice, it is a hazard. To sever heads might work to our advantage, but I doubt we shall succeed against de Ruyter himself, while perhaps the cost of trying may prove too high.' Faulkner paused then, looking round at the faces staring at him. He was older than them all, and they knew his

416

experience was wide. Judging the moment right, he went on: 'They have a weakness in their trade, Your Highness. We have attempted its seizure at sea before but never pursued the matter with much vigour. Admiral Holmes's raid on Vlieland had a devastating impact I am told, being in some communication with Amsterdam by way of trade myself. I am convinced that their attack on the Medway was provoked by ours at Vlie. We may anticipate the arrival of their East Indies trade off the Texel in late July or early August. They pass the ships into the Zuider Zee and on to Enkhuizen. Thus we may hurt them off the Texel, and if de Ruyter comes out to cover the Indies fleet, then Sir Edward's attack on their flags might pay off.'

There was a murmur of assent, and Rupert looked round the assembled officers. 'Very well, then. Upon my receiving reports that all our ships have fully recruited, we shall sail for the Dutch coast. I wish therefore to be ready to cruise by the first week in July.'

Rupert followed his dismissed officers out onto the quarterdeck as a matter of courtesy, talking intensely to Spragge as they left the great cabin. When they had gone Faulkner moved to the table to clear the papers and secure them in the leather satchels that made up the commander-in-chief's official files. A moment later Rupert returned to the cabin, having seen Spragge depart in his barge for his own flag-ship, the *Royal Prince*. 'A glass of wine, Sir Kit?'

The two men stood for a moment, staring through the stern windows, though neither of them took notice of the anchored fleet, or the town of Great Yarmouth stretched behind the sand dunes.

'This is an interminable war,' Rupert confided. 'To have fought two fights such as we just have and yet been unable to force a decision augurs ill. England cannot possess much more powder and shot but that we may well throw it all away once again. We have six thousand troops awaiting the order to embark the moment we have cleared the enemy coast of de Ruyter, yet I dare not embark them before that coast is clear, or they will eat us out of provisions.'

'War is always about attrition, Your Highness. On the evidence you cite, we are not likely to wear our enemy down by these bruising encounters alone, but the bruising encounters of themselves drain down our respective treasuries. While I am not in a position to know with any certainty, I may hazard the guess that His Majesty's is at a low ebb.'

Rupert grunted. 'A desperately low ebb.'

'Quite so. But there is turmoil in the United Provinces, their cities are still surrounded by undrained water from the inundation that stopped the French advance, their commerce must thereby be affected and the arrival of the East India fleet consequently awaited eagerly. If we may interpose ourselves between the Zeegat van Texel and the India ships coming north-about round the coast of Scotland, then we may succeed in striking the master stroke.'

Rupert clapped him on the shoulder, in an obviously more cheerful frame of mind. 'I chose my Captain-of-the-Fleet well, Sir Kit. We may yet trounce these Dutchmen.'

'One other thing, Your Highness.'

'What is that?'

'Whatever his protestations, I would not include M'sieur D'Estrées in your calculations of force. I notice Mynheer de Ruyter does not.'

Rupert stared at him for a moment and then nodded.

The fleet put to sea in July and cruised ineffectually off the Dutch coast. De Ruyter sailed in pursuit, but when the wind came away from the north and the Anglo-French fleet stood towards him to give battle, the wily Dutch admiral retired behind the shoals and into the Schelde with his inferior fleet. Then, in early August, word came south from Scotland that a Dutch fleet had been seen off the Hebrides. These were the ships of the Dutch East India Company, and Rupert at once gave orders to sail; but so too did de Ruyter, and he did so a day or two in advance of the Anglo-French squadrons. Faulkner's plan therefore miscarried, and they caught only a distant sight of the riches of the Indies being borne away under de Ruyter's guns, though one East Indiaman, the *Papenburg*, was seized as she straggled some miles astern of the main convoy.

Frustrated and furious, Rupert and D'Estrées kept the sea, tempting de Ruyter to re-emerge after seeing the East India convoy safely into the Zuyder Zee. The huge Anglo-French fleet of ninety sail proceeded to manoeuvre off the Zeegat van Texel, the entrance to the Zuyder Zee, just clear of the off-lying shoal, the Haak Sand. On the evening of the tenth of August the Dutch were seen creeping down the coast, their familiarity with the locality and their shallower drafted ships allowing them to edge south under the northerly breeze. The wind dropped away during the night, but by daylight on the eleventh it had veered and blew off the land; Faulkner was called from an uneasy doze, to be informed that the Dutch were making sail, bearing down to engage.

Buckling on his sword he ran on deck, glass in hand; Rupert joined him a moment later. He called for the signal for line of battle to be hoisted, though the fleet lay in commendable station, D'Estrées ahead in the van, Spragge astern with the rear division.

A gun was fired to draw attention to the signal as Faulkner took his station. Next to him John Wetwang acknowledged a report that the flagship's crew were closed up at their battle-stations. Sir William Reeves was in discussion with his sailing master and they were briefly joined by Prince Rupert as the first sounds of gunfire were heard. A moment later Rupert crossed the deck and spoke to Faulkner, who in turn summarized the dispositions of the two fleets as the Dutch were allowed to overtake the allied line and match ship for ship.

All along the allied line the ships were spilling wind both to keep station and to allow the Dutch to come up. Spragge's squadron had already opened fire as the leading Dutch ships passed them to draw level with D'Estrées, ahead of

Rupert's centre.

'Who commands the Dutch van?' Rupert asked Faulkner, studying the enemy line as it led past them, just out of range.

'Banckerts. He cut D'Estrées out at Sole Bay and our last encounter.'

'He's doing it again,' said Rupert, not taking his eyes from his glass. 'He's passing his damned ships through D'Estrées' line to engage from leeward.' Rupert lowered his glass with an expression of furious exasperation. *'Mein Gött!* D'Estrées is lost to us once again. He will fight another private action!'

As the two lines of ships converged, those of the Dutch van turned to starboard, intending to pass between the intervals in D'Estrées' line and then swing again parallel to the French squadron and nailing D'Estrées against the shallows off the Dutch coast. A moment later Faulkner lost sight of D'Estrées and Banckerts as they exchanged broadsides, then clouds of dense smoke interposed.

Meanwhile the English centre edged away, necessarily drawing the Dutch offshore into deeper water, but thereby playing into de Ruyter's hands. With D'Estrées again detached from his ally, the old master tactician could bring a superiority of his inferior fleet against a now weaker portion of his enemy. The thunder of the guns now grew intense and the world once more became an anarchic chaos of death and bloodshed as the squadrons began to engage and became locked in their life-and-death struggle. Rupert's centre, vigorously attacked by de Ruyter, swung slowly to starboard, turning in the course of the following two or three hours from a southerly to a northerly heading. The Dutch men-of-war clung tenaciously to Rupert's flank as the thunderous cannonade went on for hour after relentless hour. The ships' decks trembled as the discharged gun carriages rumbled inboard, driven by recoil, and a few moments later rumbled out again after reloading.

Half-blinded by smoke, utterly deafened by the concussions, ears popping in the changes in air pressure, Faulkner tried to observe the progress of the action and keep Rupert informed as they stood upon the shot-torn deck. From time to time Faulkner went up onto the exposed poop-deck to get a better view before returning to the quarter-deck. Spars and splinters, loose ends of shot-away halliards, lifts and braces fell about them, entangling their legs and restricting their movements. The whistle of ball and bullet flew across the quarterdeck, killing in an instant Sir William Reeves, Rupert's flag-captain. In the waist men died at their guns, cut in two by bar-shot, eviscerated by round-shot, knocked off their feet by balls from the swivel-guns in the enemy tops. Yet they screamed like devils and played their own fire with equal devastation.

For some time, where possible through the dense smoke, both Rupert and Faulkner had been studying the conduct of Spragge's rear as it too became increasingly detached from Rupert's centre division. Faulkner, his long-glass to his eye, strove to determine what was happening. His eyes grew sore with the strain, and he frequently lowered the telescope to wipe them, unconscious in the confusion that he did so with a silk handkerchief that had once belonged to his late wife and which he had stuffed into his pocket as a remembrance.

'Perceive now,' Faulkner roared into Rupert's ear, 'the miscarriage of Spragge's plan!' He pointed with his telescope to starboard where, amid dense gun-smoke, a continuous twinkling of fire from the muzzles of two dozen men-of-war marked a ferocious engagement centred on a duel between Spragge's flag-ship, the *Royal Prince*, and Tromp's the *Gouden Leeuw*. ''Tis another private action!'

'All our plans miscarry!' Rupert roared in response as a hail of shot swept the deck.

Faulkner met the first ball, which came inboard over the rail to strike his cuirass and crush his chest. He stood for a moment, unable to breath, and *saw* the second ball which carried away his head. His body fell at Rupert's feet, and only the Prince observed what happened. Later, much later, when night drew its cloak over the carnage, others found Faulkner's plumed hat and his wig – with what remained of his head inside it – lying in the scuppers on the far side of the quarterdeck. The telescope Rupert's uncle had once given Faulkner was also picked up and passed to the commander-in-chief.

In the *Royal Sovereign*'s battered cabin Rupert took the old glass and turned it in his hand, reading its inscription. 'This was the property of a most gallant officer,' he said sadly, laying it aside and picking up his quill.

Edmund Drinkwater received the package containing the telescope together with a letter in the Prince's own hand.

Sir,

This is to Inform you of the Unhappy News that your Kinsman, Captain Sir Christopher Faulkner, died at My Side during the late action against the Dutch off the Texel, one of the hardest fought actions in this present, or any previous war.

Sir Christopher was well known to me, as was also his wife, whose devotion to My Late Mother was Exemplary. I wish You to know that I held him in the Highest possible Esteem and the King's Service and the Country as a Whole in the Poorer for Your Loss. It was Necessary that his Body was committed to the Deep; he Lies in Goodly Company. Please Accept my Sincere Condolences.

Rupert P.

Edmund laid the letter aside and picked up the telescope. He was looking at it when he sensed a presence in the room. For a moment his blood ran cold, and then a small voice asked, 'Is that Grand-father's telescope, Father?'

Edmund looked round. His son Nathaniel stood in the doorway and came closer to look at the glass which he had seen Faulkner use from time to time when embarked in the *Hawk*. The boy stared at the brass tube which his father held out to him. 'I think that you should have it. Your Grand-father would have wanted you to, I think.'

'Is he dead?'

Edmund nodded. 'Yes. Like your Mother and Lady Kate.'

'Well, they will all be together now, won't they?' the boy said with conviction.

Edmund Drinkwater ruffled his son's hair. 'I do most certainly hope so.'

Author's Note

As with the previous two novels in this trilogy, many of the characters and most of the major events affecting the life of Kit Faulkner are real. I have taken liberties with the personalities of the less well-known of the people involved, but the main events, from the Restoration of King Charles II, by way of the Plague and the Great Fire of London to the Dutch attack on the Medway, are based on contemporary accounts. Other background events, such as the comings and goings of the Brethren of Trinity House, derive from my own original research. 'Honest George' Monck, first Duke of Albemarle, a man who saved the nation as surely as Winston Churchill, deserves an occasional remembering, despite the controversies attaching to his reputation, which included accusations of murder and bigamy. I hope I have done honour to his shade here. Other men such as Sir Henry Johnson, the principal builder of East Indiamen then at Blackwall, or Samuel Pepys and John Evelyn, were prominent enough figures who would have been known to Faulkner. As for Ensign John Churchill, the later Duke of Marlborough, he participated in Albemarle's funeral procession.

The rendition of the three Regicides from Delft

is a fact, and the parts played by Abraham Kick, Major Miles and the mysterious Armerer are based upon what little is known of the detail of a secret state abduction. One wonders if this last-named was perhaps the Nick Armourer mentioned by John Evelyn as a familiar of the Queen of Bohemia. At any rate, it was he who spirited John Okey, John Barkstead and Miles Corbett from Delft. It was said that he engineered the getting of a boat into the 'little canal' near the Rathaus and then conveying the prisoners to Helvoetsluys where Captain Tobias Sackler awaited them in the *Blackamoor*. Though usually referred to as 'a frigate', the *Blackamoor* was in fact a small, pink-built man-of-war.

The architect of the act of rendition itself, Sir George Downing, is worthy of mention in detail, not least for the fact that he was a product of the age and his personal moral ambivalence mirrors that of the society in which he functioned. Born in 1623 he was the son of a Puritan attorney who emigrated to Massachusetts in 1638. George Downing was among the very first to graduate from Harvard University whither he had been sent thanks to the sponsorship of John Okey. Downing afterwards returned to England. Here he was caught up in the Civil War, becoming chaplain to Okey's Regiment in the New Model Army then being raised by Cromwell. (Okey himself had a chequered career; a Baptist Puritan turned colonel of dragoons, he had opposed Cromwell as Protector, been cashiered several times and was dismissed by Monck before fleeing abroad.)

After the execution of King Charles I in 1649 and the establishment of the Commonwealth, Oliver Cromwell appointed Downing scout-master-general. This was a highly confidential post, actually the director of intelligence for the nascent English Republic. In 1657 Cromwell, now Lord Protector, sent Downing to The Hague as 'resident', the Protectorate's ambassador. He also served as a Member of Parliament, surviving the Restoration of King Charles II, who confirmed his appointment to The Hague. It was during this period that he bungled an attempt to abduct the Regicide Edward Dendy in Rotterdam, but in early March 1662 successfully seized Okey, Corbett and Barkstead.

In 1667 Downing was appointed to the Treasury Commissioners and was equally active in financial reforms and modernization of the state's borrowing, with mixed success. He later held an appointment on the Board of Customs and if not remembered today, is regularly if inadvertently commemorated by references to Downing Street. It is an inescapable irony that our present Prime Minister's residence stands on land developed by a man involved in many things, of which rendition was but one.

On the scaffold John Okey said of Downing: 'There was one, who formerly was my chaplain, that did pursue me to the very death. But both him, and all others, I forgive.' Pepys, who owed some of his own advancement to Downing, said of his part in the seizure of the Regicides that he was like 'a perfidious rogue, though the action is good and of service to the King, yet he cannot with good conscience do it'. Later, in 1667, on Downing's appointment to the Treasury Commission, Pepys remarked that it was: 'A great thing ... for he is a business active man, and values himself upon having of things do well under his hand, so that I am mightily pleased in ... [the] choice.'

With regard to other details of the background, the Restoration of the Monarchy in 1660, though generally accepted by the greater part of the population, was not universally welcome and some wished it otherwise. Plots against the King were hatched not least because there were those who held to their Puritan principles, regarding them as sacred. Several groups comprised these 'Irreconcilables', among them the Anabaptists, Independents, Presbyterians and Fifth Monarchy men, even a wing of those people of peace, the Quakers. History records only the deeds of men in such affairs, but the Puritan age conceded considerable licence to the views of women, mixing this with an ancient prejudice against any they considered witches. The presence of Elizabeth, the 'Winter Queen' of Bohemia, under Lord Craven's roof at Leicester House, is a matter of record, while her son, Prince Rupert of the Rhine, cannot pass ignored in this turbulent period of English history. Although the plague killed a terrifying fifth of London's population, it was possible to survive it – even be unaffected by it (Pepys was, though he moved his household to Woolwich and his office to Greenwich), while the Great Fire which followed burned fiercely to the west of the Tower, but did little damage down-river.

As for Faulkner's part in these events, I have used some freedom in my yarn. However, someone must have co-ordinated Armerer's rendezvous with Sackler, just as someone carried the King's letter to Albemarle, anchored in The Downs prior to the Four Day's Battle of the first to the fourth of June 1666 – 'the greatest naval battle in the Age of Sail,' as Nicholas Rodger has called it. I saw no reason why it should not have been Faulkner, though the *Albion* is my own invention.

Daniel Defoe's *A Journal of the Plague Year* proved useful while the *Diaries* of Pepys and Evelyn have naturally proved valuable sources for details. Among other snippets Pepys records the sound of Dutch gunfire off Harwich being heard in Bethnal Green, and Evelyn the defection of seamen to the Dutch, thanks to their lack of pay prior to the attack on the Medway. Evelyn also lays charges of incompetence and lack of money causing the catastrophic failure to commission the fleet in the spring of 1667, while Albemarle's biographers, Thomas Gumble and Sir Julian Corbett, state he was sent to Chatham by the King during the Dutch raid. Details of the Dutch attack are confusing and, at times, conflicting, particularly in terms of culpability, but the consequences are not. One third of the naval fleet in the Medway was destroyed or taken by the Dutch.

What is of passing interest is that so much that went on in these years mirrors our own time: corruption in high places, natural and unnatural disaster, economic meltdown, a run on the banks and the consequential panicky movement of people. Besides such examples, one finds in these years other parallels: religious intolerance and fundamentalism, neglect of the navy and a failure to invest in essential infrastructure, to say nothing of unlawful rendition and draconian punishment.

In an uncertain world it is some comfort to realize that a past period of similar mighty upheaval was eventually stabilized and ordered – at least to some degree.

Finally, to avoid complication and for purposes of chronology with reference to the years in which the story takes place, I have used the modern Julian calendar.